Praise for Claire Lorrimer's novels:

Ortolans

'A sweeping saga of powerful passions, mystery and a house full of secrets'   *Woman's Realm*

'A story of three women's passion and turmoil within the house they love'   *Bookseller*

'A hefty romantic saga of love, mystery and romance'
                                                                Bookworld

Frost in the Sun

'Passion in the bloody battlefields of the Spanish Civil War . . . a huge and powerful novel' *Evening Standard*

'A magnificent international historical saga' *Bookseller*

'A sizzling read . . . exciting to the end'
                                                                Woman's Realm

'[The] setting is sheer glamour'   *Evening Telegraph*

Last Year's Nightingale

'Matchless storytelling . . . a fine historical saga'
                                                                Yorkshire Post

'Unashamedly romantic'   *Evening Telegraph*

'Grippi   eller*

Claire Lorrimer wrote her first book at the age of twelve, encouraged by her mother, the bestselling author Denise Robins. After the Second World War, during which Claire served in the WAAF on secret duties, she started her career as a romantic novelist under her maiden name, Patricia Robins. In 1970 she began writing her magnificent family sagas and thrillers under the name Claire Lorrimer. She is currently at work on her seventy-first book. Claire lives in Kent.

Find out more about Claire: www.clairelorrimer.co.uk

Also by Claire Lorrimer and available from Hodder

CLAIRE LORRIMER

THE SILVER LINK

HODDER

First published in Great Britain in 1993
by Bantam Press
A division of Transworld Publishers Ltd.

This edition published in 2015
by Hodder & Stoughton
An Hachette UK company

1

A CIP catalogue record for this title is available from the British Library

Paperback ISBN 978 1 473 61655 4
eBook ISBN 978 1 444 75074 4

Typeset in Sabon LT Std by Palimpsest Book Production Ltd,
Falkirk, Stirlingshire

Printed and bound by Clays Ltd, St Ives plc

Hodder & Stoughton policy is to use papers that are natural, renewable
and recyclable products and made from wood grown in sustainable
forests. The logging and manufacturing processes are expected to conform to
the environmental regulations of the country of origin.

Hodder & Stoughton Ltd
338 Euston Road
London NW1 3BH

www.hodder.co.uk

For Phyll Gartside,
who has such close literary
and personal links with my family
– with affectionate regard.

ACKNOWLEDGEMENTS

I would like to thank the following people who have assisted me with technical information necessary to ensure the veracity of the story; and those who have given me support and encouragement in its execution: Donald McDonald, Dover Coastguard; Graeme Clark, Hot Air Balloon Club; Joy Tait, for sailing terminology; Queen Victoria Hospital, Pathology Department; Frederick L. Griggs, whose book, *Highways and Byways in Sussex*, I referred to for Sussex dialect and old medical remedies; Eve Sutton, for French geological information; Victoria and Albert Museum, for costumes of the period; C. A. Hallam, for details on firearms and performance; Sevenoaks, East Grinstead and Edenbridge Public Libraries; Penrose Scott, for her efficient, apt and tireless research; and not least, my editor, Diane Pearson, for her invaluable advice, patience and encouragement.

CL
1992

'It is the secret sympathy,
The silver link, the silken tie,
Which heart to heart, and mind to mind,
In body and in soul can bind . . .'
                                    'Lay of the Last Minstrel'
                                            Sir Walter Scott

PROLOGUE

1779

'There are times, my darling Nadine, when I find myself wishing that I had never married you! If I had only known . . .'

'Then I give thanks to God that you could not see into the future!'

Sir Matthew Carstairs' young wife ran to her husband's side and kneeling down, took both his hands in hers and leaned her cheek against his. Her dark eyes were filled with love – and a pity she could not disguise.

The man lying on the wicker day-bed gave a deep sigh as he raised his hand to stroke the silky ringlets that hung in soft clusters to Nadine's white shoulders. At thirty she was even more beautiful than she had been as a young girl when he had first met and fallen in love with her. Two years later he had brought her back to England from her home in Normandy and the idyll of their married life had begun. Theirs had been a wild, passionate union, resulting quickly in the birth of their first child, Adela – a little girl with as wild and passionate a nature as the love that had conceived her.

Sir Matthew's blue eyes clouded with renewed distress as he recalled how eagerly they had both anticipated the next child, hopefully the son Nadine wanted but was never to have. A year after Adela's birth, he had set sail for America with his regiment. The following year, during a bitter encounter with the American troops fighting for their independence from Great Britain, he had sustained injuries so severe that he had been rendered immobile from the waist down.

At first Nadine, aided by his physicians, had convinced him

that, given time, he might recover the use of his legs, but gradually, as his general health had begun to improve, they allowed him to hear the truth – he would be bedridden for the remainder of his life.

Not yet in his forties, Sir Matthew was devastated by the thought that not only would he never soldier again, but he would never again be able to make love to the wife he adored. Recalling all too clearly how eagerly Nadine had responded to this aspect of their marriage, he could not bring himself to believe that he was to be denied the pleasures of married life, or that Nadine too must also be deprived; and, moreover, that they would never be able to add to their family. As so many times before, Nadine tried now to comfort him when such feelings became too great to keep to himself.

'Can you not see in my face how entirely happy and content I am?' she enquired, turning to look directly into his eyes. 'You should not torment yourself in this unnecessary fashion, my dearest. I love you with all my heart and I know that you love me. Is that not enough? I am entirely happy here in Sussex with you and Adela and our friends. You indulge my every wish and I lack for nothing I could want.'

Sir Matthew's voice was low and rough with pain as he said meaningfully, 'Does your body never crave for more than kisses and caresses, my lovely Nadine? Look over there beneath the mulberry tree! See how your brother has his arm around Camille's waist; how they look into each other's eyes! Tonight he will hold her, embrace her as once I could hold you! And see, too, how her body swells. Your sister-in-law is with child again and I can give you no more children. Better I should have died of my wounds and you be free to marry a man worthy to be called your husband!'

Nadine rose swiftly to her feet, her white skin colouring a deep pink as she protested, 'I will not listen to you speaking in this fashion again. It is you I love, Matthew, and even as you are, I would rather share my life with you than with one of a thousand other virile men who might get me with child.

What nonsense you speak, my dearest. As for children, I am happy enough with our darling Adela. Though she be a little minx on occasions, I see so much of you in her. She may have my looks but she has inherited your character – even Hugo has remarked upon her courage. She is quite fearless – and for a child only six years old, she is quick enough in her intelligence to keep pace with her cousins.'

The indignation in her voice gave way to one of indulgent amusement as she added, 'See there, my darling – that is our Adela climbing to the top of the tree. Nou-Nou is sending Titus – or perhaps it is Barnaby – to fetch her down!'

Successfully diverted, Sir Matthew turned his head to stare out across the expanse of green grass to the big oak tree some fifty yards distant. He could see his small daughter, dark hair tumbling down the back of her muslin frock, white frilly petticoat in full evidence as she reached upwards for a still higher branch in the tree. Some fifteen feet below stood Nadine's old French *nourrice* – the nurse who had come from France with her beloved mistress when Nadine had married him. Gazing up were Parson Mallory's identical twin boys, Titus and Barnaby, six years older than his daughter, together with their younger sister, Patience, her frequent playmates.

One of the boys was even now starting to climb after little Addy but, as always, it was impossible to tell, even at close quarters, one twin from the other. Both had thick, wavy, fair hair and deep brown eyes – a combination of colouring inherited from their maternal grandmother. Even at their present youthful age of twelve, the boys were already as tall as their mother and matched the height of their rotund, chubby father who had not only proved his worth as a splendid choice of parson for the parish of Dene, but was an excellent neighbour. Since his own wounding in the war, the man had become a personal friend, spending as much time as he could spare at the big house, playing games of chance or chess or in long intellectual discussions about the war, politics, religion.

Reverend the Honourable Leonard Mallory was, like

himself, a highly educated man, the youngest son of a family
no less noble than his own, and Sir Matthew was grateful for
the frequent diversions he provided. Nadine, too, seemed to
welcome the companionship of the man's gentle, sweet-natured
wife and frequently accompanied Mrs Mallory on her visits
to the poor or sick parishioners. Not least of these advantages
of such neighbours was the fact that the parsonage was only
a mile distant and little Adela was as much at home with the
Mallory children and as often there, as the younger Mallory
children were at Dene Place. The twins idolized Nadine, whose
beauty far outshone that of their own rather plain mother;
and Nadine, without sons of her own, acquired great pleasure
from their company.

As sometimes happened when he found himself in a trough
of despair, Sir Matthew now chided himself for his self-pity,
realizing that he had a great deal to be thankful for. He loved
Dene Place, the great, grey stone building that was his family
home and had been so for the past two hundred years. It was
still possible when the weather was not too inclement, for him
to be carried out to one of the carriages for drives round the
beautiful Sussex countryside with Nadine and Adela beside
him; and, in the summer, to reach the sea-port of Rye where
the fresh salt air of the English Channel mingled with the
scents of the trees and flowers growing in the cottage gardens
and hedgerows. They would halt the carriage to watch for a
while the comings and goings of the fishing boats, and this
past year, the billowing white sails of the Mallory boys' sailing
boat – a much-treasured gift for their eleventh birthday from
their wealthy grandfather, a former naval commander.

Although Nadine showed concern for the boys' safety when
they took to the seas, Mrs Mallory had no such fears, for they
were always accompanied by Jacques, their lackey, groom,
valet and watchdog – a veritable sovereign of a servant whose
loyalty to and affection for the twins was unsurpassable. The
fellow was Nadine's contemporary and his mother, Nou-Nou,
had been nursing Jacques when she had been called upon to

wet-nurse Nadine. Although they were of French nationality,
neither servant had thought to remain in their own country
when Nadine came to England and, although Nou-Nou had
stayed in her mistress' service to become nurse to Adela, Sir
Matthew had his own English servants at Dene Place and he
had found the present position for Jacques with the Mallorys.
By the time the boys were six years old, Jacques had taught
them to ride and later to fish, to shoot, to become accomplished
with the bow and arrow, and now to sail a boat. Nou-Nou's
husband had been a *matelot* who had taught his son the ways
of the sea, lessons Jacques had not forgotten although his
father had been drowned before Jacques had reached
maturity.

'Oh, *mon Dieu*!'

Nadine's sudden cry, spoken in French as was her custom
when emotionally disturbed, brought Sir Matthew's thoughts
back to the present. Following his wife's pointing finger, he
could see his little daughter hanging perilously from a high
branch from which she had clearly lost her foothold. On a
lower branch one of the twins was reaching upwards and had
hold of her skirt. Nou-Nou and young Patience Mallory were
screaming.

Unaware of her parents' agonized fears for her safety, Adela
clung more tightly to the branch with her aching arms, confident that in a moment or two she would be rescued. Near by,
one of the twins called out in a reassuring voice, 'No need to
be frightened, Addy! Jacques and your cousins are fetching
the hammock to hold beneath you. They will be back at any
minute. Just hold tight!'

'I am holding tight and I am not in the least frightened!'
Adela declared untruthfully, for she would have died rather
than admit her fear to the boys. In fact, her arms were aching
dreadfully and the ground seemed horribly far below.

Titus shifted his grip from her skirt to her round, white-
stockinged leg, wondering if he would have the strength to
take her weight if she did fall. At least she was not panicking

as was his young sister, Patience. So, too, were Addy's four
French cousins who were even now staring up with horrified
faces, the eldest, Eugénie, looking as if she were about to have
the vapours!

With a sigh of relief, Titus saw the short, bandy-legged
figure of the faithful Jacques hurrying towards them with his
swaying gait. It was only when he was on horseback that the
good-natured fellow managed to look all-of-a-piece. Barnaby
now took hold of one end of the hammock. With the de
Falence cousins holding the sides and Jacques the other end,
there was now a safety net spread beneath Addy's small figure.

'Jump, Miss Adela!' shouted Jacques. 'Let go of the branch
and jump!'

For a moment, Addy hesitated. Suppose the hammock was
not strong enough to support her? Suppose she hit the ground
and was killed? She did not in the least want to die – especially
not today when she was so very happy. Not only had Patience
and the twins come to play but her beloved French cousins
were on a long summer visit, and all manner of exciting entertainments were planned for them.

'Do as you are told, Addy! You will be perfectly safe!'

Titus' voice, warm and reassuring, gave her the spur of
courage she needed. Closing her eyes, she let go of the branch
to which she had now been clinging for nearly five minutes,
and fell.

Although the hammock did not break, her weight was
sufficient for it to sag drastically, bouncing her once into the
air, and as she hit it a second time, to allow her to bump
uncomfortably hard against the ground. For a few moments,
she lay still, partially stunned and totally winded. She recovered
her senses to see Barnaby staring anxiously down at her.

'Are you all right, Addy? You have not broken anything?'

'She be right as rain, surely!' Jacques said, picking her up
and dusting her down. In the seven years he had lived with
the Mallorys in England, he had acquired a good grasp of
English flavoured with a Sussex accent and idioms he had

picked up from the other servants. His freckled face was creased in a broad grin mingled with affection as the colour returned to the little girl's face. 'Take more'n a bump to make you cry, eh, Miss Addy?'

Biting back the tears of shock pricking the backs of her eyes, Adela tossed her curls and lifted her chin.

'I cannot think why you are all staring at me!' she said. 'As a matter of fact, I liked falling. I felt like a bird flying down from the top of the tree!'

'Devil take it, Addy, you were nowhere near the top of the tree! As to flying like a bird – you dropped like a stone!'

Titus' voice, gently deriding, brought the tears perilously close again. If there was anything in the world she desired, it was the twins' admiration – and here was Titus berating her for her fib! She supposed it was Titus, not Barnaby, although, as always, she could never be sure. Even their own mother could not tell one twin from the other and they did not make it easier since they often pretended the other's identity.

But now her cousins were hugging and kissing her, telling her in their voluble French how brave she was. Eugénie, at fourteen, was the eldest; her brother, Philippe, two years younger. Louise, the delicate one, was a youthful eleven and Marguerite only a year older than Adela. Although the four children spoke English, they did so haltingly and since Adela, with her French mother and nurse, was bilingual, they slipped quite naturally into the French language.

'You must come straight away to your bed and lie down, my precious!' Nou-Nou was saying as she fussed over her small charge like an anxious mother hen. 'You must carry her, Jacques, the poor little angel!'

'For pity's sake, Nou-Nou, stop fussing!' Adela protested, pushing the old woman's hands away. 'I do assure you I have suffered no injury. And do not dare tell Mama or Papa I fell, else I shall be punished for climbing the tree and you and Jacques will be punished also for permitting it!'

The twins shot each other an admiring glance, marvelling

at the quick-thinking of this high-spirited child who, whenever
she could, followed them round like an adoring puppy. They
found her mischievousness amusing and tolerated her as they
did not their young sister. Patience was a nervous, timid little
girl, prone to tears when they teased her and disinterested in
their boyish pursuits. Addy, though fractionally younger, was
fearless and always ready to join in any adventure. She was,
however, too familiar a playmate to sustain their interest for
long. Both twins were old enough at twelve to be aware of
the extraordinary beauty of the eldest of Adela's French
cousins.

Although it would be two years yet before Eugénie de
Falence would be of marriageable age, already she was
attracting the glances of the opposite sex. Dark haired, with
skin as white as porcelain, her large grey eyes fringed with
curling black lashes, she was the epitome of feminine beauty.
Her tiny, slim figure had this past year developed the curves
of womanhood and the Mallory twins were already hopelessly
enamoured of her. In clumsy, boyish fashion, they vied with
one another for her attention, seeking ways to show off their
not inconsiderable accomplishments, delighting when they
succeeded in evoking a smile and oblivious to the fact that
the young girl was playing one against the other. But newly
conscious of her ability to arouse such open adoration, she
was happily experimenting with the heady powers of
flirtation.

Aware that the boys were no longer paying her any attention, Adela scowled and linked her arm through that of her
youngest cousin, Marguerite.

'If you would care to accompany me, it is time for me to
go and feed my pet lamb!' she said. 'It was one of several
orphans and Papa has allowed me to have sole care of it. I
have called her Twinkle and I have to give her milk from our
nanny goat four times a day.'

'Shall we come with you, Addy?' the boys asked in unison,
for although they had many pets – dogs, cats, ponies and a

talking parrot from Africa – they did not have a home farm. Whenever they walked the short distance from the parsonage to Dene Place, they never failed to visit the farm, begging rides on one of the big, heavy shire-horses, collecting brown, speckled eggs from the hen-house or carrying the heavy pails of swill for the fat, pink pigs. In the summer they rode the hay carts and carried ale to the sweating corn-cutters or cooled themselves in the dairy where the farmer's wife churned the thick, yellow butter. Adela, with a perspiring Nou-Nou scurrying in her wake, was their ever present shadow. As often as not the little girl would successfully evade her nurse's vigilance, and it would fall to the twins to make sure she came to no harm – no mean feat since she thought nothing of climbing into a nursing sow's pen to stroke the squalling little bodies of the piglets, or of feeding sugar to the big white stallion who had once come close to killing a groom to whom he had taken a dislike. She seemed to have a special affinity with the animals, even the most ill-tempered tolerating her. It was the same with people. Her bright, quick smile and ready laughter brought affection in response, and her parents adored her. Sir Matthew Carstairs doted on his only child and although Nadine did likewise, she was too wise to permit the little girl to become too spoilt, not an easy task since every member of the household loved her for her bright, sunny nature.

Titus was the elder of the twins by a mere half-hour, although as he had been born at a quarter to midnight and Barnaby at a quarter past, their birthdays were a day apart. Perhaps because of this, Titus was the more dominant of the two. Only by watching the boys at play was it sometimes possible for their parents to distinguish one from the other since it would more often be Titus who led whilst Barnaby followed. There was little difference, however, in their physical strength or in their choice of pursuits or activities, or, indeed, in their choice of friends. Now, for the first time in their lives, they found themselves in the company of a beautiful young French girl who aroused in them similar stirrings of masculine awareness. Adela's cousin, Eugénie, had made slaves of them both and when it was suggested that she might accompany Adela and her sister to the farm to see Adela's pet lamb, the twins vied with one another as to which of them should escort her.

Adela listened to their entreaties with a frown of displeasure. In point of fact, she did not dislike her eldest cousin who she also thought very beautiful; but she did dislike the way Titus and Barnaby were fawning upon her. She considered their attentions to her cousin quite silly and, without understanding her own jealousy, was determined that Eugénie should not command their interest if she could not do so herself.

'I have remembered that it is still too early for me to feed Twinkle!' she said, tossing back her dark curls and scuffling the dry grass with the toe of her chamois leather shoe. 'I must go and see Papa. He depends upon me to read to him from my story-book each afternoon. He says he enjoys my reading even more than Mama's!'

This was not strictly true, as well she knew, for not even she could vie with her mother for Papa's love. Although both her parents professed to love her equally as well as they loved one another, she knew by the way her father's eyes followed her mother's every movement and by the way Nadine was forever touching his cheek or holding his hand, that they shared a special closeness which excluded her. For the most part she did not really mind. Above all, she wanted her father to be happy. It saddened her beyond bearing to realize that he would be confined to live without movement for the rest of his life and her greatest consolation was her mother's assurance that his little daughter's company always brought her papa great joy and pleasure.

'Childhood is fleeting, my precious, and all too soon you will be grown up and leaving home to marry a handsome young man,' he had once told her. 'So I must make the most of the years you are here with me.'

'I shall never leave you, Papa!' Adela had vouchsafed,

hugging him passionately. 'If I am ever to marry, it shall be to you.'

Her father had laughed.

'That you cannot do, my darling, for I am already married to your dear mother. Besides, I should be much too old a husband for you.'

'Then I shall marry Titus and Barnaby!' Adela had declared. 'Then I shall remain close by and shall continue to see you every day!'

'Titus *or* Barnaby, for you cannot have two husbands any more than I can have two wives!' her father had explained. 'You will have to choose between them.'

'And how, pray, can I do that when I cannot tell one from the other?' she had argued.

'It would be difficult, I agree. Perhaps the problem would be solved if one and not the other were to choose you for a wife?'

Adela considered such a prospect unlikely, for the twins shared their tastes as closely as their looks. They wanted identical white ponies; identical lead soldiers; identical quill pens and books. If one wore a red neckcloth the other would do so, and no amount of cajoling from their parents would persuade them otherwise.

'It would make life so much easier for everyone if they would just have a pocket handkerchief that was of a different colour,' the gentle Mrs Mallory once said to Adela. 'I did once attempt it when they were younger but they merely exchanged them when my back was turned! If one has been naughty, I am obliged to punish both or neither since they refuse to confess which one is guilty! Your mama is fortunate, Adela, to have only you to manage!'

One of the boys was now regarding Adela with a quizzical look.

'A little while past you said your father had instructed you to accompany your cousins to the garden so that you could all enjoy this bright spring sunshine.'

'Oh, do stay here with us, Adela!' Marguerite cried. 'You can read to your papa later, can you not?'

'Why do we not go to see the animals without Adela?' Eugénie said equably. 'We should not deprive dear Uncle Matthew of Adela's company, and the boys have offered to escort us.'

Watching the twins' eager faces from beneath her lashes, Adela said sharply, 'You must not feed Twinkle. Only I can feed her!'

'But of course!' Eugénie said sweetly. 'Have no worries, *chérie*. We will see you later.'

With an air of unconcern belying her true feelings of dismay, Adela turned and walked back across the garden in the direction of the house. Nou-Nou trailed patiently behind her whilst Jacques accompanied the twins and the de Falence children along the rutted cart track leading to the farm. At this moment, Adela thought miserably, there was nothing she would rather be doing than going with them. She could still hear their voices and an occasional burst of laughter. How happy they sounded – and how miserable she was, the more so for knowing that she had brought her isolation upon herself! It was not even as if, try though she might, she could hate Eugénie who was not only beautiful but sweet and kind and gentle like her own mother! If she hated anyone, it was Titus and Barnaby for preferring Eugénie's company to hers. The boys were *her* friends, not Eugénie's!

At least it would only be for three more weeks that she would be obliged to share her friends, she told herself as she neared the house, for the de Falence family would be returning to their home in Paris next month. There was the whole summer ahead of her before the boys departed to their new boarding-school – a prospect she dreaded, although they were eagerly anticipating the new adventure. In all probability, they would spend many days down at Rye sailing their boat – and Papa would not give his consent for her to accompany them no matter how hard she pleaded – but there would be many more days when she would go to the parsonage on her pony to join them for long rides across the surrounding countryside; when they would spend happy hours in the walled garden gathering strawberries and raspberries and gooseberries for Mrs Mallory's conserves; or they would track badgers and foxes in the beechwoods on the Dene Place estate. There would be days when the twins would come to help with the haymaking; when they would go blackberrying or play croquet in the garden or have picnics in the tree-house the boys had built last summer. There would be wrestling or bowling matches to watch on the village green and maypole dancing, and long hours spent listening to Papa recounting from his newspaper stories of recent battles in the war raging in America. Mama would sit quietly, busy with her embroidery, whilst the boys moved their lead soldiers into the positions Papa indicated; and they would sometimes let Adela move the cannons or the horses if she took care not to upset the battle-field spread out on the stone terrace at their feet.

Comforted by such expectations, Adela had regained her customary good spirits when she entered the long, sunny drawing-room where her father lay on his day-bed by the wide windows overlooking the garden. She ran to his side and hugged him.

'You did not hurt yourself when you fell out of the tree, my darling?' he enquired anxiously, holding her away from him so that he could see her the better.

Adela shook her head.

'Of course not, Papa!' she declared although she was already conscious of numerous bruises to which her pride would not allow her to admit. 'I have come to read some more of our story!' she said quickly, twitching her small nose as she leaned over to kiss him and felt the tickling of his wig. His eyes brightened with pleasure.

'Why, Addy, I had not thought to see you this afternoon. Are you not enjoying the company of your cousins?'

'Well, yes, Papa, but they have Titus and Barnaby to entertain them and . . . and I do not see why I should permit them to spoil our special reading time.'

'That is most thoughtful of you, my darling. I was indeed feeling a little lonely. Your mama has had to leave me to attend to one of the kitchen-maids who has cut her finger, so you have chosen an excellent moment. Let us by all means read for a little while, but then I think we should set aside our "special reading time" whilst your cousins are here so that you may make the most of their company. I have your Uncle Hugo here to entertain me. As you know, he is as keen a chess player as I, and we have much to talk about. You must not, therefore, feel obliged to keep me company, my little one, much as I love to have you with me.'

Whilst the child settled herself in the crook of his arm, he stroked her hair with his other hand, his eyes dark with foreboding. She was immeasurably precious to him, as indeed was his beloved Nadine, and, paralysed though he was, he could still by word of mouth ensure their well-being and their happiness. But for how long? Not even Nadine was aware that his friend and physician had finally admitted that his state of immobility was affecting his internal organs and that he could not rely upon surviving many more years . . . if, indeed, as long.

In the four years since he had been wounded, the muscles of his once strong body had deteriorated to a point where his legs were little more than pathetic sticks; his weight was dangerously low and that despite the excellent nursing of his faithful attendant and Nadine's personal supervision of the most nourishing of meals. He hated now to look at himself in a mirror, for his gaunt visage was that of a man twenty years older and his hair had turned completely grey.

Sir Matthew was not afraid of death. Although not a fanatically religious man, he had spent many hours in the company of his friend, the Reverend Leonard Mallory. The parson had strengthened his belief in a life hereafter, and his fear of dying lay only in his dread of leaving his beautiful

young wife a widow and his child fatherless. Of late, he had
begun to talk to Nadine of a future when he might not be
with her and had tried to persuade her to the notion of
making a second marriage. Not only was she in her prime
but still young enough to bear further children; and he would
be leaving her more than well provided for. She would not
lack suitors. But even the mildest of suggestions in this vein
would bring the tears to her eyes, and her distress was such
that he could not bear to be the cause of it. He could but
hope that once she was reconciled to his passing, she would
remember his wishes for her and find another husband.

Later today he would speak of it to Nadine's brother, Hugo;
enlist his promise to persuade Nadine that, for the child's sake
as well as her own, she must find someone to replace him.

Adela was by now reaching the end of her favourite story
in her book of Aesop's tales. She closed the book and regarded
him thoughtfully.

'In that story the son is beautiful and the daughter ugly,
yet their father loves them equally. Would others do the same?'

Sir Matthew paused before replying for Adela's small face
was unusually serious and the question unexpected from one
so young.

'Most certainly they would, if the ugly child had a beautiful
nature, for that is of far greater worth.'

'Why then should Titus and Barnaby prefer Eugénie's
company to mine?' Adela asked, suddenly close to tears.

With difficulty, Sir Matthew concealed a smile of
amusement.

'Do they, indeed! Could it be because your cousin is not
only beautiful but the possessor of a charming disposition?
You must not be jealous of others, my darling, for jealousy is
an ugly trait!' Seeing that her tears were about to fall, he
relented and said gently, 'Believe me, Addy, you are very far
from ugly as your mama and Nou-Nou have doubtless told
you a hundred or more times; and even if you were so, have
you forgotten the story of the ugly duckling who turned into

a swan? One day, when you are as old as Eugénie, you will be almost as beautiful as your mother for you greatly resemble her.'

Adela's tears dried instantly and her green eyes sparkled.

'Then the twins will prefer me to Eugénie and will want to marry me after all. I shall have to decide which of the two I prefer. You will have to help me choose, Papa, for I love them equally and you said I cannot marry both.'

Sir Matthew laughed, but no sooner had his little daughter left the room than the shadows fell once more across his face. Ten years from now he would not be here on earth to guide or advise his daughter, and who could tell what the future held either for her or for the delightful boys she had seemingly already selected as possible suitors! Although it was true that Adela greatly resembled his beloved Nadine, it was only in looks. The child had a wild, passionate streak and a strength of will more befitting a boy than a girl. She would need a strong man as well as a loving one to make her happy. It was far too early to surmise whether either Titus or Barnaby Mallory would fit the bill for charming, well-mannered boys though they were, they were still too young to have proved themselves.

'We shall have to wait and see!' he told himself before recalling once again with an aching heart that he would not live long enough to do so.

PART ONE

1783–1789

PART ONE

1783-1789

CHAPTER ONE

1783

It was growing dark in the cellar. It must be nearing five o'clock – perhaps even later, Adela thought. It was the time of day when she most feared her cold, damp prison. By now she would have been locked in for more than eight hours. If today were to be the same as yesterday, there would be still a further hour or more to go before her stepfather unbolted the heavy oak door and demanded the price of freedom.

If she were not so terrified of the total darkness of the night, she would not pay that price, she thought, glancing uneasily at the lengthening shadows in the corners of the room. The big casks of wine and spirits which lined the walls were beginning to take on strange shapes. It was all too easy to imagine ghosts, smugglers, story-book monsters waiting to spring out at her; and, on this bitter January afternoon, it was cold . . . so very cold.

Dolly, the orphan girl who had been hired to assist Nou-Nou to look after Adela, had managed to secrete a moth-eaten, fur-lined carriage rug behind a stack of ale barrels. Crouching beneath the iron-barred window high above her head, with the aid of the rug, the ten-year-old girl was able to control her shivering.

Dreading the forthcoming confrontation with her stepfather, Adela tried to concentrate her thoughts elsewhere. Late last night, when at long last she had finally succumbed to Sir Henry's will and acknowledged him as her stepfather, she had been allowed to leave the cellar and sleep in her own bed. Dolly had crept in to console her as she lay weeping with humiliation. Dolly, she had discovered, was very far from being the dim-witted, Cockney 'good-for-nothing' Nou-Nou had feared. The fourteen-year-old girl was proving not just a friend but, in the dreadful circumstances in which Adela was now finding herself, a wise one.

'Wot's in a name, Miss Addy?' she'd whispered. 'Your pa would've understood.'

'But that hateful man is *not* my papa!' Adela had sobbed.

'I knows that as well as you, Miss Addy, but it's best to do as the Master tells you. 'E ain't able to tell you wot to think, not nohow, and that's wot matters!'

In one way, Adela thought now, she could see that Dolly's advice was sensible; but still she could not agree with her philosophy. To call her hated stepfather by Papa's name was to accept him – and that, she had resolved, she never, ever would do. Yesterday, when she had come down to breakfast and bid Sir Henry 'good-morning', there had been no answering greeting, no smile, no pat on the head as had been his custom during the months he had been courting Mama, begging her to marry him; to allow him the right to take care of her and 'her little Adela'; to set aside her grief at the death of her beloved husband. Throughout that one long year preceding the wedding, he had attempted to align Adela on his side, knowing that if she were not so opposed to the marriage, Mama might more willingly consider it.

Tears spilled from Adela's eyes as she remembered for the hundredth time those terrible weeks when Papa lay dying; how inconsolable her mother had been; how even the servants had cried during the funeral and Adela herself had buried her face in kind Mrs Mallory's mantle so that she could not see Papa's coffin disappearing into the vault. After the funeral Mama had been very ill and she, Adela, had been sent to stay with the Mallorys where Titus and Barnaby had done their utmost to amuse and distract her.

Very gradually she had started to come to terms with her father's death and so, less easily, had her mother. They had managed somehow to find happiness again and a growing closeness. But Nadine found the management of the estate beyond her capabilities, despite the assistance of the steward; the family lawyer who came down from London; the learned day-to-day advice from the Reverend Mallory. It was always Papa, she had said tearfully to Adela, who had seen to such things, and were it not for the growing political unrest in France, she might have considered returning to her native country.

Such a suggestion had appalled Adela, for although she was fond of her French cousins, Dene Place was her home and she loved every inch of it. Moreover, it contained all the precious memories of her beloved father and she pleaded with Nadine on this score alone, never to leave it. The parson and Mrs Mallory had added their persuasions to hers and at Adela's request, Titus and Barnaby had added theirs. Mama had finally ceased to think any more of going back to Normandy and all might have continued well had not Sir Henry Nayland (Adela could barely bring herself to say his name) come upon the scene.

From her first meeting with the middle-aged man, Adela had disliked him. Describing him after that meeting to the twins, she had screwed up her nose and declared that the former soldier who professed to be a friend of Papa's, had watery blue eyes, and ginger hairs on his hands; that he laughed too loudly and kept patting her head as if she were a dog! He had behaved as if he were an old friend of her father's whereas Mama could not even remember Papa speaking of him.

Titus and Barnaby had laughed at her description. They tried to console her with the suggestion that she might never see this unpleasant gentleman again; that perhaps her mama welcomed more adult company then Addy's and especially if, as had been the case, Sir Henry was able to speak about Sir Matthew's soldiering adventures – the only part of their life together that her mother had been unable to share.

'You are just jealous because your mama gives him so much attention!' Titus teased her.

'All green-eyed people are prone to jealousy!' Barnaby had added. 'It is only right your mother should have her own friends!'

Adela, whilst arguing the point, nevertheless took it to heart and tried, for her mother's sake, to like the man who called more and more often to visit them. Outwardly he did his best not only to charm Nadine, but to charm Adela. He never came empty-handed. There were flowers, sugar-candied sweetmeats or fruit for Nadine; toys for Adela; pretty ribbons or a lace kerchief for each of them. Nadine was indeed charmed, and was distressed by her small daughter's antipathy to this former friend of her beloved husband.

'He wants to marry you, Mama!' Adela had protested. 'Nou-Nou said so! She said she knew the signs. She likes him no better than I do.'

'Nou-Nou is a silly, gossiping old woman and does not know what she is talking about,' Nadine had insisted. 'As if I would consider marriage to anyone! Papa was the only man I could ever love and I could not bear the thought of being a wife to another man!'

But six months later, her mother had begun to speak of the possibility of marriage to Sir Henry.

'He is so good and kind and helpful, Addy!' she had said. 'We need someone to take care of Dene Place – and us! Papa managed things so well that I never realized how many worries he carried on his shoulders. You are too young to understand what it means to be alone, my darling, and to be responsible for the great wealth your poor dear father left in my care. Sir Henry tells me my lawyer has been ill-advising me and that we are being shamefully exploited, not just by him but by several of the servants. I do not like to think about it but on one of his visits, Sir Henry made a careful inventory of your father's cellar and on checking it a few months later, there were unexplained discrepancies. I cannot believe Unwin would . . . could . . . is not to be trusted. He was Papa's butler long before our marriage, your grandfather's footman before that. No, I do not believe Unwin would . . . would do as Sir Henry suggested, but perhaps one of the lesser servants has stolen valuable wines to sell. I have left everything in Unwin's care and my lack of supervision may have caused him to become careless . . . to leave the cellar keys where a less scrupulous servant might find them. If Sir Henry were head of the household, I would be relieved of such worries. And he is so kind . . . really, Addy, I cannot understand why you do not respect him as I do. It was always Papa's wish that I should remarry. He did not want us to be alone, unprotected.'

Perhaps her mama might have paid more attention to her protests if she had had more valid reasons to back up her instinctive dislike of Sir Henry, Adela thought now as she huddled closer beneath the fur. Near by, an owl hooted and the screech of a nightjar brought renewed fears of ghosts and vampires. As her mother's wedding date had drawn closer, even Titus and Barnaby had begun to agree with her that Sir Henry's nature might not, after all, be all that it seemed. He was, they agreed, too good to be true, and their father had taken it upon himself to make discreet enquiries about Sir Henry's background. They had overheard him telling their mother that the Nayland family, though well enough connected, was hopelessly impoverished, and that far from retiring from the Army by choice, Sir Henry had been obliged to resign his commission as he was unable to meet his commitments.

Suppose, the twins had said gloomily, Sir Henry was marrying Lady Carstairs (who, so their father had said, was now an exceptionally wealthy widow) in order to gain access to her fortune?

Despite Parson Mallory's warnings, despite Adela's pleas, despite Nou-Nou's tears and contrary to the express disapproval of her late husband's lawyer, Nadine had agreed to the betrothal and finally, to set a wedding date.

'You all misjudge Sir Henry!' she had protested. 'He is the kindest of men and he loves you dearly, Addy. He was Papa's friend and you can be sure Papa would not have thought so highly of him were he not beyond reproach.'

'It is only Sir Henry who tells you Papa held him in such high regard!' Adela had argued. 'If Papa thought so well of him, why did he never mention his name?'

'He may have done, Addy, but I cannot recall all the names of his fellow officers – there were so many!'

Adela's memories of those months leading up to her mother's wedding were brought to an abrupt halt as she heard the heavy footsteps descending the stone staircase leading to the cellar. Hurriedly she jumped to her feet and carried the fur rug to its place of concealment behind the ale firkins. She had barely completed the task before the key turned in the lock and the heavy wooden door swung open.

Sir Henry Nayland appeared to the crouching child to have giantlike proportions as he stood in the doorway, his face and body lit by the candle he held in front of him. Adela could not discern his features but was left in no doubt as to his mood as he barked out, 'Come here at once, Adela. If I have to search for you, believe me, I shall not hesitate to leave you here all night!'

She might have endured a thrashing such as he had administered last night, Adela thought, but to be locked in utter darkness all night long was beyond bearing. Clasping her hands before her in a vain attempt to conceal her fear from her stepfather, she stepped forward into the circle of light.

'Well, girl, let us see if you have come to your senses at last.'

He reached out a hand and roughly gripped one of her arms.

'You will now say, "Good-evening, Papa!" after which you will say, "I am sorry for my obstinacy and my stupidity and beg your forgiveness, Papa!"'

Last night she had had the courage to remain silent until

after the cane had fallen for the sixth time across her buttocks
– she could still feel the painful sting of the weals even now.
After the seventh stroke, the pain had been sufficient to break
her resolve. Since she could not finally withstand the pain and
must eventually submit, she decided now to do as he asked,
but tomorrow at breakfast, she would again refuse to call him
'Papa'.

'Did you hear what I said, Adela?'

She nodded. Her small square chin lifted and with an effort,
she looked up and met his furious gaze, her eyes stormy.

'You wish me to say: "Good-evening, Papa!" and: "I am
sorry for my obstinacy and stupidity and beg your forgiveness,
Papa!" May I go now I have done as you asked, sir?'

'You will go straight to your room; and understand this,
my fine lady, I will brook no further insolence from you. You
will call me "Papa" on every occasion you speak to me. Is
that understood? Should you fail to do so, you will again be
punished and your punishments will increase in severity. Your
mother has spoiled you quite disgracefully. I have informed
her that from now on, you will be subject to my discipline
– not hers. I hope I have made myself clear?'

Determined not to use the name he wished again, Adela
nodded her head.

'Very well! I trust we now understand each other. You may
go to your room!'

Tears stung Adela's eyes as she ran past him out of the
cellar, up through the hall and up the stairs to her room. Dolly
was waiting for her and Adela flung herself into her waiting
arms.

'I hate him! I hate him!' she sobbed as soon as she could
catch her breath. 'He is *not* my father and I shall never, ever,
ever think of him as such. If Papa only knew . . .'

Although but four years older than the child she now held
in her arms, Dolly Brixton was, by virtue of her upbringing,
a generation older in her experience of life – and of human
nature. Brought up in London, she had first-hand knowledge

of the poverty and depravity so often forced on families like
her own. Girls as young as eleven were sold for prostitution
for the simple necessity of keeping younger children in the
family from starvation. Fathers tried to drown their hopelessness in drink and were frequently violent when they stumbled
home from the gin houses. Mothers, too, worn out with child
bearing and despair, often turned to drink and violence.
Others, unable to face the advent of a twelfth, thirteenth or
fourteenth mouth to feed, abandoned their newborn babies
as had Dolly's mother. Most died. A few, like Dolly, found
their way into orphan asylums, funds for which were raised
by the good works of the Society of Friends and other phil-
anthropic groups.

At the age of twelve, Dolly, who was a strong, cheerful girl,
had been found work as a chambermaid in a hostelry in the
dock area of London. The landlord was a hard, brutal man,
and the men who roomed at his inn were, more often than
not, thieves, smugglers, pick-pockets, foreign sailors, former
prisoners. It was only a matter of months before Dolly was
brutally raped and, despite her state of penury, had run away.
For a year she had managed to survive on the streets, begging,
sleeping rough, earning a few pence here and there when an
extra pair of hands was needed for washing-up or cleaning in
an ale house.

In that year Dolly had become wise to the ways of the
streets and might have continued to survive in such fashion
had she not one day encountered a charitable lady serving
soup to the starving outside the doors of the church where
her brother was the incumbent. Despite Dolly's filthy, ragged
appearance, the good woman had recognized her as one of
the orphan girls and, upon hearing her story, had written to
her friend Mrs Mallory, to ask if she would offer Dolly a job
of work in her Sussex home by way of a sanctuary.

'It was the Will of God!' Dolly had related to Adela, omitting stories of some of the worst of her experiences which
were unfit for the little girl's ears. The good-hearted parson's

wife employed her as a kitchen-maid at the parsonage, and when Nadine's old nurse, Nou-Nou, had succumbed to the rheumatics and could no longer care for Adela, Mrs Mallory had proposed Dolly as nursery-maid. 'She said as 'ow I 'ad proved myself most 'elpful with Miss Patience and knew as 'ow I was anxious to better meself,' Dolly had explained.

Although Nou-Nou still looked after Nadine and was still superficially in charge of Adela, Dolly managed her young charge so ably that the older woman soon relinquished responsibility to the new nursemaid. In less than a year, Dolly and Adela had become not only child and servant, but friends. It was Dolly, therefore, and not Nou-Nou to whom Adela now poured out her fears and despair.

'I am no longer to be under Mama's authority!' she wept. 'Mama understood how I felt . . . I hoped she would explain to Sir Henry . . . she promised she would speak to him . . . oh, Dolly, what am I to do?'

''Ush now, Miss Addy! 'T'aint like you to cry! Next thing you'll be 'aving Master Titus and Master Barnaby calling you a cry-baby, and you doant want that, now do you?'

The faintest of smiles filtered through the tears on Adela's flushed cheeks.

'No, I do not – and do not dare tell them, Dolly! Oh, I wish I could see them. Maybe the twins would know what I should do!'

Dolly smoothed the tumble of black hair from the child's forehead, a frown creasing her own round face.

'They was up this noontide, asking for you to go and ride with them!' she said. 'The Master was with your mama when they called, and Unwin tolt me as 'ow the Master said you was ill.'

'That's a fib – worse than a fib; it was a lie!' Adela protested, her tears drying.

'That's a fact, Miss Addy. Master Titus said but you was never ill and Master Barnaby asked your mama wot was wrong with you but the Master said it was nuffing for them to concern theirselves with and your mama 'ad a 'eadache and they was to go on 'ome.'

'Mama is not well?' Adela asked anxiously.

Dolly hesitated. According to Nou-Nou, it was worry that was making her beautiful mistress ill. Ever since the new master had come home after the wedding, things had changed. Unless there were visitors, Sir Henry no longer spoke lovingly to his wife and had set about upsetting everyone with all the changes he wanted made in the house. Any memento of poor Sir Matthew Carstairs had to be put away; the furniture moved to the Master's liking; mealtimes altered; servants dismissed and others engaged. Unwin had threatened to give in his notice but the Mistress had talked him out of it, telling him he must stay for her sake. Nou-Nou had said the same, only no one had taken notice of her for, as Dolly told Adela, everyone knew wild horses would not have dragged the old nurse from her mistress' side. When the food arrived at table, if it was not as piping hot as the new master liked it, he would send it back to the kitchen. He had even threatened that if it happened again, he would throw it out of the window! Every member of the staff was frightened of him and it did not surprise any of them that the Mistress, accustomed to the gentle, adoring ways of her late husband, was deeply shocked by and fearful of her new one. Everyone in the household now looked for ways to avoid provoking Sir Henry's anger – everyone except Adela. No one knew better than Dolly that the child had been determined from the very start not to pretend a welcome, still less a liking for her new stepfather.

For a few weeks, Sir Henry had ignored the child's behaviour, although he could not have failed to notice it. He had demanded of Nadine that she instruct her daughter to behave more civilly towards him; but not even her mother's entreaties would oblige Adela to address her stepfather as Papa.

'He is not my father; he is not, he is *not*!' she protested again and again.

To please her mother, Adela had forced herself to curtsy to

Sir Henry when she entered or left a room; she spoke politely and obeyed his orders without argument; but she would not relinquish that last – and to her, all-important – concession, she would not acknowledge him as her father.

'I shall not do so at breakfast tomorrow, Dolly!' she said now, her tears drying and her mouth set in a stubborn line. 'Not even if I have to spend yet another day in that horrid cellar!' The lines of her slender body now slackened as she added wistfully, 'I could see the sun shining outside. I *wish* I could have been out riding with the twins. Were they really worried about me, Dolly? If they call again, will you find a way to tell them what is happening to me? If Sir Henry goes out, maybe they would come to the cellar window and talk to me. It is many days since I have seen them and before long, they will be going away to that Academy of Equitation in Anjou and it will be weeks and weeks before they return from France.'

She grasped Dolly by the shoulders and, her green eyes flashing with excitement, she said, 'Dolly, you could take the twins a note from me. I will write it now, at once. I will tell them that I am a prisoner; they will tell the parson and he will come and tell Sir Henry that I must not be treated in this way. You will take my note, will you not? Please, Dolly!'

Dolly bit her lip.

'I ain't a-feared to take a note for you, Miss Addy, but I doubt as 'ow Parson can do aught to 'elp. It ain't none of Parson's business 'ow the Master runs 'is 'ouse and t'wouldn't be right for 'im to interfere.' She gave a sudden smile which transformed her homely features so that for a moment, she no longer looked quite so plain but almost comely. 'That ain't to say I ain't going to ask them young rascals to sneak up and see you, Miss Addy – that is if you do be locked in the cellar again. Mebbe as 'ow them two'll talk some sense into you. I isn' able, surely!'

Adela gave a half-hearted smile.

'If you mean my calling *that man* "Father" is sensible, then I would rather be thought the village idiot. You never knew my papa, Dolly, or you would understand.' Her voice broke as she whispered, 'He was the kindest, dearest, most courageous person you could ever meet, and he loved me and I loved him and he was a *good* man. Oh, why, why did Mama ever marry Sir Henry? He is evil, Dolly. He only ever pretended to love Mama and me, and now that he has got her and Dene Place and all Papa's money, he is not pretending any more. I cannot bear it!'

''Tis more like your poor mama as 'as to bear it, Miss Addy!' Dolly said dourly as she began to help Adela out of her clothes. 'You be'aving as you do ain't making life no easier to 'er! It doant do 'er no good thinking of you shut up all day in that there cellar and 'er not able to do naught about it.'

She untied Adela's corset and stripping off her chemise, pulled a night-gown from around the warming pan which she had placed beneath the bed covers.

'I reckon as 'ow your papa would want for you to call the Master any name he likes if it makes life 'appier for your mama,' she said, slipping the night-gown over Adela's dark curls. 'You think on that, Miss Addy!'

Adela's face paled as she climbed between the sheets.

'If I do as you are suggesting, *he* will think he has won!' she said.

Dolly looked at her young charge, her eyes filled with a wisdom far beyond her age and circumstances.

'You'll know as 'ow that ain't true!' she said. 'And I will know, and your mama'll know. You be only a child, Miss Addy, and like it or not, it ain't for you to go against the Master's wishes. It doant matter none to 'im you feel it's disrespectful to your poor late papa.'

For a brief moment Adela was silent as she meditated. Then her chin lifted and her eyes darkened.

'Maybe he will stop trying to oblige me to do as he wishes if I can hold out long enough!' she said. 'He cannot make me spend my whole life in the cellar. He could not, Dolly, could he?'

Dolly turned away from the questioning, innocent child's face.

'I ain't edicated no more than is you when it comes to the law, Miss Addy. All I know is one girl in the orphan asylum where I was 'ad been locked in an attic all her life 'cos she 'ad a birthmark down one side of 'er face – a really ugly one it were, too! – and 'er pa couldn't stand to see it. She were given food but naught else and she were like a two year old – not able to talk proper nor do anything for 'erself. She'd 'ave probably stayed there all 'er life 'cepting 'er ma died and 'er pa put 'er out in the street and someone found 'er. She were lucky she weren't put in Bedlam, 'er not talking and seeming like a lunatic. When I left the orphan asylum, she were getting on fine, though she wouldn't never be fit for service. They put 'er in the laundry, 'er liking to work the coppers and mangle and such. No, the law doant tek no account of wot chillun wants.'

She turned back to face Adela only to find that the child, exhausted by her ordeal and the violence of her emotions, had fallen asleep. Dolly pulled the covers up to her chin and gently removed the warming pan.

Perhaps, she thought as she tiptoed out of the room, it was as well little Miss Addy had not heard her story, for it could only add to her fears. She could see small hope of matters improving, for this much she did know: a husband was master in his own home and his wife, children and servants had no choice but to do his bidding. To be locked in a cold, dank cellar was not an unbearable ordeal, even for a child of ten; but this might be only the beginning. Sir Henry was only starting to tighten the reins and who could tell what next might be forthcoming!

'If only Miss Addy were less stubborn; less determined to 'ave 'er way!' Dolly muttered to herself as she went downstairs. 'Seems as if she be the only one in this 'ousehold as ain't a-feared of the new Master!'

Dolly drew a worried sigh. All the servants were agreed

that Sir Henry was a bully and not one to stand for anyone challenging his authority – let alone a child. Unwin thought Sir Henry might possibly have taken to a quiet, placid step-daughter who would not dream of defying him, but they all knew these were the very last adjectives attributable to Adela.

Half an hour later, as Dolly made her way back upstairs to the truckle-bed outside Adela's bedroom door, she felt a grim sense of foreboding. She loved the fiery, impetuous little girl; admired her spirit, and she knew that love was returned. No matter what befell them at the hands of Sir Henry, she would never leave Adela, the only human being to whom Dolly had ever given her heart.

CHAPTER TWO

1787

The long summer vacation was nearing its end and the
Mallory twins were on their way across the fields to Dene
Place in a last attempt to see Adela to say their farewells.
Although both young men enjoyed their lives at their father's
old college at Oxford and the companionship of the other
students, they were devoted to their loving parents and to
their home. Their holidays had been wonderfully free from
restrictions, their time their own to ride, fish, perfect their
fencing, their archery; enjoy the company of their friends.
There were always highlights – sojourns with their London
friends when they had pursued more sophisticated pleasures.
They had caused quite a stir, not only because of their identical looks, but because they had refused to wear the
customary wigs but wore their own hair, which they powdered
only for evening entertainments. The previous summer Adela's
French cousins had come to England for the christening of
her half-brother, Ned, and they had vied with one another
for the attention of the ravishingly pretty Eugénie de Falence
and her pert little eighteen-year-old sister, Louise.

There was to have been a return visit this summer – the
invitation including the twins who, with Jacques in attendance, were to escort Adela and her mother to the de Falence
château in Normandy. During their education at the eques-
trian school in Anjou the twins had become close companions
of Philippe de Falence, whose mother, the Comtesse, frequently
invited them to their house in Paris. Charmed by the boys'
looks and manners, she thought them ideal companions for

her three daughters. However, their departure in June was postponed on account of the serious decline in the health of Adela's mother. Now, three months later, not only had there been a marked deterioration in Nadine's condition, but according to the letter the Mallorys had received from the Comtesse de Falence, Sir Henry had inexplicably denied her request to come to England to see her ailing sister-in-law. The Comtesse's concern had deepened and she had, therefore, decided to invite the twins to France – without Adela if needs must. She was most anxious to see them, she wrote to their father, for they could give her the latest intelligence. For their part, she could assure them of some interesting stag and boar hunting with Philippe and the Comte, and a merry time when the family returned to their house in Paris for Christmas.

Loath as the twins were to be leaving poor little Addy behind, they were eagerly awaiting their departure. The promise of the hunting greatly appealed to them, as did the prospect of escorting the pretty de Falence daughters to the entertainments the Comtesse had depicted. Moreover, both boys had a young man's healthy interest in the opposite sex. Now nearing their twenty-first birthday, they were very much aware of their masculinity. Unknown to their parents, they had long since bidden farewell to their virginity in France, and for the past two years at university, had been sharing the favours of the barmaid at one of the inns in Oxford.

Now six foot tall, the boys were strikingly good-looking. Wherever they went, they enjoyed the covert looks and blushes of the young females they encountered and the more openly interested glances of their matronly chaperons. The combination of fair hair and deep brown eyes and dark lashes was not only unusual but arresting. There was, too, a mischievous glint in their eyes which mirrored their sunny natures and their ability always to enjoy life to the full. Both during their school days and at Oxford, they were renowned for their escapades, most of which were harmless enough and were overlooked by their tutors in the light of the fact that they managed somehow to pass their exams.

Such minor problems as the twins had concerned a permanent shortage of money, for they invariably exceeded their father's limited allowance; and their shared – but hopeless – adoration for Eugénie de Falence. Not only was she two years older than themselves but she was already affianced to a wealthy French baron with large estates in the Loire, and the gulf between their social standing was far too great to be breached. The enchanting Mademoiselle Eugénie moved in French court circles, and although she flirted with the twins on the few occasions they met, they were well aware that she looked upon them still as boys.

'Perhaps it is as well Eugénie is engaged to marry her baron fellow!' Titus said as they left the village behind them and took the footpath across Farmer Bane's fields leading to Dene Place. 'After all, Barny, we could not both marry her even were she to have considered one of us for such a match!'

Barnaby grinned.

'We could have fought a duel to determine which of us was to ask for her hand!'

Titus returned his twin's smile, acknowledging the absurdity of the suggestion. Their relationship was – and always had been – such that they shared or went without.

'All the same, Barny, I cannot imagine falling in love with any other girl, can you? We have adored Eugénie for as long as I can remember! When Uncle George died last year and Father inherited the title, we became a deal more eligible, did we not? If only Uncle George had not spent all Grandfather's money! For all Mama called him an adventurer and a spendthrift, I liked him. He was a game old gentleman and did not deserve such a gruesome death as to be eaten by a crocodile, poor fellow! Between you and me, I think poor Mama fears we may take after him!'

They both laughed, remembering their jovial late uncle with affection, for he had always been most generous with his tips to the boys on the rare occasions he returned from one of his overseas adventures. Their father, by contrast, was a quiet, studious man who, but for a strong spiritual calling, might well have become a university don. As a parson – and an impoverished one at that – although socially acceptable by nature of his lineage, the Reverend Lord Mallory and his wife had made little attempt to mix with the local nobility. In years gone by, Sir Matthew Carstairs had always treated them as social equals, but since Lady Carstairs had remarried they were never now invited to Dene Place. On the few occasions they met Sir Henry Nayland, he made it quite clear that their presence at the manor house was unwelcome.

Nevertheless the twins still visited – albeit secretly, for they were fully aware of the unhappy conditions now surrounding their former playmate. Jacques was a close friend of the head coachman at Dene Place, as a consequence of which he was as often as not familiar with the activities of the master of the house. The boys, therefore, were made aware if Sir Henry Nayland were likely to be absent for a few days on one of his infrequent visits to London. Taking advantage of his absence, they would make their way to the stables at Dene Place for a secret rendezvous with Adela.

When first Adela had told them of the long days when she had been incarcerated in the cellar, the boys were inclined to agree with their mother that Adela was bringing trouble upon herself by refusing to acknowledge her new stepfather. They knew what a determined, passionate nature she had and of her fierce loyalty to her adored father, and had supposed that given time, she would come to terms with her mother's new husband. However, far from improving, the situation had worsened and now not only the boys but their parents, too, were extremely worried about Adela as well as her mother.

Sir Henry was as greatly disliked by all who came in contact with him as Sir Matthew had been loved and respected. Like all servants, the staff at Dene Place gossiped, and Jacques was told horrifying tales by Dolly who described Sir Henry as a sadistic bully who was making life intolerable for his wife and family.

Adela now had a half-sister, Kitty, a little girl born in the first year of marriage; and a half-brother, Edward, who had arrived two years later. According to Adela, her mother had had no one but old Nou-Nou to attend to her during the births, Sir Henry refusing to pay for the services of the village midwife. There had been complications following the birth of the boy and there were, mercifully, no more children. Far from welcoming his first born, Sir Henry was reputed to have been furiously angry that the child was female and had behaved as if the infant did not exist. That subsequently he doted upon the boy, the much-wanted son and heir, did nothing to lessen the tension in the house. No one, it seemed, could escape Sir Henry's biting tongue, his angry tirades. If the boy so much as sneezed, his wife and servants alike were criticized for not taking adequate care of the child and, according to Dolly, not even the heir to the throne could be more carefully watched over than little Ned Nayland.

Yet for all his father's blind devotion, the two year old, with no more than infantile instinct to guide him, was afraid of Sir Henry and cried vociferously if he were picked up or embraced by him. He was still too young to realize that by showing his aversion to his father, he would bring down a further display of wrath upon his mother's or Adela's head. Sir Henry would accuse Adela of setting the child's mind against him, and yet again she would be locked in the cellar with no more than dry bread and water to sustain her. Dolly had tried bribing the little boy, offering sweetmeats as a reward if he did not cry when taken to see his father; but the tension gripping the adults in the room was so great as to communicate itself to the child, and he would struggle to free himself from Sir Henry's arms and run to his mother.

On one of the twins' secret meetings in the stables with Adela, she had told them that she could bear the oppressive, unhappy atmosphere of her home for herself; her fears were for her mother who, she confessed, was quite shockingly pale and but a shadow of her former self. 'She is even more frightened of Sir Henry than is little Ned!' she had recounted. 'I think that he beats her, for I have heard her crying out to him in the night to desist, though Mama denies it. I know him capable of it for he beats me, and although Kitty is but four years old and for the most part escapes his attention, I have seen him thrash her with a cane for no more serious an offence than to call out to Mama to assist her when she fell over. He hates poor Kitty as he hates me, and I fear that he is growing to hate Mama, too.'

'It is not our business to interfere in the domestic affairs of Dene Place!' Lady Mallory had said when the twins pleaded with their mother to intervene. 'Every time your father has called to see Sir Henry on some pretext or other, the man is civil enough, if not friendly or inclined for any intimacies. Lest your father acknowledge that Dolly or, indeed, Adela, has been running to him with such tales, he has no reason to raise the subject with Sir Henry about his treatment of his wife and children. It is simply not our concern, although I have to admit that Lady Carstairs – I mean Lady Nayland – does indeed look poorly! I did mention this to Sir Henry after church one Sunday but he put the poor lady's ill health down to the difficult births of her children. I recommended the services of Sir Matthew's physician but his reply was that he believed all such practitioners were charlatans and that Nature and Time provided the best cure for all ailments.'

The twins had seen Adela only once during the past vacation for Sir Henry had decided to forgo his August grouse shooting in Scotland and had chosen instead to enjoy the pleasures of trout fishing on his own estate. He seemed to prefer a solitary existence and was, as often as not, to be seen alone in the company of the manservant he had brought with him when he moved into Dene Place following his marriage. The servant had been Sir Henry's batman during his army service and did not mix with the other servants, seeing to all his master's needs himself. A silent, taciturn fellow, he was seldom heard but often to be seen in passages and corridors where he was least expected. Dolly was convinced he was not quite right in the head. He had his own room over one of the stables and chose to eat his meals there alone rather than in the servants' hall downstairs. He did not attend family prayers and never went to church. By and large, he was as feared and disliked as his master. His only asset was his horsemanship. A superb rider, he alone could control Sir Henry's big black stallion, Chevron – an ugly, ill-tempered brute who had come close to killing one of the stable lads who had ventured into his stall. The man's name was Alfred Higgins but the twins, inspired by Dolly, always referred to him as 'The Spy'.

'Let us hope The Spy accompanied Sir Henry to London today!' Titus said as Dene Place came into view. The sinister aspect its present occupant had lent the house was not in evidence this sleepy, sunny afternoon, and the grey stone façade of the building was softened in the haze of the heat. A thin curl of grey smoke wound upwards towards an azure blue sky, coming from the kitchen chimney where the fire was never allowed to go out.

'My faith, it is a lovely house!' Barnaby exclaimed, before adding with a sigh, 'We have had such first-rate days there, Titus! I wish it had not all changed the way it has!'

'I hate to think of our poor little Addy a virtual prisoner there!' Titus echoed Barnaby's thoughts.

'She used to be such a merry child – always laughing!'

'Unless she was in one of her temper tantrums!' Titus finished with a smile. ''Tis hard these days to realize she is still only fourteen – the same age as our Patience. She seems so much older.'

'Possibly because she tries to be a mother to Kitty and Ned!' Barnaby suggested. 'Dolly told Jacques that she and Adela spend their time attempting to keep the little ones well clear of Sir Henry's tongue. Addy does not even go riding now for fear of what might occur whilst she is absent.'

"'Tis a pity the Comte and Comtesse de Falence did not stay a second night when they visited for Ned's christening,' Titus commented. 'They might then have noticed what was happening.' Barnaby frowned.

'According to Addy, they had no choice, but were ordered by Sir Henry to leave after a terrible argument took place between the Comte and Sir Henry.'

'I suppose we must accept that Dene Place belongs now to Sir Henry and that he has the right to say who shall sleep beneath his roof. Look to yourself now, Barnaby – if we go by the vegetable garden behind the glasshouses, we can reach the stables unobserved. Jacques saw Sir Henry going through the village at a gallop this morning, but he did not see The Spy and we cannot be sure he, too, is absent!'

Despite his genuine concern for Adela, and, indeed, for her mother for whom he had a very real affection, Titus was enjoying this escapade for itself. To come to forbidden territory brought back childhood memories of games he and Barnaby had played when they tried to sneak into one another's camps; raided Farmer Bane's orchard to steal his greengages; or climbed out of their bedroom window to pay a visit to the gipsies on the common.

Now they were young men on the brink of achieving their majority and when in the company of their contemporaries, were meticulous about their attire, choosing the most colourful of silk waistcoats; fashionable tight breeches and intricately folded neckcloths. The silver buckles on their dogskin shoes were shined by Jacques to perfection; their stockings snow white and with no sign of a wrinkle. Their mother complained that they were turning into real Jack-a-dandies but secretly she was immensely proud of her two handsome sons. During the holidays, however, they tended to revert in the daytime to more comfortable, less fashionable clothes which were appropriate for country wear and afforded them the freedom to indulge in one or other of their favourite sports. This summer they had spent most of their time sailing with Jacques, and as a consequence sun and sea air had tanned their faces to a golden brown and bleached their hair an even paler gold.

Spread-eagled now on the heaps of clean straw destined for the horses' bedding, they awaited Adela's arrival. They did not have long to wait, for Dolly had been keeping watch for them and alerted her young charge of their arrival. Adela ran into the barn and flung herself down between them. Her cheeks were pink with haste and excitement.

'I am so glad to see you!' she said breathlessly, turning from one to the other. 'We may not have long together because The Spy is exercising Chevron and may well return within the hour. Dolly is keeping watch and will warn us, but we must be quick. I have much to tell you!'

The colour had left her cheeks and both boys now noticed the dark violet shadows beneath her eyes; the lines of anxiety creasing her forehead. Titus sat up and gently stroked her long, raven black hair. Her ribbon had come loose and the ringlets fell about her face in an unruly fashion.

'Come, my sweeting, Barny and I are here to help you if we can. Tell us what is wrong now?'

Tears filled Adela's eyes.

''Tis Mama!' she said huskily. 'I fear for her life! She is so thin and listless and I think she has abandoned the will to live. Only yesterday she told me that she thinks only of the day she can go to join Papa. Sir Henry will not have it that she is dangerously ill although she can no longer support herself and lies all day in her bed. I take the little ones to see her but she turns her face away and will not speak to or even look at them. 'Tis as if she does not wish to be reminded that she is their mother and has a duty to remain in this world to take care of them.'

'Will Sir Henry not permit the physician to visit her?' Barnaby asked.

'I do not think he cares whether she lives or dies!' Adela said bitterly. 'He never loved her – it was all pretence. He wants only this house, this estate, Papa's money.'

'It is not your own dislike of Sir Henry prompting such an opinion?' Titus enquired. 'You cannot be certain these are the facts of the matter!'

'But I can be certain!' Adela cried, her green eyes flashing suddenly with anger. 'Nou-Nou told me last night that when Uncle Hugo was here for the christening, he took it upon himself to make enquiries about Mama's financial affairs. He had discovered that Sir Henry was penniless when he married Mama; Uncle Hugo challenged him on the matter and Sir Henry forbade him ever to enter Dene Place again or to communicate with Mama or me. Nou-Nou told me this for she had learned the truth from Mama the night Uncle Hugo and Aunt Camille departed.'

She turned from one twin to the other, her expression intense as she added, 'Do you not understand what this means? It explains why I have never received any letters. Sir Henry must have withheld them. Even if my aunt and uncle did not wish to countermand Sir Henry's ruling, Eugénie or Louise would have written to me. He is an evil man, and he is allowing Mama to die!'

The twins looked at one another and at Adela's trembling body. They longed to be able to help but could think of no way to do so.

'If I relate this story to Father, perhaps he can find some excuse to call upon Lady Nayland!' Titus said.

'Or Mama might call with the gift of some of her damson conserve as a pretext,' Barnaby intervened, 'but if your mother is as ill as you say, the physician should attend her.'

'Sir Henry will no longer permit *anyone* to see Mama,' Adela said despairingly. 'He insists that her indisposition is imaginary; but it is not; it is *not*! Can you not understand? We are all virtual prisoners in this house and we see no one.'

Barnaby put his arm round Adela's shoulders, his heart twisting with pain at the thought of this unhappy, frightened girl prey to the whims of such a man.

'He has not ill-treated you, Addy?' he asked anxiously. 'He does not beat you?'

'On occasions!' Adela admitted but quickly waved such considerations aside. 'He is reconciled now to the fact that I *will* not call him "Papa" except in the presence of Mama or the children, and he pretends to be unaware that I address him simply as "sir". But if I intervene when he is chastizing little Kitty, he will beat me instead. I am accustomed to it but I cannot endure what is happening to Mama. In the days when she was married to Papa, I cannot recall her ever having a day's illness, and she always looked so pretty! There are times . . .' Adela's voice dropped to a whisper '. . . times when I think of ways to kill him! And you should not smile, either of you, for I am in earnest. If I could devise a means of doing so without detection, I think I would have rid this house of that evil man long since. I would do so openly but for the knowledge that I would be apprehended, and then who would take care of the little ones? Mama gives them no attention now and they have only me to love them.'

Even more shocked than Titus by this violent declaration, Barnaby drew a worried sigh.

'Could you not run away with the children? Come with us to your uncle and aunt in France? They would care for you all.'

'And leave Mama?' Adela cried. 'Even if we could escape without Sir Henry's notice, she is not fit to make a journey to the village, let alone to Normandy. And even if we *could* take her with us, how long would it be before Sir Henry found us and obliged us to return?'

'If 'tis only your mama's money, Dene Place, the estate, he wants, would he not permit you all to go?'

'Perhaps it might suit his purpose, although I believe he takes pleasure in torturing us,' Adela said. 'But Dene Place was Papa's family home; and he is buried here in the church-yard. Mama would never leave. She is determined to be put to rest beside him.'

'We will speak to our parents again,' Barnaby said. 'Maybe there is something they can do. Father quite frequently plays chess of a winter's evening with Judge Ballister. If the judge were willing to look into the matter, Sir Henry would surely realize the need to temper his behaviour!'

Jacques' head appeared round the open door of the barn.

'You must leave at once,' he said, his brown, weather-beaten face screwed into lines of anxiety. 'Dolly signalled to me from the window that 'Iggins were riding towards the 'ouse!'

The boys rose quickly to their feet and turned to look uncertainly at Adela. She was close to tears – their brave little Addy who they knew to be as loath to cry as their sister was prone! Jacques was urging them both to make speed, but one of the twins hesitated. He reached into his coat pocket and withdrew a hare's foot, neatly fitted into a band of gold.

'Here, Addy, you have it. A gipsy gave it to me – he swore it would bring me luck. You keep it!'

'Demme if you will not get us all caught, Titus, if you dally much longer!' Barnaby called from the doorway.

Tears spilled slowly from Adela's eyes as she attempted to voice her thanks. Longing to comfort her, Titus put his arms around her and for a moment she stood quietly in his embrace, her head against his shoulder. Then he placed a hand gently beneath her chin and lifted her face so that he could kiss her.

'We will come and see you immediately on our return from France!' he promised. 'And we will write to you and address our letters to Father. Things will get better – I am sure of it!'

'Oh, Titus, if I could only believe that!' Adela whispered. Yet for all her hopelessness, she was strangely comforted in the safe circle of Titus' arms. Other than the faithful Dolly, she had no one now to love her. Her mama was already living in another world; her papa long since absent from her life. The kiss Titus had given her reassured her that there was still someone who really cared.

'You must go, Titus!' she said in a firmer voice, remembering Jacques' warning.

'Maybe 'tis Barny who holds you thus!' he said teasingly in an attempt to make her smile. 'It matters not, Addy. We both love you! Now, I fear, I had best be on my way!'

For a long moment after the twins had disappeared with the valet, Adela stood in the doorway of the barn, gazing in the direction they had taken. She knew that her stepfather's manservant would arrive at any moment but she was loath to return to the house. Her hand reached up to touch her lips where, if she concentrated, she could still feel Titus' kiss. It was the first time she had been kissed on her mouth and only now, in the memory, was she conscious of the strange emotions the touch of Titus' lips had aroused within her. Her heart was beating at double its usual pace – and not, she knew, from fear of detection. Her cheeks felt hot and her body languorous. Was it possible, she wondered, that this was what the poets tried so hard to describe – love? It seemed unlikely. She had known both Titus and Barnaby all her life and loved them as a sister might; as they had loved her. Yet this was somehow different. She felt a deep yearning that was both pleasurable and painful at one and the same time.

Perhaps Dolly would know why a kiss should arouse in her such strange feelings, she told herself. Dolly was always such a fount of information. It was she who had explained, two years ago, why Adela had suddenly started to bleed and that she had now become a woman! It was Dolly who had told her to be proud of her newly developing breasts and small waist for they would help her to win the affections of the man she would one day hope to marry. But for all her wisdom, Dolly had not been able to explain how it felt to fall in love.

Perhaps she would not after all tell Dolly about Titus' kiss! It would be her secret – something she could remember when she was alone in her bed at night. Meanwhile, although it would be six long months before she could hope to see Titus again, she had his lucky talisman. Adela returned to the house undetected and not a little comforted by the hope that Judge Ballister might be persuaded by the parson to come to her assistance.

The twins, however, were quickly disabused by their father

that there was anything positive which could be done to help Lady Nayland or her children.

'I have already spoken to Judge Ballister of my concern for that poor woman,' Lord Mallory told his sons. 'He confirmed what I have already said: the law would support Henry Nayland and would give no protection to his wife or children.' He gave his sons a sudden gentle smile. 'Believe me, if there were anything I could do – even at the risk of losing my living here – I would not hesitate to do it.'

Lady Mallory, who had been sitting quietly in the background, now said in her soft voice, 'You could repeat in your sermon that passage from St Luke, is it not? "*It were better for him that a millstone were hanged about his neck, and he cast into the sea, than that he should offend one of these little ones,*"' she quoted.

Her husband smiled.

'Quite right, my dear, chapter seventeen, verse two, I think. However, I have to say I do not consider Sir Henry to be a man much influenced by religious teachings. Uncharitable though it may be, I am of the opinion that it is only the fear of hell and damnation which prompts his regular attendance at church; or, indeed, that timely payment last winter for the repair of the roof!'

Despite the gravity that had given rise to this discussion, the twins looked at one another and exchanged grins. It was only on the rarest of occasions that their father displayed his cynicism at the behaviour of his fellow men. But their humour was short-lived as they recalled the desperate appeal in Adela's green eyes when she had bade them goodbye.

'Addy is convinced her mother is dying,' Titus said quietly. 'There *must* be something we can do!'

'We can do nothing,' the parson said gently. 'It is in God's hands. His will be done!'

The twins were crestfallen as they wandered out into the parsonage garden where their sister, Patience, was tending her herb garden.

'Patience will want news of Addy,' Barnaby said thoughtfully. 'It will serve no purpose to tell her of our concern.'

''Tis best to leave her in her innocence!' Titus agreed. 'But what are we to tell Addy? That we can do nothing to help her or Lady Nayland? Knowing Addy as we do, we might have thought she was exaggerating had these been the old days. Remember how she loved to embroider her stories – so much so that we were hard put at times to distinguish fact from fiction?'

'Addy is no longer the child we used to know!' Barnaby said frowning. 'If anything, I think she makes light of her own sufferings. Unless Jacques is exaggerating when he repeats Dolly's account of events, then it is no light thrashing that brute of a man inflicts upon her. She is beaten as no female should be – far more severely than we were beaten by the masters at school!'

'I cannot bear to think of it,' Titus said, shaking his head. 'What makes it worse to contemplate is the memory of how happy they all were at Dene Place when Sir Matthew was still alive. There was only love and laughter in that house – and now there are only tears!'

'We must enlist the help of the Comte and Comtesse de Falence. After all, the Comte is Lady Nayland's brother.'

Titus nodded as he said, 'This will give Addy some hope.'

'Meanwhile, she knows we both love her and that she is as dear to us as our own little sister.'

'Loving her is not enough!' Titus replied as they went in search of their sister. 'We have to find a way to protect her – and Lady Nayland, too.'

But for Nadine, their desire to help was too late, and by the time the twins reached France, Adela's mother was dead.

CHAPTER THREE

1788

It was a perfect May morning. The sun was shining, its bright gold light reflected in all the east-facing windows of the Château de Falence. A gentle breeze was swaying the branches of the trees to the north, the opposite direction to that of the English Channel which, the Comte had told the twins, posed possible dangers for their day's adventure.

Titus and Barnaby regarded one another with ill-concealed excitement. Of all the many pleasures they had enjoyed since their arrival in France last autumn, today would undoubtedly be the greatest. An army officer, Monsieur le Marquis d'Arlandes – a contact from their days at *L'Académie d'Equitation* – was about to take them into the sky in his magnificent balloon. Thirty foot in diameter, when filled with inflammable air it would support in the basket suspended beneath not only themselves, but the Marquis and their host, Comte Hugo de Falence.

Eugénie, with her mother, sisters, Philippe, most of their neighbours and all the Château de Falence servants, were gathered in the open meadow in the northern grounds of the château, their faces a combination of apprehension and curiosity.

Eugénie moved nearer to the twins. Although her expression was one of anxiety, she looked as charming and graceful as always in a simple, white, silk chemise gown with a wide, black sash. Black ribbons decorated the crown of her Lunardi hat and she had draped a black pelisse over her shoulders to protect her from the breeze.

'Promise me that you will take the very greatest care,' she

begged. 'I cannot forget the terrible death of Monsieur Pilâtre de Rozier!'

Although this had occurred some three years previously, both Titus and Barnaby were familiar with the account of the fateful last balloon flight of Monsieur Pilâtre de Rozier, who, together with the Marquis d'Arlandes, had made the first ever manned flight. Subsequently, in an endeavour to cross the English Channel, the brilliant, ill-fated scientist had fallen fifteen hundred feet to his death on to the rocks outside the port of Boulogne. He had attempted to combine the principles of hot-air ballooning and gas ballooning, but when he had heated the vitriol gas in the inflated balloon, it had exploded into a ball of flame. There had been many manned flights since then but it was still considered a hazardous occupation and Eugénie, devoted as she was to the two young Englishmen, was deeply concerned for their safety.

A year ago, the middle-aged baron to whom she was affianced had met his death by shipwreck on his way to the French colony, the Île de France, where he was contemplating starting a sugar cane plantation. Attacked by pirates, all on board had perished and thus had ended Eugénie's four-year-long engagement. Since love had never entered this planned *manage de raison*, Eugénie was quite pleased to have regained her freedom. Although twenty-three years of age, her porcelain beauty was so remarkable that neither her parents nor the society in which they mixed doubted that she would soon find another husband. Meanwhile during a respectful period of mourning, she had been enjoying a continuation of the delightful, harmless flirtation with the Mallory twins which had begun at Dene Place.

Without the financial means to buy commissions in the Army following upon their training at the Anjou academy, the twins, having left university were now enjoying their sojourn at the de Falences' château in Normandy where they had been taking part in the boar hunts in the forests surrounding the estate. Their French now perfected, the two attractive and likeable young men had been much in demand, and during the Christmas festivities had received many invitations to enjoy themselves in Paris. They were frequently called upon to escort Eugénie, it being considered that since Titus and Barnaby were never apart, the young girl would be adequately chaperoned. Eugénie's younger sisters adored the boys and Philippe, now approaching his twenty-first birthday, was their admiring and devoted contemporary. With three young men constantly in attendance upon her, Eugénie was in no hurry to surrender her freedom to a new fiancé.

'You should come with us, Mademoiselle Eugénie,' Titus said persuasively. 'The Marquise de Brossard and the Comtesse de Bouban have both ascended in a balloon, so if other ladies have dared venture aloft, will you not dare to be as brave?'

'They were no more than eighty feet aloft!' Barnaby interjected. 'And there were ropes attaching them to the ground, whereas the Marquis d'Arlandes has said we might travel fifty kilometres or more today if all goes well!'

He was not as anxious as Titus that Eugénie should go with them. Sharing one another's thoughts as they had always done since childhood, he knew that his twin was very much in love with Adela's French cousin, and although he, too, was genuinely fond of Eugénie and aware of her feminine attributes, she was quiet and reserved by nature, and lacked the kind of spirit he found attractive in the opposite sex. He supposed it had to do with the rare differences that were emerging between himself and Titus. Gradually over the years, Titus had shown himself the more resolute, the more dominant of the two. Ever more frequently, Titus was the leader, he the follower; although this difference was so slight as to be unnoticed by others. Not even their own mother was aware of it.

Perhaps it was as well they looked for different attributes in females, he told himself as Titus increased his persuasions to Eugénie to join them, for they had long ago realized that when the time came for them to marry, they could not select the same wife! As far as he was concerned, he had not yet encountered a young girl in whose company he felt entirely at ease – with the exception of little Adela Carstairs. He thought of her quite often and did so now, knowing that she would not hesitate to jump at the opportunity to go aloft with them in the balloon whatever the danger! Occasionally, they received news of her of a kind from Jacques.

Jacques had accompanied them to his homeland but from time to time, he had returned to England and to Dene where he had for many years been engaged in smuggling activities. Lord Mallory knew nothing of the nightly sorties Jacques and his English associates made, smuggling brandy across the Channel and secreting it in various caches along the south coast until such time as it could be profitably sold. Indeed, Sir Henry Nayland was one of Jacques' regular outlets – a fact which had become known to the twins on their sixteenth birthday. They had begged Jacques to take them on one of these sorties but he would not hear of it. 'What I do is my own affair!' he had told them. 'But your parents would never forgive me – and rightly so – if I knowingly permitted you to break the law. What you choose to do when you come of age will be your own business.'

Both excited by their discovery and anxious for Jacques' safety – for smuggling was a risky business and if Jacques were detected, he could be hanged, or at best deported to one of the colonies – the twins had no option but to keep their valet's secret. They knew that he was slowly accruing a sum of money which would allow him to take a wife and support a family. It was only during their six months in France that Jacques confessed he would have asked young Dolly Brixton to marry him were there not so big a gap in their ages. The twins were astonished by Jacques' preference for Adela's maid who was very far from being comely, and an unlikely female to take any man's fancy! Nevertheless, Jacques' desire to see Dolly whenever he could suited them well, for Dolly gave their manservant news of Adela and the progress of her life with her stepfather.

The facts Jacques gave them did little to reassure them that their childhood playmate was reconciled to Sir Henry Nayland's sharp discipline. When they had occasion to speak of their home in England, they contrasted the strictures of Adela's life with their own enjoyment of these pleasurable months in France and remembered her with an uneasy degree of guilt. They agreed that it was most unfair that life should be so entertaining and amusing for them whilst she languished, a virtual prisoner, in her home. But they were young and healthy and were soon caught up once more in the pleasures so willingly provided by their hosts. Paris was a very Mecca of delight, and if they bemoaned anything at all, it was the lack of money so sorely needed to attire themselves in the latest fashions; to pay for their seats at the opera, the *Comédie-Française,* the *Ambigü Comique*; for the card games and for the hire of *fiacres* to and from these places of entertainment.

When their father had agreed to their acceptance of the de Falences' invitation, he had managed somehow to increase their allowance, but they were nearly always short of money and would have felt the lack far more had it not been for the generous hospitality of their host and that of the de Falences' friends who invited them to their homes and parties. The extra *livres* with which their father had provided them were soon dissipated during their promenades down the boulevards of the Palais-Royal. There it was all too easy to spend their money drinking in the cafés, watching the farces in the *Variétés Amusantes*, buying lace or trinkets for the de Falence daughters, throwing coins to the tumblers and jugglers performing for the vast cosmopolitan crowds who strolled in these avenues and arcades.

The kindly Comte de Falence, well aware of the twins' penury, thought nothing of sending them on these pleasurable outings with purses bulging with coins, leaving them greatly indebted to him since he was not even a distant relation. The Comtesse was equally generous. Tonight she was giving a masked ball to celebrate their coming of age on the morrow and Philippe's the following week. Many of the family friends had been invited from Paris as were the nobility for many miles around the château. Such lavish entertainment would have been unthinkable at home in England where the Mallorys lived almost reclusive lives, their father going no further afield than to visit his parishioners; their mother venturing once a year to London to visit her widowed friend who, with her brother, ran a charitable organization for the city's poorest inhabitants. Despite his newly acquired title, the Reverend Lord Mallory had no inclination to mingle in society and even had he felt inclined, he had not the means to do so. His twin sons, he had told them before they departed to France, would have to find themselves rich wives if they were to continue to mix with wealthy people like the de Falences!

'All is in readiness for you to embark, *messieurs*!' the Marquis called out.

'I shall pray for your safe return!' Eugénie said, and with her sweet smile, she stood on tiptoe to plant a kiss on each young man's cheek.

'Have no doubt about it,' Titus said, 'I have every intention of attending your mama's ball tonight; and it is my hope that you will permit me to be your partner for at least one each of the quadrilles, minuets and gavottes! Have I your promise?'

'Indeed you have. Both you and Barnaby are such accomplished dancers!'

Titus grinned cheerfully, for it meant he would have her for his partner not thrice but six times since it would not be difficult for him to persuade Barnaby to give up his dances with Eugénie. Unable to distinguish between them, she would be none the wiser when he took his twin's place!

The large silk sphere of the balloon was now fully inflated. Some of the Comte de Falence's servants were holding the basket into which he and the twins now climbed. The servants removed the bags of sand which had been hung on the outside of the basket to prevent the balloon's ascent. Almost in slow motion, it floated gently across the open ground as it gained height.

'We shall not travel far, I think!' the Marquis said. 'The

wind is but six or seven kilometres an hour. However, it will enable you, gentlemen, to observe the terrain beneath us at your leisure!'

So gradual had been their ascent that the occupants of the balloon were barely conscious of the upward movement. Looking down over the edge of the basket, Titus and Barnaby could see the de Falence family and their servants seeming no bigger than lead soldiers as they waved excitedly to the departing balloon.

'I shall attempt to gain height as quickly as possible,' the Marquis announced, 'since the horses and cattle are frequently terrified by the sight of my balloon.' He smiled as, to lighten the load, he threw out several handfuls of sand. 'Indeed, the peasantry, too, are often frightened by this strange phenomenon in the skies above them,' he added, 'although fortunately they do not stampede like the animals but will more often fall to their knees and pray, fearing some visitation from the heavens!'

The twins watched in fascination as they floated over the countryside some three hundred metres beneath them. The Comte was equally entranced.

'I had never thought to see my entire estate spread out beneath me in one panoramic canvas!' he declared. 'I am most grateful to you, Monsieur le Marquis, for the experience. I have seen these balloons before in the environs of Paris, but never could I have imagined how the earth would seem from above. I am surprised, too, that there is so little sensation of movement.'

The Marquis smiled.

'That is because we are moving at the same speed as the wind and not against it, as one does for example in a carriage or on horseback! However, I am a little concerned by the lack of wind. If it decreases much more we shall be becalmed.'

'And if that were to happen?' the Comte enquired.

'Let us hope it does not!' the intrepid aviator replied. 'It is possible there might be a greater wind speed at a higher altitude, but all the time as we travel, the gas in the balloon is slowly leaking out, as a consequence of which we descend. However,

I am reducing weight by throwing a little of this sand overboard so that we can maintain level flight or, as I am hoping, even ascend. Unfortunately, we do not have unlimited ballast, and since we cannot select the direction in which we are travelling and must go where the wind takes us, we must be sure we have a smooth area for landing before our ballast runs out.'

He gazed anxiously at the distant terrain.

'We are drifting further to the east than I had anticipated. It is to be hoped that we are not carried over that forest I see ahead of us.'

Titus and Barnaby exchanged glances, for they had detected a real note of concern in the Marquis' voice. Eugénie's reminder of the fate of the late M. Pilâtre de Rozier was in both their minds as they considered the possible dangers of landing in the topmost branches of trees. The dark mass of the forest below seemed suddenly to become very much closer, and judging by the direction in which they were gliding, they could see no way to avoid it.

The Marquis had reached the same conclusion. He made a quick inspection of his supply of sand and said reassuringly, 'Have no fear, mes amis. We shall safely traverse the trees and still have sufficient lift to find ourselves a comfortable meadow on which to descend.'

For several minutes after the first of the trees had passed beneath them, both Titus and Barnaby forgot everything in the novelty of seeing the tiny shapes of the stags and hinds gathered in the small clearings in the forest. Excitedly they pointed out to one another the even tinier shapes of a family of boars. Disturbed by the big balloon passing overhead, the forest birds soared frantically into the air scattering in every direction in panic.

This entertainment was short-lived, however, for under his breath the Marquis gave vent to an oath.

'I fear the worst has happened – we are becalmed!' he exclaimed. 'I will go higher!'

He did not draw their attention to the fact that they had

but one bag of sand remaining, and that after its use they would be forced to land regardless of the terrain below.

Five minutes later, the balloon began to move once more, but painfully slowly; and instead of taking them straight across the forest, it was carrying them diagonally – a longer route than their pilot had anticipated.

'I think we are in trouble!' Titus whispered to Barnaby, partly in fear and partly in excitement. He thought with gratitude that Eugénie was not with them. Barnaby, equally apprehensive, was remembering the day long ago when Adela had fallen out of the tree and they had cushioned her fall with the hammock. There would be no such cushioning if the Marquis was forced to land amongst the trees of the forest.

A further ten minutes passed whilst the Marquis studied their direction with increasing anxiety. Below, the trees were dense, and realizing that he must now land as soon as possible, his eyes searched for sight of the farm land he knew lay beyond the edge of the forest. From his map, he could see the line of the River Bresle, and suddenly the wide bright ribbon of water, sparkling in the sunlight, came into view. Grateful though he was to see it, its flow was in the same direction as their own. Would he, he asked himself, be able to cross to the far side? He doubted it very much for they were now only a few metres above the tree tops.

He squared his shoulders.

'If we fail to reach the far bank of the river,' he said quietly, 'I am afraid there is nothing for it but to swim. Remove your coats and boots and when I give the order, you must jump, for the water will afford us a softer landing than the rocky ground or hedges.'

They were descending with alarming rapidity. Where before they had been gliding, now as the balloon began to deflate, the ground seemed to be rushing up to meet them. There was a scramble in the confined space of the basket as the occupants struggled to carry out the Marquis' orders and remove their boots and coats.

The Comte de Falence, who was standing beside the twins, said quietly, 'I am unable to swim! The physicians forbade it when I was a boy and I have never learned the art!'

Simultaneously, the twins said, 'We are strong swimmers, Monsieur le Comte. We will go into the water together!'

Almost before they had finished speaking, at a height of no less than three metres, the Marquis gave the order to abandon ship. As Titus surfaced and looked anxiously about him, for a moment he could see no sign of the Comte. From behind him, Barnaby shouted, 'There he is, over there to your right!'

From the balloon, the river had not seemed very wide but now, as the boys grasped the Comte, each supporting him beneath an arm, they realized that the nearest bank was at least a hundred metres away. Though not quite panicking, the Comte was floundering helplessly. A robust man weighing at least fourteen stone, he was no easy burden even when the twins managed to turn him into a floating position on his back.

Meanwhile the balloon – its weight lessened considerably by the evacuation of the four men – had risen once more and was rapidly disappearing in the distance.

The boys had neither the time nor the inclination to see how the Marquis was faring as they struggled to swim towards the nearest bank with the Comte de Falence between them. He was now flailing his arms as he fought instinctively for survival.

'For the love of God, be still!' Titus begged as he tightened his grip on the older man.

Believing himself to be close to death, the Comte now lay silently on his back, gasping occasionally as the cold river water washed over his mouth and nose. The current was against them. The flow was down river, and the boys quickly realized that it was dragging them with it. It was only as they neared the bank that the pressure against their bodies eased and they were able to lighten slightly their hold on the Comte. Their shoulders and legs ached unbearably, and had the pull of the current not eased when it did, neither was certain how much longer they could have continued to fight against it with their burden.

Unnoticed by them, the Marquis had long since reached the safety of the river bank, and was now waiting to drag them from the water. From a nearby farm, a group of peasants had gathered and were standing open-mouthed watching this spectacle from a safe distance. Since they had neither news-sheets nor means of obtaining information from areas far beyond the confines of their homesteads and farms, they knew nothing of this new form of conveyance that miraculously transported men through the skies. They were convinced that the balloon, which had appeared so unexpectedly from above the forest only to disappear again, had carried no less than devils or angels from celestial regions. Now their natural caution prevented them from going too close to offer assistance.

Gradually their confidence grew as they noted the familiar rich attire of the gentleman on the bank; heard his voice calling to the swimmers in a Parisian accent; saw that none of the balloonists had either wings or horns. It was a situation to which the Marquis was well accustomed and having seen de Falence brought safely to dry land by the young Englishmen, he beckoned to one of the farmers.

'We are all soaked to the skin, as you can see. Send someone to the nearest house and ask if we may kindly borrow a carriage. The quicker you are the larger will be your reward. Be off with you now!'

'Ain't no big houses 'ceptin the Duke's, your Lordship, and that be all of ten kilometres distant!' the farmer replied, removing his hat and scratching his head as he tried to think of a speedier method of earning the reward. He was anxious to comply, for times were harder than ever with the high taxes; there were tithes to be paid to the Church – one tenth of his harvest; and the price of bread alone had gone up to three sous for a pound loaf! Since he received at most five sous for ten hours' work, it was nigh impossible to feed his family. All too frequently, the Lord of the Manor would ride over his land when hunting but offered no redress for the resulting damage. Moreover, he could charge his tenants whatever sum he pleased for the use of his ovens to make their bread; for grinding their corn, or for use of his winepress. There was no question but that he could do with the reward, the farmer muttered to himself uneasily.

The Marquis solved the problem for him as he said sharply, 'Then bring a horse and cart if you have no better means of travel, and put plenty of clean straw in it.'

As the farmer gaped at him in shock at such a lowly form of transport for these airborne gentlemen, the Marquis gave him a gentle shove.

'Away with you man or we shall catch our deaths of cold.'

From his prone position on the river bank, the Comte was coughing up the quantities of water he had swallowed during his ordeal. Titus and Barnaby were sitting on either side of him, still breathing heavily from their exertions. There was a hint of warmth in the May sunshine and their cambric shirts were steaming, as were their white silk stockings and breeches. The fair hair that had been flattened against the twins' heads, began to curl as it dried. On jumping from his balloon, the Marquis had lost his wig and now one of the farm workers who had followed it down the river, was attempting to retrieve it with a pitchfork. The Marquis came to stand beside his friend.

'I cannot apologize strongly enough, *mon ami*!' he said, his voice deepened by concern. 'That such an accident should occur when you are my guest! *C'est affreux*!'

The Comte attempted a smile.

'It was not your fault! You had warned me that there could be danger and I was only too eager to take any risks for such an experience. Calm yourself, my dear sir. *Grâce à Dieu*, we are all safe and sound!'

'Thanks to these young men!' the Marquis said, turning his attention to Titus and Barnaby. 'You showed great intrepidity! You are also very fine swimmers!'

'I am deeply indebted to you both!' the Comte spoke now with genuine warmth. 'But for your assistance, I would most certainly have drowned. Your bravery will not go unrewarded.'

His clothes dripping with water, the Marquis seated himself on the warm grass. He appeared quite unconcerned about his lost balloon, but both Titus and Barnaby were by now accustomed to the fact that all these aristocrats, unlike their own family, were so wealthy as to be able to disregard such losses. Like the Comte de Falence, nearly all had large houses in Paris as well as their country estates. They had innumerable servants and equipages; were always adorned in the latest fashions and entertained in the most lavish way.

Although neither twin had a glimmer of the mercenary in his character, both had been determined since their days at the *Académie* to re-establish their family's wealth by whatever means presented themselves. As young boys they had jokingly discussed the merits of piracy and, indeed, of following Jacques' example and indulging in smuggling contraband! But they were too steeped in the high, moral ethics of their father to consider these options seriously. To marry into wealth seemed the only possible solution, but this would mean either wedding an exceedingly plain girl who could not otherwise attract a husband; or, as often happened in France, the daughter of a middle-class fellow such as a wealthy Secretary of State who, having purchased a noble rank from the Monarch, now sought further ways of aligning himself with the aristocracy by marrying his daughter to a title.

There were two main reasons why Titus and Barnaby had given no serious thought to making profitable marriages. One was that under the present French king, Louis XVI, the nobility had put an end to alliances with the middle classes, determined as they were to keep the privileges of their society for themselves. The second reason – that of Titus alone – was that he believed himself to be deeply in love with Eugénie de Falence and could not entertain the idea of marriage to any other female!

The distant barking of a farm dog diverted Titus' attention to the welcome sight of rescuers cresting the brow of the hill. Two large oxen were being driven slowly across the meadows dragging an empty wagon behind them. Barnaby too had seen them and was grinning.

'Not quite the kind of vehicle befitting our host and the Comte!' he murmured in an undertone. 'But better than none, eh? Remember how we used to ride the hay-carts at Dene Place farm?' he added in a louder voice. 'It seems a long time since those happy days when Sir Matthew was still alive.'

'Nine years almost to the month!' the Comte interposed sadly. 'I cannot tell you how concerned my wife and I are about those children. When you return to England later this summer, you must make a point of going to Dene Place so that you can write a report of the conditions there. I am sure Jacques exaggerates when he tells you these dreadful stories about Sir Henry Nayland. Much as I abhor the man – and I use the word advisedly – I cannot believe he can be as dastardly as Jacques implies. Meanwhile, I am glad to say I am feeling much better. When I tell the Comtesse of your bravery, she will be eternally in your debt for saving my life, as indeed, am I!'

It was not, however, the Comtesse de Falence's approval Titus wanted, he reminded himself, but that of her eldest daughter, Eugénie.

As the wagon drew alongside them, Titus and Barnaby rose and assisted the Comte to his feet. Titus settled himself on the straw-covered boards between them and became once more aware of the damp clothes clinging to him. He hoped very much that the journey back to the château would not take very long as he was anxious to have a hot bath and change into his new evening finery in which he hoped to impress Eugénie. Before he and Barnaby had left Paris, the Comte had sent them to his own tailor with a commission to equip both young men with evening attire befitting the celebration his wife had planned for their anniversary.

The twins had not, so far, had occasion to wear their new clothes but on the last fitting, Titus had had only to regard his twin to appreciate how well he himself would look when he did so. They had selected jade green velvet for their breeches and coats, and the tailor had chosen the finest Italian gold silk for their waistcoats to complement the gold embroidery trimmings. They had new Mechlin lace cravats, and lace ruffles as cuffs to their fine linen shirts.

To complete their attire, they had been sent by the Comte to the court wigmaker, an earnest old man who, having insisted they cut their hair short, had produced identical Grecque perukes, deceptively simple but with two long curls on either side of the head and a tail *à la Panurge*, tied with a jade green silk bow.

Aware that he had never been so handsomely set up, Titus was in excellent good spirits as the wagon jolted them surely – if slowly – over the rutted cart tracks leading to the Château de Falence. When, several hours later, he and Barnaby descended the big staircase at nine o'clock for the start of their birthday ball, he had little doubt that Eugénie would recognize him despite the obligatory mask, and be suitably impressed. As well as Barnaby, there would be other young men present, of course, but he had the advantage of height above most of the Frenchmen. Moreover, he was hoping that after today's adventure, perhaps Eugénie would be even more kindly disposed towards him for saving her father's life!

Titus was too devoted to his twin, however, to be chagrined when as they reached the foot of the staircase, Eugénie came hurrying towards them and rewarded Barnaby, as well as himself, with a kiss.

CHAPTER FOUR

1788

'It ain't right, Miss Addy!' Dolly said, her round, freckled face creased with concern as she brushed Ned's ringlets and settled them over the white muslin dress he was now wearing. ''Tis long past 'is bedtime and 'e should be tucked up in 'is cot, same as Miss Kitty!'

She and Adela were in the day nursery – now the only room in the house where Adela cared to be. A coal fire burned in the grate day and night, and on this damp November evening the room smelt sweetly of the children's freshly ironed clothes which hung over the wooden horse to air. On the scrubbed wooden table, the remains of the evening meal had still not been cleared away, the kitchenmaid too busy preparing for the party downstairs to come up to collect the dishes. Near the fireplace stood the big tin tub in which both Kitty and Ned had been bathed, their daytime clothes still scattered in heaps beside the damp bath towels. It was a homely scene, reminiscent of her own childhood, Adela thought as Dolly put the three-year-old child into a high chair where he could not dirty his clean dress.

Dolly was right to complain about Sir Henry's disregard for Ned's proper bedtime. The little boy would be tired and fretful tomorrow. But this was the least of their concerns, she told herself with a long, painful sigh. In fact, there was so much to worry about these days that she could no longer sleep soundly at night; but tossed and turned in her bed so racked with anxiety and distress that when the cock's crow announced the coming of each dawn, she welcomed the day.

At least activity did, to some extent, prevent her mind twisting and turning down endless, hopeless byways.

It was over a year now since her beloved mother had died – had, so Adela believed, willed herself to death. At the time, it had seemed as if she could suffer no greater unhappiness. Now she knew better. There were days when she could even be glad her mother was no longer alive to see what was happening to her children.

She stooped to help Dolly pick up the garments, her dark hair falling about her thin face, her eyes pricking with unshed tears as she did so.

'I will speak again with Sir Henry,' she said quietly. There was no need for her to add that she had no hope that her request to her stepfather would be granted. He was not in the least concerned with Kitty's welfare, any more than he had ever been concerned with hers, but he had assumed total control over little Ned's life and indulged the child quite monstrously. He would brook no interference with his dictates, and Dolly knew this as well as she did. Dolly might be an ignorant Cockney servant girl, illiterate and without book learning of any kind, but she had a heart of gold and she was Adela's confidante and only friend in what had become the bleakest of existences. But for Dolly, she would not have been able to endure the conditions in which she was obliged to live.

It was not even as if she had the stolen visits from the Mallory twins to look forward to, Adela thought as she tucked Kitty into her bed and kissed her good night. They had been in France this past year, first in Paris and Normandy with her cousins, the de Falences; and then visiting the many friends they had made during their schooling at the Royal Academy of Equitation in Anjou. On the brief occasion Adela had seen them last summer, they had told her, laughing, that they were enjoying life as young bachelors far too much to wish to be trapped into matrimony. 'Besides which, Addy,' Barnaby had said, 'Titus is hopelessly in love with Eugénie – and as for me, I shall wait until you are old enough and then I shall marry you!'

'Ned go down to Papa now! Ned wants to see Papa now – *now*!'

The child's voice calling imperiously put paid to Adela's momentary reminiscences.

'Hush, Ned!' she said as he began to kick his heels impatiently against the wooden footrest of his chair. His large, dark eyes were stormy, the lashes long and curling; his cheeks were flushed a deep pink. He was an exceedingly pretty child who, until his father had intervened, had had a happy, friendly nature and was already showing a degree of intelligence beyond his years. The days when he had been terrified of his father had long since disappeared. He now knew that he had but to tug at the skirts of Sir Henry's coat and smile at him prettily, to be given whatever he wanted. As a consequence of this spoiling, Adela's and Dolly's task of managing the little boy was made all but impossible. If he did not get what he wanted, he would scream himself into a stupor; and if he could escape their clutches, he would run to his father to report the reasons for his distress. Disregarding the need for the child to be disciplined, Sir Henry would allow Ned to achieve his objective, docking Dolly's wages as a punishment and banishing Adela once more to her familiar prison environment, the cellar.

This excessive pandering to his small son had now developed a stage further – and Adela was deeply concerned. Tonight, Sir Henry would be yet again entertaining his friends – friends that Dolly referred to disdainfully as riff-raff. The gentlemen were so coarse in speech and manners, she told Adela, that they barely deserved the name; and the ladies, without exception, were strumpets. Adela had been innocently unaware of the meaning of this word and it had fallen to Dolly to enlighten her.

With no mother to explain the vagaries of human nature to her, Adela had listened to Dolly's explanations with a mixture of curiosity and dismay. The fact that these unsavoury details had been relayed in her maid's unemotional, matter-of-fact Cockney voice, made it easier for her to receive such basic education concerning the sexual relationships between men and women. Though delivered by Dolly without embarrassment, it had not lessened Adela's horror on realizing that her stepfather had replaced her sweet, gentle mother with women whose morals were of the basest; who sold their bodies for money instead of surrendering them for love.

Until she had been thus enlightened, Adela's only knowledge of love had been derived from the novels in her father's bookcase – Horace Walpole's *Castle of Otranto*, Fanny Burney's *Evelina*; and from the romantic verses of poets such as John Donne, Milton, and, not least, from the sonnets of Shakespeare. Now, it seemed, Ned had become the plaything of these loud-voiced, painted women who arrived in coaches from the city of London to drink and carouse the nights away with Sir Henry and his drunken friends.

Although Adela had shut herself far away in her bedroom on such occasions, Dolly was always called upon to help the serving girls refill the guests' speedily emptied tankards. Having served in a London gin shop in the notoriously drunken area of St Giles, Dolly was neither frightened nor particularly shocked by the bawdy scenes in the big dining-room. However, when on one such evening Sir Henry had demanded that she bring down his small son and heir to show 'the ladies' what a pretty boy Ned was, Dolly was outraged.

At first Ned had cried and tried to cling to her, she had reported to Adela, but one of the females – a big, blond-haired, bosomy woman most favoured by Sir Henry – had taken the little boy from her and fed him sweetmeats. Within minutes the child's tears had dried and soon he was being passed from female to female who, as they teased and tickled him, stuffed his little mouth so full that he was later violently sick.

So popular had this game become that Sir Henry now made it the custom to send for Ned as soon as the repast had ended. No matter how late the hour, Dolly was instructed to put the boy into a pretty dress and bring him downstairs to entertain his lady-friends.

'It ain't right, Miss Addy!' she said for the third time. 'Next thing 'e'll be asking for Miss Kitty to be brought down, too, and I dursn't think what that'll do to 'er, poor little mite!'

Adela's face paled. Now five years old, Kitty was a timid, sickly little girl, the reverse of her younger, robust brother. Having grown up in a household terrorized by her father, she cried at the slightest cause and if in the presence of any adult other than Adela or Dolly, would hide behind the nearest piece of furniture. At night she would pull the bedclothes over her head and, as often as not, Dolly was disturbed by the little girl's cries as she awoke from constant nightmares. Neither Adela nor Dolly had yet cured her of wetting her bed.

'Let us pray that never happens, Dolly!' Adela said. 'I think it unlikely. You know how Sir Henry dislikes Kitty. I am certain it is because she so resembles me!'

Dolly grinned.

''E can't abide you because of the way you stand up to 'im, Miss Adela! 'E ain't never been master of you and 'e knows it. Now I'd best go downstairs with Master Ned. I've been too long as it is!'

She gathered the child into her arms and lifted him out of his chair.

''Appen 'e'll vomit again tonight!' she said wryly as she turned to leave the room. 'Pity 'e don't do it when 'e's sitting on that Mrs Mackey's lap!'

'I'll light your way, Dolly!' Adela said, picking up the candle. 'One of these days, you'll tumble on those steep stairs – and then what would I do if you broke your neck! Ned's getting far too heavy for you to carry!'

As she opened the door, the sound of the revelry in the big dining-room carried up the stairs, the shrill laughter of the women; the raucous laughter of the men. At the foot of the stairs, a footman nearly collided with them as he hurried past with a tray of brimming pewter tankards.

Seeing the child, he shook his head disapprovingly.

'Not one of 'em sober!' he said, nodding at the dining-room door. 'No place to be taking the boy, Miss Adela!'

'I know, Alfred!' Adela replied, 'but the Master has ordered it!'

As the servant opened the door with his foot, a man pushed past him, obviously in a hurry. His wig was tilted sideways over one shoulder; his lace cravat was undone, the ends flapping over the embroidered silk waistcoat. He had removed his brocade coat, and his linen shirt was deeply stained beneath the armpits. The strong odour of sweat mingled with the overwhelming perfume of his scent.

In the same second as Adela and Dolly observed him, the man lurched forwards and collided with the footman. Ale from the foaming tankards splashed on to the bodice of Adela's white, low-necked cotton dress.

'Demme if I have not ruined that pretty dress, m'dear!' the man said. Tipsy though he undoubtedly was, his eyes had quickly noted the soft swell of Adela's breasts; the astonishing beauty of her large, green eyes; the smooth creamy whiteness of her youthful complexion. She was far too young and virginal to be one of Sir Henry's harlots, he thought. Nor was she one of his host's serving wenches. 'Captain Bruce Armitage, at your service, madam!' he said. 'Allow me to express my most sincere apologies!'

Although his voice was slurred, he was at least attempting to make amends, Adela thought as he handed her his Barcelona silk snuff-handkerchief.

'It is nothing to be concerned about, sir!' she said, for the dress was an old one of her mother's and already far too small. Like the quilted petticoats beneath, it was shabby and fraying beyond the repair of her needle. Pride forbade that she ask her stepfather for money to have new clothes made for her and it was not his custom ever to enquire if she needed anything. She had managed until now to alter her late mother's wardrobe.

'And may I enquire who I have the honour of addressing?' the man asked smoothly, for he had noted her speech as well as her charming appearance, and his curiosity was aroused.

'My name is Adela Carstairs – I am Sir Henry's step-daughter!' Adela replied, leaning backwards in a vain attempt to avoid the captain's beery breath. 'Now, if you will excuse me, sir, I shall go and change. And you, Dolly, had best take Ned into the dining-room without further delay.'

As she curtsied and hurried back up the stairs, Adela quickly forgot the man who had introduced himself as Captain Armitage. She had neither noticed nor would have cared had she done so, that his eyes had been bright with admiration. There were only two men in her life whose admiration she wanted – Titus and Barnaby – and since they were so far away in France, she gave little thought to her appearance. She was unaware of how in this past year she had changed from girl to young woman, her hips swelling gently below her tiny waist; her bosom rounded within the partial confines of her stays. The childish contours of her face had thinned with worry and unhappiness, and now it was a perfect oval in which her dark-lashed, green eyes looked larger and more luminous than ever.

Captain Armitage, however, had noted all these things, and having relieved himself in the earth privy at the rear of the house, he returned to the dining-room with one thought in mind – to see the girl again.

'You chary old fox, Nayland!' he said as he reseated himself at the table. 'Unwilling to trust your friends with that pretty stepdaughter of yours, eh?'

Sir Henry disengaged himself from the embrace of the large blond female on his lap and frowned as he replied, 'The girl's but fifteen years of age, Armitage – and even if she were old enough to amuse you, you would have no more time for her than I. Proper little wild cat, she is, and I would not wish her on my worst enemy.'

Captain Armitage grinned.

'Needs taming, eh? I'll take on the task, Nayland. I like a spirited female.'

The other men in the room joined in the laughter.

'We will break in your filly for you, Nayland.'

'You will do no such thing!' Sir Henry said sharply. 'I aim to get that girl married and off my hands as soon as I can. I'll not have her despoiled!'

Captain Armitage nudged his neighbour with his elbow, winking.

'We will behave ourselves, Nayland. Personally, I found her quite agreeable – not at all the spitfire you describe. Be honest now – admit you do not consider us proper company for her, eh?'

The thin, dark-haired female who had earmarked the captain for the more intimate adventures to come when the feasting was over, now flung an arm possessively around his neck.

'Who wants children spoiling our fun anyways!' she said in her shrill voice.

Sir Henry's blond companion looked across the table to yet another woman who was fondling little Ned as she fed him a slice of candied pear.

'Leave off, Nellie!' she shouted as the woman's hand slid beneath the boy's petticoats. 'Be a while yet afore you get a rise out of that young man!'

The loud laughter that greeted this sally was momentarily deafening. The women began to vie with one another as to whose turn it was to have the child on their lap. Smiling at each of them, well aware that he was the focus of their attention, Ned made no demur as they smothered him with kisses. Understanding nothing of the sallies which became coarser by the minute, he knew only that he was attracting everyone's attention; that the women's warm hands on his bare flesh felt very agreeable and that with no more than a smile, he could have whatever he wanted.

Sir Henry regarded him fondly. In that small frame existed the only human being in the world whom he had ever loved. He looked upon women as objects provided solely for the gratification of his needs. In Nadine, he had found only limited pleasure but although he had enjoyed her body whenever the desire took him, it was for her money he had married her. At the time, he had not been concerned about siring a son to follow in his footsteps, still less a daughter to dandle on his knee. He had virtually ignored the advent of his first child; but when the midwife had put Ned into his unwilling arms, he had felt a totally unexpected surge of paternal pride. It would not be long, he had told himself, before the infant was old enough for him to mould to his own image. A few years and he would rid the boy of his dresses and petticoats and start to teach him the ways of manhood. He would make sure that Ned went to the best schools, wore the finest attire and moved in the highest circles. He was to achieve the place in society he himself had never acquired. Who knew but he might even find a place at court!

Meanwhile, however, it amused him to see how even at this tender age, the child could exert his charm upon the opposite sex. When first he had instructed Dolly to bring the boy down to show his guests, he had had no thought of allowing him to become a regular entertainment for the women. The truth did not cross his mind that the maternal instincts of these harlots had been suppressed by the need to be readily available for sex and that his son was a beautiful little boy. Because he was clean and prettily attired, his skin so white and he so chubby and sweet-smelling, they expressed their emotions in the only way they knew – by petting and fondling him. One of the women, more daring or perhaps more tipsy than her companions, even parted the lace edged bodice of her dress and exposing one of her breasts, encouraged the child to play with her nipple.

The long oak dining-table was brilliantly lit by a dozen wrought-iron candelabra. Dolly stood quietly in the shadows beyond the pools of light, her round face taut with concern. Yesterday Ned had tried to put his little hands beneath the bodice of her dress and now she understood what had prompted him. He had also begun to show an inordinate interest in his own extremities. At this rate, she thought ruefully, it would not be long before he was hopelessly corrupted, his innocence lost even before he could speak the King's English properly.

Despite the intense heat of the great log fire burning in the inglenook, she shivered, hating the thought that she must warn Adela what was happening. It was years now since Dolly herself had been forced to face the more salacious facts of life. Not only had she been raped but there was little degradation she had not witnessed during her life in the slums. Nothing, she believed, could ever again shock her; but with Miss Addy it was quite different. Her young mistress knew nothing whatever of life beyond the confines of this house; her companions had been the parson's children and the gently reared French cousins. It had been a nasty enough shock for her to learn that the Master was using her home – her father's family home – as a place to entertain the riff-raff which he brought down from London. A gentleman, Dolly very well knew, might frequent the bordellos, drinking houses and gambling dens where such females abounded, but he did not use his own home for such purposes. Sir Henry, however, was a law unto himself. Now that he owned most of Dene village, he cared nothing for his reputation, nor, it would seem, for the good name of his family. Little Ned, of whom Dolly was genuinely fond, seemed destined to become the replica of his father. He even had the same ginger-coloured hair and freckled complexion! It would break Miss Addy's heart to see her little half-brother thus corrupted.

Dolly's eyes went to the face of the man at the head of the table. Hot and perspiring, Sir Henry was leaning back in his chair, his corpulent stomach stretching the seams of his embroidered silk waistcoat as he rested his gaze proudly on his little son.

'Always said the boy was intelligent!' he was muttering. 'Even at his age he knows what's good for him, by Jupiter!' He gave a loud belch before turning his attention back to the captain. 'Tell you what, Armitage, since you seem to doubt my word about that stepdaughter of mine, next time you come to dine,

I'll see she is here to sit next to you, eh? But no firky-toodling. She is to remain a virgin!'

He turned to Dolly.

'You can take the boy back to bed,' he said. 'And tell Miss Adela I shall wish to speak to her in the morning.'

As can happen in large families, there is often a rotten apple in the barrel and Henry Nayland, though well bred, was born without that instinct of chivalry which was his birthright. The unpleasant facets of his nature had quickly surfaced and his family had been pleased to see the back of him when he had joined the Army. He very soon became as unpopular with his fellow officers as with his men, but instead of trying to rectify the sadistic side of his nature, he had given it full rein. Well aware of his unpopularity, but unwilling to admit its cause, he became ever more intolerant and resented even the mildest challenge to his authority. The instinctive dislike, born of mistrust, that Adela had portrayed, even at the tender age of eight when he'd first come to Dene Place, irked him to such an extent that he had grown to hate her. When she had openly defied him despite the cruel beatings, he had threatened turning her out of the house. That he had not done so was for no better reason than that as she was a minor, the officers of the law would very quickly have returned her to him since like it or not, she was his responsibility. Nor could he tolerate the thought that anyone should consider him, a magistrate, incapable of disciplining a mere child.

As the years had passed, Adela took care for the most part not to defy him openly, and kept out of his way. Outwardly she appeared docile and obedient but by the look of contempt in her eyes, he knew she despised him. It had become something of an obsession with him to find a way to bend her to his will. Now, as he considered the degree of impropriety that would be involved if he ordered a fifteen-year-old girl of her breeding to mix with the whores he invited to his house, he quickly set aside his qualms. To oblige her to sit at the table with such women would be a very subtle form of humiliation, and the longer he considered it, the more attractive such a notion became. The servants, of course, would gossip but there were few, if any, in the village who would dare to criticize him. From bailiff to the lowest cow herdsman, the smith to the chimney-sweep – all were dependent upon him for their livelihood. Even that worthy Parson Mallory, and his plain, sanctimonious wife could do little more than complain to the bishop who, Sir Henry was well aware, would not risk offending such a generous patron as himself.

Money gave a man the power to do as he pleased, Sir Henry had learned long ago. He had planned his seduction of Lady Nadine Carstairs long before the death of her ailing husband who he knew to be one of the wealthiest men in the south of England. He had succeeded with the fewest possible difficulties in persuading the sorrowing widow into marriage, and thus, with the greatest of ease, had acquired sums of money way beyond his expectations. So wealthy was he now that only on principle did he resent the fact that Sir Matthew Carstairs had left a sum of money in trust to his only child, Adela, to be paid to her as a dowry, or on reaching the age of twenty-five. She knew nothing of her future inheritance for she had been too young at the time of her father's death to comprehend such things. Subsequently he had determined not to enlighten her for it was his intention to see her humbled before she discovered that she would not always be indebted to him.

As Adela stood before Sir Henry the following day, her eyes were stormy and her chin was raised defiantly as she said, 'You cannot force me to be present!'

Forewarned by Dolly as to the extent of the dissipation that was now taking place whenever Sir Henry was entertaining his London friends, and of little Ned's involvement, Adela had no intention of complying with her stepfather's demands that she should play hostess at his next dinner party.

He was standing, legs astride, in front of the fireplace in the morning-room, impeccably attired in riding coat and top boots, his tall hat and crop clasped in one hand, his York tan gloves in the other. His thin lips were pressed together in an ugly line as he stared down at her threateningly.

'We will see about that, my fine lady!' he shouted. 'Is it your wish to return to the cellar. Because I warn you, this time you will remain there for as long as it takes to enforce your obedience to my wishes.'

Adela had anticipated such a threat.

'I would prefer the solitude of the cellar to the company of your . . . your obnoxious friends, sir!' she said coldly. 'And, indeed, I would prefer the bread and water you so generously provide for me than the handsome fare you choose for their indulgence!'

Sir Henry took a step forward, his spurs clinking when he raised his crop as if to strike her. Adela flinched but did not step backwards.

'Oblige me to be present as you do your son and I will tell your friends exactly what I think of them. I am sure you would not wish them so embarrassed.'

'You will keep your opinions to yourself, my girl!' Sir Henry shouted. 'I will not have a chit of fifteen tell me what is befitting my son.'

He was the more angry for being uncertain how to proceed. If Adela were to be absent on the next occasion Bruce Armitage was present, he would be at pains to find an adequate excuse; for he had given his word she would be there. On the other hand, past experience had taught him that this vexatious girl meant what she said, and other than to punish her for her disobedience, it served no purpose to lock her in the cellar.

Watching his hesitation, Adela guessed that they had arrived at an impasse. In the same instant, the mention of Ned had brought the child's predicament to mind, and she now saw a way by which she could protect him.

'There is one condition which might change my mind, sir!' she said quietly. 'Were you willing to grant it, I would do my best to be civil to your guests!'

Not a little surprised, Sir Henry was nevertheless wary.

'That condition?' he enquired tersely.

'That Ned is not also present. I will not condone the use of my half-brother as a plaything. As you have stated, it is not for me to tell you what is or is not befitting a three-year-old boy, but my mother would not have tolerated it and nor would any decent human being.'

At last she had had the courage to speak her mind, Adela thought. Her legs were trembling and her heart beating furiously as she waited for the tirade she was convinced would come. To her astonishment, her stepfather's face cleared and he gave a loud guffaw of laughter.

'Devil take it! We have a martyr in the family . . . a little saint who will go to the gallows to protect her brother! 'Pon my soul, I never thought to see you, Adela, go meekly to the stake! So be it, then. I agree to your condition.' His face darkened once more and his tone was no longer one of amusement as he added, 'You show one moment of incivility to my guests and Ned shall take your place. Understand me, my girl, I will have no surly looks; no churlish behaviour. In the meanwhile, get your sewing woman to make you a fashionable gown. You look little better than a servant girl. You may wear some of your mother's jewellery – I will give you something suitable on the night for I'll not have you shame me. Is that clear?'

Dolly was appalled when Adela repeated the conversation to her.

'You dursn't, not even for Master Ned's sake!' she gasped, almost in tears. 'When those men 'ave drink inside of 'em, there's no knowing what they'll do. 'Arken to me, Miss Addy! You be in real danger!'

Adela attempted a smile.

'Save your breath, dear, kind Dolly. I have not forgotten all you have told me about the behaviour of such men, and I will not permit any one of them to lay a finger on me. I am no longer a child and I shall take care of myself!'

'Oh, Miss Addy!' It was all Dolly could say before she burst into tears. Despite her young mistress' brave declaration, Dolly knew – even if Adela did not – that she *was* still a child, and despite all her own efforts to enlighten her, Adela was no more able to take care of herself in such company than was poor little Ned.

CHAPTER FIVE

1788

One by one, Adela laid out the sparkling brooches, pendants, necklaces and rings that had been Nadine's. Memories flooded back of her mother, dressed in one of her beautiful evening gowns, stopping by her cot to kiss her good night before descending the stairs to join Sir Matthew for dinner. Her green eyes, so like Adela's own, had sparkled with love and happiness as brightly as the emeralds or diamonds around her throat. She had seemed then, to her little daughter, to resemble a queen or a princess and Adela had been loath to let her laughing mother leave the room.

Dolly's mouth gaped in wonder as she gazed at the jewellery lying before her on the dressing-table.

'I ain't never seen nothing like it!' she gasped. Her eyes clouded as she frowned. 'Fancy the Master 'aving them locked away all these years since your poor mama died! Knowing the way 'e goes on, you'd 'ave thought as 'ow 'e'd 'ave 'anded them out to 'is lady-loves!'

Adela shivered as she fastened one of the ruby pendants around her throat. The deep red glow of the precious stones enhanced the whiteness of her skin and gave a touch of warmth to the white sarsenet of her new dress. Gazing at her reflection, she felt a momentary glow of pleasure. The dress made her look quite grown-up and, as Dolly had only recently commented, prettier than either of them had imagined. The tight lacing of the embroidered Pierrot bodice accentuated the size of her small breasts, the close-fitting material clinging to her tiny waist. With her dark hair dressed in loose ringlets and lightly powdered, she could pass for a young woman in her twenties.

Without warning, Adela found herself wishing that the Mallory twins could see this transformation. Would they be as admiring as Dolly? Would Titus, in particular, be surprised to see her thus attired? Without knowing how it was she could be so certain, she was convinced that it had been Titus, not Barnaby, who had held her so gently in his arms that afternoon in the stables. How long ago it seemed, and what a long time it would be before she could hope to see either of the boys again. If only there were some magic means by which she could be transported to her cousins' home looking as she did now! What happiness that would be!

Dolly, however, had no such dreams. She was even more aware than Adela of the young girl's beauty and her heart was heavy with anxiety as she contemplated the hours to come. Would any of the so-called gentlemen present at the Master's table tonight respect her young mistress' innocence? With sufficient wine inside them – and none knew better than Dolly how much they poured down their throats – would they keep their hands off so tempting a prize? Somehow she very much doubted it. Nor, indeed, could she convince herself that Sir Henry would honour his declared intent to protect his young stepdaughter.

If only there were some way she, herself, could protect Adela, she thought. More and more often of late she had asked herself if there might not be some means by which they could run away. Miss Addy had professed herself more than willing to go anywhere in the world, so long as she could take little Miss Kitty and Master Ned with them; but how could they even contemplate such a prospect of freedom without money to support them? Those few coins she had managed to save from her wages would not feed them for a week! And where, she asked herself, would they live?

Dolly caught her breath as her eyes turned once more from Adela to the jewellery spread out before them. There, within their reach, lay riches beyond her imaginings. The sapphire-and-pearl necklace with cupid's bows linking a miniature of a child's face alone must be worth a fortune! Suppose they were to leave now, this very night, taking the late mistress' jewellery with them? They could find lodgings in London – sell a ring, a bracelet, a pendant until she could find work and earn enough to support them, and be free of Sir Henry Nayland's persecution.

Dolly's heartbeat quickened as her mind raced. How often, she asked herself, had she heard Miss Addy saying that she no longer loved Dene Place; that it had ceased to be her home; that she would be happier anywhere else in the world than within these walls where all but Ned lived in fear of her stepfather?

Dolly swallowed nervously and her voice was hoarse as she said aloud, 'Sit you down, Miss Addy. There's something I want to say to you – something I just thought of what'll come as a shock.'

Adela looked at her maid in surprise. The tone of Dolly's voice was one she had never heard before. Obediently she sat down on the ottoman.

'Make haste then, Dolly. There lack but five minutes before I must go downstairs. I dare not risk Sir Henry's change of mind and his demanding little Ned's presence in preference to mine!'

Dolly nodded, her thoughts elsewhere.

'The jewels, Miss Addy – has the Master given them to you?'

Adela gave a wry smile.

'You cannot really suppose such an unlikely event, Dolly! I have to return them in the morning. Sir Henry keeps them locked in his bedchamber.'

'Then we would have to go this very night!' Dolly muttered as much to herself as to Adela. She knelt on the floor and clasping Adela's hands, looked intently into her face. 'They are rightfully yours – they was your mama's!' she said in a rush. 'So it wouldn't be stealing if we took 'em, Miss Addy.

I knows a pawnshop where we could exchange them for money!'

Adela gaped in astonishment.

'Sell Mama's jewellery – for money?' she repeated. 'But how could we explain it to Sir Henry? And why – why should we sell them? Besides, you know as well as I that everything of Mama's now belongs to Sir Henry. It would be stealing.'

'We'd not be in this dratted place to answer for it!' Dolly said breathlessly. 'And pawning ain't selling – it's borrowing. The pawnbroker gives you a ticket and when you pays the money back, he gives you back your belongings. And as for the Master – we'd not be 'ere, Miss Addy. We'll go to London – you and me and the little 'uns. I'll get work – the way we've talked about. I know places we could go where 'e'd never find us. You don't know what it'll be like down there, Miss Addy.' She nodded vaguely in the direction of the dining-room. 'You'd not stand for it – and then Ned would be asked for and we both know what that's been a-doing to 'im!'

Adela's cheeks had flushed a deep pink as Dolly clarified her meaning and she realized that the possibility of escape – so often discussed but without any hope of being realized – had now presented itself. Last year, after the twins' farewell visit, she had gone on hoping that somehow Lord Mallory and his wife might have found a way to intervene. As the months had passed, she had been forced to realize that nothing would – or could – be done to rescue her or the children from their step-father's domination. If they ran away, even were he glad to see the back of her and little Kitty, he would leave no stone unturned to find his son. Without money, they had had no hope of travelling any great distance, and such refuges as the parsonage – even were the Mallorys to agree to concealing them – would all too quickly be searched.

Now, if they were to sell the jewellery as Dolly suggested, would they after all be able to make their escape? Did she have the courage to dare such an attempt? There would be no second chances, she knew, for if she were apprehended, it was not only likely but almost inevitable that her stepfather would thenceforth keep her under lock and key; and she would lose what little opportunity she had to protect the little ones. Moreover, there was no knowing what cruelties he might inflict upon Kitty; nor what nefarious indulgences he might find by which to corrupt his small son.

'We would have no man to protect us!' she whispered. 'You have told me many times of the dangers facing those who live in the city of London – cutpurses, footpads – even murderers. I do not fear for myself but the children . . .'

'Are they in less danger 'ere?' Dolly countered. 'And you, Miss Addy! That Captain Armitage 'as 'is eye on you – and for all 'e promised your stepfather 'e'd not deflower you, I reckon as 'ow 'e's no more to be trusted than any of 'is like. You should see yourself, Miss Addy – pretty as a picture – and I'll not stand by and see you debased like what I was!'

Adela shivered, yet it was partly excitement that was coursing through her veins. If Dolly had the courage to run away, so, too, had she! Her eyes went to the gems lying on the dressing-table. Dolly had said they were worth a great deal of money, and that she knew how to dispose of them. If she were to write a letter to the twins telling them where in London they were hiding, when Titus and Barnaby returned from France, they would surely come to their assistance!

If only they could go to France to the safety of her aunt's and uncle's home! she thought wistfully; but as Dolly had so often pointed out, the de Falence family would be one of the first places Sir Henry would look for them, and Ned would be dragged home to England even if she and Kitty were not.

Never a day passed now when Adela did not rue the change in her small half-brother. How horrified her poor mother would have been to hear his shrill voice demanding attention; to see the unnatural interest he had in his body, expecting Dolly or herself to laugh when he exposed himself! And he was but three years old! At least she could be thankful that Nou-Nou no longer lived in Dene Place to witness events. Jacques had been able to buy a tiny cottage in the village to which her mother's old nurse had retired. The only time Adela saw her now was in church on Sundays when, as Sir Henry conducted them down the aisle after the service, she was able to smile at the old woman seated in one of the back pews. Sir Henry himself never acknowledged his former servant and would not permit Adela to speak to her or to any of the villagers.

'You mun make up your mind, Miss Addy!' Dolly's voice was sharp with urgency. 'If we're a-going, I'll need get a few bundles of clothes together; and food for us to eat. We dursn't 'ire no carriage afore we gets a good few miles away from Dene, and it'll tek time to walk with the little 'uns.'

For a moment her voice faltered as she contemplated the difficulties of executing her plan; but now Adela was leaning forward eagerly, her eyes bright with excitement.

'We will manage somehow, Dolly! If we are apprehended, I will insist that I forced you to accompany me and then the worst that can happen to you is that you will be given notice. I am certain Lady Mallory would find you another position if she knew the circumstances behind your dismissal. As for me . . . Sir Henry cannot kill me and at least I would have the consolation of knowing I had done all I could to protect Mama's babies.'

Dolly grinned as her momentary fears abated.

'You'd best go on down now, Miss Addy,' she said as she started to put the jewellery back in the casket. 'Tell Mr Unwin I've been taken ill so's I ain't expected to serve tonight. Tell 'im I'm covered in spots and you's afeared I've something catching; then 'e'll not argue I'm well enough to do extra duties tonight!'

Adela stood up and smoothed the flounces of her skirt. Her heart was beating fiercely as she turned towards the door.

'How shall we manage to get Kitty and Ned out of the house undetected?' she said. 'Suppose they call out and someone hears?'

Dolly grinned again.

'Miss Kitty'll not make a sound if I warn 'er what'd 'appen if we're caught; and I'll give Master Ned a few drops of laudanum. 'E'll not wake, Miss Addy, though 'e'll not be walking, neither, so I'll 'ave to carry 'im.'

'You could take the handcart, Dolly!' Adela suggested with a flash of inspiration. 'We can pull it between us!'

'I'll get the little 'uns ready and down to the 'aybarn by midnight!' Dolly said, reaching up to straighten one of the tendrils of Adela's hair. 'Won't no one notice what I'm a-doing whilst them downstairs is enjoying theirselves! I'll put out clothes for you to wear soon as ever you can get away. You ain't going to change your mind, Miss Addy?'

'No!' Adela whispered. Her hand on the door-latch, she turned once more to smile at her faithful servant. 'And don't forget to take Mama's jewels. We would get no distance without them!'

Despite the ordeal immediately facing her, Adela, having spoken to Unwin, was still smiling as she entered the dining-room where Sir Henry and his friends were already seated. Buoyed up by the prospect of escape, her head was high as she went over to her stepfather and dipped in a respectful curtsy.

'My apologies for my tardiness, Papa!' she murmured. 'My maid has been taken ill with a catching disease and I have been at pains to isolate her so that she cannot pass on the infection to the children!'

Surprised by his recalcitrant stepdaughter's unaccustomed meek demeanour – and not least by her transformed appearance – Sir Henry forgot his growing irritation at her unpunctuality.

'You look charming, my dear!' he said. 'Now allow me to present a great admirer of yours who I think you have already met – Captain Armitage! My stepdaughter, Miss Adela Carstairs!'

The captain rose quickly from his chair and taking Adela's hand, kissed it with alacrity. His eyes covered her body with unconcealed appraisal.

'May I be the first to endorse Sir Henry's compliment. 'Pon my soul, I have seldom seen a more fetching young lady.'

There was a murmur of 'Hear, hear!' from the other gentlemen as the captain conducted Adela to the empty chair beside his own.

Adela was aware that the females were all staring at her with undisguised curiosity as she sat down. She felt herself blushing beneath their scrutiny and try as she might, she could do no more than nod her head as Sir Henry introduced them one by one before ordering the butler to commence serving the meal.

Beside her, Captain Armitage said unctuously, 'Your father has deprived us of such beauty far too long!'

Despite her intent to get through these last few hours in Sir Henry's household without contention so that he might be lulled into believing in her ready compliance with his dictates, Adela could not allow this remark to go uncorrected.

'Sir Henry is not my father but my stepfather!' she countered. 'I am the daughter of the late Sir Matthew Carstairs.'

'But of course, I should have recalled the fact!' the captain said smoothly. He was excited by this first indication of the fire within the delicate beauty of the girl's appearance. 'Now may I recommend this burgundy? Your stepfather has an excellent cellar and a glass or two will whet your appetite!'

With unwelcome intimacy, he took one of Adela's hands and placed it round the stem of her goblet, his face uncomfortably close to hers. Adela leaned quickly backwards, her senses baulking at the smell of brandy which her table companion must have consumed earlier.

One of the women opposite her who had overheard the conversation gave a shrill laugh.

'Leave her be, Brucie-boy! She's too young for liquor, ain't you, love? One glass afore she's ate anything and she'll be groggy as a gawk on pay-day!'

Those who heard this sally joined in the laughter. Adela's blushes deepened. Only now was she beginning to understand the kind of company to which her stepfather was subjecting her. Dolly had described these women as 'common trollops', 'doxies', 'loose-moralled', 'wantons' – women whom Adela's Mama and Papa would never have allowed in their home, let alone as guests. 'Them's unfit company for any lady, let alone a young girl the likes of you, Miss Addy!' Dolly had declared, deeply shocked.

So be it, Adela thought as the first of the many dishes of food was placed in front of her. She had no appetite but toyed with her knife and fork so that she need not engage in conversation with the men seated either side of her. Captain Armitage was not to be ignored but plied her with small attentions. Beneath the table and despite the wire hoops of her petticoat, from time to time Adela could feel the pressure of his leg against hers. She hated this touch, slight as it was, as greatly as she abhorred the sight of her red-faced stepfather feeding morsels of food to the woman beside him whom he addressed as Florrie. Now and again, this woman glanced in her direction and, puzzled, Adela detected a look of concern on her face. She was convinced she must be mistaken, for the woman's behaviour towards Sir Henry was little short of lascivious. She was even now shrieking with laughter as a piece of crust from the game pie on Sir Henry's fork slipped into the cleft between her large breasts. Nor did she demur when he took his time fumbling to retrieve it.

'And why no smiles upon that pretty face of yours, my angel?' the captain whispered in Adela's ear. 'With me as your protector, you have no cause to be fearful. I shall see you come to no harm. You have my word upon it!'

Far from reassured as the man took possession of one of her hands imprisoning it between his hot, sweaty palms, Adela said coolly, 'I was unaware I had cause to be afraid, sir. Please return my hand to me so that I may continue to enjoy my dinner!'

Captain Armitage grinned at this childish attempt at

haughtiness. Keeping hold of her hand, he leaned closer to her as he whispered, 'A forfeit, Miss Carstairs. If you will give me a kiss, I will return your hand. That is a small price to pay, do you not agree!'

'You have no right to take possession of something that does not belong to you and which has not been freely given to you!' Adela returned sharply. 'Kindly release me, sir!'

'And if I do not?' the captain enquired with a provocative leer.

Adela had not the slightest idea how to proceed with this unwelcome contretemps, but before she could think of a cutting reply, a voice from the far end of the table called across to her.

'I have drunk too much wine and now I am obliged to relieve myself. I 'ave quite forgot the way to the privy. Will you conduct me there, Miss Carstairs?'

For a moment, Adela made no move, so astonished was she by the request which, if at all, should have been addressed to one of the servants. She was shocked by the woman's crude reference to her bodily functions for it was no subject for a dining-table! But the opportunity to escape from the clutch of the man beside her had been presented, and quickly, she stood up.

None of the men bothered to rise from their chairs as Adela followed the woman out of the room, although Captain Armitage made pretence of doing so, conscious as he was of Adela's good breeding. He suspected Florrie's motives, and rightly so. No sooner had they left the room than the woman dragged Adela to a dark corner of the hall and said urgently, 'You ain't got no place in there! Mark my words, child,' she whispered. 'I mean you well for all you may despise me! I know your stepfather 'ates you – 'e's tolt me so many a time. For all 'e calls 'isself a gentleman, 'e ain't no more one at 'eart than I'm a lady. 'E's a bad lot Miss Carstairs, and 'e can't abide the way you've always seen through 'im. It's rankled so bad 'e's going to break your spirit sooner or later. Take my advice – get away from 'im afore 'e sees you ruined.'

'How . . . how do you know this? I thought you were . . .' Adela's hesitant voice broke off, unwilling as she was to insult this woman who, incredible though it might be, was clearly trying to befriend her.

Florrie grimaced.

"E'll tell me anything when 'e's in 'is cups – and that's as often as not. As to my being 'is doxy – for that's what you meant, ain't it? – I use 'im same as 'e uses me. I've two kids to support and 'e pays me well. Ain't no other way I can keep my kids, and I'd sooner whore than see them starve. Now listen to me, Miss Carstairs. In a while I shall start complaining to your stepfather that you're spoiling our fun; that it puts me off me stride 'aving a young lady like you watching when 'e paws me.'

She gave a wry smile as she added, 'And that'll be no more than the truth. Like as not, 'e'll tell you to leave but only if 'e thinks you doant want to – that's how contrary 'e can be. So it's up to you now. Play along with that Armitage fellow – let 'im 'old your 'and or give you a kiss or two if you 'as to. It won't do you no 'arm and it could save you from a great deal worse if I'm any judge of 'ow this evening will end! For all your stepfather said 'e wants you kept a virgin so's 'e can get you quickly married, 'e'll not be in any state to call a 'alt once the brandy is down 'im. Now, will you do as I say? Believe me, I've been around long enough to know what I'm talking about and you – you're a babe-in-arms. Your ma would turn in 'er grave if she could see what's become of you!'

Adela needed no further convincing. As she waited in the hall while Florrie visited the closet, she knew she could not allow her to return to the dining-room without thanking her.

'You have taught me more than one lesson tonight, not the least of which is that I had greatly misjudged you . . . and perhaps those others like you. You have been very kind, and I am very grateful. I will do exactly as you say and . . . and please forgive me.'

Florrie patted her arm in a motherly way.

'Soon as you can, you find yerself a nice young gentleman to marry you and take you away from 'ere!' she said softly. 'Lord love you, but you're pretty enough – and young enough – to find yourself an 'usband! They'll be lining up in droves just waiting to fall in love with a nice girl like you!'

'Do you really think so!' Adela said wistfully. Her thoughts despite the gravity of the conversation had turned involuntarily to Titus. 'I had not thought of myself as . . . as pretty!'

Florrie patted her arm once again.

'Don't you 'ave no doubt about it! 'Cept for my kids, I'd give everything I ever owned in this world to 'ave your looks. There ain't a man alive as wouldn't give 'is right arm to 'ave you for 'is wife!'

Or his mistress, she thought cynically as she preceeded Adela back into the dining-room. As Sir Henry reached out an arm and slapped her coarsely on her rear, she laughed obligingly and wriggled her hips before seating herself once more beside him. She could play her part more easily now – without the bitterness of resentment which lay deeply hidden beneath her loud laughter and suggestive smiles. Just this once, she had outwitted Sir Henry, and, she sincerely hoped, said enough to his young stepdaughter to deprive him very soon of this captive butt for his cruelty. Hopefully, she told herself, Adela would elope with the first presentable young man who fell for her, and Sir Henry would have to look elsewhere for someone to bully.

Adela could not know as she raised her goblet of wine to her lips, that Dolly had already packed their few belongings into the handcart which she had dragged to the haybarn. She had covered the boarded floor with hay to make a soft bed for young Ned; and had stolen enough food from the pantry without being observed. There were warm cloaks waiting for Adela and the children and the old fur carriage-rug from the

cellar for added warmth. This, Dolly knew only too well, was
no time of the year to be travelling on the road. The Romanies
had caravans for shelter but she, Adela and the children would
have to take shelter in barns. What little money they had they
would need to pay their passages on the stage-coach to London
once they had put sufficient distance between themselves and
the surrounding villages which the Master would certainly
have searched.

Now there remained only the laudanum for little Ned which
she would not administer until Adela returned to her room.
The late mistress' jewels she had packed safely in two chamois-
leather bags fastened with leather thongs, with the exception
of several rings which she had sewn into the hem of her serge
skirt. She tied the bags securely around her waist, for her years
on the streets of London had taught her caution, and none
knew better than she the horrors of being penniless. This time
she would not only have herself to take care of but the vast
responsibility of her young mistress and the two children. It
was a daunting prospect, Dolly thought as she awaited Adela's
return to her bedchamber.

As the minutes and then the hours passed, her confidence
began to wane. She had no idea of the true value of Lady
Carstairs' jewellery, and therefore no way of knowing how
long the money it realized would last. Moreover, having failed
in the past to keep herself from starvation, how could she
hope to support these gently reared children? Admittedly she
was nineteen now and no longer a child; but this was barely
reassurance enough. Perhaps, she thought, they should all
postpone their escape at least until the summer!

It was past midnight when Adela came hurrying into the
room where Dolly sat disconsolately beside the embers of
the fire, her candle guttering in its holder. Seeing the tears
glistening in Dolly's eyes, Adela forgot the horrible ordeal
of submitting to Captain Armitage's ever more ardent flirtation. She forgot how her flesh had crept when he had kissed
her cheek; how nauseous she had felt when his hot, sweaty

hand had encircled her waist and his elbow brushed her breast. Somehow she had managed to play her part, sustained by the occasions when her eyes had met those of her unlikely new friend, Florrie, and seen her nod of approval. Now she could think only of Dolly's distress and her fears for its cause.

'What has happened, Dolly?' she cried as she knelt down in front of her. 'Were you detected? Does someone know of our plan?'

Sniffing back her tears, Dolly recounted her misgivings.

'T'weren't naught but madness to think on it!' she ended. 'Lunnon town ain't no place for a young lady as is unprotected. And it 'ud be all my fault, Miss Addy, if you and the children came to 'arm. We dursn't go!'

Adela drew a deep breath. She could understand Dolly's fears and did not underrate them. Nevertheless, she was even more determined to leave now than she had been when they first discussed the plan. Had not Florrie warned her to get away from the house? Had she not experienced this past few hours exactly what the future here must hold for her? Or if not for her, for Ned? Perhaps, in time, for Kitty?

'Of course we must go, Dolly!' she said. 'You cannot be fainthearted now!' She essayed a smile. 'I am ordering you to come with us! It is your duty to do as I say, and if you do not, I shall dismiss you!'

Despite her misgivings, Dolly returned the smile.

'Oh, Miss Addy, you ain't got the right. It's the Master what pays my wages. 'E's the one what would dismiss me!' She stood up. 'Everything's ready, Miss Addy, if'n you be certain sure you wants to go!'

'I am as sure of it as I am that the sky is blue!'

Dolly grinned as she reached in her apron pocket for the small phial of laudanum.

'Ain't very blue right now, Miss Addy. 'Tis black as pitch out there and the moon's that watery we'll like as not 'ave rain afore morning.'

'Then I'll say I am as sure as the sea is blue!' Adela said, reminding herself involuntarily of the blue waters of the English Channel across which were Titus and Barnaby, sleeping peacefully, no doubt, and without the slightest inkling of the dangerous adventure upon which she was now about to embark.

CHAPTER SIX

1788

'I am hungry, Addy! Where are we going?

'Why is it dark?'

Kitty's voice, muffled by the fur rug covering her, penetrated Adela's consciousness. She had been half asleep this past hour as she and Dolly dragged the handcart down seemingly endless lanes and farm tracks. When she had last heard the soft chime of the silver-cased verge watch in her pocket, she knew it was past five o'clock and that dawn could not be far off. They had been trudging through muddy puddles of water for nearly five hours, and for all her youth and good health, she was exhausted. At least little Ned was still sleeping, she thought gratefully. When he woke, he would be querulous and demanding, unlike Kitty who was always so quiet and obedient that it was easy to forget she was there.

'We will have something to eat in a short while, my sweeting!' she replied. She decided it was better not to tell the child where they were going for if they were apprehended, the less Kitty knew the better. 'It is dark because it is night-time. Dolly and I thought it would be exciting to engage in a little adventure, so our destination will be a surprise. Now try to sleep just a little longer like a good girl!'

As the child settled once more, Adela turned to look at Dolly.

'How far do you think we have travelled?' she asked anxiously. 'One thing we can be certain of is that Sir Henry will come looking for us the moment he discovers we have gone.'

Dolly reached up a hand to pull the hood of her cloak closer about her face. She was less tired than her young mistress for she was accustomed to late hours and early risings; and to being on her feet all day. Nevertheless she, too, was nearly at the end of her resources and would welcome a rest and some sleep.

'No more'n eight miles at the rate we're going!' she replied. 'We'll make better time when we dares go on to the coach road.'

They had already decided that they must keep to the drovers' lanes and byways at least until they reached Northiam, or 'Norgem' as Dolly pronounced it having heard of the staging post from Jacques. It was an area so much used by the smugglers that the local gang with whom Jacques had dealings were more in command of it than the proper authorities. 'The Excise dursn't go near there after dark if they value their lives,' Dolly had said. 'So if Sir Henry sends men out looking for us, like as not they'd fare worse'n what we might!' For this reason, they had decided to travel only at night and conceal themselves somewhere by the roadside in the daytime.

'At least we are halfway to our destination!' Adela said as she tried to muster the last remaining strength in her body. 'As soon as the sky lightens, we must start looking for shelter.'

Although Dolly had attached a lanthorn to the handcart, they had forborn to light it save when they passed through woods, for mercifully, the rain had held off and though misty, the moon afforded sufficient light by which to keep on the tracks. Despite the hastiness of their departure, Adela had thought to bring with her her father's compass as well as his time-piece, and every now and again when they reached a fork or turning, she stopped to check that they were travelling in a northerly direction.

Once the frenzied barking of a farm dog had frightened them into a loss of direction as they had hurried away from the nearby farmstead. Although the farmer would almost certainly have given them shelter, both Adela and Dolly were determined that no one, were they questioned, could claim to have seen them as they headed for London town.

It was nearing six o'clock when they came upon a derelict charcoal burner's hut in the forest through which they were walking. Although part of the roof had collapsed and a faint glimmer of dawn light shone through it, the ground was dry beneath one wall and would afford shelter from the wind now blowing in from the coast.

With a sigh of relief, Adela sank down on to the fur rug Dolly laid on the earth floor. Involuntarily her heavy eyelids closed, and although she raised them once to see Dolly lifting the children down from the cart, she passed quickly into a deep sleep. It was Dolly, therefore, who unwrapped the bundle of food and jollied the children into believing this picnic was part of the game they were playing – a game of 'search and find' with their Papa, she improvised. Kitty was at first nervous, for she felt instinctively that this childish entertainment was not one which her irascible father was likely to enjoy. Ned, however, considered it an excellent way to pass the time and readily agreed to Dolly's request to keep his shrill voice lowered to a whisper. Fresh from his night's sleep, his energy was boundless and when Dolly permitted him to make little boats of twigs and sail them in the puddles that had formed beneath the open roof, he settled happily to his play.

Kitty looked at Adela's sleeping form and her blue eyes, too large in her thin face, filled with anxiety. 'Why does Addy not waken?' she asked. 'She is not dead like poor Mama, is she?'

Kitty had been of an age to remember when Nadine died and she had been taken to see her mother's body before it was put in the coffin. The memory still haunted her dreams.

'Miss Addy ain't 'ad no sleep all night long, Miss Kitty! Nor more 'ave I! When she wakens, it'll be my turn for a nap.'

'How long will we stay here?' Kitty asked, looking fearfully round her and aware of the tall, dark trees outside the hut. 'Are there wolves in the forest?'

'I dare say!' Dolly said adding firmly, 'But they doesn't dare come near us. They's scared of people and doant never eat 'em lessen theys starving!'

'Suppose they are starving now!' Kitty suggested.

'Not with all them pheasants and rabbits abounding!' Dolly stated with a conviction based on hope rather than knowledge. 'That were a cock pheasant you 'eard callin' just now! Them birds is a lot tastier nor you be, Miss Kitty, and that's for sure!'

When Adela woke some four hours later, she was ravenous; but seeing that the bundle of food was fast diminishing, she took only a little, urging the two children to eat their midday meal without restraint. At least they had plenty of water in the cask Dolly had put in the handcart, Adela told herself thankfully whilst her stalwart maid snatched a few hours' sleep.

By now Ned had long since tired of playing with his boats and, indeed, of the stories Adela made up for the children. For a little while, they played catch with her fur muff; hunt the thimble with a button she found tucked in the lining; and finally, when they complained of the cold, Ned's favourite game, 'The Little Dog'. The smallness of the hut was restricting, for one of them had to touch the shoulder of each of the others in turn whilst they squatted on the ground, saying: 'I have a little dog who will not bite you, will not bite you . . .' but when they called: 'But he will bite *you*!' that child was required to jump to his feet and chase the caller.

The noise of the game disturbed Dolly who, rubbing her eyes, climbed awkwardly to her feet.

'What time be it, Miss Addy?' she asked. 'Seems darker'n it were afore I slept!'

Adela looked at her watch. It was after four. Somehow the long day had passed without mishap. The worst that had happened since they had left the house was that her skirts and Dolly's were muddied inches above the hems and the children looked like chimney-sweeps!

'Another hour and we can be on our way,' she told Dolly. 'We will use a little of our water to clean the children before putting them in the cart to sleep.'

Fractious now, Ned demanded to be taken home. He wanted to sleep in his own bed. He wanted Papa to kiss him good night. He wanted his lead soldiers!

'You be wanting a good 'iding, Master Ned!' Dolly said finally as her patience was exhausted. 'Now stand still this minute whilst I wipe your face!'

When Ned started screaming, it was Adela who felt obliged to smack his hand, for his shouts could be heard a furlong away, possibly endangering them all. Dolly grinned as the boy's wails quietened.

'Any more nonsense, Master Ned, and Miss Addy and me'll leave you 'ere by your ownself!'

This threat more than Adela's chastisement finally achieved Ned's willingness to behave himself. With his papa not here to countermand any orders he did not like, he knew there was little to be gained from further tantrums.

By five o'clock the last of the rooks had settled in the treetops and from behind the hut, a vixen shrieked. It was pitch dark and loath though they were to do so, Adela and Dolly were obliged to light the lanthorn. Now their progress was even slower for one of them was needed to walk ahead lighting the way whilst the other pulled the cart. Until now they had shared the burden, and it was almost more than Adela could accomplish single-handed. Dolly, buxom and by far the stronger, therefore took longer spells at the task.

The forest was far behind them as some four hours later, they halted on the crest of a steep hill. Away in the distance they heard the sound of a church clock striking the hour. The wind had increased in strength and despite the warmth of her fur-lined pelisse, Adela shivered. It was impossible to keep both her hands within the muff when she was holding aloft the lanthorn, and her fingers were numb with cold. The short spell of fitful sleep she had had was proving insufficient to

sustain her energies and the elation at having passed the first
twenty-four hours without Sir Henry's detection, was rapidly
dimming.

As her spirits flagged, she began to appreciate the enormity
of the action she had embarked upon. Although she had known
there could be no going back without horrifying repercussions
for herself and Dolly – and perhaps for Kitty, too – the possible
consequences awaiting them now could be even worse. Dolly
had warned her of the dangers of life in England's capital,
and she had swept them aside without stopping to consider
them. But for her thoughtless impulse they would all be safe
in their beds at Dene Place.

The memory of her home brought with it the recollection
of her stepfather's dinner party and with it, the nauseating
face of Captain Armitage; the smell of his brandy-fumed
breath; the touch of his body. Sir Henry's guests would still
be in the house, their loud raucous voices filling the rooms,
the scent of their unwashed bodies polluting the air. She wanted
no part of it, she reminded herself fiercely; and it could be
only a matter of weeks – at worst a month or two – before
the letter she intended sending the Mallory twins reached
them. She knew from Jacques, who had returned to England
last June when Nou-Nou had fallen ill, that the twins had
departed for the eastern Mediterranean on a sight-seeing
journey with Philippe de Falence. According to Jacques, they
expected to be back in France in time to spend Christmas
once more in Paris with the family.

As Adela trudged forward listening to the creak of the cart
and Dolly's laboured breathing, it occurred to her that they
should have stayed their departure to London until Jacques
had been there to accompany them; but Nou-Nou had recovered from the bout of ague which had afflicted her earlier in
the year and Jacques had taken advantage of his young masters'
absence to rejoin his smuggling friends in France.

Despite Dolly's protest, Adela handed her the lanthorn and
purposefully took hold of the handcart.

'I shall manage very well – it is downhill now, Dolly—'

She was suddenly silenced as Dolly pressed her hand against Adela's lips.

'Sshh!' she whispered. 'I can 'ear something!'

Adela held her breath. Now she, too, could hear the sound of approaching hoof beats. Someone on horseback was coming swiftly in their direction. There was no time to take cover and they could do no more than crouch down behind the cart, the wet earth muddying their petticoats still further.

'Whoever it is must've seen the lanthorn!' Dolly breathed.

There was no time for Adela to reply for the dark shadow of a horse and rider had come into sight. A few seconds later, the rider halted beside the cart, the animal breathing noisily from its gallop.

'Identify yourselves!' The voice was loud, peremptory as the rider broke the silence. He leaned from his saddle and roughly snatched the lanthorn from Dolly's grasp. Holding it above them, he gave an audible gasp. 'Devil take it, females!' he exclaimed, shining the light in Adela's face. As he nudged his animal nearer to the handcart, Adela placed herself between it and his horse.

'Keep away from them!' she cried. 'They are only two children sleeping!'

The man hesitated, his face dark with suspicion. He had caught the educated cadence of Adela's voice and was even further perplexed as to who these unlikely night travellers might be. But a short while ago, he and his gang of smugglers had become aware of the winking light of the lanthorn ahead of them, and after a short consultation, had reached the conclusion that this must be a rival gang of smugglers trespassing on their territory. They themselves were taking a wagon load of contraband to Northiam, distributing part of their cache at various points on the way. Extremely well organized and fully prepared to use whatever violence might be necessary, they were unprincipled, armed ruffians. Anyone suspected of betraying them to the militia was quickly disposed of, the result being that they went about their business without needing too much recourse to the various secret passages and tunnels used by their counterparts.

For the most part, the local population welcomed the smugglers since they made it possible for even the poorest farmer to enjoy the tea and brandy that they brought in from France; their wives the lace that was otherwise denied them. This particular gang, of which the man, George Robinson, was the leader, was not involved with the outward smuggling by 'owlers' of English wool to France, although they had, upon occasions, supplied a wagon to replace a broken one in an emergency.

'And just exactly what might you be doing out 'ere at this 'our?' the rider said impatiently, addressing his question to Adela. Even by the faint light of the lanthorn, he could discern her youthful beauty and was amused by the proud uplift of her head. Her hood had fallen away from her white, oval face and if she were frightened, those big, green eyes of hers gave no indication of her fear.

'My maid and I are on our way to Northiam where we hope to join the stage-coach to London!' she said. 'If we trespass upon your property, I ask your indulgence. Are you the landowner?'

George Robinson laughed.

'Lord love you, no!' His face became guarded once more as he added, 'Yours is a likely story, and one that doant deceive me! A young lady like yerself doant journey abroad unescorted. Quick now, the truth! I've no time to 'ang about!'

His tone had become threatening, and for the first time, Dolly spoke.

'You mind your manners. This be Miss Carstairs of Dene Place you be speaking to!'

Realizing instantly how revealing her remark had been, she covered her mouth with her hand; but the man's voice held only scorn as he said, 'Indeed, now! Dene Place! You'm a relative of Sir Henry Nayland, then, God rot his soul!'

Adela's trepidation gave way to hope as she realized the implications of this expletive.

'We are running away from Sir Henry's tyranny,' she said quietly. 'He is my stepfather. You know of him?'

George Robinson tucked his pistol back into its holster.

'Who ain't 'eard of 'im in these parts!' he declared. 'It were 'e, no less, as sent one of my men to the gallows – and 'e be the one 'as benefited above others from our supplies. Magistrate 'e be – and still is for matter of that! – sitting there in court like the Lord 'isself denouncing us smugglers with 'is cellars full to brimming with our cognac! Cognac what we risk our lives to bring to the likes of 'im. Too canny, 'e were, to let our lad speak out for justice, knowing what story 'e 'ad to tell. Oh, I knows Sir 'Enry well and better for 'im 'e doant meet up with me on a dark night!' He spat on the ground and grimaced as he added, 'Meanwhile I makes 'im pay a price for 'is goods as gives 'im a right belly-ache!'

Adela stepped forward eagerly.

'Then you, more than most, sir, will understand why we are leaving his house. By now he will be searching for us, which is why we travel at this hour. You will not betray us if you meet with anyone enquiring as to our whereabouts?'

The man grinned.

'No more'n I trust you'll make no mention of seeing me!' he said. 'But you've quite a ways to go yet if it's your 'ope to catch the first stage.' He glanced at the handcart and scratched his head thoughtfully. ''Appen we can lighten your load, miss. Do you wait 'ere whilst I tell my lads to bring up the wagon!'

Without waiting for Adela's agreement to his suggestion, he swung himself on to his horse and galloped back in the direction from which he had come.

'Oh, Miss Addy! I thought as 'ow I'd betrayed us!' Dolly cried as soon as he was out of ear-shot. She was close to tears. 'Do you think as 'ow we can trust 'im, 'im being an outlaw-like?'

Adela smiled wryly.

'We are outlaws too, Dolly, so we can count ourselves fortunate that we are amongst friends. As to your betraying us, that too was a stroke of good fortune, for how else should we have discovered that Sir Henry was as hated by him and his men as by us?'

Dolly was only partly reassured as they heard the creak of wagon wheels and the sound of muffled voices approaching. However, the smugglers were not only friendly but highly efficient as first they transferred the two children into the wagon and then lifted Dolly and Adela in beside them. It was a tight squeeze between the big casks of spirits, but they were made comfortable enough leaning against the bales of lace that made up the load.

Both Kitty and Ned had been awakened and were watching sleepily as this transference took place. Only Kitty looked anxious as she gazed at the men's rough attire. Her eyes fastened upon an eye-patch worn by one of the men.

'Is he a pirate?' she enquired tearfully as she clung to Adela's arm.

'No, my precious, he is a man like the valet, Jacques. You remember him, do you not? Nou-Nou's son!'

Reassured, it was but minutes before lulled by the swaying of the wagon, Kitty fell asleep once more. Soon both Adela and Dolly were sleeping too, and the sun was already rising before they awoke on the outskirts of Northiam. The wagon had halted beneath a vast oak tree and the men were removing the first of the casks and carrying them into a timbered house near by.

George Robinson came round to the back of the wagon and grinned as he nodded towards the house.

'You'll be safe enough there 'til the stage comes!' he said. 'The Mistress be a good friend of mine and will not say aught about you if'n she be asked.'

Ned was scowling as he gazed around him.

'I do not like this place!' he announced. 'Why is the house so small? I want to go back to my home!'

'Hush, Ned!' Dolly began but the man beside her laughed.

'Our good Queen Bess 'ad a banquet prepared for 'er in that 'ouse!' he said. 'Ate it 'neath this very oak tree, she did. So wot's good enough for 'Er Majesty's good enough for you, young sir!'

Although his small face was mutinous, Ned thought better than to continue the argument with this large, disreputable-looking man. He allowed himself to be lifted down to the ground.

'Be a good 'alf 'our yet afore the stage comes!' George Robinson told Adela as he helped her out of the wagon. 'The mistress is preparing a breakfast for you.' He grinned at Ned as he added, 'A banquet fit for a queen, mark my word! Bread fresh out of 'er ovens and cold tongue to go with it!'

Both Adela and Dolly were suddenly ravenous and even Ned, when he was finally seated at a table before a large log fire, eagerly partook of the excellent food. At a table near by, the band of smugglers were consuming even larger plates of food washed down with big mugs of ale. They seemed perfectly at home, but suddenly vanished – as had the casks long since – when a lad came hurrying into the room with a warning shout that the stage was on the brow of the hill. At the same moment, they heard the sound of the guard's horn warning of their approach.

Hurriedly Adela started to pay for their food with some of Dolly's money, praying that there would be sufficient left to pay their coach fares. By a stroke of good fortune, the landlord seemed more interested in acquiring their handcart and suggested they settle their bill by leaving it with him since they had no further need of it. Collecting their portmanteaus of clothes and the fur rug, and with Kitty and Ned clinging to their skirts, they hurried out into the wintry sunshine where the stage was now standing.

'Best travel outside, Miss Addy!' Dolly whispered for she had once travelled on a stage-coach whereas Adela had never done so. 'It'll be a lot cheaper!'

Adela looked up dubiously to the roof of the coach where a number of passengers were already seated. If it rained before they reached London, they would become drenched, she thought; but the interior of the coach with its number of seats limited to six, was, on this cold November morning, already crowded. At least if they were outside, the children could enjoy the passing view, she comforted herself. Moreover, only six of the ten seats were occupied, and she and Dolly would have no need to hold them on their laps, at least until the next staging post was reached.

The guard blew a loud blast on his horn and the driver whipped his four fresh horses into action. It was bitterly cold and by the time they had crossed the River Teise and driven through the tall overhanging trees of Bedgebury Forest, they were all frozen for there was little shelter from the east wind. When finally they reached the Chequers Inn at Lamberhurst where they halted for a meal, they were numb with cold.

Throughout this leg of the journey, a portly gentleman from Rye had been eyeing Adela and her small party with curiosity. From her voice when she had spoken to the children and her delicate appearance, he had quickly ascertained that she was both very young and unaccustomed to public conveyances. Neither she nor her maidservant had seemed anxious for conversation, but he was a chivalrous man and now he saw his opportunity to make his fellow travellers' acquaintance.

'Pray allow me to escort you into the parlour!' he said politely, offering his arm. 'It will be noisy and crowded inside, as possibly you are aware, and perhaps I may be of assistance?'

Adela had been deliberately avoiding any possibility that might oblige her to introduce herself. Neither she nor Dolly had yet thought to adopt pseudonyms, and she knew that if Sir Henry were persistent enough, he might succeed in following upon their heels if a chance word put him on their trail. He was not a man to be thwarted. Now, however, she saw an opportunity to cover their tracks. If questions were asked at the coaching inn, it could not be reported that an unattached lady and two children had been there this day if she were to be accompanied by this gentleman.

'That is exceedingly kind of you, sir!' she said quickly. 'My name is Mrs Annie Porter. This is my maid, and these are my children, Edward and Katherine.' Lowering her voice so that the children would not hear her, she added a further lie. 'Their father is very ill and I would prefer you do not mention him as they are concerned that he is not with us. I am taking the children to their aunt in London.'

Her companion led her into the bustling inn and found places for them at one of the long polished-wood tables. The air was stale with wood and pipe smoke but at least it was well warmed by the fire burning in the huge hearth. Only a little light filtered through the leaded windows, but the well-polished lamps hanging from the ceiling had been lit and the atmosphere, though noisy, was both busy and jolly.

As a large tureen of hare soup was placed before them and served by a girl Adela assumed to be the landlord's daughter, she felt herself relaxing. Her only worry at this moment was that Dolly's money would not be sufficient to pay for this meal. It would be more than a little embarrassing were they to be obliged to produce one of her mama's rings by way of payment – even if the landlord would accept such an offering. He might think the ring stolen – or of lesser value than would meet their dues.

She might have been a great deal more concerned had she realized that her kindly companion had disbelieved her story. Not only were her small white hands without the circlet of a wedding-ring, but in this better indoor light, he could see that Adela was far too young to have a daughter who must be five if not six years old! He supposed Adela to be his own daughter's age – in the region of fifteen or sixteen at the very most. His curiosity deepened still further. How came her skirts and those of the other three to be so muddied? Why did her maidservant refer to her as 'Miss Addy' when her name was supposed to be 'Annie'?

Long before the bread and pie had been brought to the table, his keen eyes had observed the young servant counting the coins she had taken out from her shabby pocket. Her freckled face had looked anxious, as if she were concerned there might be insufficient money to pay for their meal. When the coachman sounded his horn to warn the travellers that it was time to return to the coach, he was sufficiently intrigued to offer help to the young fugitives, for he was now certain this was what they were. It pleased him to act the Good Samaritan to this pretty young girl seated beside him.

'Since I invited you to join me for this repast, you must permit me to settle the account!' he said. As Adela began to protest, he put a fatherly hand on her arm. 'Pray do not deprive me of this small pleasure, madam. I have enjoyed your company.'

Without waiting for her further protests; he rose to his feet and paid the landlord, tipping him generously with a three-penny bit for the food had been both hot and of excellent quality. He had, moreover, thoroughly enjoyed eating it in such mysterious company.

''E's a good gentleman and I reckon 'e's not the sort to take liberties!' Dolly whispered as she helped first Adela and then the children back into their pelisses. 'This be our lucky day, Miss Addy!'

'Let us hope so!' Adela whispered back. With a smile she withdrew from her pocket the hare's foot charm Titus had given her. 'Perhaps this is working its magic for us,' she said, 'although I am far from certain Mama would have agreed to our being beholden to a stranger, however fortuitous his offer.'

Dolly held no such scruples. Life had taught her never to look a gift-horse in the mouth, and she had time to say as much to Adela before their benefactor returned.

It was not, after all, destined to be their lucky day. It was late in the afternoon and the sky had darkened still further with threatening rain clouds when the coach horses wound their way through the heavily wooded forest of the Weald. They were obliged to move at walking pace as the state of the road deteriorated and became ever more rutted. Adela's kindly protector had left the coach at Tunbridge Wells and his seat had been taken by an ill-tempered spinster whose scowls deepened when Ned started crying. Nothing Dolly could do would stop him. Wearily, Adela brought out the silver verge watch and permitted the little boy to listen to its chimes; but he was only momentarily diverted.

It was the noise of his increasingly loud wails which drowned the sound of approaching hoof beats. The guard perched on the back seat caught sight of the two horsemen as they gained upon them, and called out a warning to the driver. Cut-throats and highwaymen were known to frequent these lonely stretches of forest, and although the drivers and guards were always armed, so, too, were the robbers.

In a vain attempt to outpace their pursuers, the driver urged his horses into a gallop; but the coach was now lurching dangerously from side to side and the lead balls fired by the guard from his blunderbuss went wide of their mark. He had no time to reload his weapon before the horsemen had over-taken them and brought the four steaming horses and coach to a halt.

Adela and Dolly stared at the two men in horrified recognition. Attired in black cloaks and hats, black scarves concealing the lower halves of their faces, they were unquestionably high-waymen. Adela put her arms protectively about the children.

Whilst one of the men stood at a slight distance pointing his pistols in their direction, the other flung open the door of the coach.

'Your money and valuables!' he demanded peremptorily in a hoarse voice. 'Quick now, if you value your lives!'

There were screams from the ladies inside the coach and murmurs of dissent from the men; but they were powerless to refuse the highwayman's demands. Within a matter of minutes, the highwayman was on the roof. Ned let out a wail of terror whilst Kitty hid her face beneath Adela's pelisse. The terrified spinster lost no time in handing over the contents of her pockets.

'Yours, too, lady!' the highwayman ordered, turning to Adela. As she hesitated, he added, 'Confound it, girl, make haste lest I take that noisy bantlin of yours hostage!'

'I have no money! See for yourself!' Adela said quickly. Drawing Ned closer to her, she emptied the contents of her pockets.

Finding them indeed empty of all but a lace handkerchief and a hair comb, the man turned to Dolly. With a despairing look at Adela, Dolly instinctively clutched her hands to her sides. With a muffled oath, the highwayman tore open her cloak, and seeing the tell-tale bulges beneath her skirt, he dragged it quickly above her knees and wrenched the two chamois-leather bags from her. His eyes above his scarf glinted as he saw the contents. He had assessed at a glance the immense value of this unexpected haul. Not bothering to search the children or indeed, to remove the pendant from around Adela's neck, he leapt to the ground and joined his companion. After exchanging a few words, the two men remounted their horses, and before either the guard or the driver could reload their blunderbusses, they had disappeared amongst the dripping trees.

Dolly looked at Adela, her face white with shock.

''E's robbed us of everything – *everything*!' she whispered. 'Oh, Miss Addy, what'll we do now?'

As shocked as her maid and no less frightened, Adela refused to give way to tears.

'It was not your fault, Dolly! There was nothing you could do to prevent them robbing us.' She put a comforting hand on her arm. 'I still have my pendant!' she said. 'And Ned has Papa's watch!'

Suddenly Dolly remembered the rings she had sewn into the hem of her travelling dress. It had been a precaution lest they were robbed in London by footpads or pickpockets, but although it had been highwaymen who were the thieves, her chariness was now proving to mean the possible difference between survival and starvation.

Adela's attention had been diverted by the need to attend

to the spinster who was having an attack of the vapours. She would tell her mistress about the rings later, Dolly thought, her spirits lifting. She herself was confident that they would survive now until Master Titus and Master Barnaby returned from France and came to their assistance, hopefully bringing Jacques with them.

'There now, Miss Kitty!' she said, taking the weeping child in her arms. 'There's naught to cry about. Me and Miss Addy will take care of you. T'will not be long now afore we 'ave you tucked up in a nice warm bed!'

But she knew without looking at the watch still clasped in Ned's hands that it would be several hours yet before they crossed Westminster Bridge and reached the safe anonymity of London town.

CHAPTER SEVEN

1788

Despite the roughness of the Channel crossing which had laid low most of the passengers on the packet to Dover, Titus, Barnaby and Jacques remained on deck, all being excellent sailors and familiar with even rougher days at sea in the twins' own sailing boat. There had, too, been a memorable Channel crossing in stormy conditions when, for a lark in their student days they had stowed away on the schooner belonging to Jacques' smuggling friends.

They were seated now in the dining-room of the Lord Warden Hotel, the remains of a large meal spread out in front of them together with pint-size pewter tankards of foaming ale. They had managed to obtain passages on the last packet to leave Calais that day, and since it was dark by the time they docked, they had decided to spend the night at the inn before proceeding at dawn to London. With close on eighty miles to travel and speed essential, they had already made arrangements to hire a post-chaise. Even with frequent changes of horses *en route*, they did not anticipate reaching their destination until after dark the same day.

Jacques had coincided his arrival in Paris two days previously with their own return from their long and enjoyable sojourn through the European towns and cities on the Mediterranean coast. They had been warmly welcomed by the de Falence family but Titus had nevertheless been downcast to learn that the beautiful Eugénie had once more become betrothed – this time to a chevalier who owned the estate adjoining that of the Comte de Falence. Titus had therefore been forced to accept that he could no longer hope one day to win her hand.

By then the twins had been absent from their family for almost a year, with only one brief summer vacation to lighten their separation. It had been their intention, therefore, to leave for England after the Christmas balls and entertainments were over. However, when Jacques told them the story related to him by George Robinson on a recent encounter with the smugglers, they had immediately advanced these plans. Leaving Jacques out of the account, the twins had informed the Comte, and with his blessing and a handsome purse of gold *louis* to assist them in effecting his niece's rescue, they had taken his post-chaise for the long journey to Calais. A broken back axle-tree had delayed their arrival, as a result of which they were behind their planned schedule.

Titus now called to the landlord to bring him quill and ink to a quiet corner in the parlour. As soon as the three were reseated, he went through the time-table of events yet again with Jacques.

'Your cutter reached England with its contraband on Monday, yes?' he questioned. 'Then you met Robinson close by Dene on the Tuesday?'

Jacques nodded.

'It was at night, of course! To tell you the truth, Master Titus, Master Barnaby, I thought it best to go back 'ome quick as I could lest Miss Addy'd got scared and 'ad gorn back to Dene. There was a right to-do all over the village, and Dene Place were in a turmoil. Sir 'Enry weren't there, nor 'is man, and most of the grooms and those as could sit a 'orse 'ad been sent out searching. So I called in to see the Reverend.'

'Poor Mama! She must be dreadfully concerned!' Barnaby said, knowing how devoted to Adela Lady Mallory had always been; and how fond of Dolly, too.

'The Mistress were in tears 'til I tolt 'er they been seen safe and sound getting on to the stage at Norgem!' Jacques said.

'So that must have been on the Saturday!' Titus muttered

as he studied the dates he had filled in on the paper in front of him. 'Robinson would not have returned to Dover before Sunday at the earliest. Now let us consider: on the Wednesday you returned to Paris and it is now Friday – so Miss Adela and Dolly and the children have been gone for close on a week.'

'We knew before we departed that we would have no chance of overtaking them,' Barnaby commented with a worried frown. 'Unless, of course, they have not gone straight to London but have stopped at a village on the way.'

'Begging your pardon, sir, but I think if they'd been on the 'Astings to London road, London would 'ave been where they was 'eading. Dolly knows London like the back of 'er 'and, and seeing as 'ow you said they was unlikely to 'ave much money to support them, like as not she is planning to get employment there if'n she can!'

'We can enquire at the coaching inns when we reach London!' Titus said thoughtfully. 'The trail cannot have gone entirely cold in so short a time. Someone must have noticed them!'

'It is to be hoped Sir Henry does not hear word of them first!' Barnaby muttered. 'Whatever the reason for their disappearance, I am convinced they left home on his account; and he is not the man to take such a matter lightly. 'Tis common knowledge how he dotes on his son, and I dread to think what punishment he might inflict on Addy for taking the boy from him.'

Jacques nodded. 'The whole village is aware of their disappearance and most folk is saying: "Small wonder!"'

Both Titus and Barnaby remained silent, unable to prevent thoughts of the possible consequences if Adela were apprehended. Sharing their thoughts – as happened so often – they tried not to worry at this stage as to what they would do when and if they found Adela. It was unlikely she would seek help from any of her family's former friends for Sir Henry was no fool and would have any suspected place of refuge searched. The law was on his side and he would therefore have its support and assistance.

The future did not seem very hopeful, all three of them decided as they made their way up to bed. Rooms had been provided for the twins with cheerful fires in the grates, copper warming-pans in the feather beds and clean fresh linen for their use. Nevertheless, neither slept well for there was a constant barrage of noise from the busy kitchens below and from the stages arriving with passengers who were to embark for France on the morning tide.

The twins were already up and dressed when at five o'clock next morning there was a loud knocking on their door and Jacques came in with one of the Mallorys' stable lads. The boy had brought with him a letter from Lady Mallory. He was grinning broadly as he told them that his mistress had instructed him to watch for their arrival at the inn, no matter if he had to wait a week or more, he recounted. It was of the utmost importance that he give them the letter the very moment they set foot on English soil.

Only when the twins broke the seal did they realize why their mother had considered such urgency to be vital, for the letter was from Adela.

The children, Dolly and I are newly arrived at The Rose and Thistle situated at Charing Cross.

she had penned in her large, round script.

I will not try to Explain the Reasons for leaving Dene Place for it would take too long. We are greatly in Need of your Assistance, so I am sending this to your Mama and a similar Missive to France lest you both be there.

We were beset by Highwaymen on our Journey to London and have very little Money to support ourselves. Nevertheless, I remain Determined never to go back to Dene Place so long as Sir Henry is alive. I would not thus

Burden you with my Misfortunes were I not convinced
of your True Love and Friendship. We are Tired, but in
Good Health, and Dolly is a Tower of Strength to me.
   From your Devoted, Adela

'So she is safe and well, and now we know where to find her!'
Barnaby said joyfully. Titus shook his head.

'She is very far from safe, Barny. Sir Henry will surely question the landlord at every London inn where stages arrive
from the south. No matter what promises of silence Adela
may have extracted from the landlord of The Rose and Thistle,
you can be sure he will not gainsay the law; and Sir Henry's
guineas will loosen most tongues and elicit support even if
the law does not!'

Barnaby's handsome face lost its hopeful smile.

'You are right, of course. But surely Addy will have thought
of this danger for herself? 'Tis possible she has moved further
afield and left word for us at The Rose and Thistle.'

'To whom might she entrust such a letter?' Titus questioned.
'Addy is of sufficient intelligence to know that the landlord
would of a certainty hand it over to Sir Henry if there were
sufficient reward offered.'

Throughout the breakfast the three pursuers hurriedly
partook downstairs, they debated their chances of finding
Adela before her stepfather could do so. Titus remained apprehensive although Jacques was inclined to support Barnaby's
belief that they would discover Adela still ensconced at The
Rose and Thistle. They were all agreed that the sooner they
could be on the road, the better were the prospects of success.
Before even the sun had risen fully over the rim of the horizon,
they were making fast pace in their hired post-chaise towards
their first staging post at Canterbury.

Adela paced the floor of her room at The Rose and Thistle with
growing unease. It was now three hours since Dolly had left
with the pendant and her mother's rings to find a pawnshop,

promising that she would not be long. Ned was playing happily enough in front of the fire with some paper horses Adela had fashioned for him and an upturned soap dish he was using as a make-shift carriage; but Kitty was lying listlessly in Adela's feather bed. Her cheeks were flushed, and every now and again Ned's childish patter was overshadowed by her cough. There could be little doubt that she had caught a severe chill whilst they had been on the road and Adela was now reminded how delicate the little girl had always been. Yet again, she was assailed by doubts as to whether she had been justified in taking the children from the comparative safety of their home.

Kitty, however, was inadvertently reassuring.

'We are not ever going back, are we, Addy?' she asked again and again. 'Papa cannot make us go back, can he? He will not come here, will he?'

Clearly, she was far more afraid of her father than she had begun to be of the highwaymen. All she had had to say on that topic was a relieved, 'Those naughty horsemen did not hurt us, did they, Addy? They did not have a cane like Papa's.' She was too young and innocent to have been aware that they had pistols and could well have killed them!

Adela bathed Kitty's feverish forehead with a cool cloth and smoothed her pillow before returning to her window. At least the sights within her view were a distraction from her worries. Apart from carriage rides to such ports as Rye and Winchelsea – and on one memorable occasion to Hastings – she had never witnessed the sight of so many people, carts and carriages crowded in one street. Hastings she recalled from the memory of a four year old, when the family had visited a venerable old friend of her father's – an eccentric old man who had, so her father told her, copied out the works of England's great poet, Shakespeare, in his own hand ten times; and the tenth volume had been shown to her to marvel at.

Grief for the loss of her beloved father brought tears to Adela's eyes but she brushed them away quickly and lifted Ned up to the window.

'Have you ever seen so many people?' she said. 'Look, there goes a knife-grinder! And see there – that is a sedan-chair. See what fine liveries the two men have who are carrying it. Can you count the horses pulling that dray? That is quite right, there are four. Just listen to all the church bells! Oh, dear, that poor woman has been knocked over and the apples in her basket are rolling into the gutter!'

She paused to wipe the frosty panes of glass which had misted over as they breathed.

'If we look hard enough, we might see the dome of St Paul's. You have never before seen a cathedral, have you? St Paul's has a whispering gallery and if you are a good boy, Dolly and I will take you to see it. 'Tis said to be one of Sir Christopher Wren's masterpieces.'

She was still thus engaged in amusing Ned when a breathless Dolly returned.

'Oh, Miss Addy, I ain't done well for us, not no way,' she gasped as she removed her cloak. 'That pawnbroker were a cruel man and reckoned as 'ow I must 'ave stole the jewels, so 'e didn't give me the 'alf of what 'e ought. 'E said if'n I didn't redeem 'em like I'd said I would, they'd be that 'ard to sell.'

Adela bit her lip.

'Maybe I should have taken them myself, Dolly! He might have believed the valuables were mine!'

'Oh, no, Miss Addy! You dursn't be seen round about lessen someone takes note and word reaches the Master!' Dolly cried. 'I kept back your pendant and four of the six rings!' she said as she tipped out the coins in her pocket and bade Adela count them. 'But these won't keep us for long, Miss Addy – not lodging at this inn, not nohow! And whatever else, us doant want to get into the 'ands of them pestilent money-lenders.'

She shook her head, and drew her brows downward in a worried frown. ''Sides, it ain't safe for us to stay 'ere. The landlord's wife stopped me on my way out, and she were that curious about you and the little 'uns. I said your uncle would be coming afore long to fetch you,' she added, 'but I doant think 'er believed me. It just ain't proper for a young lady like you to be 'ere alone in a place like this, Miss Addy.'

Dolly's warning made sense but Adela was reluctant to agree to a move. Not only was little Kitty ill but she had told Titus and Barnaby in her letter that it was here at The Rose and Thistle they could find her. If only she could be sure they had received one or other of her letters, she thought! But there was no certainty that Titus and Barnaby had returned from their sojourn as expected, and for all she knew, they could be ignorant still of her predicament.

'I suppose I could leave another letter here for the twins!' she spoke her thoughts aloud. 'The landlord could give it to them when they come enquiring for me!'

Dolly shook her head.

''T'aint safe, Miss Addy. Lunnon folks is out for every penny they can make, and that there landlord's no different, mark my words. 'E ain't got no cause to keep your counsel, not if'n Sir 'Enry comes asking for you!'

Reluctant to sever the life-line to which she had clung ever since she had made up her mind to leave Dene Place, Adela hesitated. Dolly was right to take every precaution; and move they must if they could not afford to pay their board and lodging here. After the finery of the only home she had ever known, Adela found it hard to believe that this noisy, shabby inn was beyond their means. Never having handled money, she was ignorant of its values, but she trusted Dolly to know best and accepted the need for economy.

'I suppose I could write again – once we are settled at a new address,' she said slowly. Her face brightened. 'Of course I can, Dolly! We shall manage on our own for a further week or two, shall we not? We have managed so far without mishap!'

Much relieved by her young mistress' agreement to move, Dolly set about packing their few belongings. They had brought only one change of clothing each for, being winter-time, they needed flannel petticoats and night shifts as well as stout boots and shawls. Knowing they must walk quite a distance before they dared join a stage-coach, one portmanteau had seemed quite enough to carry, for they had believed that with the money acquired by pawning Nadine's jewellery, they could purchase what else they might need when they reached London.

Now, with the necessity for economy in the forefront of her mind, Dolly suggested that they make their way to the cheaper district beyond Covent Garden market. Lodgings would be less costly there although the narrow dark streets shadowed by overhanging houses would be a very far cry from the conditions her young mistress was accustomed to. The gutters would be dirtier; the smells which she had remarked upon already, even more noxious; the inhabitants rougher, coarser than Miss Addy could imagine.

Adela swept such misgivings aside when Dolly voiced them. 'We cannot be certain how long it will be before Master Titus and Master Barnaby come to our assistance,' she said as she lifted Kitty's hot little body from her warm bed. 'Nor even how long it will be before you can obtain work, Dolly. You must stop thinking of me as someone who must be pampered and waited upon! And believe me, no horrors can be worse than that cellar at home where I spent so many hours; nor, indeed, that last night in the presence of Sir Henry's guests. You will not hear me complain!'

Dolly was by no means reassured, for she understood very well that Adela had no conception of how the poor of London existed. No gently nurtured young girl could begin to imagine the squalor, the vermin, the language of the gin-drinking females; the sight of half-starved ragged urchins. From her own experience, Dolly knew that such people were often kind to one another, offering such succour as they could to their fellows; that their sympathy for one another was but a glimmer of good in otherwise cruel, indifferent surroundings. Unlike Adela, she was only too well aware of how precarious their situation was. The pawnbroker had robbed her, for she was in no doubt that the rings he had taken were worth a hundred times more than he had allowed her; but there had been no alternative to selling them for the landlord's wife was unwilling even to serve them breakfast before they had paid for their night's lodging.

Outside, it had begun to rain – a cold, hard downpour that deepened Adela's concern.

'We cannot let Kitty walk in this weather even if her condition permitted it!' she said. 'She has a fever!'

Dolly felt the little girl's forehead although she could see from her flushed cheeks that she was burning hot.

'I'll go down and pay our dues and see if by chance there's a wagon going to the market. It ain't far, Miss Addy!'

'I want to go in a wagon!' Ned said suddenly, for there was nothing he had enjoyed more than a ride in the hay carts in the fields at his home. 'I want to go in a wagon *now*!'

'Hush, Ned, Dolly's going to see about it!' Adela said, grateful that the small boy who could be so truculent when the mood took him was not demanding a ride in a respectable carriage! She glanced down at her muddy skirt, glad that she had not, after all, worn her clean dress, for it would certainly be dirtied still further riding in a farm wagon.

'My head hurts, Addy!' Kitty said in a small, hoarse voice. 'Can I go back to bed, please?'

'In a little while, my sweeting!' Adela replied as she wrapped the child's cloak more tightly about her thin body. She was once again filled with anxiety. If Kitty's fever worsened, they would need to call a physician to see her. Would Dolly know where to find such a man in this vast city? And how much money would he charge for his services? Her ignorance about such matters worried her deeply. Until she acquired some knowledge about these things, she must rely upon Dolly. It was strange to consider that for all her own education, it was the illiterate Dolly upon whom she must now depend.

Whilst she rocked Kitty on her lap as she awaited Dolly's return, her thoughts conjured up a summer's afternoon before her Papa had died, when the twins had been taking dinner

with them. It was nearing five o'clock and they had finished
the two main courses and were enjoying the cakes that
followed. Mama, seated as ever close beside her father, was
pouring tea for him from her favourite Sèvres china teapot
which she had brought with her from France when she was
married. Only six years old at the time, adult conversation
seldom held any interest for Adela, but on this occasion Papa
had started talking to the twins about their future. Loving the
boys as she did, Adela had paid attention. Her father was
trying to encourage Titus and Barnaby to purchase commissions in the Army as soon as they were old enough, recom-
mending it as a most enjoyable way of life for a young man.
Young as she was, it nevertheless crossed Adela's mind that if
the boys became army officers and fought in wars as her father
had done, they too might end up paralysed as he was, and
that was unthinkable. She was enormously relieved therefore,
when they informed Sir Matthew that their uncle's legacy had
been very small and that their father had advised them it was
inadequate to meet the costs of such a career.

Matters of finance were seldom mentioned thereafter but
Adela was nevertheless aware that unlike her parents' other
friends, the Mallorys were poor despite their gentle birth. Now,
suddenly, it struck her that even whilst the twins would almost
certainly come to her aid and help her in any way they could,
they might not have the means to help support them, however
modestly she and the little ones were prepared to live.

Adela had no time for further unhappy reflections for Dolly
had returned. Hastily, she bundled them down the narrow
staircase to the cobbled courtyard where an impatient
waggoner was awaiting them. It was not until later that
afternoon, when Dolly had gone out in search of a physician,
that Adela once more considered their future. Despite her
reassurances to Dolly that she was perfectly content with their
new-found accommodation for the time being, she was secretly
appalled. For one thing, the two little rooms in the attics
which they had rented were so cramped as to be little bigger

than her clothes closet at home. She and Kitty were sharing one big tent bed with a hard, lumpy flock mattress; Dolly and Ned were in the even smaller room adjoining. She had been deeply shocked to discover something live when they were hurriedly making up the bed for Kitty with the coarse linen sheets their landlady had provided. 'Them's bedbugs!' Dolly had whispered lest the children overheard. 'I'll buy a sulphur candle at the apothecary whilst I'm out. It doant smell nice so we'll burn it tomorrow when we can take the little 'uns for a walk. I'll buy a few grains of mercury, too. It stops the itching if we gets bit!'

Adela was convinced she would not be able to sleep in the bed, and it was with the greatest reluctance that she had placed Kitty in between the sheets. The fever had not subsided and the little girl had difficulty swallowing the sips of water Adela held to her lips. When Dolly had told the landlady they would pay to have a fire lit in the empty grate, the woman had obliged readily enough; but the low-ceilinged room which had been so cold was now so stuffy that they all had difficulty in breathing. She had opened the small casement window but the stench from the gutters was so horrifying, she had quickly closed it again.

They could not remain here for more than a few days, she told herself, no matter how reasonable the weekly rent! What hope had Dolly of cooking adequate meals for the children on the filthy fire downstairs in what the landlady had called her 'kitchun'? Accustomed as Adela was to the big, airy kitchen and scullery at Dene Place, she could not imagine how they would manage. She had expected the dinginess – but not the dirt. Up here in their attic rooms, a black oily dust clung to everything.

For the third time, Adela questioned her wisdom in taking the children from their beautiful home. Turning her head she saw Ned, his small nose pressed against the window pane, staring at something which had caught his attention in the street below. As she joined him at the window, she realized what had attracted him – the antics of a man and woman sheltering in a doorway. The man had one hand in the bodice of the woman's dress; the other grasped the curve of her buttocks. Clearly Ned, like herself, was reminded by this spectacle of the lecherous behaviour of Sir Henry's dinner guests, for he said, 'Ned wants a sweetmeat! Ned wants a candied fruit! Ned give you a nice big kiss, Addy, if you give me a sweetmeat.'

The doubts she had been harbouring were swept away; and her resolve to keep the children with her whatever the hardships, was reinforced when Kitty moaned yet again, 'Papa will not come and take us home, will he, Addy? Papa will not find us here?'

'No, my sweeting, we are quite safe here. Lie still now. The physician will be here shortly and will give us something to make you feel better!'

She was interrupted by a loud knock on the door, and without waiting for Adela's reply, the landlady came in.

'Physician's come with that girl of yourn. Yer ain't ill, is yer, missis? I doant want no sick folk in my 'ouse!'

'My little girl has a slight fever!' Adela said quickly. 'I am sure it is nothing very serious – a childhood ailment, I expect.'

The woman glanced at Kitty and, with more curiosity, at Adela. She had known at once that this was a young lady of quality despite Dolly having done all the talking. Curiosity vied with cunning. Quality meant money, and that was her priority. Nevertheless she could not fathom what Adela could be doing in a house like hers. The girl looked too young to be mother to the elder child, she thought; not that you could always tell! Maybe she had been got at when she was a youngster and her parents had married her off to anyone who'd give the kid a name. They looked like fugitives – the both of 'em – and like as not they had done a bunk. Well, good luck to them – she, herself, had had a basinful of men who'd beaten her; stolen her hard-earned money; run off and left her to fend for herself. She'd no time for men. They were good for one thing only – money; and now that she was way past the age when she could earn her living on the streets, she'd found a better way to keep herself, even if letting rooms to lodgers was plain drudgery from dawn to dusk.

She glanced once more at Kitty. It did not do to have sickness in the house, she thought. Word got round in no time and people was scared of illness, most of them not having the wherewithal to pay for medicines and the like. In this part of the city, if you did not get better on your own account, you died. Kids, especially, died every day.

When the physician arrived with Dolly, however, she was respectful as she held open the door for him. She shooed away the crowd of urchins who were gathered round his phaeton, then went to the landing outside the child's room so that she could overhear his diagnosis.

Adela was far from reassured by the man's appearance, for his clothes were shabby and his manner abrupt, the more so when he pronounced that there was nothing seriously wrong with Kitty.

'I am a busy man, Mrs Porter,' he said, using the false name Adela and Dolly had agreed on, 'and I have little time to spare for those who are not seriously ill. However . . .' he paused, staring more closely at the young woman he presumed was the child's mother '. . . it is your business not mine if you wish to waste your money paying my fee.'

Like the landlady, he was consumed with curiosity as to what this well-spoken young woman was doing in these back streets of London. Had she no husband . . . no father to protect her? Her hands, he noted, were smooth and white, and clearly unused to work. The children too, he suspected of being accustomed to very different circumstances from these. As for the young woman who had requested his services, it seemed reasonable to suppose that she was a servant – a nursemaid, perhaps.

However, years of working in these poverty-stricken streets had taught him that it was simpler not to ask questions as to his patients' circumstances. The fees he charged were small enough and all too often remained unpaid. Not knowing who Dolly was, he had demanded payment in advance and been agreeably surprised to be given it. Now, having encountered Adela, he understood why he had been called out for so minor a complaint. He was usually only asked to visit a patient when they were *in extremis*, such as a woman whose neighbours had been unable to birth a child for her and who feared the expectant mother would die; or a girl bleeding to death from an attempt to get rid of an unwanted child. Those who were dying of old age or starvation did not waste money on a physician; and those less sick came or were carried to his rooms for medicines or to have a broken leg mended.

He picked up his portmanteau and three-cornered hat and bowed.

'You know where to find me if the fever worsens!' he said. 'Meanwhile keep the child warm, keep the casement shut and give her nothing to eat for a day or two. Now I must be on my way!'

As he closed the door behind him, Adela drew a deep sigh as she recalled the charming physician who had attended her father until his death; and who had called regularly to see her mother until Sir Henry had dismissed him after an argument over the cause of her deterioration. His manners were impeccable as well as respectful, unlike those of the man who had just departed. What effrontery to remark that she was 'wasting her money' – even if that had proved to be the case, she thought indignantly.

With a sinking heart, she realized that for the time being she must accustom herself to a very different world from the one which she had been used to. She had only to look at the shocking condition of her dress and shoes to feel embarrassed. As for Ned, who had been playing on the bare-boarded floor – he looked no cleaner than the children she had seen in the streets.

'Tomorrow we must buy Ned some boy's clothing!' she

said to Dolly. 'Breeches will not gather the dirt as do those dresses of his.'

Dolly gave a cheerful grin.

'And if'n we cut 'is 'air, there'd be less chance of 'im being rekkernized!' she agreed.

With a lightening of her spirits, Adela, too, smiled.

'Perhaps I, as well as Ned, should have my hair cut!' she said half in earnest.

Dolly gave a gasp of horror.

'Not no way, Miss Addy – not that beautiful 'air of yourn. But I dare say it 'ud make you less to be noticed if'n we got you a dress like mine. They'll be searching for a lady – not a servant! That is, if'n you didn't mind too much, Miss Addy?'

'On the contrary, I think it an excellent idea!' Adela replied as she moved over to Kitty who, mercifully, had once again fallen asleep.

'Time young Master Ned 'ad a nap, too,' Dolly said, taking the boy by the hand. 'Then, if'n you agree, Miss Addy, I'll go out and see if I can find some work whilst you mind the little 'uns. The sooner I can get a job the better, though it mightn't be that easy without no references.'

'I could write one for you!' Adela suggested, but Dolly quickly vetoed the idea.

'If'n it were taken up, Miss Addy, the Master would find out where I was, and it 'ud not be long afore 'e came looking for you, knowing we was together. It ain't worth the risk. I'll find something, never you fear!'

But a week later, Dolly had still not found employment, and their small residue of money was coming perilously close to an end.

CHAPTER EIGHT

1788

'This is accursed weather, Barny!' Titus said. He was attempting to regain the circulation in his hands and feet before a huge fire in the room of the Crown Inn where they had taken lodgings whilst they continued their search for Adela and the children. Despite trudging the streets for the best part of every day for the past three weeks, they had discovered no trace of them. As November gave way to December, the weather had steadily deteriorated, as had their optimism.

'It lacks but a week to Christmas!' Barnaby remarked. 'Father and Mama will expect us home and I think we should go before the roads become impassable.'

'Right enough, Master Barnaby!' Jacques agreed as he struggled to remove Barnaby's top-boots so that he, too, could thaw his feet. 'If we have a heavy fall of snow . . .'

Titus frowned.

'I am loath to give up the search,' he said quietly. 'If we are finding life disagreeable, what must poor Addy be suffering?'

Barnaby nodded.

'I cannot understand it!' he muttered. 'Addy promised to write. I am in no doubt that if she had written a second time to the parsonage, Mama would have forwarded her letter. Addy should know of our address here in London by now and of our reasons for being here.'

'How can we be certain that Sir Henry has not already apprehended them and taken them home to Dene Place? If we were to return to Dene, we could find out if they were there.'

'Mama would have written to tell us were that the case,' Barnaby reasoned, 'although I suppose it is possible that he has taken them elsewhere?'

'God rot his soul!' Titus swore vehemently. 'If I come face to face with that man, I'll not answer for my actions!'

'Nor I!' added Barnaby.

With a grunt, Jacques succeeded in removing Barnaby's second boot and began stuffing it with sheets of the *Morning Chronicle* before placing it near the fire.

''Twas being said in the village that Lady Nayland's jewellery had been stolen and that Sir Henry believed Miss Adela 'ad took it. If that be the case, she'll not be without the means to survive,' Jacques volunteered.

Titus shook his head.

'But even if Miss Addy took the jewels, the highwaymen would have robbed her of them,' he said. 'If only we knew where she was. She needs us! Her letter made that clear. I cannot bear to think of her all alone in this pestilent city!'

Barnaby sighed.

'We cannot even be sure she is still in London. We could be wasting our time, Titus – and what little money we have left.'

Titus shook his head.

'I am reluctant – as I am sure you are, Barny – to draw on the credit the Comte said he would arrange at the London branch of his bank. Jacques is right – we should return home and discover what Sir Henry has been up to.'

'Is it possible 'e 'as stopped searching?' Jacques enquired.

Simultaneously, the twins shook their heads.

'He'll not give up his son! 'Tis common knowledge he dotes on the boy to the point of insanity. That is why *we* must find Addy, for he will never forgive her for abducting young Ned.'

They had arrived at The Rose and Thistle not three days after Adela and Dolly had departed, but despite the boys' offer of a handsome bribe, the landlord had no knowledge as to where they had gone. Sir Henry's man, Higgins, had already made enquiries and promised a reward if the fugitives were found, he informed them; but he had nothing to relate, other than that the women and children had departed in one of the dozens of wagons leaving for Covent Garden market. His wife had suspected something might be amiss, he told them eagerly, hoping such a snippet of information might lead to one of the guineas in his enquirer's hands; but the reward was not forthcoming when he was obliged to admit that both he and his wife had been too busy to look further into the matter.

'Stages come and go all day long and at night!' he had reiterated. He could not be expected to take note of where his customers came from or whither they were going. All he could say was that they had arrived on the coach from Hastings – a fact he recalled quite clearly since the stage had been robbed *en route*.

This news underlined what the twins already feared – that Adela might well have been obliged to hand the jewellery over to the highwaymen.

In the busy market at Covent Garden, their enquiries had been met with barely concealed derision. Wagons came in from farms as far away as Hertfordshire and Surrey, the porters had told them. The young lady and her companions might be anywhere from Suffolk to Kent; or they might have dismounted and be in the environs of the market!

Three weeks of visiting every inn and respectable lodging house in the immediate surroundings of the market had proved equally unavailing, and now the twins were beginning to despair. Jacques was as concerned as they – and not only for Adela and the children, but for Dolly. He was genuinely devoted to her and had every intention of proposing marriage to her as soon as he could afford to do so. He had acquired sufficient money from his smuggling activities to buy his mother the tiny cottage in the village; but with only one bedroom upstairs and one kitchen-cum-living-room down, it was not large enough also to accommodate him and a wife. His mother was now seventy-six and very frail and needed the attention of her neighbour – payment to whom was a further drain on Jacques' income. He could, he knew, obtain better paid employment in a wealthier family than the parson's, but his loyalty to the Mallorys was absolute. The parson was a fair, kindly employer, as was the Mistress, who visited his ailing mother every week, taking a basket of food from her own kitchen and vegetables and fruit from the garden. Nor could any wage tempt him from the two young men whom he had looked after since they were little lads of four. He loved them as he would his own flesh and blood and would readily lay down his life for either of them. Their good nature, their ready humour and enthusiasm for any adventure appealed to him as greatly as their attitude to him which was unfailingly considerate. Besides these particular attributes, he respected them for their fearlessness as much as for their physical skills. They could both outclass their opponents at swordplay and were a match for any gentleman in marksmanship, with fisticuffs or driving a four-in-hand. They were also skilled at the handling of a boat.

Jacques could well understand why his two young masters were so popular with the ladies! Apart from their identical good looks – which always drew attention – there was a glint in their eyes which suggested they were on the brink of laughter. These past few weeks, however, they had been unusually sombre and totally dedicated in their pursuit of little Miss Adela and the children. Jacques' feelings towards Sir Henry Nayland were no less violent than theirs, and he heartily endorsed their desire to do Sir Henry some mortal harm.

Jacques' reflections were only momentarily diverted by the landlord's buxom daughter who came in bearing a large tray heavily laden with his masters' evening meal. Whilst the young men exchanged sallies with the smiling girl, he went down to the yard to wash his face and hands in the freezing cold water of the pump. His thoughts returned to the immediate future. Ever since he had joined the local band of smugglers, he had known of the underground passage which ran from the church to Dene Place. He had been sworn to secrecy before this knowledge was imparted and had so far never revealed the

information, even to the twins when, forbidden to call at the
house, they were obliged to meet Adela clandestinely. He had
given his oath upon his life and could well understand the
need for keeping such hiding places from becoming general
knowledge. If there were others in the village who knew of
it, they never spoke of it, any more than had Sir Matthew
who must have been aware of the history of his family home.
Sir Henry, Jacques was convinced, was unaware of the
concealed entrance from the cellar, and if the Reverend knew
that one of the old vaults in the churchyard provided an ideal
exit to the secret passage, then he, too, kept the fact to himself.

Now, however, Jacques could not help but wish that he had
imparted the secret to Dolly for it would greatly have assisted
their escape from the house. It had worried him as much as
it had the twins, to think of such young women walking alone
at night all the way to Northiam – and Robinson had been
clear that this is what had occurred. Though it was too late
now to be of use to Dolly or Miss Addy, he realized that he
had this easiest of means to get into Dene Place unobserved
and perhaps learn from the servants what developments there
might have been in Sir Henry's search for the runaways.

'We mun go back home!' he reiterated emphatically to Titus
and Barnaby as he served the meal to them in their private
room which was now warmed by the additional pile of logs
the serving girl had readily brought up. Overcome by the
flirtation of the two identical young gentlemen, she welcomed
any excuse to serve them.

'We be only three in number,' Jacques continued, 'and I'll
wager a gold piece Sir 'Enry 'as a deal many more men than
that out searching . . . and the law to assist 'im! If Dolly and
Miss Addy was 'ereabouts, 'e'd 'ave found 'em, surely.'

'Jacques is right!' Titus said instantly. The thought brought
an unhappy frown to his face. Barnaby nodded.

'If Addy writes to us again, we would receive her letter
telling us her whereabouts the quicker if we were at home!'

They turned simultaneously to Jacques and bade him start

packing their valises. Now that the decision was made, they were impatient to be gone, but the weather was so bitter that they knew it would be folly to start such a long journey at night.

'We will leave at sun-up!' Titus announced reluctantly.

'If there is any sun!' Barnaby commented ruefully. 'I cannot recall when it was last so cold in December!' He put down the leg of guinea-fowl he had been gnawing and drew his chair closer to the fire. 'I pray that Addy is not suffering from the cold!' he muttered. 'I had the most unhappy dream last night in which I came upon her floating in a river, and although she waved to me, I was stuck fast in the mud on the riverbank and could not go to her aid! She was blue with the cold and her eyes—'

'No more of this, Barny!' Titus broke in quickly. 'I had a dream not dissimilar.' He knew that such dreams could be omens, and that a soothsayer hearing of them would almost certainly warn of imminent danger, if not death. 'We are worried quite enough as it is and . . . and we should speak of other things.'

Appreciating his brother's train of thought, Barnaby forced himself to smile.

'If it is pleasant thoughts you want, Titus, I suppose we must listen yet again to you extolling the fair Eugénie's virtues!'

Glad to have this happier topic of conversation, Titus laughed, albeit ruefully.

'You may mock me as much as you please, my dear fellow, but you cannot deny she is quite ravishing to look upon and more captivating in her ways than any other girl we know!'

'Oh, I will grant you her beauty, Titus, but I question your conviction that there is no other female in the world to match her. I ask you to consider those extraordinary green eyes of Addy's! Or, indeed, the sound of her laughter.'

Titus looked surprised.

'But Addy is only a child!' he protested. 'I was speaking of the appeal Eugénie has to our more masculine instincts!'

He raised his eyebrows in sudden surprise as a thought occurred to him. 'Do you realize that this must be the first time in our lives we have not agreed as to our likes and dislikes? And I had thought you admired Eugénie as much as I but out of the goodness of your heart, were refraining from competing with me!'

Barnaby grinned.

'I will admit that I was not unmoved that night of the masked ball when, thinking herself to be in your company, Eugénie kissed my cheek!'

'The devil she did!' Titus exclaimed with an answering grin. 'Well, since you admit as much, I will confess that I was not unmoved when I held our little Addy in my arms when last we said farewell to her. In a year or two's time, she will be stealing all hearts.'

The faces of both boys suddenly clouded as they were reminded that Adela's life, even were they to find her, would not be one where she would be permitted to attend normal parties; or to enjoy the company of gallant young swains who sought to woo her. Even were Sir Henry to forgive her this present escapade, it was inconceivable that he would change his ways and introduce her into society as her parents would have done.

'One of us will have to marry her!' Titus said thoughtfully. 'Since I can no longer hope to win Eugénie's hand, maybe I should propose myself. I am very, very fond of her!'

'As am I!' Barnaby said quickly. 'If she were wed to one of us, Sir Henry would have no further right to control her life.'

'But he could forbid the marriage. He is her guardian – and she not yet sixteen years of age.'

Barnaby laughed.

'We could go to Gretna Green where, as you know, you can marry without the necessity for a parent's consent. Now that I have thought of it, I am quite taken with the notion for it would solve all Addy's difficulties. She could live at home with us. Do you not agree, Titus, that if this proves to be the only solution for her, we must propose ourselves and let her choose which of us she would prefer for a husband?' His smile was short-lived as he added, 'We may not need such a drastic remedy. If we can conceal her for a while until Sir Henry gives up hope of finding her, I have no doubt that the Comte and Comtesse de Falence will give her sanctuary. Once Sir Henry has assured himself she is not in France with them, he may cease to search for her there.'

Titus gave a sudden yawn.

'It has been a long day and we are rising early. Let us to bed, Barny! You, too, Jacques. We forget, I fear, that you are a lot older than we are and need more sleep!'

Jacques returned his grin as he laid out the two linen night-shirts on the large, curtained bed.

'I'll wager a gold piece that I can go longer hours than you without sleep, Master Titus!'

'He will win for sure if you take his bet, Titus!' Barnaby said, slapping his twin gleefully on the shoulder. 'You are forgetting our friend here is accustomed to losing a night's sleep when he is busy playing cat and mouse with the Excise men.'

'Do you realize you are helping to deplete the King's coffers, Jacques, my good fellow?' Titus supplemented as his valet pulled off his breeches. He yawned again, adding sleepily, 'Speaking of the King, I was informed by a gentleman today that he was close to death last summer and that his mind has been affected and he is no longer capable of conducting public affairs!'

As Jacques went to assist Barnaby, Titus untied his muslin cravat and removed his frilled shirt.

'Doubtless Mr Pitt will manage the country ably enough until he recovers,' Barnaby commented.

Titus gave another yawn and donning his night-shirt, he fell into bed. ''Tis either our good landlord's excellent wine, or else this odious London air which is making me so sleepy,' he said.

'It will be good to breathe fresh Sussex air again,' Barnaby agreed, settling himself for sleep beside his twin. 'Be off with you, Jacques, and snuff out that candle, there's a good fellow!'

He closed his eyes, hoping as he did so that he would not have yet another ominous dream about their little friend, Addy, for he was finding it hard to forget the desperate look in her eyes as she appealed to him in vain for help.

I cannot understand why Titus and Barnaby have not come to our aid, Adela thought as Dolly put the last of their precious supply of coal on the fire. Her glance went to the bed where both children were now sleeping. Ned would not settle in Dolly's room if she, too, were not in bed and they now put him down with Kitty until later in the evening when Dolly would lift him and carry him to her room.

Adela reached for the candle and drew it closer. She was stitching the hem of a purple satin dress which must be completed by morning so that it could be returned to the theatre company in time for their next performance. Dolly, in her search for employment, had been told that a seamstress was required who was able to repair the players' garments that had been damaged during a performance. It was only by chance that she had mentioned the work to Adela for she herself could no more ply a needle than spin yarn. The repairs to Nadine's and Adela's clothing had been accomplished by Nou-Nou who had learned her skills in France as a girl; and these she had passed on to Adela in the years of Nadine's widowhood. After Nou-Nou's dismissal, either Adela had mended her own and the children's attire or it had been sent to a woman in the village.

The theatre work entailed stitching at night by candlelight, often until the early hours since there were times when the wardrobe mistress could not keep pace with the sewing. Although Adela had been given the job, the work was intermittent, the pay was meagre and the costumes had to be collected and delivered whatever the weather, with no allowance made if a hackney had to be hired to protect the garments when it was raining.

Dolly had been shocked when Adela had suggested *she* undertook the work for the theatre company.

'It ain't fitting!' she had said over and over again, and was only mollified when Adela agreed that Dolly should be the one to collect and deliver the sewing. The fact remained that despite the pawning of the last of Nadine's rings, and, far more distressingly for Adela, her father's silver watch, they had barely enough money left to pay the next week's rental and for their food. Adela had insisted upon buying little luxuries to tempt the convalescent Kitty who was, even Dolly agreed, far too thin. Both she and Dolly, too, had lost weight these past weeks and only little Ned remained as chubby as ever. He asked less frequently for his papa now and was far more amenable to the gentle discipline Adela and Dolly exerted.

Unlike Kitty, who was nearly three years older, he was quickly forgetting his old life and seemed to enjoy spending a great deal of time at the bedroom window from which he could look down upon the ceaseless hurly-burly of city life being enacted beneath him. He loved to see the huge shire-horses pulling their drays. He liked to watch the mongrels fighting over a bone; the antics of the monkey on the organ-grinder's shoulder; to listen to the street cries of the pie-sellers, the dust-man's chant of 'dust-ho', the porter house-boy calling for the pewter pots, the milkmaid, the orange-seller, the watchman.

Most of all Ned liked to watch the rag-and-bone man with his cart and the dappled horse which stopped of its own accord at every house as his owner shouted, 'Any old rags?' On one occasion, Adela had permitted Ned to take some snippets of velvet from a villain's black cloak she had shortened and allowed him to keep the farthing the rag-and-bone man had given him.

Only on the rarest of occasions had she ventured out with Ned. It was far too cold to risk Kitty's delicate health and there was the further risk that one of Sir Henry's men might sight them. Although Ned, in his new breeches of which he was inordinately proud, looked like a cleaner version of the urchins who played in the streets, Adela knew she could not so easily disguise herself. She was unfortunate, she had realized, in the colour of her eyes which, as Dolly had pointed out, was quite unusual.

Now, however, she was a great deal wiser about the value of money than she had been but a few weeks earlier. She could see from the small pile of coins Dolly had laid on the table before her, that they could not survive much longer with such irregular work as Dolly was bringing back from the theatre.

'Whatever the risk, I must go there myself in the morning!' she spoke her thoughts aloud. 'You must stay here and look after the children, Dolly. Maybe if I go in person I can persuade the wardrobe mistress to give me more to do!'

'It ain't right!' Dolly said, shocked beyond measure that her lovely young mistress should be reduced to circumstances where she must beg for work. 'If'n I try again at The Crown, they'll surely 'ave washing up or else for me to do. Landlord said they need extra 'ands at Christmas time. They'd be needing 'elp now if t'weren't for this dratted weather. I never knowed it so bitter!'

Adela shivered, pulling her shawl more closely about her shoulders.

'It really is cold!' She blew on her fingers to warm them and picked up her sewing again. 'If only I knew where Titus and Barnaby were! Surely they cannot have remained on their travels now winter has come! And where is Jacques? If he has been home, he will know of our escape and come looking for you, Dolly. It is my belief that if it were not for the big difference in your ages, he would have come courting you!'

Dolly blushed.

''Tis true 'e's that fond of me 'e'll want to find me. 'Appen that George Robinson will tell 'im 'e seed us if'n Jacques meets up with 'im.'

Adela sighed, her forehead creasing with lines of worry.

'The smuggler knew only that we were going on the stage-coach,' she reminded the maid. 'Unless Titus and Barnaby have received one or both of the two letters I sent, they will not know where we are. 'Tis ten days – if not two weeks – since I wrote that second time saying we were here.'

She would have been no happier to learn that her second letter could never reach its destination for it had been waylaid by their landlady. Whilst Dolly had been out in search of work, Adela had trustingly handed it to the woman who was about to go to the market, requesting that she give the letter to a post-boy. None came down this unlikely street except on the rarest of occasions when there was a letter to deliver. Few of the people living there could either read or write! Adela had sealed it with wax and never doubted that it would remain sealed.

The landlady, however, whose curiosity had deepened with each day that passed, had been unable to resist the temptation of breaking the seal and, since she could read if the words were simple enough, of perusing the contents. She was in no doubt now that Adela was of gentle birth if not a child of aristocratic parentage. It was not only her appearance and her voice which had given rise to this conviction but Adela's behaviour. For one thing, she and that servant of hers were forever cleaning! The rooms smelt of carbolic and she had noticed that even the curtains had been washed. For another, there was a conspicuous lack of visitors. Everyone had relations, family of some sort, friends. The girl was far younger than she had first supposed and must, presumably, have parents? And, she had asked herself, where was the uncle who was supposedly coming to collect them when he could get to London? He, if he existed, had had three weeks to do so and that was long enough to travel from as far away as Scotland – a journey which could be accomplished by coach in five days.

Unable to read the longer words or, in places, to decipher Adela's script, the landlady had nevertheless found out enough to determine that her suspicions were justified. '*We will never return home, no matter what the law may say . . .*' The words had caused her a stab of fear. She wanted no trouble with the runners. There were enough folk in this street already as were the wrong side of the law! And even she was not without guilt. If the friends to whom Adela was appealing for help were to betray her – and they living in the house of a God-fearing, law-abiding man like a parson! – they'd like as not be a-feared to come to the young lady's assistance, she reflected. Next thing, the runners would come charging down the street, hammering on *her* door and like as not taking her into custody for hiding the young lady and those brats of hers! If there was one thing she most feared next to death or starvation, it was the confines of Newgate!

Her decision to tear the letter into pieces and throw it into the flowing gutters was reinforced by her belated realization that she would be unable to renew the wax seal without detection. Since the blame for such interference could only be laid at her door, she did not for a moment consider attempting it. A week later, she had forgotten the whole incident, and the fragments of Adela's letter to Titus and Barnaby had long since floated down the gutter into the stinking waters of the Fleet and thence into the Thames to be carried out to the sea.

'I will write another letter as soon as I have finished this gown!' Adela said with a deep sigh. 'Sooner or later, the twins must return home from France.'

But by the time Adela had completed her task, the candle had guttered and she was so weakened with exhaustion that Dolly had perforce to undress her and assist her into bed.

Dolly woke her next morning soon after cock's crow. Whilst Adela dressed, she heated a cup of hot chocolate which she insisted her young mistress should drink before she left the house. Even then, Adela could not leave directly for first Ned had to be placated when she refused his demand to accompany her; then Kitty needed to be comforted as, tearfully, she begged Adela not to leave her.

The child's querulous voice followed Adela when, hardening her heart to Kitty's anxious pleas, she made her way downstairs. By now people had emerged from the houses like ants from their nests and were scurrying on their way about their business, slowing Adela's progress. It was freezing hard and her breath frosted on the air as she picked her way carefully down the icy road. No matter how unsavoury the conditions, she could not afford to hire a chair.

Following Dolly's directions, Adela kept a tight hold on the bundle beneath her arm, and elbowed her way through the indifferent crowds. As she reached the Strand, a passing carriage pulled by four beautiful greys swept past her, the hooves of the animals and the wheels of the coach bespattering her cloak with mud as they splashed through the frozen puddles, their weight breaking the thin layers of ice on top. People hurried as best they could, heads tucked down in their shoulders to escape the bitter wind, and they jostled one another and Adela as they fought for passage on the edges of the road. Several times Adela was obliged to step down into the gutter which, as she neared the market, was filled with floating cabbage leaves and other such vegetable refuse tossed from stalls or fallen from farm wagons or from the baskets balanced precariously on the porters' heads.

With a sigh of relief, Adela saw the door of the theatre and hurried into the overhanging portico of the entrance just as, without warning, the skies opened and a deluge of hail descended from the heavens. Dolly had told her that she must go round to the stage-door on the far side of the building, but were she to search for it now, not only she but her precious burden would be drenched. Even were she late with her delivery, she had no alternative but to wait for the hailstorm to pass – which it must do eventually, she comforted herself.

She stood there for close on five minutes before she was joined by a second fugitive from the storm. At first she paid no attention to the tall, black-hatted figure beside her although she was aware that he carried a gold-topped cane and that he wore hussar buskins of fashionable design. It was only as he spoke that she realized the companion who shared her shelter was, like herself, of gentle birth.

Removing his hat, shaking it free of the white hailstones that had settled in the brim, he made an elaborate leg.

'Clarence Fortescue Esquire – at your service,' he introduced himself in loud, ringing tones. With a grand gesture, he swept some hailstones from the hem of his caped coat. ''Pon my faith, this is accursed weather, is it not?' he remarked, his voice deep and resonant. 'I trust those are raindrops on your cheeks, my dear young lady, and not tears?'

Adela felt herself blushing and then, realizing the theatricality of her companion, she could not resist a smile.

'Indeed, sir, they are neither tears nor raindrops, but melted hailstones!' she said. 'May I enquire if you are an actor, sir?'

Where, before, the man's interest had been no deeper than that he might have for any member of the public whom he could impress with his dramatic persona, his curiosity now became far more personal. This was no London wench, he realized, despite her shabby appearance. The girl's voice was perfectly pitched and melodious – an educated voice; and when she smiled, she was remarkably pretty.

'That is the case, my dear young lady!' he replied to her question. 'I am also the manager of the company of players who have the honour of entertaining the patrons of this theatre. And now may I know to whom I have the pleasure of speaking on this most loathsome, most fiendish, most obnoxious of days?'

Adela's smile deepened as she realized that the gentleman beside her much enjoyed the sound of his own voice. It was on the tip of her tongue to give her true name, but even as her mouth opened, she remembered Dolly's caution never to reveal her identity.

'My name is Mrs Porter!' she said. 'I am returning one of your players' costumes which I have repaired!' Remembering the second and more important reason for her presence at the theatre, she was struck by the opportunity this chance meeting had provided for her. 'It is a task I very much enjoy, but alas, the costumes you provide for your players are of such good quality they need little attention and I fear I shall return home empty-handed and shall once more be without work to do.'

Clarence Fortescue regarded Adela with even greater interest. Already middle aged and with his once slim figure now owing its shape to corsets and his well-muscled legs to discreet padding, he was no longer a suitable choice for the young male lead roles. His leading ladies were already showing a preference for the younger male actors; and his conquests with the lesser-part players were growing fewer. He knew that the young women now accepted his favours only in the hope of acquiring more prestigious parts when he was casting a play. No longer did he receive those exciting little *billets-doux* from the ladies of society who came to see his performances, inviting him to enjoy a 'late supper' with them at their homes. Such assignations were always carried out in the most discreet manner, as often as not when the ladies' husbands were absent, or else in houses large enough for marital suites to be far apart. It was also a very, very long time since he had, by sheer charm and the attraction of his good looks, enjoyed the seduction of a female of such tender years.

This young girl, he surmised, whatever her background, must be without the protection of husband, parents or guardians for otherwise it was not only inconceivable that she would be out and about without a chaperon, but that she was in need of work.

'Pray allow me to be of assistance, Mistress Porter!' he said gallantly. 'I have no doubt my company has need of a skilled seamstress to design new costumes. Someone who takes an interest in the theatre – someone with imagination and taste . . . yes, indeed . . . good taste, might prove invaluable to me. Would such work be of interest to you, my dear?'

Adela's eyes glowed with excitement. She could not believe in such timely good fortune. Her eyes were luminous as she looked up at the man beside her.

'You would not find me without imagination – and, I trust, good taste!' she said eagerly. 'I am greatly in need of regular work, Mr Fortescue. You see, I have two young children to support!'

The actor's dark eyebrows lifted. Two children and no husband to support her? What easy prey this could prove to be!

'You surprise me, madam. I would not have thought you old enough to have such responsibilities – if you will excuse such a personal remark. However, if nothing else, life has taught me that even the least deserving can meet with misfortune – and I can see that the good Lord has not thought fit to treat you kindly.' He gave a soft chuckle. 'But let us hope we speak of the past, and your future will be far happier for you. Now the storm, too, has passed, and I will accompany you to my office where we shall decide what place you might be found in my company.'

'You are very kind, sir!' Adela said sincerely. 'It is good of you to take this interest in someone who is a complete stranger to you!'

Gently, her companion removed the heavy parcel from beneath her arm and tucked it beneath his own.

'We are not strangers, my dear young lady, for are we not all brothers in the eyes of God?' It was a line from one of his more recent productions and he recalled it without difficulty as he delivered it to Adela in his most telling tones. A hint of religion did much to allay any feminine anxieties as to his motives and he was quickly aware that Adela was looking little short of rapturous as she followed him into the theatre.

As Adela stared in wonder at the rows of empty seats and the big unlit stage with its looped crimson curtains, for the first time since she had left her home, her heart was singing with excitement, relief and joy.

CHAPTER NINE

1788

Not only the theatre but the rooms and passages were deserted but for an old caretaker who emerged from the shadows and bowed to Mr Fortescue as he opened the door of the office which also served as the actor's dressing-room.

'Your gold-laced, scarlet knee-breeches is fresh ironed, Mr Fortescue, sir!' he said. 'Can I fetch aught for you or the young lady, sir?'

Mr Fortescue smiled at Adela.

'A bottle of wine, do you think, to warm us up? 'Tis perishing cold in here, Burrows. You may light the fire since Mrs Porter and I have much to discuss and will be here some time. Then you may fetch a bottle of claret.'

He reached beneath his coat and drew out a purse from which he took a guinea. He tossed it to the old caretaker who, with a grin, caught it expertly as if well accustomed to this gesture.

'Let me take your cloak, my dear!' Mr Fortescue said paternally to Adela. 'You are doubtless as wet as I!'

He ushered her into a gilt chair with a violet-coloured velvet seat and suggested Adela remove her bonnet. Mesmerized by her surroundings as much as by her companion, Adela silently obeyed these commands. Her hair, which she had hastily pinned up before leaving home, was loosened by her actions and now fell to her shoulders.

Observing her from the corner of his eye as he removed his own outer garments, Clarence Fortescue realized that not only was this girl far younger than he had supposed, but even prettier. She was blushing most becomingly as she tried to re-fasten her flowing dark ringlets into some sort of order.

He sat down at his dressing-table and smiled at her reflection.

'Seeing you as you are at this moment, young lady, I'd be of a mind to cast you in the role of Juliet – one of the most rewarding of my Shakespearean productions, I think.' He stood up suddenly and facing Adela, lifted his hands and chin towards the ceiling.

'*When he shall die, Take him, and cut him out in little stars* . . .' he quoted, his voice carefully articulating each word which resounded in the confined space of the little room.

'*And he will make the face of heaven so fine That all the world will be in love with night, And pay no worship to the garish sun,*' Adela completed the quotation shyly.

The actor swung round to face her, a look of pleasurable surprise on his face.

'So you are familiar with this passage!' he said. 'And so charmingly spoken, if I may say so!'

Adela smiled.

'You are very kind, Mr Fortescue, but I do not think I spoke the words as you would have spoken them. But yes, I am familiar with that passage from *Romeo and Juliet* – and many more besides. My father was a devotee of Mr Shakespeare's works, and as a small child, I read them to him so many times that they were easy for me to memorize after . . .' her voice faltered '. . . after he died.'

Clarence Fortescue leaned forward and took one of her hands in his. The familiarity of the gesture was softened by his words as he said in a low, deep voice, 'I can see the memory still saddens you. Poor child to lose such an erudite – and I am sure – loving parent. Your mother, too, must mourn him.'

'She, too, has died!' Adela said, her eyes filling suddenly with tears which her companion's sympathy had unexpectedly evoked. 'Of grief, I think!'

In ringing tones, Mr Fortescue quoted:

'Fear no more the heat o' the sun,
Nor the furious winter's rages;
Thou thy worldly task hast done,
Home art gone and ta'en thy wages;
Golden lads and girls all must,
As chimney-sweepers, come to dust.

'*Cymbeline*, Act Five,' he added in his ordinary voice.

'You are most knowledgeable, sir!' Adela said, impressed by the actor's erudition which, strangely, reminded her once again of her father.

He bowed at her compliment and smiled.

'We digress, Mrs Porter. It has occurred to me that with your voice, which is pure and melodious, your looks and your familiarity with Mr Shakespeare's plays, I might indeed feel justified in offering you the role of Juliet.' His smile deepened as he added, 'Do you not think acting upon the stage a far more enjoyable occupation than mending costumes? More rewarding, too,' he said quickly, for he had noted from Adela's attire that though of good quality, her gown was as shabby and as worn as her boots. As he had correctly assessed her breeding, he had now recognized all the signs of poverty.

Whilst Adela stared at him in undisguised astonishment, Clarence Fortescue was considering his impulsive suggestion more seriously. It had been made for no better reason than to impress and attract her for he was certain of one thing – that he wanted this girl-child for his mistress. If it were necessary for him to risk his reputation as being one of the most popular actor-cum-managers in London, was he willing to go to such lengths to entice her to his bed? he now asked himself. He knew instinctively that she would not surrender herself for money, and he was no longer able to delude himself that his appearance – or indeed his fame – would tempt her, as it had so many others in the past.

He sighed inwardly. For the time being, such a decision need not be made. He could justifiably offer the bait as a possibility, well hedged by 'ifs'. She would expect no less.

Adopting his paternal role once more, he patted her hand.

'Of course, I could not guarantee you such a huge step forward into fame and fortune. Much would depend upon your ability to memorize your lines; on your stage presence; on the pitch of your voice, for considerable volume is required if your words are to carry to the back of the theatre. Even the redoubtable Mrs Siddons failed at her first attempt. Good actresses are hard to come by! And then there is the question of the time you would have to give for rehearsals. For all that this life on the stage may appear one of excitement and ease, I can assure you it is largely a matter of long hours and hard work.'

'Can you really be in earnest, sir?' Adela asked, finding her voice once more. 'I know nothing of the theatre. I have . . . I have never even been in one before. I have lived all my life in the country, you see, and my father was an invalid so . . .'

She broke off, remembering the need to retain her anonymity at all costs.

'I come from Northumberland!' she said quickly, her eyes averted as with reluctance she voiced the lie.

He guessed that she was not speaking the truth, though he gave no sign of it. He was further intrigued. Already he had learned quite a bit about her and *ingénue* that she was, it would not be long before he learned a great deal more!

Too cunning to press his advantage, he turned to the tray with its wine bottle and glasses brought in by the caretaker.

'You must have a thousand things to do,' he said casually, 'as indeed, have I. So let us drink to your possible future and agree meanwhile to meet on the morrow to discuss the prospect further. I want you to think very seriously about my suggestion, and tomorrow you will do me the honour of dining with me and you can give me your decision.'

At his last words, Adela's expression became downcast. How could she possibly dine with this charming, friendly man when she had no evening gown? He was a famous actor and would expect his dinner guest to look at the very least respectable. If only she had just one of her mother's necklaces – or even a ring to wear! As to the need of a chaperon, she trusted Mr Clarence Fortescue implicitly. His manners were impeccable and his attitude to her had been perfectly correct – fatherly, in fact – and she, for all he was aware, of no more import than a poor sewing girl!

Adela thought suddenly of her stepfather; of his florid hateful face; his over-hanging belly; his straggly red hair; the bloodshot, watery pale blue eyes; the thin, cruel mouth. How could her mother have married such a man, however courteous and attentive his behaviour towards her had been when he was wooing her? The actor, now helping her to her feet, was the very antithesis of Sir Henry, and for that alone, her heart warmed to him.

She decided upon being as honest as her circumstances permitted.

'I would be honoured to dine with you, sir,' she said with quiet dignity, 'but I do not have suitable attire for . . . for the occasion you have suggested. Nevertheless, it was kind of you to invite me.'

'Come, come now, we have a wardrobe of gowns upstairs, one of which must surely be appropriate for a quiet little dinner party. I had thought we might go to Vauxhall Gardens.' Seeing her look of incomprehension he added, 'If you have not been there before, you might find it quite entertaining. They are the most popular of pleasure gardens, where you may listen to music and mingle with the fashionably dressed Londoners enjoying the paintings and observing the delightful arches and other such structures. We can dine there most satisfactorily in a discreet booth away from the curiosity of the vulgar public; and the food is excellent. I shall myself select something youthful and yet fashionable for you to wear, and one of our errand boys shall bring it to you. So, my dear, our little assignation is agreed, is it not?'

Speechless once again, Adela nodded. Having delivered her parcel to the caretaker and been assured by Mr Fortescue that he would see further work was sent round to her address that same day, she readily gave him the name of her street and the number of her lodging house and hurried home to tell Dolly of the morning's extraordinary encounter.

Dolly was busy boiling up some mutton-bone broth for Kitty when Adela returned. She listened in silence as, breathless with excitement, her young mistress related the events. When she turned to face Adela, her expression was both frightened and concerned.

'No matter how nice you thought the gentleman, Miss Addy, you cannot be sure 'e is not one of Sir 'Enry's spies on the lookout for you and was just being friendly-like to find out your address. I tolt you, didn't I, that there's posters up offering a big reward to anyone as can give news of our whereabouts. They was in the bars of both those inns where I tried to get work – them as is the ones where the stages come and go. I doant doubt them posters is in many another, too. That actor may 'ave read about them missing chillun and guessed 'twas you!'

Adela gave an uncertain smile.

'I do doubt it very much, Dolly! I saw myself in the big mirror in Mr Fortescue's dressing-room and I was quite shocked by my appearance. I looked exactly what I have become – a working girl!'

'That there Mr Fortescue did not think so, did 'e, Miss Addy?' Dolly said sharply, her frown deepening. 'You tolt 'im you could recite Mr Shakespeare to 'im; that your papa had taught you! Working girls like me doant learn such things. And 'sides, Miss Addy, no matter what, you still look like what you is – a young lady – what with your small 'ands and feet and your face an' all!'

Although unable to express herself adequately, Dolly was in no doubt that she was right. Her young mistress was of gentle birth and would never look otherwise.

'There's another thing, Miss Addy!' she said. 'This stage job 'e were offering you . . . I know you 'aven't made up your mind as you could do it, but even if'n you could, it ain't a fitting way of life for you, not nohow. And 'ad you thought on this – there's all of London would be sitting there staring at you if'n you did get up on that stage, and there'd be no better way of letting the Master know where we are than that!'

Adela gasped, unable to believe that she had not herself thought of such a possibility. So entranced had she been by her first and only pleasurable contact since she had last seen the twins a year ago, she had entirely forgotten she was in hiding.

'Mr Fortescue was so charming, he quite put our plight out of my mind!' she admitted ruefully. 'You are right, of course, Dolly! Even if you were not, I very much doubt if I could have lived up to Mr Fortescue's expectations.' Despite the gravity of the moment, her eyes lit up in a mischievous smile. 'Although I would dearly have loved to attempt the task, Dolly. Think on it – me taking the part of Juliet, speaking those wonderful lines before an audience!'

Aware that Kitty and Ned as well as Dolly were staring at her wide-eyed, she could not yet relinquish the excitement of the morning. Stepping back so that there was space between them, she flung out her arms as Mr Fortescue had done and in ringing tones, cried, 'O, *swear not by the moon, the inconstant moon, That monthly changes in her circled orb!*'

Dolly's worried expression gave way to a grin.

'That do sound a bit of orright, Miss Addy!' she said. 'Though I doant know as 'ow I unnerstood what you was a-saying!'

Adela laughed.

'It means to make a promise on something more constant than the moon!' she explained. 'If you swear on your life, Dolly, that would be more reliable than the moon, would it not?'

The smile left Dolly's face as she said urgently, 'Then you

swear on your life, Miss Addy, that you'll think no more on becoming a player?'

Adela sighed.

'I shall have to tell Mr Fortescue tomorrow that I do not have the time; or perhaps that I should be too nervous. It is to be hoped he will not take offence, for it is a great honour, I think, to be considered for so important a role. I would not want him to be so put out that he will refuse me further work on the stage costumes!'

The following evening, however, though clearly disappointed, Clarence Fortescue accepted her decision without argument. He had selected for her a green satin gown with a fichu, sleeve frills, a plumed Lunardi hat and green-satin, silver-buckled shoes. He had even provided her with elbow-length gloves, a pretty lace fan, a beauty patch and a generous quantity of powder for her hair. The green of her gown was a paler shade than that of her eyes, which only enhanced their colour the more.

Adela looked astonishingly beautiful and considerably older than her years, her companion thought as they made their way to their private booth. He was conscious of the many openly admiring and envious glances from the other gentlemen and was more determined than ever to make her his property. Without doubt, he thought, staring at her across the discreet, candle-lit table, she was the most desirable female he had met in his long life of conquests; and he was quietly wondering how best to go about her seduction.

Aware of his admiring glances but not of his intent, since she judged him to be some forty years older than herself and therefore beyond the age of romantic inclination, Adela was none the less flattered. Dolly had dressed and powdered her hair most becomingly, and although some of the other females had huge elaborate hair-styles with lavish decoration, she was quite happy with her appearance. After these past weeks of living in comparative squalor, she was spellbound by the astonishing novelty of their glamorous surroundings and was appreciating the elegance of her escort, the excellent food and wine. Now that her companion had taken so well her refusal to attempt the role of actress, she was happy to be enjoying this unexpected treat.

Seated opposite to this glowing girl, Clarence Fortescue found it hard to reconcile her with the drab apparition he had met the previous day whilst sheltering from the hailstorm. How right his instincts had been, he congratulated himself. He must now see if he had been as right in guessing that she had something of a serious nature to conceal.

'Tell me, my dear, what tragic circumstances brought you from your home in Northumberland to so unfashionable a part of London?' he enquired as a servant replenished their glasses of burgundy. 'Carters Lane is hardly a suitable area for a young lady.'

The glow left Adela's face and, to her annoyance, she blushed as she attempted to think of a plausible reply.

'My . . . my parents left me penniless!' she fabricated. 'I had no alternative but to come to London to find work.'

'But did you not tell me your name was Mistress Porter? That you were a widow? Did your late husband not leave you adequately provided for?'

Adela's blush deepened for she had quite forgotten this earlier fabrication. Her confusion was such that words escaped her.

Her companion leaned forward and covered her hand with his. In a low-pitched, gentle voice, he said, 'Dear child, will you not do me the honour of trusting me? I would like to be your friend and my instinct tells me that you have need of one. I can see that you are too young to have had much experience of life which, alas, is all too full of pitfalls! I would dearly like to be of assistance to you.'

His eyes were warm and friendly and reminded her once more of her beloved papa. How well she could recall running to him with her childish problems! How patiently he had listened to them! How easily he had found solutions! He, too, had always known when she attempted to deceive him with a fib to avoid a punishment for some childish misdemeanour! If Dolly had met the kindly Mr Fortescue, she would not have doubted his motives. Even to consider that he might reveal her whereabouts in order to gain the reward was to insult him. He was a successful theatre manager and famous actor, so what need had he of money? Whereas she . . . she had never been in greater need of a friend.

So intense was her longing to confide in him, she decided to do so – but only to a degree.

'I have to confess that I have not been entirely truthful with you, Mr Fortescue!' she admitted in a low voice. 'The name I gave you is an invention. Nor am I a married woman. The children I spoke of are my half-brother and sister. It is true that my parents are dead but . . . but for reasons I cannot explain to you, I could not continue to live with my guardian.'

With his own mind filled with salacious thoughts, Adela's declaration regarding her guardian caused him to tar the fellow with the same brush as others might have painted him. The man had most probably tried to take advantage of his ward, he decided, and who in all conscience could blame him? The girl was a most tempting bud on the very brink of flowering! Perhaps the fellow had gone about the task in boorish fashion and frightened her into flight! He was too wise to make the same mistake and would approach her with subtlety. Kindness, flattery, casual caresses could soothe a young girl's fears and in time, she would unfurl her petals to the soft probing of the honey-bee's tongue!

'So you ran away?' he prompted her gently.

Adela nodded. Suddenly, the sadness left her eyes and they flashed brilliantly as she added, 'I do not regret it, for all it is not . . . not very easy. My maid has been unable to find work, for she has no references, and the only talent I have is needle-work. That is why the sewing you provide for me is so important.'

'But quite unsuitable!' Mr Fortescue said softly. 'That is to say, a young lady of quality should not have to work at all!'

'I do not mind my lowly occupation!' Adela's chin lifted and her voice was firm. 'I will do anything rather than return to my guardian. You will understand now, why I cannot appear upon a stage. I could be recognized!'

'Of course! Of course! Nor, indeed, do I think your parents would have wished you to become a player. That, too, would be a quite unsuitable occupation! You must permit me to advise you – as a parent might have done. First, my dear young lady, if Mrs Porter is not your name, may I know another by which I may address you? At least permit me to know your Christian name – or since you so resemble my conception of Juliet, perhaps I should call you that. You are of similar age, I think, for all I know you would wish to be thought older?'

The question was posed so casually, Adela smiled as she said, 'I am in my sixteenth year, Mr Fortescue. It will shortly be my birth date, and you may call me Annie, sir, although that is not my real name either.'

Once again, Clarence Fortescue was obliged to call upon his acting skills to conceal his surprise. He had supposed her to be at least two years older.

'I admire your courage, and I respect your reticence, my dear, so I shall not ask what unhappy event obliged you to leave the safe sanctuary of your home. I must applaud your eximious valour, however, for life can be very difficult – and dangerous – in this big city of ours. So I was right in my belief that you do need a friend, and I very much hope that you will permit me to fill that role.'

Adela relaxed, certain now that she had not said too much and that her new friend was not intending to press her for further details.

'You are very kind, Mr Fortescue, though why you should trouble yourself with my affairs—'

'Say no more, Annie, I beg of you. We are none of us without experience of life's vicissitudes, and if we cannot look to our fellows for support, where would we be?' He leaned forward once more so that he could the better see her expression. 'Have you no other relatives, friends, to whom you can turn?'

Adela's eyes clouded.

'Such relations as I have, sir, live abroad. As to friends, I do have two very dear ones to whom I have written, but . . .' her voice faltered as tears came unbidden to her eyes '. . . but they have not so far replied to me. I fear my letters cannot have reached them else they would surely have come to my aid. I have known the twins all my life and as children we were very close.'

Momentarily she fell silent, remembering the tall, handsome boys with their fair hair and laughing brown eyes, especially Titus. She was still certain it was he, not Barnaby, who had kissed her farewell on their last encounter. It had been such a loving kiss! Or had she just imagined it held something more than comradeship?

Forgetting her promise to Dolly that she would tell Mr Fortescue nothing of Dene Place or her life at home, her face became animated once more as she said, 'The twins are identical!' She was so happy to be speaking of them that she hurried on. 'Not even their mama can tell them apart although . . . well, sometimes I have thought that I can. You see, it is more often that Titus is first to speak although their answers are nearly always the same! I think, perhaps, that as they have grown up, Titus has become the leader and Barnaby the follower. They have been like dear brothers to me.'

Brothers! thought Clarence Fortescue. For a moment, he had thought by the tone of Adela's voice when she had spoken of this Titus fellow, that it was something more than a sisterly affection the girl had for him. He was relieved to know that neither twin had replied to her pleas for help.

'Since you speak of them as your contemporaries, I assume they are of similar age to yourself. I do not wish to distress you but I think I should remind you that a youth in the first flush of manhood is likely to be very preoccupied with his own affairs. Little sisters, however dear, are apt to be forgotten by a young man wooing his first lady-love!'

Adela's face fell as unbidden came the memory of the twins' attentions to her pretty cousin, Eugénie. Then there was Louise who must be nineteen now, and perhaps as beautiful and sweet-natured as her sister, to take their fancy. Were they the reason Titus and Barnaby had departed so eagerly to France; stayed there so long; were reluctant to come home?

'I have upset you!' Mr Fortescue interrupted her thoughts. 'Forgive me, please. For all we know, I am probably quite mistaken!'

'But you may not be!' Adela cried softly. 'You may even have provided me with the very reason why I have had no reply to my letters. Until now, I have been convinced that the twins did not receive them, although I could think of no good reason why they should have gone astray.'

'Then let us suppose that for whatever reason, you cannot now expect them to assist you. What then? Have you given thought to your future?'

Adela shook her head. Indeed, she had not thought beyond the need to escape from Sir Henry's household and remain in hiding until Titus and Barnaby thought of a means of conducting her to some place where her stepfather would never find her or the children. Considering the matter through her companion's eyes, her actions seemed irresponsible, foolhardy, doomed to disaster. Nevertheless she declared vehemently, '*I shall never go back home!*'

It was a vow she had made to herself and now, whatever the difficulties, she would face them. It needed only determination and courage and she was not without either.

'I see that your mind is resolved on this point!' Mr Fortescue said, for he had noted with satisfaction the resoluteness of her declaration. 'So we must ensure that you have the means to support yourself and your little family as best we can!'

For the first time, Adela felt a moment of unease. Pleasant as he was, Mr Fortescue *was* a stranger and yet in the space of a day, he had assumed the familiarity of a friend, coupling their names together as if they had entered a partnership. He had asked her to trust him – and such was her inclination – but she had no reason to do so.

Nor, indeed, to mistrust him, she told herself firmly. Besides, the very last place Sir Henry would think of finding her would be in the company of an actor! If he walked into the dining booth now, it was questionable whether he would give her a second glance! She smiled at the idea even whilst she took a quick look around her – just to be certain!

'This is perhaps too public a place for you to be seen!' Mr Fortescue remarked suddenly as if he had read her thoughts. 'When next we dine together – as I very much hope we will, little Annie – then it might be safer if we were to do so in my rooms. Of course, you must bring your maid with you as it would not be proper otherwise!'

As he had supposed, this was a safe enough gamble, for almost certainly, the maid would have to be left behind to look after the children.

'Tell me about the little ones, my dear!' he said, for it was as well to know as many facts as possible, and this was not the moment to pursue the matter of their next tête-à-tête. The look of indecision left Adela's face which at once became animated.

'They are being so good and patient!' she declared. 'Little Katherine, who is only five years old, has been quite ill yet she has made no complaint. Edward is still too young at three to understand what is happening or appreciate the change in our circumstances. I was obliged to bring them with me as my . . . my guardian ill-treated them both . . . in different ways.'

'How brave you are – and so young! I cannot adequately

express my admiration – and it endorses my desire to help. Now listen to me, Annie! I will speak tomorrow with our wardrobe mistress. I did not do so today because I believed . . . I hoped very much . . . that you would tell me you had decided you might like to be an actress. Now I know why that cannot happen – a fact I deeply regret – I have an alternative suggestion. It may well be possible for you to assist Mrs Millet in dressing the cast. We open tomorrow night in *Hamlet* and as always, we are short-handed. You would receive a not ungenerous salary, but, of course, you would be required to spend a large part of your afternoons and evenings at my theatre. Could you manage this?'

Adela's eyes shone.

'I am quite sure I could, Mr Fortescue. Dolly will take care of the children. Since I live close by, it will be no inconvenience to walk home at night.'

Mr Fortescue looked shocked.

'That is out of the question. It is unwise for you to walk the streets of the city alone after dark. I will arrange for a chair to carry you safely to your door. Really, my dear, it becomes ever more clear to me that you do need a friend and mentor. Whatever would your poor dear parents think were they alive to know of their daughter's behaviour?'

Reassured once again by the man's fatherly attitude, Adela smiled her thanks.

'You are really very kind,' she said, 'and I can think of no other work I could do which I would prefer. Will Mistress Millet instruct me in my duties?'

'But of course! And I shall be around, too. You must always feel at liberty to come to my office whenever you wish.'

'I trust I shall have no need to trouble you, sir!' Adela said genuinely.

There was only the briefest of pauses before he replied, 'On the contrary, my dear, I hope you will look to me to advise you for I can think of no greater pleasure than being the one to instruct so brave and charming a young lady!'

It was not until later when Mr Clarence Fortescue drove her back to her dingy lodgings in his phaeton, that Adela reconsidered his compliment and wondered whether she had made the right decision after all.

CHAPTER TEN

1789

'Devil take it, Scrimgeour, I will have no more of these excuses! Damn it all, man, I have paid out enough money to support an army! What, in the name of God, is everyone doing?'

Sir Henry's face was puce, his wig awry, his expression thunderous as he regarded his lawyer. He was seated in an armchair in his rooms in London; his left leg, white stockinged, rested on a footstool, for he had been suffering severe twinges of gout. The condition was painful and not improved by his physician's insistence that the only real cure was to curtail his drinking. Despite this advice, he held a moderate-sized tumbler of brandy in his hands – a palliative he had not offered his lawyer who was standing like a fearful schoolboy before his headmaster.

None knew better than Mr Herbert Scrimgeour how merciless Sir Henry could be. He disliked the man as intensely as he abhorred the many transactions he had been obliged to contract for his employer. Sir Henry had first engaged him in the days when he had been thrown out of the Army for unpaid debts. Fortunately for him, he had not been cashiered for he was allowed to resign in preference to the regiment having to face any unpleasant scandal attaching to its good name.

At the time, Scrimgeour was desperately attempting to earn his living and not always by transactions that were strictly lawful. He could not afford then to refuse Sir Henry's patronage however minimal his fee. After Sir Henry had married the Carstairs fortune, it would have been folly to do so, although on the few occasions he had been to Dene Place and met Lady

Nayland, he had returned to London with renewed feelings of disgust and self-recrimination. The avaricious side of his character had, however, prevailed over his scruples and he had no intention of losing the patronage of the only titled client he had!

"'Tis being said that this is the worst winter the country has suffered since 1709!' he essayed. 'Travel is nigh impossible, Sir Henry, and those men whom I employed to make enquiries outside the city have been having the greatest difficulty in getting about.'

'The devil they have! Even if what you say is true, Scrimgeour, it is of little moment. I am convinced that the girl is in London. My man is a damned sight more efficient than half a dozen of your so-called experts. Dolts, the lot of 'em! Higgins has reported three different sightings to me – and what have your men discovered? Not a thing!' He glared angrily at the impassive face of his lawyer.

'With respect, sir, Higgins had the advantage of time on his side. You did not call in my services until two weeks after the . . . the departure, by which time the trail had gone cold.'

Despite his need to vent his frustration on the lawyer, Sir Henry had no answer to this statement. That Adela and the children had stayed the night at The Rose and Thistle was but one very early sighting last November; that she had been seen with her maid and the children dismounting at the market in Covent Garden, another. As to the third – from a beggar anxious to claim the proffered reward who insisted that he had seen Adela going into His Majesty's Theatre – who in their right senses would give credence to that? Sir Henry had himself questioned the fellow – a filthy, crippled, illiterate tramp – and realized instantly that there could be no truth in his babblings. For all the girl he had described had resembled Adela in age, height – even in the colour of her hair and eyes – she had been most fashionably attired and in the company of a well-known actor from whose phaeton she had alighted. There were no children with her and her companion had addressed her as 'Annie'. No, it was inconceivable that this girl could have been Adela. Although Higgins had suggested that he might keep watch on the theatre lest she put in another appearance, he had instructed him not to waste his time.

Since then, neither Higgins' nor Scrimgeour's men had come forward with any further intelligence.

'Sir, if you would only permit me to call in the services of the newspapers, I am in no doubt they would print an appeal on behalf of a gentleman of your standing—'

Scrimgeour got no further before Sir Henry roared out his dissent.

'Dammit, man, have I not told you often enough that I will not allow this matter to become public knowledge? Are you so rattlebrained that you think I wish to be questioned, sympathized with by my club members, my friends and acquaintances? What kind of a fool would they think me, allowing a chit of a girl to disappear with my son – my only son?'

His colour deepened an even darker red as words momentarily failed him. Even now, eight weeks after Adela and the children had vanished, he refused to consider that he might have lost Ned for ever. He would find him soon enough. For one thing, there were not that many people who would give refuge to Adela knowing that they were contravening the law of the land; that she had abducted the children – *his* children! Had that interfering parson not admitted as much? The man had been insulting, inferring that it was his treatment of Adela and the children that had obliged her to take such drastic measures; that he would himself have given her a refuge were it his legal right to do so!

His late wife's family had been even more forthright. Although he was convinced that the Comte and Comtesse de Falence would do everything possible to deny him access to his offspring, he had nevertheless travelled to France before he had gone to London, expecting to find the children there. As far as he was concerned, the de Falences were welcome to keep his stepdaughter, and his daughter, too – but not Ned;

not his son! However, when Hugo de Falence had sworn by his life and his honour that Adela and the children were not beneath his roof, nor, to his knowledge, anywhere in France, Sir Henry was obliged to acknowledge that he had been mistaken.

He had secondly suspected the Mallory twins of being Adela's accomplices. According to their parents, the young men had not yet returned home from their prolonged sojourn in Europe and could not, therefore, have been involved in Adela's disappearance. His enquiries in Dene village confirmed that neither Titus Mallory nor his brother had been seen for many months and, frustrated yet again, Sir Henry had been obliged to abandon this line of detection.

Only very occasionally, usually when he had reached the point of becoming maudlin after a heavy bout of drinking, did Sir Henry allow himself to wonder whether it was possible that all three children were dead. If such had been Adela's and Kitty's fates, he would shed no tears. His dislike for his pale, sickly daughter who from infancy had screamed at the mere sight of him, was no less than that he entertained for Adela, who had always so openly defied him. But Ned . . . Ned was more important to him than anything in his life. Not even his love of wealth could begin to match his love for his son. Not only did the boy resemble him in looks but he had preferred his father's company to any other, young though he was.

Sir Henry had been eagerly awaiting the time when Ned would be of an age to start making a man of him. He envisaged the days when he would teach him to handle a gun, a rod; teach him to hold his drink, to tell a good wine from a bad. Even at the tender age of three, the boy could sit on a pony, laughing, fearless, as, tied into a small basket chair fastened securely to the saddle, the groom walked him round the grounds.

'Devil take it, Scrimgeour, the boy must be found – and quickly!' he now bellowed. 'Be damned to the weather! Set more men to the search, and double the size of the reward.

And find an artist – a copier – and send him down to Dene Place to make a likeness of my stepdaughter from that oil painting that used to hang in Sir Matthew Carstairs' bedroom.'

The lawyer's mouth tightened nervously.

'The girl was little more than an infant when Sir Matthew died! I have to say that I cannot believe it would assist in her discovery to show such a drawing to landlords and the like!'

To his surprise and relief, Sir Henry's colour faded and he actually grimaced.

'There are times when you manage to earn some of your over-generous fees, Scrimgeour! So, we will forget the artist; but I want the search intensified, do you understand, whatever the cost! Now get out and stop wasting my time. Next time I see you, I want results, not excuses!'

As he left the room, Scrimgeour decided that it had become necessary to employ the services of London's more criminal element of whose existence he was very well aware; for knowing Sir Henry as he did, he was in no doubt of the consequences to himself should the boy not be found.

Sir Henry's frustration was equalled only by that of Titus and Barnaby as the old year gave way to the new and they remained virtual prisoners in the parsonage. Heavy falls of snow followed by bitter frosts had made the roads impassable except for short distances on foot. No one ventured out but from extreme necessity. The farmers round about were having the greatest difficulty in feeding their live-stock for the ground was too hard to dig up the stores of beet and swede, turnips and potatoes harvested the previous summer. The rivers had ceased to flow and the mill-wheel had stopped so that the miller could no longer grind his grain. Only those who had stores of flour could still bake bread. Sheep which had been unable to find shelter lay frozen, unburied like the dead whose corpses could not be given a resting place in the graveyard since no grave-digger could break the ground.

The people of Dene village were suffering great hardship

for such was the severity of the weather that their wood-sheds were all but empty. The elderly, the sick and the newborn were dying at an alarming rate and Lord Mallory was kept busy from dawn to dusk as he tried to ease the suffering of his flock. For the first time ever, he cancelled Sunday services at the church which was as cold as a tomb since there was no way to heat it.

Titus, Barnaby and their mother were giving what assistance they could to the villagers. The two strong young men had trudged many miles in the biting east wind to deliver a little food or milk to the starving. Such clothes and blankets as Lady Mallory could spare had long since been distributed, as had been the reserves from her pantry. Now there was little more any of them could do; and with the lack of occupation, the twins had more time than ever to think of Adela and the children.

It had been small comfort to learn from their parents that Sir Henry had departed for London at the same time as they had returned home; that as a consequence, he was more likely to be the first to find the children. Despite the constant reminders by their mother that both Dolly and Adela were resourceful and courageous and would withstand all manner of hardships, they could not bear to imagine Adela alone, more especially now that the unprecedented severity of this winter was making even the simplest of tasks difficult.

'I could almost wish Sir Henry would find Addy and bring her home!' Barnaby said, sighing as he threw another log on the fire. They were in their father's library warming themselves after their labours in the village. Yesterday, he and Titus had cut down one of the old apple trees in the orchard, and the wood, unweathered, smoked and hissed rather than flamed as it burned.

Titus frowned as he poured himself a second glass of mulled wine.

'I understand your meaning, Barny, but you cannot have given thought to the punishment Sir Henry will, of a certainty, inflict upon Addy if he finds her!'

'Better she should be punished than that she should die!'

Titus slapped his hand against his leg, his voice rising as he said, 'Be done with such melancholic speech! You are becoming a positive Niobe!'

Barnaby grinned at his twin's reference to the daughter of the mythical Greek king.

'If it gets much colder, I shall – unlike Niobe – be turned to ice, not stone!' he said.

Titus sighed. 'This frost cannot continue much longer. It will thaw soon and we shall want to set out at once for London, so I think I will reply to that letter we received from Eugénie! Unless, of course, you wish to undertake the task?'

Barnaby shook his head.

'She is your paramour, not mine, my dear fellow!' he teased.

Titus returned his smile, albeit ruefully.

'Was, dear boy, not is! By June she will be the wife of another, and you and I will be but guests feasting at her nuptials!'

Barnaby's smile widened.

'Somehow I cannot bring myself to believe that your heart will be broken, for all your despondency. Your reactions to her letter telling us of her intentions to be married this summer were not exactly those of a lover prostrated by grief!'

'And how, pray, do you know that I did not entertain the notion of drowning myself? Disappointed lovers have been known to plunge from the heights of Beachy Head to be dashed to pieces on the rocks below.'

'Huh!' said Barny. 'Beachy Head is all of thirty miles distant and you would have thought better of it long before you reached there! In any event, you would have had to postpone your premature decease since we were in London searching for Addy when Eugénie's letter arrived. To be serious, Titus, it was as well we left France when we did, else we might have met up with Sir Henry there. I have no doubt the Comte gave him short shrift. He dislikes the man no less than we do.'

Titus nodded.

'Speaking of dislikes, Jacques said last evening that if Sir Henry harms one hair of Dolly's head, he will not live to see another day! And what is more, Barny, I do not doubt he would carry out his threat! Was any man so much hated!'

'I wish we had better news to impart to Eugénie!' Barnaby said wistfully as his brother went to the bureau to find quill and paper. 'You must inform her that we will resume our search as soon as we are able. If only Addy had written and told us where she is! Surely she must do so soon!'

'We can but hope and pray!' Titus muttered as he tipped his quill into the tiny well of black ink.

Not only Titus and Barnaby, but Mr Scrimgeour, too, might have felt a great deal easier in their minds had they known that there was one man in London who could tell them exactly where to find Adela and the children. Mr Clarence Fortescue, however, was keeping this knowledge very much to himself. Not a week after his offer to give employment to Adela in his theatrical company, he had by chance seen one of the posters in the bar-room of The Crown Inn in Holborn. Where before his meeting with her, he would not have given the bold black print a second glance, he had read it with growing interest and then excitement.

MISSING:
Young GIRL aged sixteen years, black hair, green eyes, medium height.
Also GIRL aged five years, blond hair, blue eyes, small in stature.
BOY, aged three years, red-haired, blue eyes.

REWARD for INFORMATION
leading to the discovery of their whereabouts.
Apply to:
Herbert Scrimgeour Esquire, lawyer, of Took's Court, Cursitor Street.

The amount of the reward was not stated but Mr Fortescue was in no great need of money. Of that he had a-plenty. What he wanted was the young, green-eyed girl whose virginal beauty haunted his nights and from whom he could not keep away during the day. Far from being put off by her childish indifference to his carefully contrived touches – for she reacted to the pressure of his hand or the gentle pat on her shoulder as might a daughter to her father – it had merely inflamed his growing lust for her. He sought for ways to detain her after the cast and stage-hands had departed; but she would insist that she must return to the children – to the little girl in particular, who would not rest easy unless she were present; to her maid, who also worried about her, though not, Clarence Fortescue surmised, for the same reasons. Dolly, it seemed, was highly suspicious of him. Dolly, according to his little Annie, was not as innocent as her young mistress and could see no good reason why he should take such a personal interest in someone who only a few weeks ago was a stranger. Dolly, so Adela told him sadly, did not believe that men, especially older men, could be motivated by mere friendship!

Dolly was proving quite a stumbling block, thought Mr Fortescue, and he had not yet made up his mind what to do about her. He had tried, unsuccessfully, to undermine Adela's confidence in the girl, but she refuted any suggestion that an orphan from the London slums was no fit companion for her. 'I would lay down my life for Dolly – as she would for me!' Adela had declared. 'I wish you would agree to meet her, Mr Fortescue. You would then see for yourself what a stalwart, kind person she is; and she would see that you are a perfect gentleman and that I have every reason to trust you! To thank you for your many kindnesses to me.'

'One of these days he'll be wanting more than a thank-you for them!' Dolly had pronounced when yet another box of toys for the children, or bouquet of flowers had arrived for Adela. 'Mark my words, Miss Addy, it ain't a daughter 'e's wanting. Them actors've not got no morals. Look on that female, Florrie What's-it your stepfather used to entertain – she were an actress! That there Mr Fortescue ain't up to no good, I'm telling you.'

'I will be very cautious, Dolly!' Adela had said, laughing. 'And in the meanwhile, here are my wages. Mr Fortescue has raised the amount yet again – because he thinks I work just as hard and as efficiently as Mrs Millet now I know my way around the theatre!'

Dolly had counted the coins carefully and placed them in the tin on the mantelshelf without comment. Adela was angry, her disappointment acute for she had expected Dolly's praise for her efforts; but she quickly forgave her. What could Dolly know of the theatre or those who peopled it? They were far less conventional than ordinary folk, greeting one another with kisses and endearments or, at times when they were being temperamental, losing their tempers and using language that would never be heard in polite drawing-rooms. At least Mr Fortescue's language when he addressed her was always scrupulously correct even if he was a trifle more familiar in some ways than other gentlemen would consider quite proper.

He was kindness itself, Adela thought, as she hung up the last of the cast's costumes in the wardrobe-room. If she could voice any objection to her benefactor's behaviour, it would be to his habit of staring at her. She had begun to notice of late that whichever way she turned, his eyes were gazing in her direction. Since the glances were in no way venomous – on the contrary they were exceedingly friendly – she could not understand why they made her so uncomfortable.

Adela wished very much that she could control her blushes. They came far too readily, her cheeks burning each time Mr Fortescue complimented her – and even when members of the cast teased her about her lady-like voice and ways! They had nicknamed her 'The Princess' although this did not stop them ordering her to fetch and carry for them.

Noticing that one of the lace cuffs of Hamlet's white shirt had come unstitched, Adela sighed as she sat down on a stool and reached for her work-basket. It would take but a minute to repair, but her back ached and she was tired. Moreover, she was worried about Kitty who had yet another cold and who was always restless unless she was with her. Unlike Ned, the child had not forgotten her father and lived in dread that he would burst in and take her away before Adela returned in time to rescue her.

Adela bent over her sewing, shivering as the draught stirred the rows of gowns hanging from their rails. The theatre had been almost empty at tonight's performance – which was hardly surprising seeing how bitter was the cold. Only those who must would venture out in such weather, she reflected. At least she and Dolly had saved a little money to buy coal, she comforted herself, thanks to Mr Fortescue. She finished the last few stitches and put away her needle and thread. He would be waiting for her in his dressing-room and, on this bitterly cold night, must be as anxious as she to get home, so she did not want to delay him.

'Romeo taking you home again tonight, love?' one of the actresses called out as she bade Adela good night. 'One way to keep warm, I s'pose!'

Adela did not understand quite what the woman meant, although she knew that 'Romeo' was the nickname they had recently given Mr Fortescue. She thought the tag a little unsuitable, despite his having recently played the role. Since he was both middle aged and portly, she had always supposed that the part of Romeo – and indeed that of Hamlet which he was currently playing – would have been acted by a younger man, if not a boy! If anyone were to be properly cast in those roles it should be Titus or Barnaby, she thought. What handsome actors they would make! How stirring it would be were Titus, for example, to stand upon the stage, his fair head turned in profile to the audience as his voice cried out in grief at the graveside: *I lov'd Ophelia: forty thousand brothers could not, with all their quantity of love, make up my sum.* Even to imagine it was to cause Adela's heart to flutter, whereas when

Mr Fortescue spoke the same words each night, however deep the throb of his voice as she listened to him in the wings, she was unable to ignore his somewhat portly figure and wonder how Ophelia could be so deeply enamoured of him that she had drowned herself for love!

With a sigh Adela set aside such thoughts as she knocked on the door of Mr Fortescue's dressing-room. He called her to come in and rose at once to take her arm and conduct her to the chair beside his dressing-table. As always, it was littered with grease-paints, powders, rouges and variously styled wigs propped up on their stands. He had removed his stage costume and wig, and was informally attired in white breeches and a cotton shift open at the throat. His face still bore the make-up he had applied for his performance and was heavily coated with a ghostly white powder. This, together with the bright red splashes accentuating his cheeks and lips, and the heavily blackened eyebrows, gave him the somewhat grotesque appearance of a clown.

Adela might have been amused by this ridiculous image of the imposing performer had he not at that moment given her a smile which even further distorted his painted visage.

'Sit down, my dear, sit down!' he said, seemingly unaware of the absurd figure he cut. Was it possible he believed that at close quarters he still looked the same romantic character he played on stage? Adela wondered. 'I have some Madeira here which I think you might enjoy.'

Adela's face fell.

'It is a kindly thought, Mr Fortescue, but I really feel I should be getting home. It is later than I had thought and—'

He reached forward and took possession of both her hands. His voice held a gentle rebuke as he interrupted her, 'Come, come now, my little Annie. I was hoping you would agree with me that my performance tonight was exceptionally good, and that we might celebrate. I took eight curtain calls – quite a record, do you not agree?'

Adela hesitated.

'Yes! Yes, of course! It certainly deserves a celebration; but . . . one small glass, then, if you insist!'

Mr Fortescue had already filled the glasses – as if he had taken her compliance for granted, Adela thought unhappily. Not wishing to seem ungrateful, she took one from him and raising it to meet his, forced a smile to her face.

'Please forgive me if I did not praise your performance earlier. It is just that . . . that I am a little tired; and . . . and although we do not have far to go, the weather is so cold that . . .'

'My dear child, it is I who should be asking you to forgive me for my thoughtlessness.' He put down his glass and gently took hers and placed it beside his own. Reaching forward, he drew her to her feet and closed the distance between them, so that she was leaning against his knees. She was instantly repelled by the proximity and by the rivulets of perspiration which scored the white-powdered countenance with dark exaggerated wrinkles. His eyes glittered as he said in a low voice, 'You can have no idea, my sweet Annie, how very charming you look even with those violet shadows beneath your lovely eyes!' His voice thickened as he added, 'I do worry about you, you know – far more than you can imagine. If I could have my way, I should ensure that you were never again tired, or cold, or in distress . . .'

Embarrassed and shocked by this unexpected and unwanted familiarity, Adela's body stiffened and she tried to ease herself backwards; but his hands tightened their hold on hers. His knees parted and he drew her even closer. Whilst she was still trying to think of words that would put an end to this unwelcome ardour, he released her hands but fastened his own about her waist. She could feel the heat from his palms through the fustian of her gown and was suddenly reminded of Captain Armitage. No, I am being absurd! she told herself as her skin prickled with fear and disgust. This man is my friend! He is like a father to me. He is only trying to be kind . . .

His next words, however, quickly disabused her of such a

notion. She listened in mounting horror as in a hoarse intense voice, he said, 'Do you understand what I am trying to tell you, Annie? I am quite hopelessly in love with you. I will do anything – anything at all to please you; to make you happy! Tonight as I spoke Hamlet's words of love, I could think only of you. I am determined not to frighten you by too hasty a declaration, but I must know that you have at least a little fondness for me in your heart; that you will give me more of your time, your thoughts!'

Shocked beyond speech, Adela tore her eyes away from the repugnant face, distorted as it was with passion, that had held her mesmerized whilst he spoke.

'I cannot . . . I do not . . . Mr Fortescue, I beg you to release me. I am sorry if I have, by word or deed, given you reason to suppose that I . . . that you . . . let me go, please. I insist!'

Far from obeying her request, his hold upon her strengthened. His eyes narrowed and there was an unmistakable threat in his voice as he said, 'So, I have no attraction for you – I, Clarence Fortescue who has been fêted, applauded, wanted, yes, desired, by some of the most beautiful and influential ladies in the land! Who are you, then, to reject the devotion of a man who has shown you nothing but kindness? Are you really so innocent that you suppose I have no more than a charitable interest in you? That it was for *charitable* reasons I gave you employment here in the theatre? That I pay you so handsomely – you, an ignorant, inexperienced chit of a girl who is wanted by the law? You should reconsider your position, little Miss Unknown, who chooses to call herself Mistress Annie Porter! Do not make the mistake of taking me for a fool! I can find out easily enough who you really are; why you have run away from your rightful guardian – yes, and taken two young children with you!'

He reached up and touched Adela's cheek before allowing his hand to travel down her neck and rest for a moment on her breast. She was trembling violently, partly with nausea and partly with anger. Had the man before her but known it, his threats were to deny him rather than achieve him what he most wanted, for now Adela recognized her danger and her mind was racing furiously as she listened to him. Clearly he had discovered part – if not all – of the truth. For the moment anyway, she must try to pacify him and then make her escape before he could expose her.

Gently but firmly, she pushed his hand away. Somehow she managed to steady her voice as she said quietly, 'You spoke just now of not wishing to frighten me – but surely you must realize that ignorant as I was of your . . . your feelings towards me, I was alarmed to hear you speak in such a fashion. Your sentiments do me great honour for I am well aware of your immense fame and . . . popularity, and of my own . . . youth. You are right, too, in thinking that I sounded most ungrateful for your . . . your assistance to me; but please believe me when I assure you that I am very conscious of your patronage, your sympathy, your generosity. However, you will admit that I have been taken greatly by surprise and that I need time to think . . . to appreciate . . .'

She had no need to elaborate further for she had given him what he wanted – a belief that in a day or two she would reconsider her attitude to him. His pride still smarted for, believing himself still able to seduce females with words and deeds if not looks, he had expected she would have succumbed far more readily to his charms. For a moment, it had seemed as if, on the contrary, his Annie had been repulsed by his advances. He must make allowances for her youth, he reminded himself, and for the fact that a girl such as herself would have been strictly reared to the conventions. Undoubtedly, he had spoken too hastily. He felt himself relax as she actually smiled at him.

'Will you forgive me, Mr Fortescue?' she asked disarmingly. 'Tonight I am really too fatigued to be good company; but perhaps tomorrow we might dine together and by then I shall have realized how childish I was to have thought of you only as a kindly father. You have been so much more to me – the very best of friends. How ungrateful you must think me!'

Reminding himself of the need to proceed more cautiously, Mr Fortescue stood up and mollified by her speech, he did no more than lay a reassuring hand on her arm.

'It is I who was at fault, my dear! After all, a lover should be both father and friend, and as you say, we can most certainly advance our friendship tomorrow night after my performance. Much as we shall miss you here in the theatre, I shall give you the day off so that you will have time for once to pretty yourself – that most feminine of pleasures, I believe! May I suggest that you wear that green gown once again? It becomes you well, and perhaps I shall have a little something that would go charmingly with it. Now I shall escort you home!'

Steeling herself yet again, Adela did not draw away when he put an arm around her shoulders in the phaeton; nor turn her face aside as he kissed her cheek when she alighted outside the house. She even managed a smile as he bowed over her hand and looking deep into her eyes, intoned, '*Parting is such sweet sorrow!*'

Two minutes later, she arrived breathless and close to tears in the room where Dolly awaited her.

'We have got to leave, Dolly – now, tonight. That man . . . Mr Fortescue . . . he is evil. You were quite right to suspect him. He is not the gentleman I thought him. And Dolly, even worse, he must have seen one of those posters and has implied that he will find out my real name if I do not submit to him. Do you understand? We are in danger – real danger. You must start packing, and however late the hour, we must go. We must leave now – at once; for if I do not meet him tomorrow as I have agreed, he may tell my stepfather where to find us, and all these past weeks of suffering will have been in vain.'

CHAPTER ELEVEN

1789

Three days after Adela and Dolly had departed so hastily from their lodgings in Carters Lane, the twins received her third letter telling them they would find her there.

> We have been in rooms at this address for three weeks now and I have been fortunate to find Employment as a Dresser in His Majesty's Theatre which is close by,

she had written.

> The Manager, a Mr Fortescue, has befriended me and pays me a very Fair Wage which buys us the Essentials we need. However, we cannot remain here indefinitely as it is no Fit Place or Life for the Children, and it is my dearest Hope that you will somehow find a Way to help us to France where I am sure my Aunt and Uncle will assist me. I long for News of you, but fear you may not yet be back from France or you would surely have answered my last Letter.
> I am signing myself by the Name
> I have assumed,
> Your Troubled but Ever-devoted Friend,
> Annie Porter.

The twins were overjoyed. They hastened to tell the good news to their parents that Adela could now be found; that they would leave at once for London and see what could be done to secure passages for Adela and the children on a packet to France.

'Since Sir Henry has already made enquiries and satisfied himself that they are not with the Comte and Comtesse, I do not think he will go to France again!' Titus said when his father expressed doubts as to whether Adela would be safe from her stepfather in France.

'And the de Falences have so many friends, I am certain one of them will give Adela and the children refuge if Sir Henry should turn up unexpectedly,' Barnaby added.

Despite the bitter weather, they set off immediately for London, their hopes high as they chafed impatiently at the delays when they stopped to change their horses. Both were confident as they crossed London Bridge, that it was only a matter of hours now before they would see their beloved Addy again.

When they called at Carters Lane and learned from the disgruntled landlady that Adela had disappeared in the night like some common thief, they were so bitterly disappointed that they stared at the dishevelled woman open-mouthed. Sensing that the young gentlemen might be persuaded to part with some money, her tone of voice became whining. Mrs Porter had left the rent that was owing, she admitted, but had given no notice. She had been unable to find another lodger and was hard put to pay her own rent. For all Mrs Porter's airs and graces, she complained, she had proved herself no better than a fly-by-night.

In the hope of obtaining some inkling as to where Adela might have gone – or indeed, why she had left in such a hurry – Titus gave the woman a guinea with the promise of another if she could give them an address where they might find her. Regretfully the landlady could offer no information other than that she knew her lodger had worked at the theatre and was often escorted home by a middle-aged theatrical gentleman.

Realizing that this must be the Mr Fortescue Adela had mentioned in her letter, Titus and Barnaby remounted their horses and made their way round to the theatre. There was a rehearsal in progress, but it was only a matter of minutes before the twins were taken by the stage doorkeeper to Mr Fortescue's office.

The actor had guessed immediately from the doorkeeper's description of his two visitors, that these must be the young men to whom Annie had so often and so lovingly referred. Since they were aware of his name and his whereabouts, there seemed little advantage in a refusal to receive them, and he had made up his mind to brazen it out and do what he could to white-wash his own part in Adela's affairs. The manner he now assumed was frank and open.

'Sit down, gentlemen, please. May I offer you some refreshment?'

The twins declined the offer and came straight to the point. Mr Fortescue had been employing a young lady who went by the name of Mrs Annie Porter, Titus said. Was she still working for him and could he please give them the address of her present lodgings?

'Would that I could, my dear fellow!' Mr Fortescue said with a doleful shake of his head. 'The young lady left my employ five days ago and, I have since ascertained, left her lodgings in Carters Lane at the same time. I have been very concerned about her welfare. To be perfectly honest with you, I was deeply hurt that she should have left my employ so suddenly . . . and without a word of explanation – and after all I had done to befriend her!' He drew a deep sigh. 'Perhaps it was foolish of me to expect a little consideration . . . gratitude. But that is so often the way of the young, is it not?'

Titus and Barnaby were regarding one another in dismay.

'So Addy – Mrs Porter – gave you no warning that it was her intention to leave? Did you, perhaps, have the impression that she was . . . well, in danger of any kind?' Barnaby enquired.

Mr Fortescue spread out his hands in an exaggerated gesture of resignation.

'Ah, you have put your finger upon the answer, I believe. Some while ago Mrs Porter confided in me that she was in hiding from her guardian. Now you may consider I was wrong to assist her as I did and that knowing she was a minor, I should have felt it my duty to see that she was returned to those responsible for her. However, she had placed her trust in me and my nature would not permit me to betray her. I stand condemned by my weakness and will most willingly accept such reproaches as you feel justified in making.'

'On the contrary, you are to be praised for your kindness!' Titus said quickly. 'Mrs Porter's guardian is a cruel and evil man, and my brother and I have every intention of keeping her from his clutches!'

'Ah, so my instincts have proved sound!' Mr Fortescue said, adding regretfully, 'However, there is little I can do to assist you. Had Mrs Porter remained in my employ . . . but there, we must not make judgements when all the facts are not yet revealed. I had grown very fond of your young friend – as a father might feel affection for a daughter, you understand – and I have been beset with worry on her behalf!'

'Clearly, you were her friend at a time when she was most in need of one,' Barnaby said thoughtfully. 'That being the case, she may yet get in touch with you at some future date. Should this happen, will you write at once and notify us? You are the only link we have with her!'

'Rest assured, gentlemen, that I shall do as you ask!' Mr Fortescue promised as Barnaby handed him his card and he rose to see them out. He had no intention of fulfilling this promise. In the unlikely event that the girl contacted him, the last thing he wanted was for these two young men to take her under their wing. He had been foolish to rush matters with her and was still smarting at the thought of his folly in frightening her with premature advances. Were she to return, he would try to regain her confidence and then . . . Her elusiveness had only made her the more desirable and he could not bring himself entirely to give up hope of seeing her again.

'There is nothing for it but to return home and wait for a further letter!' Titus said to Barnaby as they left the theatre, each as dejected as the other.

'If one of Sir Henry's men had been close on Addy's heels, it would explain her leaving her lodgings and her employment so suddenly!' Barnaby commented as they rode back to the inn. 'Who knows but she has been apprehended and is even now being taken back to Dene Place! We could search the streets of London for months on end and see no sign of her. With no further clues to her whereabouts, there seems little point in our remaining here.'

They completed their journey home in silence, each lost in their own unhappy thoughts – that it was now over two months since Adela had left Dene Place and that it was beginning to seem ever more likely that they might never see her again.

'Where the devil can they be?' Titus swore softly as he pulled the velvet collar of his caped greatcoat more tightly about his neck. 'Jacques said midnight – and it is near the quarter-hour past!'

He and Barnaby were standing huddled beneath the old yew tree in Dene churchyard from whence they could keep watch on the Carstairs family vault. The snow and ice had disappeared but now the bitterest of March east winds was whistling through the trees and hedgerows, and icy rain was sleeting against the moss-covered gravestones and statues. Near by, the kissing-gate swung to and fro, creaking eerily on its rusty hinges.

The twins had arrived early for their assignation with the smuggler, George Robinson, for Jacques had warned them that the man's innate caution had taught him always to put safety before punctuality! It was how he had managed to continue conducting his illicit trafficking for so many years without being caught by the Excise men. This evening he was delivering a consignment of tea and brandy to Sir Henry Nayland. Sharing the universal dislike of this unworthy magistrate, the smuggler nevertheless did business with him, taking a particular pleasure in demanding a far higher price for his contraband than he normally charged his customers. Sir Henry had recently returned from London; and following upon tonight's transactions, he, Robinson, would be making his way back from the house by way of the secret passage exiting in the churchyard. This clandestine method of approach to and from Dene Place was a precaution he deemed necessary for such was his distrust of Sir Henry that he would not have been surprised to find Excise men lying in wait for him in the driveway.

'If you are willing to meet with 'im in the churchyard, George says 'e 'as information for you about Miss Adela's whereabouts – but 'e'll expect a goodly reward. 'E'll not tell me what 'e knows!' Jacques had grinned when he recounted this intelligence to the twins the previous day. 'Reckon as 'ow 'e thinks 'e'll strike a better bargain with you two young gentlemen than 'e might with me.'

The twins were aware that Sir Henry had promised a big reward to anyone able to enlighten him as to the fugitives' whereabouts, and they were grateful to Jacques' smuggling friend for keeping what information he had from Sir Henry. According to Jacques, although George Robinson was not a local man, he was nevertheless aware of Sir Henry's reputation; and whilst the smuggler was prepared to risk trading with the Squire, his sympathies lay with the runaways. Were they not, like himself, outside the law? he had commented to Jacques with wry humour.

Before Titus could give further vent to his impatience, the heavy iron grille of the vault swung open silently, for Jacques kept the hinges well oiled, and he emerged, followed by the smuggler. They were both attired in black-cloth greatcoats, their heads covered by black, flat-topped round hats, the broad brims turned down. Had Titus and Barnaby not been expecting them, it was doubtful if the men would have been observed.

Simultaneously the twins moved forward. Robinson eyed

their sodden clothing and touching his forehead, grinned as he said, "'Tis fine weather, surely, for the ducks, is it not?'

Titus returned his grin.

'And for those who have no business to be about at this ungodly hour! So let us not tarry longer than we need. My brother and I will be most grateful to you for any assistance you can give us. We are deeply concerned for Miss Carstairs and the children. Have you seen them? *Do you know where we can find them?*'

Robinson wiped the rain from his face with a corner of the grubby kerchief tied round his neck.

'I reckon I knows where they is – or where they was last week when I were in Lunnon!'

'Tell us, please!' Barnaby broke in eagerly. 'We shall reward you well, as I am sure Jacques has told you!'

'Aye, he did, surely, sir. Well, I were in The Blue Boar Saturday night – that were a week back last Saturday – ten days ago by my reckoning. That be a hostelry down by the docks and popular with the sailors who put into port there. 'T'aint somewhere as young gentlemen like yourselves would go for you'd 'ave your pockets picked afore you'd downed your first pint!'

As he paused to scratch his head, Titus said impatiently, 'Go on, man, though I must admit I cannot see what this might have to do with Miss Carstairs.'

Robinson nodded.

'Right enough, sir. 'Twas the last place on earth you'd expect to see the likes of 'er. Well, it were busy as an ale 'ouse on market day, and there was two girls as were serving what I'd not noticed at first for they was dressed same as you'd see any wench in a like place. Then I 'eard a commotion nearby the bar, and reckoning on it might turn to fisticuffs – and that's not unusual for the likes of The Blue Boar – I wanted no truck with the runners so I downed my pot and was going through the door when of a sudden, it all went quiet.'

'And then . . .?' Barnaby prompted.

'Then there was just the three of 'em standing by the bar
– landlord, the tar and this girl. Seems the sailor were a
Frenchie and didn't speak no English. Far as I could make
out, 'e'd not paid the proper money for 'is brandy and the
landlord weren't 'aving it. So this girl steps up and says she
can speak the Frenchie's lingo and can she 'elp. Next thing
the Frenchie is smiling and so's the landlord and it's all settled
friendly like. That's when she turned and I saw 'er face. She
were the same young lady as I 'elped that night at Norgem
– or that's what I thought then, gentlemen. Black 'air, green
eyes and near the same 'eight as I remembered.'

Titus and Barnaby turned to face one another, a look of
acute disappointment on their faces. The girl Robinson had
seen could not by any miracle have been Addy, for all she had
the same colouring. It was inconceivable that she would be
serving ale to the riff-raff of London's docklands.

Seeing their reaction, Robinson said quickly, 'I know what
you both is a-thinking! The Blue Boar ain't no place for a
young lady to be, not no way; but arter I'd thought on it a
while, I reckoned there wasn't no serving wenches in Lunnon
as could speak a foreign tongue like it was their own. Now
I knowed Jack 'ere were Frenchie born and 'is ma were nurse
to Miss Carstairs, so I reckoned it could 'ave been 'er. When
Jack tolt me you was still a-looking for the young lady, I made
up my mind to tell 'e what I seed.'

'And you were right to do so!' the twins said in unison.

'Can you tell us more, Robinson – anything at all?' Titus
persisted.

The smuggler shook his head.

'Only thing were the other wench as was serving. She 'ad
freckles, same as that maid as were with the young lady at
Norgem, but I wouldn't swear to it. I'd a mind to go back
next night and take another look, but . . .' he broke off, a
grin spreading across his face.

'Well, man, speak up!' Titus cried.

'It were like this, sir – what with the weather being that

contemptible these past months, we ain't done much business since afore Christmastide. It being a bit better now, I didn't 'ave no time to waste, seeing as 'ow it might 'ave been a wild-goose chase, if you take my meaning! Then, being otherwise occupied, as you'll understand, sir, it slipped my mind 'til I met up with Jack, 'ere, and 'e remembered it to me. 'E said as 'ow you'd be wanting to 'ear and that you'd be wanting to see me personal so's you could ask questions, like.'

'Good man, Jacques!' Barnaby said, turning to the valet. 'At least we now have hope, however unlikely it may seem, that it was Miss Addy and Dolly who Robinson saw. We must go directly to this ale house you speak of. Down by the docks, you say?'

Robinson nodded, and gave them the name of the street, but added, 'You'd best take Jack 'ere with you else I'd not answer for your safety. Some as go there'd cut your throat for a few guineas!'

Titus nodded.

'You are to be thanked for the warning, Robinson, but my brother and I are quite handy with our fists, as Jacques will tell you. Nevertheless, we shall take him with us.' He drew out his leather pouch and tipped the contents into Robinson's cupped hands. 'That would seem fair reward for your story. We shall see if you were right, and if it was Miss Carstairs you can expect as much again.'

Robinson had already counted the coins and was nodding his head.

'Very fair of you, sir! And there's one more thing you might like to know – the other wench . . . like I said, I weren't paying her no attention but now I come to think on it, she were the same 'eight and build as the young lady's maid – buxom, as you might say. Now, beggin' your pardon, sirs, I'd best be on my way. I'll wish you both good fortune – and a safe journey. The roads to Lunnon ain't good. What with the snow melting and all this rain, they's flooded in places deep enough to drown a cat!'

'We will fare well enough, but thank you!' Titus said, holding out his hand to shake that of their informant. 'And a safe journey to you too, Robinson, for I think you may face far greater dangers than we do!'

The sound of their shared laughter, albeit muted, echoed amongst the gravestones as Robinson slipped away into the darkness. By now it was raining still harder, but neither Titus nor Barnaby was aware of it. They were too filled with mounting excitement to be conscious of their discomfort as together with Jacques, they made their way back to the parsonage.

'Get our things packed, Jacques!' Titus said as they slipped into the house via the servants' entrance. 'We'll leave at daybreak. And wake Tom and tell him to have our horses saddled and ready.'

It was only as they were removing their wet clothing in preparation for the few hours' sleep that remained of the night, that a little of their excitement abated, for, as Barnaby said, Adela's circumstances must be singularly dreadful if she were reduced to the status of a serving wench in a notorious alehouse like The Blue Boar.

It was Dolly who had found work for them there, and a room in the attic for the four of them to live in. When they had left their lodgings in the dead of night to avoid any chance of Mr Fortescue tracing them, they had been obliged to spend the little money Adela had saved from her wages on the hire of a room at one of the coaching inns to the east of the city. In order not to draw attention to themselves, they had awaited the arrival of a stage-coach which had come from Chelmsford and passed themselves off as travellers. They could not remain there however, neither having the money to pay for a further night's lodging nor wishing to expose themselves in so public a place.

With a sinking heart, Dolly announced that she was going to seek work at an alehouse she knew of called The Blue Boar.

It was dirty, disreputable and no fit place for a decent girl to work, she told Adela, but they were often short-handed and if they took her on, she would earn enough to pay for one room and food of a kind – at least until she could find something better.

By a stroke of good fortune, the landlord was indeed short-handed. The severity of the winter had taken its toll on a good many of London's poor who, half starved and unable to afford fuel, were succumbing either to inflammation of the lungs or to an excessive consumption of alcohol, he grumbled to Dolly. His last two girls were now too sick to work and he needed to replace them. Although Dolly insisted that it was only she who was looking for employment, and accommodation if it was available, he was quick to see that they were desperate for a roof over their heads. Dolly's employment was conditional upon Adela helping out of an evening when he was most busy, he said firmly. They could have the attic bedroom, but they must both work, he stipulated.

'It ain't fitting! It just ain't, Miss Addy!' Dolly had wailed when Adela insisted they take the room. 'What would your poor mama say if she knew . . . and Lady Mallory and Nou-Nou. No, it ain't fitting, not noways, Miss Addy!'

She had put her apron over her head and wept. Immediately Kitty had burst into tears and Ned, not to be outdone, had joined in.

'Enough, all of you!' Adela said. ''Tis my fault, not yours, Dolly, that we are in this predicament. I should never have trusted Mr Fortescue. If I had listened to you . . . Ned, will you stop that noise this minute or I shall tell Dolly to give you such a hard smack, you will not want to sit down for a week! And you, Kitty! You are just aping Dolly. Now be quiet, all of you. We are going to make this into a nice little home until we can find something better.'

Kitty had cheered immediately on hearing that they would all be sleeping together. Always nervous, she was delighted by the shrinking area of their living quarters. She had not, at that moment, realized that from her bedtime onwards, neither Adela nor Dolly would be sitting with her to keep 'the nasty ghosties and witches away'.

'Suppose Papa comes to get us!' she had whispered tearfully to Adela when the time came for Adela to join Dolly in the tap-room. Young as she was, she knew she must not mention her papa's name in front of Ned who by now only very occasionally mentioned him.

'Papa will not find us here!' Adela had said with more conviction than certainty, for if Mr Fortescue had indeed seen one of Sir Henry's posters and took his revenge upon her by reporting that he had been employing her, her stepfather would almost inevitably renew his search, if he had ever abandoned it.

There had been no alternative to leaving their previous lodgings in Carters Lane. Of that she had no doubt. Dreadful as this fetid area of the city was, at least it was unlikely that anyone from the theatre would patronize the inn; nor indeed would Sir Henry believe her to be living in such squalid surroundings. The smell of rotting vegetables – perhaps worse – floating down the Thames outside the buildings, combined with the feculent gutters and doorways heaped with fly-blown refuse, was beyond her own worst imaginings; and she had needed all her courage to take refuge here.

As before, she and Dolly had spent the day destroying the bedbugs and cockroaches, the bluebottles on the windowsill. They had scrubbed the floor and few rickety pieces of furniture, polished the grimy window panes, washed the curtains. There was nothing they could do about the bedding since there was no way with the rain pouring down that they could hope to dry the coarse blankets and lumpy feather quilt before evening. Dolly had gone out with their last few shillings and purchased a rat trap, two cheap cotton sheets and a case for the bolster. With her remaining pennies, she had bought bread and a bit of cheese and some salt bacon for the children, for whilst she and Adela were to be fed from the fare provided for their customers in the kitchen, the landlord had refused to feed the children.

Although Adela's and Dolly's wages were ridiculously small, and half of the money they earned was deducted by the landlord for their board and lodging, they were, after one week, able to feed the children adequately and, indeed, save a few pennies. With Dolly working from mid-morning until midnight, and Adela from six in the evening until the early hours of the morning, there was nearly always one or other of them to mind the children. There remained the problem of how Adela could sleep in the daytime, for although the weather had taken a slight turn for the better, it was still too cold for Dolly to keep the children out of doors for any length of time.

Gradually exhaustion had overcome Adela and she could now sleep despite Ned's constant chatter and Dolly's movements around the room.

The lack of undisturbed sleep, so much needed after the long hours spent on her feet, did not perturb her to the same degree as the work itself. As Dolly had foretold, she was totally unfitted to serve the rough, often drunken, clientele from the wharfs and warehouses lining the banks of the Thames. The lewd comments of the men, their coarse gestures and their straying hands were almost more than she could bear.

She said nothing of her repugnance to Dolly who constantly worried about her, for she had determined that she would not give up and go home when all that was required of her was a further degree of courage. The men's words and touches could not harm her, she reminded herself. It was only her pride which was suffering. These rough prurient sailors supposed her to be no more refined than any of the other serving wenches with whom she worked whereas Captain Armitage had been very well aware of her background and upbringing and for all his fine words, had behaved in as lewd a manner as her present customers.

Mercifully there had been only two fights, one when she had actually witnessed a foreign sailor pull out a poniard and attempt to stab another before the pair were flung unceremoniously out into the street; and the other when a customer had an argument with the landlord over payment. In this she herself had intervened for the man spoke no English and she had been able to interpret his French, thus resolving the dispute.

Demeaning though she found it to be serving such loutish men, few of whom had the manners of the lowest farm labourers on her father's estate, at least such people would not suspect she was the 'young lady' Sir Henry had advertised as missing on his posters, she told Dolly. She wore the same yellow-and-amber striped linen dress, white kerchief and large white apron as the other serving girls, her hair was hidden by a white mob-cap, and she spoke so rarely that many of the men supposed she was dumb. More often than not, a nod and a smile sufficed to do her job.

It was now mid March and she was convinced that Titus and Barnaby must be back in England. She had written yet again telling them of this further change of address. Meanwhile, she told herself each night as she tucked the children into bed, she and Dolly were managing to evade Sir Henry – and to support themselves and their little family. The twins would surely come to their aid before much longer and so it was not as if they were condemned to spend the rest of their lives in these lowly circumstances.

It was a Wednesday morning and Dolly had taken the children down to the quayside where a large schooner had docked on the night tide. For once, the sun was shining, although there was little warmth in it and knowing that it would be a busy night with the new arrival of sailors, Dolly was anxious to allow Adela as much sleep as she could get whilst they were absent. Since the two children were happily occupied watching the frenetic activity as the ship was being unloaded, she lingered until shortly before midday before setting back to the inn.

As usual the narrow streets were crowded. Many had no pavements, and they were obliged quite frequently to huddle in doorways as a wagon or carriage went past, throwing up great splashes of filth from the puddles. One such carriage came from behind them as they neared the inn, travelling far too fast for such congestion. Grabbing the children by their hands, Dolly attempted to pull them into an alleyway, but a one-legged tinker who had been sheltering there, decided at the same moment to hobble forwards on his crutch. The tray of trinkets he was carrying on his free arm caught Ned a glancing blow on the shoulder, bowling him sideways into the path of the on-coming carriage.

The liveried postilion, mounted on one of the two front horses, saw the danger and appeared to be on the point of trying to halt them, but from within the chaise, the occupant shouted, 'Get on with it, man! We've no time to stop! Get on, I say!'

Her mouth opened in horror, Dolly would have darted into the street in an attempt to pull Ned to safety, but with astonishing strength, Kitty clung to her arm, screaming in fear. In the matter of seconds before the carriage passed her, Dolly saw two things – the face of the man inside, and that miraculously, the wheels of the chaise appeared to be passing either side of the boy who lay stretched full length, but seemingly unharmed, between them.

Several people rushed forward to pick Ned up, inspecting him for broken bones. Finding none, they dragged him back to Dolly. For once, he was not crying; but he was deathly pale and shivering from shock.

All around them, voices protested vociferously at the lack of concern of the gentry.

'Might as well be vermin for all the likes of them care!' one woman said bitterly.

'Didn't bleeding well stop to see if the poor little kid was dead!' said another, spitting into the gutter in disgust.

'You orlright, missis?' asked a third, seeing Dolly's dumbstruck face. 'Thought the little lad was a gonner, didn'cher?'

But Dolly was no longer concerned about Ned who, though

filthy, had not so much as a scratch on him. Her concern was
for the possible danger they might be in, for she had seen the
face of the gentleman in the coach and recognized him immediately. *It was Sir Henry Nayland.*

The excitement over, the crowd around them began to
disperse; but one of the women lingered.

'I live next door but one!' she said. 'You come with me,
dearie. Wot you needs is a drop o' gin.'

Dolly hesitated, her mind racing. For Sir Henry Nayland
to be in such a quarter as this could mean only one thing – he
had discovered Miss Addy's whereabouts. He was heading in
the direction of The Blue Boar, and if that was his destination,
he would reach there before she could – unless she ran. She
knew these streets like the back of her hand, and there was
a short cut through an alley which would bring her out at the
back door of the inn. As a rule, she did not take the children
down there for what went on in that dark passageway was
not fit for any decent person to witness, let alone youngsters.
But if she ran . . .

'Would you take care of the little 'uns for a few minutes!'
she said. 'I wouldn't ask the favour but I'm not their mum
and I think as 'ow I should fetch her.' With sudden inspiration,
she added, 'She'll be that grateful to you, she'll reward you,
surely. She's a real lady, she is!'

Despite Kitty's wails and Ned's timely sobs, as soon as the
woman had given her consent, Dolly darted into the alley and
raced down it to the back door of the inn. She was trembling
with fear that Sir Henry had reached there before her and that
Miss Addy might already have been taken away by him. As
she ran up the rickety back staircase, she could hear no unusual
sound of voices . . . certainly none that sounded like Sir Henry's.

She burst into the room, scarlet-cheeked and breathless.
Adela was in bed, sound asleep.

'Wake up, Miss Addy, wake up!' she gasped, tugging on
Adela's arm. 'Oh, please wake up, Miss Addy. We's in mortal
danger.'

It was a moment or two before Adela, still drowsy, could make sense of Dolly's frantic urgings and the reason for them. Immediately she did so, she sprang out of bed, pulled her striped dress over her night shift, slipped her feet into her shoes and without stopping to tie her shoe-strings she grabbed her cloak and muff. It took her no more than three minutes before she was ready, but as she and Dolly were about to leave the room, she paused and ran back to get the tin box from beneath her pillow in which she kept the few coins she had saved.

'Hurry, Miss Addy! Hurry, do!' Dolly wailed. Then her voice died away as from down below she heard the sound of shouting. Her finger to her lips, she froze where she stood.

'Get the landlord this minute, you stupid dolt! Are you halfwitted? I do not care if he is asleep. He can be talking to the King for all I care. I want him here, now, at *once*!'

Now it was Adela who, moving silently past Dolly, urged her down the stairs. Keeping well to the shadows, they crept into the passage leading to the kitchen where Adela nearly cried out as one of the kitchen boys came out of the scullery and stood gawping at her. As he was about to speak, she placed a hand over his mouth and whispered, 'Not a word, Tom! You have not seen us, you understand? Here – here is a halfpenny for you. Not a word to anyone – promise?'

As the boy held out his hand, grinning, she pushed the coin into it and pulling Dolly after her, went out into the street. Only when they had put a hundred yards between themselves and The Blue Boar and Dolly had told her of the near accident involving Ned, did she speak.

'Someone must have told Sir Henry where we were – but who? It cannot have been Mr Fortescue for he did not know where we had gone! No matter – we have evaded Sir Henry, and we must thank the good Lord for providing us with the timely warning of his arrival.'

'Or 'appen Mr Titus' 'are's foot be keeping our luck working for us!' Dolly said grinning. 'There's good luck too, that Master Ned weren't 'armed.'

Only then did the irony of the situation strike Adela – *that it was Ned's doting father who had so nearly killed him!* Who had failed to stop after the accident to see what injuries the child might have sustained! If only she could confront him with the facts! And not the least of the ironies was that by his callous behaviour, he had alerted them to the fact that he was near at hand!

'I think we have more than a lucky charm, Dolly,' she said. 'We have a guardian angel to protect us.'

'Then I 'ope as 'ow 'e's thought on where we's to go now,' Dolly said with a lop-sided smile, 'for *I* ain't got no idea. I'm thinking we'd best get out of Lunnon, Miss Addy. 'Appen we should go back to Dene – ask Lady Mallory to 'elp us!'

'We'd have to walk, Dolly,' Adela said, shaking her head, 'for we have no money for fares. But you have given me an idea – one I should have thought of long ago. Could we not ask for help from Lady Mallory's friend – the one you once met who lives in London?'

Dolly's face lit up.

''Er wot runs the charity wot gives soup to the poor . . . the one as 'elped me that time I were starving! Oh, Miss Addy, I doant know where she lives, but I knows where we might find 'er of a night. 'Appen she'll be outside St Stephen's same as she always was – lessen something's 'appened to 'er since I knowed 'er! Mrs Critchley, 'er name were.'

As they reached the door of the dingy house where Dolly's cockney Samaritan was caring for the children, Adela's thoughts returned to the man who had so nearly killed his own son. No one – not even she – would have suffered as Sir Henry would have done had Ned been under rather than between the wheels of his carriage. But what could have led him to The Blue Boar? Who could have enlightened him when the only two people in the world to whom she had entrusted the information were Titus and Barnaby? Had Sir Henry somehow managed to intercept her last letter to them? They would never betray her. And where – oh where were the twins when she needed them so much?

Adela would have been none the happier to know that thanks to George Robinson, at this very moment Titus and Barnaby were crossing London Bridge; for by the time they reached The Blue Boar, it would be to find that she, Dolly and the children had gone, yet again leaving no address where they could be found.

CHAPTER TWELVE

1789

'Oh, Addy, you *do* look pretty – like a princess!'

Kitty's treble was higher than ever with excitement as Mrs Critchley fastened a bow of apple-green ribbon amongst Adela's curls, securing it with a diamond pin. It matched exactly the sprigs of flowers painted on her chintz day dress – a simple enough gown but one which, to the child who had become accustomed these past months to seeing Adela in drab working clothes, was worthy of royalty.

Lady Mallory's kindly friend had found clothes for Dolly and the children as well as for Adela, and on hearing their story, had without hesitation given them refuge. A letter had been despatched immediately to the parsonage and three days later, a reply had been received from Lady Mallory. Titus and Barnaby were in London searching for Adela, she had written. Mrs Critchley had sent a courier to advise the twins of Adela's present location, and they should be arriving at any time.

Mrs Critchley had also received a letter from Lord Mallory which she had not shown to Adela, for it contained advice as to the future of the children. They must not go back to Dene, he maintained. On the occasions Sir Henry had called on him since their disappearance, the man had been choleric with rage and threatened dreadful retribution upon Adela when he found her. Despite his failure so far to do so, he had not the slightest intention of abandoning the search, for he wanted his son home beneath his roof and would leave no stone unturned until he achieved his aims. Lord Mallory had written:

My wife and I have debated long and hard the ethics of the Matter. We are agreed that both legally and humanely, Sir Henry has a right to Possession of his own Flesh and Blood. Nevertheless, what we now know of the man's Morals lead us to question his fitness to bring up the boy. As a Man of the Cloth, I should uphold the law of the land – and indeed, the Christian Doctrine that Sanctifies the unity of the Family. As a Father, however, I could not countenance the upbringing of my own Dear Sons by such a man, and I therefore hesitate to advise that young Edward be returned to his Father.

I have come to the Conclusion that it must be for the Children's Uncle, the Comte de Falence, to make this fateful Decision regarding their future. I have, therefore, instructed Titus and Barnaby to escort the Children to France at the earliest opportunity, and I am sending you a Draft to cover the expenses they will incur. I have also written to the Comte to advise him of their impending Arrival, and have given him a brief Outline as to what has been taking place.

In the meanwhile, we must Thank God that Adela and the Children are safe and sound in your keeping; and both my Dear Wife and I are most grateful to you for providing them with this Sanctuary.

With a smile, Mrs Critchley turned to stroke Kitty's head.

'You are quite right, my dear child – your sister looks as pretty as a princess, and so do you. As for young Ned – I declare you look quite a little man in that skeleton suit!'

Unexpectedly Kitty burst into tears as she surveyed her young brother in his buttoned jacket and nankeen pantaloons. His red hair was neatly brushed, the fringe touching his red eyebrows.

'He looks just like a little Papa!' she sobbed, hiding her face in Adela's skirt.

Mrs Critchley turned hurriedly to Dolly, suggesting she take

Ned down to Cook to see if by chance the gingerbread men she had been baking were out of the oven. Turning back to Adela, she said gently, 'Let us go down to the drawing-room, my dear. You may come with us, Kitty, as you are such a good, quiet little girl. You may look at the pictures in my nature book whilst Adela and I do our embroidery.'

Finding occupations for the little ones was not proving easy for they had all agreed that on no account must Adela, Dolly or the children venture out of doors.

It is a Miracle . . .

Mrs Critchley had written to Lady Mallory,

. . . that they were not observed by one of Sir Henry's men long since. I shudder to think how close they have come to capture. I think Adela must be right when she says they have a Guardian Angel. Can you imagine, My Dear, what awful fate might have befallen her at the Hands of that dreadful Actor? And to think that I had admired him in that Performance of *A Midsummer Night's Dream!* It is a Mercy the poor Child seems unaffected by her nearness to Danger! Doubtless her Innocence in such matters limits her Understanding of the Profligacy of such a Reprobate! This Fortescue fellow might so easily have taken fuller Advantage of her Ignorance. It is the greatest Pity she did not seek my Help earlier!

Relaxed, at ease now that she was momentarily relieved of responsibility for her precipitate actions, Adela had the same regret as, seated opposite her motherly protector, she plied her needle to the bell-pull she was embroidering. But when she had left home she was not even aware of Mrs Critchley's name; nor, indeed, that she was godmother to both Titus and Barnaby. The good lady had never to her knowledge visited Dene Parsonage, and it was Lady Mallory who always made the journey to London to maintain their friendship. 'I shall be paying a visit to my dear friend in London next week!' Lady Mallory had often remarked in the past, without mentioning her name. But for Dolly recalling it and knowing where Mrs Critchley could be found, they would not be here now.

A smile played at the corners of Adela's mouth as she worked, for she knew that very soon now Titus and Barnaby would be there. Her heart quickened its beat each time she thought of their nearness. Were they already in London – perhaps only a street or two away? How she longed to see them! She could picture in her mind every detail of their appearance – the Nordic fair hair, the dark brown eyes with lashes longer even than her own! The straight Grecian noses and strong, firm jawlines. Most of all, perhaps, she remembered how tall and strong Titus had seemed as he had bent to touch her lips with his that afternoon in the haybarn.

At such a point in her reflections, Adela always paused, as she did now, to wonder if she had been mistaken; if, after all, it had been Barnaby who had kissed her. Something deep inside convinced her that it had been Titus. Would she know one from the other when they came to this house? If she could not *see* the difference, surely she would feel it. She did not understand why she wanted it to be Titus since there was really no tangible difference between the two boys – not that they were children now, any more than she was a child.

In the midst of their difficulties, neither she nor Dolly had been aware that early in January her sixteenth birthday had passed unnoticed. She had left her childhood behind her when she had left her home, she thought now; and in the new dress Mrs Critchley had given her, she knew that not only did she look but she felt like a young woman. As for the twins, they must be nearing twenty-two, and after their travels abroad, they would be young men of the world! Almost without notice, the days of their childhood had gone!

Perhaps her present contentment most of all lay in the wonderful feeling of cleanliness. Only in Mrs Critchley's small but scrupulously clean house had she fully perceived the horrible degree of squalor to which she, Dolly and the children had been reduced. How long would it be, she asked herself, before she once more took for granted the sweet-smelling, newly laundered sheets? The feel of soft piled carpets beneath her feet when she climbed out of bed? The pleasure of donning the clean clothes and soft shoes Dolly brought to her room each morning? How long before she ceased to notice the delicate perfume of the Hungary water Dolly poured into the tin bath? The joy of luxuriating in the piping-hot water as she sat soaking to her heart's content?

'If I had learned nothing else these past months, dear Mrs Critchley,' she said now, 'I have learned how terribly hard life is for the poor. When I was very small, Mama used to take me with her sometimes when she visited the sick tenants on our estate. We would take them fruit from our orchards and jars of calves' foot jelly. Although their cottages were dark and damp and poorly furnished, they were always clean. Even the children were less ragged and dirty than those I have seen in London.' She shivered at the memory. 'In the country, the villagers have cats and terriers to kill the vermin, but all too often Dolly and I saw mice on the food shelves and black rats in the kitchens and passageways. I gave the poor woman who cared for the children after Ned's accident half the money I had saved – little enough, I fear – but I was much moved by her charity, for she had given the children an apple apiece to comfort them, half starved though she was herself.'

Mrs Critchley nodded.

'Such unfortunates do what they can to take care of one another,' she said with a sigh. 'I only wish I could do more to help them – particularly the children. The soup I dispense is quite often the only meal they have when times are very hard – as has been the case this dreadful winter. The cost of flour has risen so high what with the millers unable to work their water wheels, that the price of bread has been beyond the reach of most families. But I have no need to tell you this, my poor child! We are told we must submit to the will of God, but I cannot bring myself to believe that it is God's will there should be such hardship.'

'Nor I!' Adela agreed. 'But Lady Mallory says . . .'

She broke off as one of the parlour-maids came into the room carrying a silver salver on which was a letter which she handed to her mistress.

Mrs Critchley's face was beaming as she read it.

'It is from my godsons!' she told Adela. 'They have just received word from home that you are here with me and sent a messenger ahead of them to advise me that they will be here within the hour! That is most satisfactory news!'

She laid down her tapestry and stood up.

'I shall go and instruct Cook to prepare something special for their refreshment. Come, Kitty, we shall go together, and Dolly shall find occupation for you and Ned in the parlour. You may come back in a little while after your sister and I have had an opportunity to talk to our visitors in peace!'

As Mrs Critchley left the room, taking a reluctant Kitty with her, Adela put down her sewing and went over to the window. A pale sun was attempting to send its feeble warmth through the ever present layer of smoke which seemed always to be hanging over the chimney tops. There were few pedestrians about on this breezy March morning, but the occasional carriage would pass down the leafy cobbled street in which Mrs Critchley's home was situated. At one end of the street an organ-grinder was turning the handle of his organ, a red-coated monkey on his shoulder. In one of the houses, a window opened and there was the clatter of a coin on the cobbles which the monkey speedily gathered. Nearer to hand a delivery boy with a basket of meat on his head passed by. His cheerful whistle mingled with the call of a candle-seller proclaiming his wares as he trundled his carrier down the road. Two carriages slowed to pass one another before going on their way, the horses' hooves clattering over the cobbles.

Adela's eyes went to the end of the street. Would the next

carriage bring Titus and Barnaby? The one after? If she closed her eyes and counted to a hundred, would it appear when she opened them again? She felt breathless with excitement – a sensation of wonderful expectancy such as she had known as a child when her father had said, 'Look under the table, my darling, and see if Papa remembered your birthday!' Once there had been a rocking-horse, large enough for her to sit on. She had called it Dobbin. Once there had been a Queen Anne wooden doll wearing the prettiest of royal robes; another time there had been a cylinder musical box which, when she turned the key, played four different airs.

Oh, Papa, how much I have missed you! she thought now as she turned away from the window, trying to curb her impatience. Almost immediately, she heard the sound of carriage wheels and she ran back in time to see the driver open the door of the chaise. A moment later the twins emerged and, identically dressed as always, bounded up the steps side-by-side to knock on the front door.

Adela's first thought was to race downstairs to greet them; but as her hand reached for the doorknob, she suddenly withdrew it. A shyness she had never before experienced had overtaken her, bringing the hot colour to her cheeks and causing her whole body to tremble. Holding her breath, she waited, listening to the sound of voices . . . the parlour-maid's, Mrs Critchley's, followed by the deep masculine tones of the twins. Before she could draw back again, the door of the drawing-room opened and they hurried into the room. One of them reached her before the other. He made a sweeping bow and then raising his head, he smiled down at her.

'I cannot tell you how good it is to see you, Addy!' He took one of her hands and pressed his lips against it. 'You have no idea how worried Titus and I have been!'

Her cheeks flaming with happiness, Adela's eyes went past Barnaby to Titus. For a fraction of a minute, their eyes locked and then he pushed past his brother and lifted her off the ground. As if she were no older than Kitty, he swung her round in a circle saying, 'You little rapscallion, Addy – always up to mischief! Was there ever such a bothersome scamp as you?'

Affectionate though his tone was and however much laughter in his eyes, his words brought an instant reaction from Adela. As in those long-ago days when Titus had loved to tease her, her temper flared.

'Put me down – this minute! I command it! I am neither a rapscallion nor a scamp; and as to being bothersome – a fine lot of bothering *you* have been doing all these weeks when I needed your help!'

Titus released her but drew her down between himself and Barnaby on the sofa. He did not, however, release her hands, one of which he retained firmly in his own.

'Still as hot-tempered as ever, I see!' he said with a grin. 'At least give one of us the chance to explain. When you ran away, Barny and I were still in France and—'

'Paying court to my lovely cousin, Eugénie, I suppose!' Adela interrupted before she could prevent herself. 'I wrote to you there as well as to your home. Surely you received one of my letters?'

'Indeed, we did . . . that is to say . . . we did not receive the first you wrote to France because we had already learned that you had left home from Jacques who had heard it from the smuggler, George Robinson. As soon as we reached England, we came at once to London, but for all our weeks of searching, we could not find you.'

'Addy knows we love her far too much to abandon her!' Barnaby said, taking her other hand. 'Believe me, Addy, we were worried out of our wits about you, but none of that matters now that we have finally found you. Oh, Addy, it must have been devilish bad for you to have left home like that. Mama told us a little of the unpleasantness to which Sir Henry was subjecting you. Upon my life, I cannot bear to think on it. That fiendish devil! It would satisfy me greatly to run my sword through him!'

Adela looked from one twin to the other. Neither was smiling now as she said in a quieter tone, 'He is paying the price. I have taken Ned away from him – the most precious thing he had. Ned cannot go back – none of us can go back. It is my hope that you will help us to escape to France and that my aunt and uncle will keep us hidden in Normandy. I would have taken the children there when I left home had I not feared that the château was the first place Sir Henry would have thought to look for me.'

'Which indeed he did!' Titus said. 'Thank the good Lord that you delayed your escape there for your uncle was able to swear upon his honour that you were not beneath his roof, nor to his knowledge in France!' He paused, the frown leaving his forehead and a mischievous smile returning to his face as he said, 'By Jupiter, Addy, you have grown up! Do you know, you have become a very pretty young lady? I do declare your eyes are larger and greener than ever! And your face is thinner. Much more of this and you will be little else but skin and bone!'

Quickly, Adela withdrew her hand, aware that her cheeks were colouring again.

'Perhaps you would be thinner if you had eaten as little as I these past months!' she said hotly. 'But if I have changed, you certainly have not, Titus Mallory. Your manners are certainly no better. A gentleman should not make personal remarks about a . . . a lady's appearance!'

Titus looked not the least put out by this set-down. He was grinning broadly as he said, 'At least your temper has not changed, but I fear you have lost all sense of humour else I would have brought one smile at least from those pretty eyes of yours!'

'Enough, Titus! Poor Addy has suffered a great deal, as well you know,' Barnaby intervened, 'and instead of teasing her, you should be applauding her courage. I can think of no one other than you, Addy, who would have dared do as you have done. I beg you to ignore this odious brother of mine and allow me to speak for us both. We love and admire you and we are here to help you. Father has given us money to assist you to France; and your uncle has also given us funds. We shall take you to safety else die in the attempt!'

'Indeed we will – take you to safety. In this past half-hour I have thought how this can be accomplished!' Titus added with yet another grin; 'but I have no intention of "dying in the attempt", for all your words have a noble ring to them, Barny. There is little doubt that Sir Henry has paid spies watching the packets to France. Even were you, Addy, and the children to travel separately, you would almost certainly be recognized – you by the unusual colour of your eyes, and Ned by his red hair. There will not be a sailor on board those vessels who is unaware of the reward Sir Henry has offered for your detection – and he has given the most graphic descriptions of you all. We can trust no one . . . no one, that is, but our faithful Jacques who, I believe, is at this moment in our godmother's kitchen paying court to your Dolly! No, we shall use our cutter and Barny, Jacques and I will sail you to a cove we know of in Normandy. It will prove an amusing adventure, will it not?'

Suddenly Adela laughed. Only Titus would consider such an undertaking 'an amusing adventure'. He must know very well that by assisting them to leave the country, they would be acting against the law; that Sir Henry would have them most severely punished – perhaps imprisoned – were they apprehended. It was even possible they could be shot if they tried to resist capture! 'An amusing adventure' was an absurdly inappropriate description for such a dangerous enterprise.

Correctly interpreting her thoughts, Titus said softly, 'Come now, Addy, 'tis not like you to be fearful. Are you afraid we shall drown you? We are good sailors, you know, for all you may think us rattle-brained!'

'Oh, Titus, I think no such thing! As to being afraid for myself, I know very well what excellent sailors you are. No, it is for you I fear. I am ignorant as to the penalties for child stealing, but to remove Kitty and Ned – me, too – from Sir Henry's jurisdiction can be no less than a very serious crime!'

'And one you yourself have not hesitated to commit!' Titus said quickly. 'Surely you do not think us lacking in courage equal to your own? Who rescued you from Farmer Bane's bull? Who helped you down from the belfry when the wooden stairway broke? Who waded in to rescue you when you fell into the village duck pond?'

Adela's smile widened.

'Except perhaps for the bull, you know very well that neither you nor Barny were ever in mortal danger on my account!' she said. She was very aware that Titus had once more taken hold of her hand and now she became conscious of the strange feelings that his handclasp was evoking. There was a hollowness in the pit of her stomach not unlike that she had felt when she had allowed her pony to gallop a little too fast; when she had swung on the bell-rope a little too high. At one and the same time, she wanted Titus to release her hand and never to let it go. She turned quickly to Barnaby who had placed his arm protectively around her shoulders.

'We will take the greatest care of you, Addy!' he said. 'We—'

He broke off as Mrs Critchley came into the room. Both he and Titus rose swiftly to their feet as she smiled at them.

'Well, dear boys, if you and Adela have finished greeting one another, I think we should waste no time in deciding what is to be done. Your Father's letter to me suggested that it would be best for Adela and the little ones to go to their uncle and aunt's home in France. He has written to tell the Comte to expect them.'

As Titus and Barnaby took turns to outline their plan, Adela rose quietly from her place and went across to the window. Standing with her back to it, she could observe the two young men whilst they addressed Mrs Critchley. Even now, could she be sure which twin was which? she asked herself. Had they changed places when they had greeted their godmother? Was it Titus or Barnaby who every now and again glanced in her direction and smiled? They were warm, intimate smiles – or seemed to her to be so – as if the two of them were linked in some secret conspiracy. It must surely be Titus! Yet he had teased her as if she were still a child – his little playmate; whereas Barnaby had spoken to her much as she imagined he would have spoken to Eugénie – with affection, but also with respect. Had Titus not noticed that she had grown up?

With an effort, she attempted to listen to the plans that were being made. She and the children were to remain with Mrs Critchley a few days longer whilst arrangements were made by Jacques to prepare the cutter. The twins, meanwhile, would hire two carriages so that they could travel separately to Rye, and thus be less identifiable were they noticed at the coaching inns. One of the twins would travel with Adela and Kitty, the other with Dolly and Ned. But which one would be accompanying her? Adela asked herself, aware that her heart was once more beating much faster than usual. Let it be Titus! she thought. How would they decide the matter? Would Titus want to be with her, or did he not care? And why should it matter to her which one of them was to be her companion during the long journey to the coast?

It was not until after the meal that Dolly was instructed to bring the children to see Titus and Barnaby. Ned had been too young when they had left for France the previous year now to recollect the twins; but Kitty stared at them anxiously before running to Adela to bury her face in her sister's skirts.

'Have they come to take us home?' she whispered tearfully. 'I do not want to go home, Addy. I want to stay here with you!'

'I fear she associates you both with an environment where she was very unhappy!' Mrs Critchley murmured in an aside to the boys. She stroked Kitty's head. 'Uncle Titus and Uncle Barnaby have come here to help you and Ned and Adela, child,' she said. 'Now, why do you not show them how you have learned to curtsy so well? Yesterday you were performing quite beautifully!'

When Dolly had once more removed the children, Titus' face was no longer smiling.

'I have never before seen so timid a child!' he remarked.

Adela sighed.

'She is fearful of all grown men,' she said sadly, 'which is not to be wondered at for as you know, her father never saw her but that he shouted at her . . . cruel things which made it quite clear that he despised her. If she saw him approaching, she would hide whenever she could, for he never passed by her without some reproof or derogatory remark.'

'He is both a bully and a tyrant!' Barnaby said. 'I shall never forget those days you were locked in that cold cellar, and Titus and I used to try to see you . . . and you only a little child! How we longed to set you free!'

'And now you will be doing just that!' Mrs Critchley said firmly, for she saw little to be gained from dwelling on the past.

It was with reluctance that the twins decided it was time for them to leave. The sooner Jacques departed for the coast and made ready the cutter, the better it must be, they said. It was not inconceivable that Sir Henry had someone watching their movements in the hope that they would lead him to Adela.

'Barny and I will hire the coaches from different posting inns!' Titus said. 'I suggest that we leave at night – it would be safer than travelling by day, for I think the possibility of our being held up by highwaymen a lesser danger than being followed by one of Sir Henry's spies! Some time tomorrow, I will send word to you when to expect us here.'

These final arrangements having been agreed, the boys departed. It was only after they had left that Adela realized one of them had kissed her hand with a new formality appropriate to a young lady, whereas the other had kissed her cheek as if she were still a child. She had no way of distinguishing between them nor, indeed, had she an inkling as to whether it would be Titus travelling with her to the coast, or Barnaby.

It does not really matter, she told herself as firmly as she could; but deep down within her, she knew that it did.

PART TWO

1791–1793

CHAPTER THIRTEEN

1791

Eugénie watched as her young cousin came across the garden towards her, her arms filled with fragrant rose blooms and sweet-smelling fronds of syringa. She smiled as Adela came nearer, and placed the bouquet of flowers on the table in front of them.

'Sit down, *chérie*,' she said, indicating the white-painted, wrought-iron chair close to her own. 'I have been thinking how fortunate we both are to have such perfect weather. So often here in Normandy we can have rain even in June.'

Adela returned her cousin's affectionate smile. In the two years since she had been living with Eugénie, they had grown very close, not least because her husband, Robert Evraud, the Chevalier de Saint Cyrille, was so often away, and her elderly mother-in-law was a semi-recluse who seldom left her rooms in the east wing of the château. As a gentleman-in-waiting to Louis XVI, the Chevalier's attendance at the French court was obligatory, and whereas at the start of her marriage in June two years previously, Eugénie had accompanied her husband, within months she had discovered herself to be with child and had retired to their country estate which adjoined that of her own family, the de Falences.

Her removal to the country had been a timely one for Adela. Jacques had brought word from England that Sir Henry was now convinced she must be in hiding in France, and although the Comte and Comtesse had been happy to shelter the fugitives for the past six months, they had decided that Adela and the children would be far safer living with their married daughter.

The cousins had subsequently become the greatest of friends despite the eight year difference in their ages. When Eugénie's little son was born, Adela was her first choice as godmother. Moreover, the French girl's sweet equable nature had a wonderfully palliative effect upon the highly-strung Kitty who was now her adoring shadow. The long journey from London to Normandy had been accomplished without mishap, but Kitty had sensed the anxiety that prevailed and for a long time refused to be parted from Adela. This was now a thing of the past. The little girl was also devoted to Eugénie's baby, and for a year now, Adela had been freed from Kitty's hands clinging to her skirts.

Ned, too, was forgetting the few memories he had of his former home and the father who had spoilt him. Now six years old, he was a sturdy little boy who liked nothing better than to roam freely with the young sons of the estate workers. That he tended to be a little aggressive at times was a trait Adela sincerely hoped he would outgrow. At least when the Chevalier de Saint Cyrille was home, he would be admonished and occasionally chastised for such behaviour. Once, when Titus and Barnaby had been visiting, which they did for several weeks each summer and again at Christmas, they had come upon the boy ducking the stonemason's son in the river, and they had taken it upon themselves to give young Ned a similar ducking. The child was at last learning that by no means could he always get his own way, and that tantrums would not help him do so.

'Berthe will be back with the children and *Bébé* Robert shortly!' Eugénie said as Adela sat down beside her. It was Eugénie's custom to spend at least an hour before their bedtime with the children when Berthe, the *nourrice*, brought them to the *salon* cleanly dressed, washed and brushed. 'So we have still a little time for you to tell me what news there was in the letters you received this morning from Titus and Barnaby!'

Eugénie's smile was gently teasing for none knew better

than she, Adela's confidante, how the mere mention of Titus Mallory's name could bring a blush to her cousin's cheeks.

'They are both well and send their felicitations to you and Robert!'

'And something a little more personal than felicitations to you, *non*?' Eugénie said. 'You know, Adela, *chérie*, it is high time you put poor Barnaby out of his misery, and told him that it is Titus you love!'

'But Eugénie, you know very well I can say no such thing!' Adela protested, her cheeks colouring. 'Titus looks upon me as a sister – a loved one, perhaps, but he feels no more than a brotherly affection for me. If Barnaby knew how I felt and were to tell Titus, I would die of embarrassment! If you want the truth, Eugénie, I think Titus is still a little in love with you. Had you given him the least encouragement, I think he would have proposed marriage to you before Robert asked for your hand.'

Eugénie laughed.

'But as you well know, *chérie*, there was never anything serious between Titus and me. In those days, I was a quite shameless coquette and was happy to have both boys dance attendance upon me.'

Adela smiled.

'I was so jealous of you when we were children. How long ago it seems! When Titus and Barny write of Dene, I find myself remembering those happy days when Papa and Mama were alive, and I become quite nostalgic. Barny says that his mother puts flowers by our family vault every Sunday, and sometimes he and Titus do so too. Which reminds me, the twins have had an unexpected surprise.'

'A nice one, I trust?' Eugénie prompted.

'Indeed, yes! When their Uncle George died, he left them a parcel of land somewhere to the north of London. It was derelict and without value so they forgot its existence. Now, it seems, the land is to be developed for it is not far distant from the New Road that connects the Great North Road and

Islington. Quite soon, work is to begin on digging a canal near by – to run from Paddington in the west to Stepney in the east, and this will cross the land the twins own. They have been offered a large sum of money for it – far more than is needed to buy an estate of their own; so they are looking to purchase a property not too far from their parents in Dene.'

'That is indeed good news!' Eugénie said. She glanced sideways at Adela and added, 'Now that Titus will have money of his own, perhaps he will contemplate marriage more seriously. He could choose no better wife than you, *chérie*! If he should do so, you would go back to England, would you not? Without the little ones, of course. They could remain here with me!'

'I could never go back to England whilst Sir Henry is alive!' Adela declared with a shiver of abhorrence at the mere thought.

'But if you were to be married to Titus, your stepfather would have no legal hold over you, *chérie*!' Eugénie said thoughtfully.

Adela drew a deep sigh.

'You forget, dearest, that I could not marry without Sir Henry's consent.'

Eugénie patted her hand comfortingly.

'Perhaps the wedding could be here in France. Both Robert and Papa have many influential friends who might arrange matters for you.'

Perhaps it was possible, Adela thought; but even to consider such a topic was addle-pated! Unlike Barnaby, Titus had given no indication whatever that his feelings for her were those of a lover! On the contrary, he paid far more attention to any other of Eugénie's young friends than he did to her. When Barny had declared himself last summer, she would have given anything in the world for it to have been Titus who was telling her he loved her. She had known that she loved him ever since that long journey from England. It was he who had ridden in the coach with her; who, when they had stopped at one of the many inns somewhere on the road to Rye, had suddenly reached for her hand across the table where they were eating supper, and told her she was beautiful; that he had only just realized it!

How swift had been her heartbeat as he had gazed into her eyes! She had seen that they were devoid of their usual teasing and had thought that there was a new expression in them. He had kept hold of her hand, telling her that he admired her beyond any other female; that he had been greatly impressed by the fact that she had not once complained at any of the hardships of their journey. 'You are a nonpareil, my little Addy,' he had concluded, 'and I cannot think how I never before realized quite how special you are – not just as a person, but to me!'

Foolishly she had allowed herself to believe that Titus loved her, although he had not declared himself. Later when they joined Barnaby on the boat at Rye, his manner had become once more that of an affectionate, but teasing elder brother. She had been bitterly hurt and disappointed; and angry with herself for reading a deeper meaning into Titus' words and looks than he intended. Soon after their safe arrival at the Château de Falence, it was Barny, not Titus, who had taken her on one side and proposed marriage to her. He had not been discouraged by her gentle refusal, which he seemed to have expected, and declared that he was still determined to win her love however long it took to do so.

If Titus knew of Barny's proposal, he never once referred to it. Only occasionally did Adela turn her head and find him staring at her, a strange look in his eyes. Eugénie had seen it also, and was convinced that not only Barny but Titus, too, was in love with her. With all her heart, Adela wished it were true; but she knew now that it was not, for throughout the month the twins remained at the Château de Falence, his manner towards her had continued to be that of an affectionate brother.

The twins were made welcome by the de Falences again the following June. Philippe, Louise and Marguerite were of

an age now to be in society, and during that summer, the
Comtesse gave soirées, card parties and ridottos for her family.
The château was always filled with young people, and Adela
was never without a group of charming and amusing young
men around her. It should have been the happiest of times;
but even whilst she smiled, danced, played croquet or went
boating on the river, her heart ached, for Titus was always to
be seen in some other girl's company. Only Barny was
constantly amongst the circle of admirers around her whilst
Titus amused himself with a dozen different girls.

It was during that summer Adela discovered that she could
almost always distinguish between the twins. If there were a
decision to be made, it would be Titus who first suggested an
answer. If there were a problem to be resolved, it would be Titus
who first found a solution. Barnaby seemed happy always to
fall in with his twin's or other people's ideas. There were, too,
moments when one of the two would walk across a lawn or a
room and, as they drew closer, she would see that strange,
searching look on Titus' face whereas Barnaby's eyes were always
openly adoring.

'It would be kinder to put poor Barnaby out of his misery
and tell him his quest is useless since it is Titus you love!'
Eugénie repeated now. The twins had been invited to spend
this approaching summer at the Château Saint Cyrille. 'There
must be times when Barnaby suspects the truth, for your face
lights up like a lantern whenever you are in his twin's company.
Titus makes you laugh, and those extravagant compliments
he pays you may not be as insincere as you suppose. If only
my dear Robert were here, we could ask his opinion! How
impatiently I await his return!'

Mention by Eugénie of her husband brought identical looks
of anxiety to her own and Adela's faces. For some time now,
there had been considerable political unrest in the country
and in the capital in particular. Not only was the King being
blamed for the hunger and poverty that prevailed, but the
Queen, an Austrian, was thought to have engineered the war

that had broken out between Austria and France. Angry crowds, many on strike, had become ever more daring in denouncing the clergy as well as their monarch.

Deeply troubled by the growing unrest of the populace, the Comte and Comtesse de Falence had decided to leave France until things were calmer; and had removed themselves and their family to London. They had wanted to take Eugénie and the baby with them, but Eugénie would not consider leaving without her husband. She had confided in Adela but a few weeks ago that Robert was planning with Monsieur Lafayette to effect the escape of their Majesties from Paris to their château in Varennes where the King believed his family would be in less danger. Since then, she had had no word from her husband although rumours had reached Normandy that whilst the fleeing royal party had arrived safely at their destination, they had almost at once been arrested; that they had been ordered back to Paris by the Assembly and escorted there by six hundred armed citizens and National Guardsmen.

At first calm in the face of such stories, Eugénie was convinced that Robert would be home within a few weeks at most; and that if he had suspected she and his child were in any danger, he would have sent word to her. Subsequently, however, with neither sight of him nor letter from him, she could no longer remain unconcerned, and it was with a deep sigh that she said now to Adela, 'There has been no rumour of fighting in Paris, so I have no fear that Robert has been harmed. Nevertheless, he is a staunch royalist and if the people are turning against the King, will they not do so against his supporters? The ugly suspicion has crept into my mind that Robert, too, might have been arrested and his freedom of movement curtailed. It would explain his long absence!'

Although the Chevalier de Saint Cyrille had attempted to explain the intricacies of the French governmental system both to Adela and to his wife, Adela had still not mastered them. Robert himself did not care for Queen Marie-Antoinette's influence upon the King, but such was his loyalty that he was

prepared to defend both of them with his life. He refused to
believe the rumours that the Queen had lovers and maintained
that even if the King were indeed a 'weak' man, this was all
the more reason for needing strong men around him.

'Ah, there is the *nourrice* with the children!' Eugénie cried,
glad of the diversion. Her face lit up as the little party came
towards them. She was devoted to her baby who was now
almost a year old, and although the birth had been a difficult
one, she longed for more children. She had also become deeply
fond of Kitty whose shy, gentle nature was much like her own;
but found it more difficult to feel affection for the boy, Edward,
who had none of the Carstairs or de Falence looks or char-
acteristics. Clearly he took after his paternal family, the
Naylands. Nevertheless, the child was her cousin and Adela's
half-brother and for these reasons, she did her utmost to see
that Ned was happy.

If only Adela could be made happy as easily as the boy,
she thought, as they followed the children and their nurse
indoors. Her cousin's nature was profoundly passionate; she
was eighteen years old, and it was time she married. There
were many quite delightful and wealthy young Frenchmen
who would happily have proposed marriage to Adela had she
encouraged them; but it was Titus she loved, and Eugénie was
convinced that although he returned her love, he would not
declare himself until Barnaby switched his attentions elsewhere.
It was breaking Adela's heart, for as one year had succeeded
another, there seemed no likelihood that the status quo would
change.

When Eugénie had voiced these thoughts to her husband
at Christmas, he had said little to reassure her. The relationship between identical twins was outside the understanding
of those who were not so born, he maintained. For one to
hurt the other would be to hurt himself. It was even known
that however far apart, one could feel the same physical pain
as the other. He was not in the least surprised to hear that
they were both in love with Adela, and had decided between

them that Barnaby should be first to declare himself. 'It would be wrong for us to interfere,' he had concluded.

It was nearly the end of June before Robert Evraud arrived home. He brought with him the news that the Austrian army were massing on the French border and that he would shortly be leaving again to join his regiment. King Leopold of Austria was considering war as the best means of aiding his sister, Queen Marie-Antoinette, the Chevalier explained. By defeating the French army and therefore the anti-royalists who were daily increasing their powers, the seeds of the revolt against the monarchy might thus be shrivelled before they could flourish further.

Since the French court was in disarray whilst the King and Queen were virtually prisoners of the Assembly, many of their friends had left Paris and emigrated to Koblenz. The Chevalier was anxious that Eugénie should do likewise, although here, in Normandy, there was no open sign of rebellion by the local peasantry who were going about their work as usual.

'It is not our land they want, but a share in our privileges!' he told Eugénie with a long sigh. 'I cannot believe that our own people will rise against us, *chérie*, but nevertheless, I would feel happier if you were to leave here. Our friend, the Marquis de Palignon is arranging for his family to remove to their *schloss* near Koblenz before the summer is over and I wish you to go with them. The Marquis will protect you on the journey if I have not returned. He has said that he will be happy to accommodate you.'

'You mean we must leave here – our home – for ever?' Eugénie cried aghast, for she knew only too well what her husband's estates meant to him. They had been in his family for hundreds of years.

'Most certainly not for ever, *chérie*!' the Chevalier said sombrely. 'We shall return as soon as the political situation is resolved. Much depends upon whether the King can agree to the demands of the Assembly without the dissenters deciding they can dispense with the monarchy altogether. As you know, the people do not care for the fact that the Queen is of Austrian birth and they suspect she has persuaded the King to abandon his country for one which has always been our enemy.'

'And what is to become of your mother, Robert? You know *Belle-mère* will never leave home. And what of dearest Adela and the children?' Eugénie enquired, close to tears. 'As you well know, they cannot return to England!'

'They will be safe enough in Koblenz,' the Chevalier said. He turned to smile at Adela. 'I have no doubt that the Marquis and his wife will be happy to give you all asylum.' He put his arm round his wife's shoulders. 'If you go to Koblenz, my dear, I will have many opportunities to see you since my regiment will shortly be leaving for the border.'

'But is *Belle-mère* strong enough to make the journey, *chérie*?' Eugénie asked with a doubtful look at her husband.

'Perhaps not! But I am not too worried about *Maman*,' he replied. 'She is an old lady and I cannot believe anyone would harm her. As you know, *chérie*, many of our servants have been in her service all their lives and I can depend upon their loyalty. Nor is there a soul in the village who does not respect her. If such is *Maman*'s wish, I will leave her here, but you and little Robert must leave, for I am deeply uneasy about the present situation. It is not only in Paris that there have been strikes, riots, ugly demonstrations!'

'This is terrible news, Robert. And their Majesties . . . it must be most hurtful to them to know of their unpopularity . . . and they must worry for their children, too.'

With no desire to distress his wife further, the Chevalier forbore from telling her that he could see every possibility of a civil war. The first signs had been there when, two years earlier, the people had stormed the Bastille and released the prisoners. So many of the poor were starving, unable to pay their taxes or earn the price of a loaf of bread. If one had any degree of humanity, he told himself, the plight of the poor was not to be ignored despite the fact that they had been born to such a lowly state. They could not, however, be permitted to claim for themselves the rightful privileges to which he and others like him had been born; still less to make treasonable insults to their Majesties. He fingered the sword at his side, knowing that he would have no hesitation in running it through the first person who dared to do so in his presence.

Despite all the efforts they made, neither Adela nor Eugénie could muster a cheerful atmosphere in the two weeks before Robert Evraud departed. As he kissed her farewell, he regarded his wife's doleful face and made a last attempt to jolly her.

'You should give one of your excellent summer balls when the twins arrive!' he suggested. 'Leave the servants to see to the packing up of our possessions. There remains a month or more before the Marquis will be leaving. As to the household staff, take only your maids and the baby's nurse. If *Maman* will not go with you, we can trust the old retainers to take care of her; and you can dismiss those others who will not then be needed.'

'*Prenez garde, mon amour!*' Eugénie whispered. 'I am more worried for your safety than for ours!'

The atmosphere did lighten, however, after the Chevalier had gone. Without his brooding presence to remind them, it was difficult to think that anything could be amiss. The sun shone brilliantly in a cloudless sky and the corn was ripening to a golden brown in the fields. In the orchards, the apples, apricots and peaches were almost ready to be gathered. The countryside was at its most peaceful and Eugénie and Adela decided to take the Chevalier's advice and plan a summer ball to coincide with the twins' arrival.

Adela did her utmost to keep busy. She wanted above all to curb the growing excitement within her. At all costs, she must not let Titus know how eagerly she had awaited his arrival. It would not be easy for it seemed an unconscionably long time since she had last set eyes on him, heard his voice, watched his quick, ready smile. Not even to Eugénie could she reveal the extent of her love for him although her cousin was very well aware that she treasured every letter that came from him, and that she kept them beneath her pillow.

At long last the day came when the twins arrived. Hot, dusty from the long journey, still wearing their greatcoats, round hats, top-boots and spurs, Titus and Barnaby strode across the lawn to the terrace where Eugénie and Adela were standing. Titus was the first to drop his gloves and riding whip and sweep Adela into his arms.

'Upon my word, you are a sight for sore eyes, my sweeting!' he said, smiling at her as he held her aloft. 'I have been counting the hours and I will swear upon my life that the road from Calais was twice as long as usual!'

As he set her down in order to greet Eugénie, Barnaby stepped forward and kissed Adela on both cheeks.

'It is good to see you looking so well, Addy,' he said quietly. He turned to Eugénie and kissed her hand. 'You too, Eugénie! We have brought loving greetings and letters from your family!'

'You shall give them to me all in good time!' Eugénie replied with a smile. 'First you will want to change out of those clothes. Then we shall take refreshment here on the terrace. It is only possible to sit here in the late afternoon when it is in shade, for the sun is quite unbearably hot even beneath our parasols.'

''Pon my soul, 'tis not like you to be so silent, Addy. Has the cat got your tongue that you cannot find a word of greeting for us?'

Adela was certain that it must be Titus who had spoken, for Barnaby never mocked her in such a fashion.

'You are both very welcome!' she said, trying to quieten her heartbeat. 'You have rooms once again in the west tower. I hope you will be comfortable there. Is Jacques with you to look after you?'

The twins grinned.

'He went hot-footed to the servants quarters to find Dolly!' one of them replied with a laugh. 'He has been bothering us to death with his worries that Dolly will have found herself a Frenchie beau! You will not believe this, Addy, but he has set his heart upon marriage to her and the girl has promised to consider the matter!'

'I know Jacques has always been very fond of her,' Adela said smiling, 'but I thought Dolly looked upon him as an elder brother. He is, after all, old enough to be her father, is he not?'

'The difference is some thirty years I believe. But perhaps your maid adheres to the belief that it is better to be an old man's darling than a young man's slave!'

'Then I shall give her my blessing,' Adela said, 'for Papa always told me there was much wisdom to be found in the old proverbs.'

The twins were both laughing as, excusing themselves, they walked away towards the *porte-fenêtre* leading into the big *salon*.

Eugénie looked at Adela's flushed cheeks and sighed.

'*Vraiment, ma petite*, I cannot see the difference between those two. How can you be so certain it is Titus you love? If I were in your shoes, I think I might accept Barnaby next time he proposes, for one is quite as handsome and charming as the other!'

'Perhaps Barny has changed his mind and will not renew his proposal!' Adela laughed away Eugénie's suggestion.

Later that evening, however, when the elaborate dinner had been cleared away and they were drinking coffee in the small *salon* Eugénie preferred to use unless her husband were home, Barnaby suddenly rose to his feet. With only the barest of hesitations, he said, 'Would anyone care for a short promenade round the garden? Titus? Addy? Eugénie? The air will be cooler now if you feel like a stroll.'

'Quite right, Barny, it should be very pleasant,' Titus said quickly. 'I, however, am far too lazy to move from my chair. Will you remain with me and keep me company, Eugénie? I am sure Addy will go with you, old fellow, for I have never known her lacking in energy!'

Adela caught her breath. Was Titus engineering moments

alone with Eugénie? Was he still so fond of her cousin that any moment alone with Eugénie was precious? Or was he simply helping Barnaby to have time alone with her? Either way, it was clear that *he* had no interest in her; and both hurt and angry with him, she allowed Barnaby to take her arm and lead her into the garden.

There was a brilliant moon rising above the dark mass of the forest, and Barnaby had no difficulty finding his way along the flagged path to the gazebo. At one point he took Adela's hand to assist her down two steps to the stone fountain where water splashed coolly from a dolphin's mouth into the basin beneath. The sound was soothing – but there was nothing that could soothe her aching heart, Adela thought wretchedly.

Beside her, Barnaby spoke in a sudden rush of words.

'This is truly a night – and a place – for lovers, is it not? And you are so beautiful, Addy. Is it any wonder that I love you? No, please do not turn your head away, for I cannot bear this uncertainty any longer. On the last occasion I asked you to marry me, you told me that you were not ready yet for marriage – nor even for a betrothal. You said that you did care very much for me – but not in the way I wished. I pray you, dearest Addy, reconsider your answer. No one could love you as deeply, as truly as I do! I have loved you ever since I was a boy. Even in those days, young as we were, Titus and I were agreed that one of us should marry you.'

Adela bit her lip.

'So, you and Titus have agreed I should wed *you*! *My* feelings, it seems, have not been considered.'

Quickly Barnaby repossessed her hand, his face distressed as he protested, 'It is not like that, Addy, and you must not think so. It is simply that Titus knows how I feel about you and has agreed that I could have no better companion for life if only you will say you care enough for me to marry me.' His voice deepened as he added in a low tone, 'Is there no hope for me, Addy? None at all? Is there someone else?'

For a moment Adela was tempted to lie to him. What

purpose could be served by telling him that she loved his twin when Titus did not care one jot for her? But there was no doubting the sincerity in Barnaby's voice and such was the depth of her affection for him, she knew she must be as honest as possible.

'I am so sorry, dear Barny!' she said softly. 'I wish I could feel the way you would like me to, but I cannot. There . . . there is someone else . . . but if you will forgive me, I really do not wish to talk about him. I cannot even explain my feelings to myself. All I can say yet again is that I am sorry – very sorry, for I am truly honoured by your proposal.'

To her surprise, Barnaby did not question her as to the identity of the man she professed to love. He turned sadly away as if he were unwilling for her to see the distress in his face. When he spoke, however, his voice was firm.

'There will never be anyone else but you in my life, Addy. I want you to know that; and that I hope we may always be friends. I would not want this to come between us. Please give me your promise that it will not do so. It is very important to me.'

'Of course we shall always be friends – dear friends!' Adela cried. 'I . . . I wish things could be different, Barny . . . I wish . . . but it seems as if God does not always intend for us to love where it is wisest.'

'Nor choose where we love!' Barnaby replied sadly. 'Did not Shakespeare say as much in one of his poems – "The Rape of Lucrece", I think? . . . *nothing can affection's course control* . . . Addy, my dearest girl, those are not tears I see? You must not weep. If words of mine—'

'No, you are not responsible, Barny!' Adela broke in as she wiped the unbidden tears from her cheeks. 'You are always so kind. I do not think I deserve it, for I know I have hurt you. It is this which saddens me.'

'Yet all I ask is for you to be happy! You will be so, Addy, I promise. I will make it so!'

Adela smiled through her tears.

'Would that it were in your power to do so, Barny, but I fear it is not. Come now, let us go back to the others. They will be wondering what has become of us. We shall behave as if we have done no more than walk.'

For the first time, Barnaby smiled.

'I do not think Titus, for one, would believe you could stay silent for so long, my dearest Addy. Nor indeed would I! Even as a little girl, we named you The Chatterbox. How you made us laugh one time when we begged you to be quiet and you replied that you were attempting to stay silent but that your mouth would not stay shut!'

It was thus, as Titus looked up to see them coming through the *porte-fenêtres* that he saw them – their arms linked, the laughter still in their eyes.

I have lost her! he thought. She has chosen Barny and now, somehow, I must force myself to show that I am pleased!

CHAPTER FOURTEEN

1791

The Reverend Lord Mallory regarded his wife's anxious face across the breakfast table.

'I do assure you, my dear, that you need have no cause for concern. I shall not under any circumstances reveal to Sir Henry that Adela and the children are with their cousin in France. As I have already explained to you, I cannot in all conscience refuse his request that I call upon him this morning. He has asked to see me as his Spiritual Advisor and, as such, I cannot refuse to give him such comfort as I can.'

Lady Mallory frowned.

'Is he really so ill, Leonard? I have known of a woman who recovered from dropsy of the belly, so it cannot always be fatal!'

Her husband sighed.

'The point is he believes he is not long for this world, and he wishes to make his peace with the Almighty. I would be failing in my duty if I denied him this chance to do so.' He gave a wry smile as he added, 'Speaking now as a layman, you know very well that I cannot abide the fellow; but he, more than anyone I know, needs to see the error of his ways. I must do my duty, Frances, however much I may dislike it!'

An hour later, as he approached Dene Place, he realized that it must be over six months since he had last seen Sir Henry Nayland. The man had closed down the house, leaving only a skeleton staff, and gone to live in London. From time to time, his servant, Higgins, had been seen in the village where doubtless he had been renewing enquiries about the missing children. The neighbour who cared for the old nurse, Nou-Nou, had been most incensed when Higgins had forced his way into the tiny cottage and pestered the poor old soul with questions. Fortunately, her extreme old age had affected Nou-Nou's mind as well as her body, and she had thoroughly confused the fellow by speaking as if Lady Carstairs were still a child living in France. Nou-Nou had even spoken in the French language!

The news had spread quickly around the village when Sir Henry returned to Dene Place a week past to take up residence there once more. He had, it seemed, become grossly fat, and it had taken four servants to carry him from his carriage into the house. Sir Matthew Carstairs' old physician had called twice to see him and there was little doubt that the man was ill. Sir Henry's letter, delivered to the parsonage the previous afternoon, had confirmed the rumour.

As the parson tugged on the heavy iron bell-pull, he pushed to the back of his mind his memories of the occasions when, over two years ago now, he had called at Dene Place only to be told insultingly by Higgins that his master was not At Home to him and wished it to be known by the Reverend that he was not to call again!

Today, however, the big door swung open immediately and he was ushered into the hall and asked if there were any refreshment he would care to have brought to Sir Henry's bedchamber. Having declined the offer, the parson was shown upstairs.

Despite the warmth of the day, the windows were closed and the curtains half drawn so that the room was in semi-darkness. Sir Henry lay propped up in the big four-poster bed supported by numerous pillows. He wore no wig but a white jelly bag covered his almost bald head. Its silk tassle hung down one side of a face that was turkey-red and so distorted by fat that he was hardly recognizable.

'Ah, Mallory, it was good of you to come!' Sir Henry greeted him. 'Be seated – here, beside the bed.' His voice had lost a great deal of its harshness although it was sharp enough as he dismissed his servant. He turned back to his visitor. 'I do not have to tell you that you are looking at the wreck of the man I was. This devilish illness is killing me! The physicians in London have been treating me with purges and leeches, but to no effect.'

'I am sorry to hear that!' Lord Mallory said, wondering what was coming next.

'They tell me 'tis dropsy of the belly, but I am no better for their remedies,' Sir Henry rejoined, his voice doleful with self-pity. 'I am therefore looking to Longman who, I gather, did wonders to prolong Matthew Carstairs' life. He has recommended Venice treacle – it has viper's fat in it which he swears will do me good; and I am to have regular infusions of purple foxglove. They are tolerable remedies, but less agreeably he is also insisting I curtail my appetite! You are looking in good health, Parson!'

'Thanks be to Providence!' Leonard Mallory said. 'I regret to find you thus, sir. How may I be of assistance to you?'

The invalid linked his fingers together and studied them intently for a few moments before lifting his miserable face to regard his visitor.

'I wish for forgiveness, Mallory – for the boundless mercy of Our Lord, Jesus Christ. Believe me, sir, I am a reformed sinner . . . yes, I humbly admit it – I have sinned most grievously. It has taken my approaching death to show me the error of my ways!'

Was it possible the man was genuine in his repentance? the parson asked himself. It would not be the first time that the fear of death brought home to a man the possibility of an eternal life in hell! Yet somehow he doubted whether this particular man could change his character so radically.

'I see you doubt my sincerity,' Sir Henry said quickly, 'and I cannot say that I blame you for it. I was lacking in all those virtues befitting a gentleman – kindness, probity, temperance, justice, morality. I behaved cruelly towards my poor dear wife and, not least, towards her children. I cannot find excuses for my behaviour, for there are none, other than that I was blind to their suffering. It was only after they – Adela – ran away, taking the children with her that I found myself asking, Why has she done this?'

'And it has taken you two years and more to find the answer?' the Reverend Mallory asked dourly. He half expected a reproach for his sarcasm but none was forthcoming.

'Far from it!' Sir Henry said. 'I realized very speedily that for the girl to have taken such extreme measures, I must have given her good cause. I have spent these two and a half long, unhappy years searching for her, hoping that I could bring her home so that I could make amends as best I could. I have spent hundreds of pounds – willingly, I might add – combing the city, the countryside. I have offered big rewards for information leading to her whereabouts, as I am sure you know, but to no avail.'

His voice thickened as he reached out a white, pudgy hand, the back of which was covered in tufts of ginger hair, and gripped the parson's arm.

'Am I to die before I can amend the wrong I have done those poor children?' he cried out in agonized tones. 'It is possible that I have but a year of life left! If only I knew where they were I could, at the very least, write to them.'

A letter could do no harm, Leonard Mallory thought uneasily. On the other hand, if the man once knew they were in Normandy, how long would it be before he sent someone over there with a legal warrant demanding their return?

The tears now in Sir Henry's pale blue eyes rolled slowly down the folds of his fleshy cheeks. Despite the parson's repulsion at the sight, his heart was moved.

'Ned . . . my boy! My only son!' Sir Henry continued. 'If you but knew how much the boy meant to me! You have two sons of your own, Mallory – surely you must understand my sentiments? Suppose they were lost to you – perhaps for ever! If I could see my son but once again before I die, I could depart this world a happier man!'

The parson turned aside, his expression troubled.

'From what you have told me, sir,' he prevaricated, 'you have forfeited that right, morally if not legally!'

Sir Henry's voice had gained strength as he said, 'Do you think I am unaware of that? But I am no longer the man I was, Mallory. And you, a man of the cloth, must recall the words of the Absolution in the Communion service . . . *our Heavenly Father, who of His great mercy hath promised forgiveness of sins to all them that with hearty repentance and true faith turn to him . . .'*

To hear such words quoted from the Common Prayer Book by this reprobate was almost beyond Leonard Mallory's credence. There had been an unaccountable number of Sundays when the Carstairs family pew had remained empty! Granted the fellow had given generously on one occasion to the restoration of Dene Church roof; but that was many years ago.

'What exactly is it you wish me to do?' he enquired cautiously. 'It is for the good Lord, not I, to forgive you!'

'Indeed, indeed! And were I fit to do so, I would come to your Sunday service and pray for the Lord's mercy. But in the meanwhile, Mallory, I am asking that you should intercede for me with the Comte de Falence. I called upon him in London when he emigrated from France, but he refused to receive me. I am convinced that he knows where my . . . where Adela and the children can be found. After all, the girls are his nieces and Ned his nephew! He cannot have allowed them to disappear as if they were no kin of his! I am asking . . . no, *begging* you . . . to write to him saying that you have seen me and that you have some sympathy for my position. I am no longer a young man, Mallory, and Death may be sitting on my shoulder.'

'I doubt very much if any word of mine would influence the Comte de Falence, even if you are right and he is aware of their abode. Much as I, myself, applaud your return to more godly ways and will pray for your strength to continue in such fashion, I have to say that by your treatment of the children, you forfeited all right to their affection or their guardianship.'

Sir Henry shifted his big frame uneasily beneath the bedclothes.

'I do not deny it! But you have to believe me, Mallory, I am a changed man . . . and a very lonely one. You have your dear wife and your three devoted children to comfort you as the years go by. I have nothing . . . no one that I love. And I loved my son as I have never loved another human being!'

There was no doubting the sincerity of this last declaration and Lord Mallory, as he searched his heart, found a measure of compassion for the invalid. That Sir Henry had brought his misfortunes upon himself was no comfort – on the contrary, it must add to his misery. And when all was said and done, it was not a parson's duty to decide what was right in this matter. Once again, it must be for the Comte de Falence, as the children's kinsman, to reach such weighty decisions.

'I will do as you ask and write to the Comte,' he said quietly, 'but I would advise you not to set too much store by his reply.'

There were genuine tears of gratitude in Sir Henry's eyes as he voiced profuse thanks and bade the parson goodbye.

'You will come to see me again – just as soon as you have word from the Comte?' he called out as Lord Mallory reached the door. 'I shall have ready a small donation for the Poor Box in gratitude for your kindness and the consolation you have given me. At least now I have some hope of being reunited with my boy!'

Was Nayland to be trusted? Lord Mallory asked himself as he drove back to the parsonage in his gig. Was it gullible of him to believe that such a sadistic reprobate could change coats so thoroughly? Or was he being overly suspicious to doubt the man – uncharitably so?

'I must voice these doubts to de Falence when I write to him!' he said later to his wife. 'I shall not try to prejudice his judgement, but if he is relying upon my opinion, I must inform

THE SILVER LINK 233

him that I cannot vouch for Nayland's transformation. If the Comte should decide to reunite Nayland with Adela and the children, then it must be upon his conscience, for I would not wish it upon mine!'

The mid-August afternoon was drawing to an end when Titus and Barnaby returned to the Château de Saint Cyrille from a day out shooting on the estate. Now bathed and changed from their hunting clothes into identical, pale-blue broadcloth coats over buckskin breeches, the twins were seated each in a comfortable *fauteuil* on either side of Eugénie in the *grand salon*. For once, neither was smiling.

'The Marquis sent his felicitations, Eugénie, and hopes to see you soon,' Titus said uneasily. 'I fear he was not in good heart, for he had but recently returned from Paris and the news he brought with him is a matter for concern.'

'The King . . .?' Eugénie's voice was sharp for she knew only too well her husband's devotion to his monarch.

'The King has been accused by the Central Committee of having deserted his post when he took his family to Varennes, and they wish to put it about that he attempted to abdicate.'

'The Marquis said they will not succeed in this charge unless the nation supports their petition,' Barnaby added. 'The Committee may choose not to recognize Louis as their king, but the people will surely not be persuaded to such iniquities!'

'Martial law has been imposed!' Titus elaborated. 'The Marquis saw fifty thousand demonstrators, unarmed and from the poorer districts, he thinks, confronted by the National Guard. When the rabble threw stones, the guardsmen replied with fire, and a number of the wretches were killed. He did not know how many!'

'But this is terrible!' Eugénie cried. 'If Robert has heard of this, he will be greatly concerned. Oh, I wish he were safely home! I do not wish to depart for Koblenz without him.'

There had been no word from the Chevalier since he had

left the previous month. Eugénie watched each day for a postboy but was always disappointed.

'And how have you ladies been passing the time?' Titus asked in a deliberate attempt to turn the conversation. He was aware of Eugénie's consternation and hoped now to distract her. 'If you are anything like Patience, you will have been exchanging gossip about the colour of your gowns and ribbons!' he added with forced jollity.

Adela's cheeks flushed, for it seemed these past weeks as if Titus, when he was not actually avoiding her company, welcomed the opportunity to mock her.

'As it happens, Eugénie and I – the children, too – were gainfully employed picking *fraises des bois* which you will be eating for dessert this evening,' she replied trenchantly.

'Quite hard work it was, too,' Eugénie said, attempting a smile, 'for we had to bend ourselves double to find them.' She must try not to dwell on the disturbing news the twins had imparted, she told herself as she rose to her feet. ''Tis time I went to say good night to the children. By the way, Barnaby, the housekeeper was searching for you a short while ago. You had asked her to repair the ruffles on your shirt, but she was unsure if you wished her to renew both cuffs whilst she was about it!'

'Then I will go and find her!' Barnaby said.

For a long moment after he and Eugénie had left the room, there was a silence which neither Adela nor Titus seemed able – or willing – to break. A little of Adela's earlier anger with him remained and yet she had not been able to bring herself to leave the room with her cousin. It was so rarely she was ever alone with Titus since, as always, he and Barnaby were inseparable. The same thought must have been passing through Titus' mind for he broke the long silence, saying, 'Just the two of us, Addy! I do not think we have been alone in each other's company since that night on the journey down from London to Rye.'

Adela refused to meet his eyes which she was conscious were fastened upon her.

'I am surprised you should remember a time so long past! I had quite forgotten!'

For once, Titus did not challenge her with the fib; nor was he smiling as he said, 'I have been wanting to ask you, Addy – is there really no hope for Barny? He loves you very much, you know.'

Adela's chin lifted. For one ridiculous moment, she had been hoping he was about to question her feelings for *him*!

'Did he not tell you I had rejected his proposal?' she said stiffly. 'I thought you shared all your secrets!'

'Yes, we do,' Titus replied calmly. 'But I was not entirely sure if you meant that decision to be final. I understand you told him there was someone else; but although I have been observing you quite closely these past weeks, I have seen no sign of another suitor!'

With difficulty, Adela suppressed a gasp. It was too late now to pretend that she entertained any special liking for one of the many young men who came to Eugénie's parties. She had shared her favours equally amongst them, showing partiality for one no more than another.

'I cannot see why it should be of any concern to you, Titus,' she said sharply. 'I do not seek to pry into your preference for one young lady over another.'

Without warning, Titus laughed.

'Do not play the hoity-toity with me, Addy. I am too old a friend to take that kind of high-handedness seriously. Of course you are of concern to me . . . far more so than I think you realize. For some long time, I was convinced that you . . . you and Barny . . . that if you did not already love him, then that given time, you would grow to do so.'

Adela's cheeks flushed a deep pink.

'Is that what you want, then? That I should wed your twin? Would you have me do so even though I do not love him, simply to make *him* happy?'

Now Titus' cheeks were burning. He rose to his feet and stood looking down at her, his eyes brilliant as he said emphatically, 'Yes, I do want Barny to have his heart's desire – if that were possible. I would do anything in the world to help him achieve happiness – but not at the cost of yours, Addy.'

He reached down and putting his hand beneath her chin, tilted her face upwards so that she had perforce to meet his gaze.

'I have been wanting to explain matters to you for days, Addy, and now at last I can. When Barny first told me he was . . .'

He broke off as one of Eugénie's footmen unceremoniously flung open the double doors and came hurrying into the room.

'Where is Madame la Chevalière, Monsieur Mallory?' he gasped. 'I must find her immediately. There is a *courrier* here in the hall with news . . . with news . . . oh, Monsieur, with terrible news! It is my master, Monsieur le Chevalier – he has been killed.' He crossed himself hurriedly. '*Hélas*, who is to tell Madame this? For of a certainty, I cannot!'

'I will tell Madame, Pierre!' Adela cried, for she had noted the man's distress, and her first thought was that such shocking news must not be blurted out in so brutal a fashion to Eugénie. 'But first tell me, is there no hope that the *courrier* may be wrong – that the Chevalier is wounded, perhaps and . . .?'

Beside her, Titus had taken her arm to steady her, and his voice was quiet and authoritative as he broke in, saying, 'We will go together to ascertain the facts from the *courrier*. Tell no one else in the meanwhile, Pierre. Try to pull yourself together, man, lest the other servants guess what is amiss. We want no maid running to your mistress in hysterics. Such terrible news must be broken to her very gently.'

The *courrier*, a young soldier from Robert Evraud's regiment, was standing in the hall, his head bowed, his uniform covered in dust, his face glistening with sweat, for he had ridden without rest directly from Paris. The Chevalier de Saint Cyrille had been returning home on leave, he told them. He had stopped in Paris in the hope of gaining access to the King but having failed to do so, he was leaving the Tuileries Palace when he heard a man in the crowd gathered outside call the Queen 'a lustful scoundrel' and the King 'an imbecile'. The Chevalier had at once drawn his sword and challenged the ignorant fellow to retract upon the pain of death; but the mob turned on him and in the *mêlée* that followed, the Chevalier had been run through with his own sword. The wound had been a fatal one and he had died instantly.

'I will go to Eugénie,' Adela whispered, although for a moment, she could not bring herself to move. 'Oh, Titus, they were only married two years ago. It is so cruel! How will she bear it?'

'Go now, Addy!' Titus urged gently. 'Eugénie will be down shortly and 'tis better she should be in her own room when you impart this tragic news, do you not agree? I will tell Barny.'

They parted at the top of the stairs, Titus turning towards the tower rooms, Adela towards Eugénie's bedchamber. As she lifted her hand to knock on the door, it occurred to her how thoughtful it had been of Titus to realize that Eugénie would not wish to exhibit her grief in public. In her room, she could weep without restraint.

'Ah, it is you, Adela!' Eugénie said with a smile as Adela entered. Her dark eyes twinkled. 'I suspect that you have something very special to tell me, *n'est pas, chérie*? Did I not engineer Barnaby's absence very cleverly? I had promised Titus that I would think of some way that he could be alone with you. He would not tell *me* why he wished to speak to you undisturbed, but of course, I guessed . . .'

She broke off as she saw the colour flood Adela's face and then recede, leaving her deathly pale.

'You may go, Blanche!' she said to the maid who had been dressing her hair. 'I will call you presently when you can finish your task.' Having dismissed the girl, she beckoned to Adela to be seated beside her on the *chaise-longue*. 'Now tell me, *chérie*, did your *tête-à-tête* not go as I had imagined? You did not quarrel with Titus, did you? I know he loves to tease you, but that is just his way of—'

'No, Eugénie, stop, I beg you. I have not quarrelled with Titus. Our *tête-à-tête*, as you call it, was interrupted, so I have no idea why he asked you to arrange for us to be alone together. He was asking me about my feelings for Barny when . . . when Pierre came to tell us that a *courrier* had arrived from Paris!'

Smiling delightedly, Eugénie clapped her hands.

'He has brought news? From Robert? Robert is in Paris? I had supposed him still in Strasbourg. Tell me quickly, *chérie*, for I have waited so long for word from him.'

Adela enclosed Eugénie's clasped hands in her own as she said, 'The *courrier* brought news *of* Robert, not *from* him. Oh, Eugénie, I fear it is very far from good news. You will have to be very brave.'

The gravity of her voice was not missed by the older girl. Her face whitened as she whispered, 'Tell me, then! Robert has been wounded? I am to go to him? What is it, Adela? I can bear anything other than his death. Why do you not speak? Is he wounded? Hurt? Ill? Adela!' Her last word was a cry of agony. As Adela nodded, Eugénie's whole body shook in terrible understanding.

'No, no, it is not true! It cannot be true! Oh, Robert, Robert, Robert . . .'

As Eugénie flung herself down on the bed, sobbing uncontrollably, Adela bent over her, stroking her hair, her own eyes full of tears. Little by little, she told Eugénie what had occurred.

'He died defending his King, Eugénie!' she said at last. 'If it had to happen, it was in a manner he would have approved. You must try to be strong now – for little Robert's sake. You will have to be both father and mother to him now.'

She doubted if Eugénie took in her words; her crying was painful to hear. Briefly, Adela left her side to send for some cognac and to instruct one of the footmen to ride to the village for the physician. Laudanum would calm Eugénie and help her to forget her suffering for a little while in sleep.

It was some two hours later before this could be accomplished and Adela was able to leave her cousin's bedside. In the meanwhile, the family physician had taken it upon himself to break the news of her son's death to his mother. The old lady had also been given laudanum and was sleeping with her devoted *abigail* close beside her. Downstairs the sombre faces of the servants were proof that Titus had already informed them of the death of their master. The twins were sitting quietly in the *salon* and rose quickly to their feet as Adela joined them.

'It is truly a terrible thing to have happened,' Barnaby said, helping Adela into a chair. 'So meaningless a death! I am far from certain that the French King deserves the life of such a good man.'

'As a soldier and a man of honour, the Chevalier could do no less than defend the King's honour,' Titus argued. 'We would have done the same had it been our King who was insulted!'

'But Robert leaves a widow and child as well as his invalid mother!' Adela protested. 'What is to become of them now? They cannot remain here and there is little point now in Eugénie and her *belle-mère* going to Koblenz.'

'We could take Eugénie home to her parents in London,' Barnaby suggested. 'She would be with her family and that would be of great comfort to her.'

Titus nodded.

'You are right, Barny, but what of the old lady? Of Adela? And Kitty and Ned? They cannot go back to England.'

'Will the Marquis not give you and Madame Evraud sanctuary?' Barnaby asked Adela. 'He knows you well, does he not? And only the other day he was saying that his children's English had greatly improved since they have been regularly conversing with you!'

'The Marquis is a family friend and I am sure that the only reason he offered to include me and the children in his entourage was because Eugénie told him she would not go to Koblenz without me. I cannot ask him for charity, nor would I wish to be beholden to him.'

'This is no time for pride, Addy!' Titus said reproachfully. 'And do not look so angry. I am concerned for your safety.'

'Titus is right!' Barnaby agreed. Seeing the look of exhaustion on Adela's face, he added softly, 'We shall think of something, Addy. For the time being, let us concern ourselves with the present. Arrangements must be made to bring the Chevalier's body home so that there can be a proper funeral. There is much to see to.'

Titus stood up and drew Adela to her feet.

'This cannot have been easy for you, Addy, and Eugénie will need you beside her when she wakes, so go to bed now and try to get a little sleep.'

His voice was very gentle – so filled with tenderness that for the second time that evening, tears filled Adela's eyes. Seeing them, Titus brushed them away with his fingertip and for a moment, held her gaze.

'Another place, another time, Addy!' He murmured the enigmatic words so softly that she could not even be certain she had heard them correctly. Then he stooped and kissed her on both cheeks.

The remembered touch of his lips lingered in Adela's thoughts, soothing a little of her distress as she went slowly up to bed.

CHAPTER FIFTEEN

1791

Robert Evraud's body was brought home from Paris and ten days after his untimely death, he was buried in the family vault. All the villagers and many of Eugénie's neighbours attended the funeral, as did a representative from Robert's regiment, the majority being unable to leave their post on the Austrian border. Most important of all to Eugénie was the arrival of her father from England. The Comte, Titus, Barnaby and the Chevalier's good friend, the Baron d'Anville, supported Eugénie who was distraught with grief. Madame Evraud, who had insisted upon being present and had been carried to the church, was remarkably composed. She had long since become accustomed to death, she told Adela, for she had not only buried her husband but her five other children as well as most of her contemporaries.

'It is to the future one must look, my dear child,' she said philosophically as she was carried back to her bed. 'Robert has left a son, and for that great mercy, we must thank our Maker!'

It was not until some hours after the last of the funeral guests had departed and Eugénie, too, had been put to bed that the Comte de Falence requested the three young people to join him in the *petit salon* where he had something of importance he wished to discuss with them.

'My poor Eugénie is in no fit state to make decisions regarding her future,' he said. 'However, I am anxious that we should all agree the plans I have in mind for her and the child. This matter concerns you, in particular, Adela, my dear.'

Adela regarded her uncle who looked sad and sombre in his black shalloon mourning clothes.

'I shall stay with Eugénie whatever you decide is best for her, Uncle Hugo!' she said quickly. 'I promised her I would not leave her. We have become very close, you see, these past two years.'

The Comte nodded.

'I am aware of that, Adela, and I am happy to say that it is my intention to take Eugénie back to England to her mother and sisters, and I see no reason why you should not accompany her.'

Both Titus and Barnaby were on their feet.

'There can be no safety for Adela in England, sir!' Titus cried.

'My father maintains Sir Henry will never give up searching for her,' Barnaby said simultaneously, 'for he knows Addy would lead him to his son.'

The Comte gave a wry smile.

'You will be surprised to learn that not three weeks past, I visited the man. I did so at the request of your father, boys, and I have to tell you that Sir Henry is a pathetic shadow of the person you all knew. I do not mean by that that he is thin – far from it! He is grossly fat and suffers the disease known as dropsy. The fellow is an invalid and may not be long for this world. More importantly, he is a reformed character!'

Adela stared at her uncle, her eyes wide with surprise – and not least, disbelief.

'In what way "reformed", Uncle Hugo? I find this difficult to credit!'

The Comte smiled.

'I felt as you did, my dear, when I received Lord Mallory's letter telling me of Sir Henry's condition. For a week, I struggled with my conscience and my doubts. Had I the right, I asked myself, to withhold from a man who may well be dying, the knowledge of his son's whereabouts? Indeed, the poor fellow was not even certain that the boy was alive! But I knew that the parson also had doubts as to whether this reformation was genuine, and I finally decided to go and see Sir Henry for myself.'

'Are you now suggesting, sir, that Adela and the children go back to live with him?' Titus asked incredulously.

'I think Adela is old enough to make up her own mind!' the Comte replied quietly. 'I see no compulsion for her to return to a life which in the past brought her only unhappiness. On the other hand, Dene Place was her father's family home – even if Sir Henry now owns it; and Adela may wish to supervise Ned's welfare. No, Titus, I am saying only that your father and I are agreed that Ned should be returned to him. I do not think Sir Henry is in the least concerned about Kitty. Eugénie has told me that the child now looks upon her as her mother and it may well be best for the little girl to remain with Adela and my daughter in London.'

Aghast, Adela looked from her uncle to Titus and then to Barnaby, her mind so filled with apprehension that her hands were trembling.

'I would not have one moment's peace knowing that Ned was alone under Sir Henry's roof. As to my returning there . . . to safeguard his upbringing . . . Uncle Hugo, you cannot expect me ever to go back to Dene Place whilst my stepfather lives there. You and Lord Mallory may consider he is to be trusted but I will *never* believe it.'

'My dear child, I do understand your misgivings,' the Comte said, laying a placatory hand on Adela's shoulder, 'which is why I am suggesting you live with us in London. As to Ned's safety, Sir Henry has agreed unequivocally that Lord Mallory shall keep a close eye upon the boy. If Sir Henry were to revert to his former ways, the good parson would be quickly aware of it.'

Titus was looking thoughtful as he now leaned forward to address the Comte.

'If you and my father truly believe that Sir Henry is a reformed character and Adela returned to Dene Place with

Ned, Barny and I as well as Father would be close at hand to see no harm came to them. We have purchased the Vernons' farmland adjoining Dene Place, sir,' he explained. 'The family have retained the house, but they require only a few acres for a garden and were willing to dispose of their farms at a very advantageous price. We had come into a little money through some land on the outskirts of London which we sold recently at considerable profit; and we decided that it would afford a useful occupation for us to administer the farms. There is considerable woodland and we plan to use some of it for a shoot.'

'So we expect to spend a great deal of our time at Dene and could watch out for Ned's – and indeed, Addy's – welfare!' Barnaby said eagerly. 'Do you think that Sir Henry is so reformed that he would receive us once again at Dene Place?'

'He has said so!' the Comte replied. 'He has assured me that your father and mother, your sister, you, yourselves, I and my family – all will be made welcome.' He turned back to face Adela. 'He is a lonely old man, broken in spirit and painfully anxious to make amends. You must bear this in mind when deciding what you wish to do, my dear; but far be it from me to force you to return against your wishes.'

'Come home with us, Addy!' Titus said earnestly. 'If Eugénie is to return to England, there will be no home for you here in France. Come back with us. We will take care of you – and if you have any trouble with Sir Henry, we will deal with him.'

Looking at Titus' bright, eager eyes, hearing the vehemence of his voice and its impassioned tone, momentarily Adela's heart leapt. He wanted her near at hand! Was she allowing her revulsion of her stepfather too great an importance? If she were to return to Dene Place, she could see Titus every day – and as to the dangers, the twins and their parents would be at hand to protect her; and she would be there to protect Ned.

The moment of weakness did not last, however, as reasoned judgement overcame her emotional reaction. Her mouth tightened and her hands were now clenched at her sides as she said, 'And how would you all protect Ned or me if Sir Henry betrayed this new-found trust you have in him? The law is on his side, as well you know. If there were trouble . . . and Ned and I sought sanctuary at the parsonage or with you, Uncle Hugo, the Law could oblige us to return. I am sorry if I cannot accept your judgement but with the best will in the world, I do not believe that so base a man can have changed.'

Her uncle regarded her uneasily.

'We must hope that you, rather than I, are mistaken, Adela. You see, there is something of significance that I have not told you. Sit down, my dear, for I fear this will cause you some concern.'

As Adela reseated herself beside him, he fidgeted with the engraved silver snuff-box he had withdrawn from a pocket in the skirt of his waistcoat.

'Although Sir Henry made no such admittance to me, it seems he told Lord Mallory that he had paid investigators searching for you in France, and has just, within the last few weeks, discovered your whereabouts. If he wishes, he can have you extradited. You have no choice, Adela. That he has not taken such action already does lend credence to his change of heart – and to the genuineness of his anxiety that you should return home of your own free will, does it not?'

Adela's eyes narrowed.

'You may think me uncharitable, Uncle Hugo, but I am not convinced. Nevertheless, I take the point you seek to make – that if Ned is not now returned to him, he will force the issue!'

The Comte nodded unhappily.

'I think there is no alternative to my plan to take you and Ned back to London with Eugénie. If you can bring yourself to do so, Adela, you should visit your stepfather. I have no doubt that Lord and Lady Mallory would accommodate you and they – or Titus and Barnaby – could escort you when you went to see Sir Henry. He is anxious to apologize to you for his past behaviour. I would not make this suggestion were it not my belief that the man is genuine in his oath that he has no intention of punishing you for taking Ned from him; that all he wants is the return of his son, and to that end, will agree to any conditions you care to impose.'

'If you will come back to England with us you need have no fear, Addy. Barny and I will take care of you!' Titus repeated eagerly.

There was such fervour in his voice that once again, Adela's heart missed its beat. Nevertheless, she remained deeply disturbed as she said, 'It is more for Ned's future than for my own that I fear. However, it would seem from what Uncle Hugo has told me that I have no option but to do as he suggests. I would be easier in my mind, Uncle, were I to have even a particle of your faith in my stepfather's reformation!'

The following morning, however, although Eugénie was calmer and came downstairs for a little while after luncheon to join her father in the *salon*, she immediately dissolved once more into tears when he suggested that she might now go to live in England with her family.

'This is Robert's home – my home!' she said. 'Robert would not have wanted me to leave it. Then there is little Robert. He should grow up in his father's house; with his father's people. It is his heritage!'

The Comte put his arm round her shoulders, his kindly face creased with concern.

'But my darling, Robert had already asked that you should leave – with the Marquis. Had you forgotten?'

Dry-eyed now, Eugénie stared back at her father.

'But that was only to be a temporary measure, Papa – until matters were calmer. He wanted us to be nearer to him . . . in Koblenz . . . where he could more easily visit us. In any case, you must have seen for yourself at the funeral that we are in no danger here. Many of Robert's servants and tenants were in tears; and I do not think one man or woman capable of attending was not present to see their master laid to rest. No, Papa, Robert would have wanted us to remain here.'

'You cannot be certain of that, my poor child. Above all,

he would want your safety and your happiness. Your mother, sisters, Philippe all want you home with them – and as for little Robert, have you forgotten that he is our first grandchild? *Maman* cannot wait to spoil him!'

Somehow Eugénie managed a smile, but seconds later, she was close to tears again.

'You have forgotten *Belle-mère*! She would never leave. She told Robert so when first he mentioned his plan to remove us all to Koblenz. "I was born here and I will die here!" *Belle-mère* told him. Finally Robert was obliged to give way on the matter for he had no doubt that she was justified in her belief that no one, no matter what the provocation, would harm an old lady who was so crippled with rheumatics that she can no longer walk.'

'Your mother would make Madame welcome in England!' the Comte said uneasily. 'However, I will speak with the Marquis. Doubtless he has a better understanding of the current political situation than I; but I have to tell you, Eugénie, the future of France is much discussed in London and matters look exceedingly grave.'

'*Belle-mère* will never leave!' Eugénie said again with surprising firmness. 'Nor can I leave her here alone, Papa. I will accompany you to England on a visit – a month or two, perhaps – as it is so long since I saw *Maman* and the family, and I long to do so. Then I must return.'

The Comte nodded, as if he were prepared to agree to this suggestion. Privately he hoped that once his daughter was back with her family, she might reconsider returning to a country so deep in turmoil.

'There is also the matter of Adela's future,' he said, as much to turn the conversation as for any other purpose. Whilst Eugénie listened attentively, he related the turnabout in the character of Sir Henry Nayland.

'If young Ned is returned to him – as I fear is inevitable – then I have no doubt Adela will choose to live at Dene Place with the boy . . . as a safeguard,' he said finally.

'It is what I would expect of my dearest Adela!' Eugénie murmured. 'I shall miss her sorely, for she is such a comfort to me, Papa, and I have grown deeply attached to her.'

'And she to you!' the Comte replied. 'There lies another difficulty, my dear, for she does not want to be parted from you.'

Momentarily Eugénie forgot her own grief and managed a smile.

'I have always known we must be parted at some time, Papa, for Adela will of a certainty marry before long.'

'To one of the twins? To young Barnaby, perhaps? You wrote and told us that he had proposed. Has Adela now accepted him?'

Eugénie shook her head.

'It is Titus, not Barnaby, she loves! I think Titus has been on the point of declaring himself, and if he has not already done so, he will do so soon.'

The Comte sighed.

'I do not see how Adela can tell one from the other, or feel differing degrees of affection for them. Both are likeable young fellows and either would make an agreeable husband – although I do not think they have a great deal to offer her in the way of wealth!'

'That would not influence Adela!' Eugénie said softly.

Noticing how pale was his daughter's face and how dark the shadows beneath her eyes, the Comte now insisted that she return to her bed. He, in the meanwhile, intended to ride over to his own château to ensure that the *gardiens* were keeping it in good order; and that his *sous-intendant* was taking proper care of his lands. In a year or two's time when France had settled down once more, it was his intention to bring his family home. In many ways he could understand why the elderly Madame Evraud was unwilling to leave. Unlike himself she did not have a wife and four children to consider. Fortunately, Camille was quite content in England where she had many friends amongst the other French *émigrés*; and the girls had been presented at the English court. Only Philippe, his son, was restless.

Philippe had wanted to come to Normandy with his father but the Comte had insisted he remain as temporary head of the household. His reason for keeping Philippe at home was that he feared the boy, once back in France, might elect to remain there. His son was an ardent royalist, and whatever the Comte's private misgivings about the character of his King, he knew Philippe would champion Louis to the last! Even as a young lad, he had maintained a childish adoration for the pretty Marie-Antoinette, and at the age of twenty-four, was still sufficiently under her spell to refuse to allow one word against her.

Philippe had long since reached manhood, the Comte reminded himself, and it was becoming increasingly difficult to keep him within the family circle. If nothing else good could come of poor Robert Evraud's death, at least it might serve as a warning to his son that danger did exist; that the family's emigration to England had not been meaningless. For too long now, Philippe had maintained that if his sister, Eugénie, could continue to live safely in Normandy, then so too could the de Falences!

Despite the Comte's efforts of persuasion, Eugénie was as adamant as her mother-in-law that she would not leave France to live in England. She needed to be near Robert's tomb which she visited every afternoon, leaving fresh flowers there even though the previous day's bouquets had not yet faded. Adela always accompanied her, and it was on their return from such a visit that the two girls spoke once again of the future.

'Papa will want to leave before long,' Eugénie said. 'I know he wishes me to undertake the journey with him, but I cannot go yet! I have not yet come to terms with . . . with Robert's death; but you and Ned must go, chérie. I will come later, in the autumn!'

'No, Eugénie, I shall stay here with you,' Adela said adamantly. 'If my stepfather is as kindly disposed towards me as Uncle Hugo has implied, then he will wait a little longer for Ned's return. I do not care how ill Sir Henry may be. I only wish I need never set eyes on him again, for all I am obliged to do so. As for Ned – it is not even as if he remembers his father, still less pines for him! No, *chérie*, I will not leave you,' she repeated.

Eugénie sighed.

'Then if Papa is in agreement, I shall be happy to keep you here a little while longer. We can travel home together with the twins when the summer is past. Adela, my dear, has Titus spoken to you yet? Alone, I mean? I know he wished to do so, although he would not tell me the reason!'

Adela flushed a deep pink.

'We have not been alone since . . . since that evening . . .' she said hesitantly. 'I know you believe he loves me; but much as I long for that to be so, I cannot share your belief. No, Eugénie, when you have noticed someone gazing at me or paying me a compliment, it was Barny, not Titus you saw!'

Eugénie shook her head.

'They are so alike, it is easy to be confused,' she admitted.

That night during dinner, Adela went out of her way to ignore Titus who seemed annoyingly determined to gain her attention. As always, he was teasing in his remarks.

'My faith, Addy, the sunshine has brought out two most winsome freckles on your nose! Do you not agree that they are very becoming, Barny?'

Aware of Adela's irritation, Barnaby said quickly, 'I had always thought your eyes were jade green, Addy, but tonight they are like emeralds!'

Titus leaned back in his chair, his eyes smiling wickedly at Adela as he quoted, '*Blue eyes go to the skies; Grey eyes go to Paradise; Green eyes are doomed to hell; And black in Purgatory dwell.* Poor old Nou-Nou used to tell us that old French rhyme. Do you recall how angry it made you, Addy?'

'Yes, I do, Titus, and I recall Papa quoting Cicero to you "*Adhibenda in jocando moderatio*" each time you said it.'

'Well said, indeed! "Moderation *should* be observed in joking." Remember that, my boy!' the Comte said in gentle rebuke.

Titus grinned.

'I only mock my dearest friends, sir. Is that not right, Barny? And Addy knows how much I love her!'

Somehow Adela managed to shrug her shoulders with a nonchalance she was very far from feeling.

'It is as well I never take anything you say seriously, Titus. Upon my soul, I think you will remain a schoolboy all your life. 'Tis time you grew up!'

'But then who would amuse us?' Eugénie countered with her soft smile as she rose to her feet. 'I think I shall go up now and sit with *Belle-mère*. She is not sleeping very well at the moment.'

''Tis devilish warm again this evening!' Titus remarked as Eugénie kissed her father good night and left the room. 'What say you to a walk down to the river, Addy? There are enough stars in the sky to light our way. Shall you come too, Barny?'

Barnaby shook his head.

'I promised Ned I would finish the little boat I have been carving for him. I have yet to varnish it!'

'I, too, have work to do!' the Comte said as Titus glanced at him. 'A letter to my dear wife is long overdue and I have vowed I will not postpone the task a day longer.'

'You will accompany me, will you not, Addy? I would much enjoy your companionship!'

There was no laughter in Titus' eyes and his voice held a pleading tone which confused Adela and started her heart racing. Unable to trust her voice, she nodded and crossed the room to gather up her silk shawl which she had laid over the arm of a chair. She was aware that Barnaby was watching her, a look in his eyes which she could only assess as sadness. Still further confused, she allowed Titus to take her arm and lead her out through the *porte-fenêtre* into the garden.

High up in the night sky, a huge harvest moon outshone

the stars which Titus had observed earlier. Small nocturnal animals hurried through the dry grasses and leaves, and from the wood came the sharp squawk of a cock pheasant. There were no glimmers of light from the farmhouses for the occupants were weary after the day's harvesting and would be up again at dawn.

'We could as well be in England!' Titus said as he walked beside Adela. 'Do you not long sometimes to be home, Addy? Do you not miss the Sussex countryside?'

'For me, Dene has only sad memories,' Adela replied. 'When I return, it will be only for Ned's sake. One day he will inherit Dene Place and it is right he should grow to love his future home.'

Her words hung between them for a long moment before Titus took Adela's arm and drew her to a halt.

'It was my hope that you would want to spend the rest of your life in Dene,' he said. 'I know you may find this hard to believe, but I love you very much, Addy, and I was hoping that you would do me the honour of becoming my wife!'

Adela caught her breath.

'Is this another of your jokes, Titus? It seems to have become your pastime to mock me. When last we spoke on this subject, you wanted me to marry Barny and you knew that he had asked me to marry him.'

'Yes – and that you refused him! Addy, listen to me. It is because of Barny I did not speak earlier of my feelings for you. You of all people must know how close Barny and I are – have always been. He was the first to speak of his love for you and I felt, therefore, had first right of opportunity to win your hand. Some might say that this only proves my love for him is greater than my love for you, but that would not be true. I love you both – but differently – and I could not hurt him. Strange as it must seem to you, I would rather be the one to suffer than to know that he was grieving.' He drew a deep sigh as he continued, 'When Barny told me that you had refused him, he was not without hope that you might have a change of heart. I knew the time had not yet come to tell him of my feelings for you. I was afraid that if he knew I loved you, he would not propose a second time. Nor could I speak out to you lest I prejudiced Barny's chances. That is why I pretended an interest in all those eligible *demoiselles* Eugénie introduced to us. I wanted you both to believe I had no personal interest in you for Barny would of a certainty have relinquished the field to me.'

'Oh, Titus!' Adela whispered. 'I have always envied you and Barny; wished I had been blessed with an identical twin. Now I see that it does not necessarily always make life easier – or happier. It is not enough to seek one's own happiness but one must seek theirs, too. I thought . . . I was very jealous of your attentions to the other girls and I thought . . . I thought you did not love me as Barny did . . . only as a friend!'

Titus put his hand beneath her chin and lifted her face to his. Her eyes were radiant in the moonlight as he said vehemently, 'I love you with all my heart, my darling Addy. I think I always have and I know I always will.'

As his mouth touched hers in a long, lingering kiss, Adela knew that she would never forget this moment of supreme happiness. If it were possible, she would have bade life's clock stand still.

When Titus released her, his face was alight with joy.

'We will be married as soon as we return to England!' he said eagerly. 'We shall have to live at the parsonage until I can have a house built for us. Father shall marry us. If he and your uncle are right, Sir Henry will not forbid our marriage.'

'I cannot believe he will be anything but overjoyed!' Adela agreed. 'I have no doubt whatever that it is only Ned he wants – not me! But Titus, we cannot hurry our wedding. I must live at Dene Place with Ned if I am to protect him. It is Sir Henry's influence upon him that I fear for I know he would not harm him physically. I must be present if I am to ensure Ned is not over-indulged, spoilt, lacking all discipline – as happened before. It is my duty, you see, if not to Ned then to

Mama. He is as much her child as I am, and Mama would expect me always to care for him. I must stay with him – at least until I am convinced that my stepfather will raise him as she would have wished. Do you understand this, Titus?'

'I understand, but I am not altogether sure I agree that so close a surveillance is necessary,' Titus said thoughtfully. 'I am impatient now to make you mine, Addy. But if I must, I can wait . . . but not too long, my darling! At least in the meanwhile we shall be betrothed, and I shall not have to fear that some other man will snatch you from my grasp. I have seen how some of these Frenchies ogle you! I do not blame them, mind you, but demme if I shall allow one of them to steal your heart!'

'I promise you that it is yours for always!' Adela said softly. 'But perhaps for the moment, it would be kinder not to speak of our betrothal . . . not when my poor Eugénie has just lost the man she loves. Let us wait until a little time has passed. It will be our secret.'

'One that will be hard to keep,' Titus said as he kissed her once more. 'There are stars in your eyes, Addy, for all to see,' he added, 'and I do not doubt that they are there in mine, too. Was any man more in love than I?'

Their arms and hands linked, they walked slowly back towards the house. Neither was aware that from one of the upstairs windows, Barnaby was watching their return, fearing with a bitter ache in his heart, that nothing would ever be quite the same again between him and his twin.

CHAPTER SIXTEEN

1791

'Sir Henry is in the morning-room, M'Lord, Miss Addy. He said he would receive you the moment you arrived!' The elderly butler who had long ago been in Sir Matthew's employ, beamed at Adela. 'May I say "welcome home!" Miss Addy. It is a real pleasure to see you, Miss.'

'Thank you, Unwin! I am glad to see you looking so well.'

Adela could not bring herself to say that she was happy to be home, for although the sight of Dene Place and its remembered beauty had brought tears to her eyes as she and Lord Mallory had driven up to the front door, her heart was full of misgivings. She dreaded this meeting with Sir Henry, knowing that nothing could ever erase the unhappy memories she retained of those years of his domination.

She had arrived from London, accompanied by Jacques, the previous evening and spent a happy few hours renewing her association with Lady Mallory. Kitty and Ned had remained in the safe-keeping of Eugénie and her family; and Titus and Barnaby were conducting some legal affairs relating to the purchase of their land. They would be returning to the parsonage in a day or two, and at the end of the week would escort her back to the de Falences' house in London.

'Do you wish to speak to your stepfather alone, my dear, or would you prefer that I stay with you?' Lord Mallory enquired with an anxious look at Adela's tense face. 'I have to say I am surprised to hear Sir Henry is up and about. I had thought him to be more or less permanently bedridden.'

'I would like you to remain with me, if you will!' Adela

replied. 'I feel there should be a witness to any undertaking Sir Henry might make.'

It was with some relief that on entering the morning-room, she saw at once that Sir Henry was alone. It was not past her belief that he would have arranged for officers of the law to be present to arrest her! As she dipped politely in a curtsy, she realized that she might not have recognized the grotesque figure in the armchair had she encountered him in strange surroundings.

'Adela, my dear child! Forgive me if I do not rise but I am, alas, confined to this miserable chair. Good morning to you, Mallory. May I say how grateful I am to you for bringing Adela to see me?'

Inclining his head, the parson remarked, 'I had thought to find you in your bed, sir. Your health has improved?'

Sir Henry's purple cheeks, puffy with fat, wobbled as he nodded his head. He placed his hands on the mustard-yellow velvet waistcoat stretched over his swollen stomach and sighed.

'My physician told me I was making a remarkable recovery!' he said. 'He thinks the improvement may be due to the fact that I am a man no longer devoid of hope or pleasure.' He gave Adela a roguish smile which sickened her as he added, 'You can have no idea how you had driven me to the very depths of despair, young lady. Not, let me assure you, that I blame you for your actions. The fault lay entirely at my door. But I am forgetting my manners. Pray be seated!'

His pale-blue eyes narrowed as his visitors obeyed his request.

'You have explained to Adela that I wish to make amends for the way I treated her, have you not, Mallory? That I am filled with remorse?'

Adela's mouth tightened.

'I am not concerned about your treatment of me, sir. If apologies are due, then I think they should be made to your little daughter, Kitty – and, indeed, to Ned!'

'Ah, Ned!' Sir Henry gave a deep sigh and insofar as his

bulk would allow, leaned forward in his chair so that he could search Adela's face. 'My son . . . how is the boy? Grown beyond my recognition, I have no doubt. Is he well? Is he here, in England? You have not brought him with you to Dene?'

His voice was trembling with eagerness and, for a moment, Adela felt a degree of pity for him. Yet his very presence revolted her and involuntarily, she drew herself backwards as far as her chair would permit.

'Ned is well. He knows nothing of my visit to you. Indeed, I fear he does not remember you.'

For an instant, Adela thought she detected a look of malevolence cross her stepfather's face but she could not be certain. He gave another long, drawn-out sigh.

'I suppose he was too young when . . . to remember me, I mean. He must be six years old now, nearing seven? Does he still resemble me?'

'He has red hair and blue eyes similar to your own, sir.' She could not deny him this.

Lord Mallory shifted uneasily in his chair. He had hoped for a better understanding between these two but the antipathy between them was almost tangible.

'Your stepfather is hoping that it will not be long before Ned returns to him. As your uncle explained to you, Adela, Sir Henry is concerned for the boy's future.'

'Yes, indeed!' Sir Henry said eagerly. 'Dene Place will one day belong to my son and I am sure you will appreciate that it is only right that the boy should be brought up here.'

For generations Dene Place had been the Carstairs family home, the parson thought unhappily. It should rightfully have been Adela's . . . and doubtless poor Matthew Carstairs would have left the estate in trust for her had she been a boy. Leaving it outright to his wife, Nadine, can only have been because he supposed Adela would eventually marry and live in her husband's home; or, if Lady Carstairs remained a widow, that she would leave the estate to her daughter.

'I quite understand why you wish Ned to return here!'

Adela said quietly. 'However, you are well aware, Sir Henry, why I took Ned and Kitty away when I left your household. Your *upbringing* . . .' she stressed the word with undisguised sarcasm '. . . was hardly befitting a child of his tender years. Mercifully those excesses have done no lasting damage; but what guarantee can you offer that they will not be repeated?'

Once again, Adela detected a flash of anger in Sir Henry's eyes, but his voice was conciliatory as he said, 'I do not deny that you have every justification for your sentiments and I have said as much to your uncle and to the parson here, have I not, Mallory? But you are no longer a child yourself, Adela. If I may say so, you have grown into a very charming young woman.' His eyes almost disappeared as he delivered the compliment with a smile that was all but grotesque in its falsity. 'You are doubtless mature enough now to appreciate that when I married your poor mother, I had had no experience of raising young children,' he continued. 'I made mistakes – many mistakes – but no one can regret them more than I. May the good Lord forgive my sins!' he added unctuously, looking at the parson. Then he turned once more to Adela.

'I shall be happy to continue with whatever disciplines to which you have accustomed my boy. Indeed I would be more than happy if you, too, would agree to come home, my dear. This house needs a woman's care and the servants a mistress' authority. Can you not find it in your heart to forgive an old man – a very sick old man – and to grant him some peace and happiness in his remaining years? Proud though I am, I will willingly humble myself now if this will convince you of my good intentions. Were I able, I would go on my knees to beg you, for your poor dear mother's sake if not for mine, to allow me to be reconciled with my son!'

Despite Adela's resolve to remain cool and controlled, this sentimental reference to her mother who, indisputably, had died from a broken heart, was more than she could tolerate.

'It was as much for my mother's sake as Ned's that I took

him away!' she said accusingly. 'How can you demand his return *for her sake*?' Her voice was full of scorn.

'Come, come, my dear!' Lord Mallory said gently. 'Sir Henry has admitted his mistakes and regrets them bitterly.'

Realizing that he had made an unfortunate error, Sir Henry hastened to rectify the matter.

'You misunderstood me, Adela. When Ned was born, your mother's first words to me were: "Now we have a son to inherit Dene Place!" She was overjoyed. It was your father's family home and she was unwilling for it to pass into a stranger's hands. Naturally she supposed that Ned would grow up here and love the place as your father did.'

Adela's throat constricted. They were words her mother might very well have spoken, for her love for her first husband had never been diminished by her second marriage; and young though she, Adela, had been at the time of her father's death, she had known this to be so. As for her father – since he had not left a son to inherit his estates, he would have wanted Nadine's son to do so. Had he not always urged her mother to remarry after his demise? As for Ned, he was more French than English and although he spoke both languages with equal facility, it was time he received an English education.

'Lord Mallory told me that you would agree to any conditions I might request if Ned is to come back here to live!' she said. 'One of those conditions would be that Lord Mallory should tutor Ned until he is old enough to go to boarding-school.'

Sir Henry's face was quivering with excitement.

'Indeed, that is a most excellent suggestion. And the other conditions . . .?'

'I am sure that you remember my maid, Dolly. I wish you to reemploy her and give me written assurance that you will never seek redress for her part in our . . . our escape!'

Sir Henry nodded his head.

'I readily agree to that request; but you, my dear? And . . . er . . . Kitty?'

'I trust you will not insist that Kitty return,' Adela said sharply. 'She is perfectly content where she is. Perhaps when she is older . . . As for myself . . .' She paused, her mind once again trying to resolve her future when Ned returned to live with his father. There seemed no way by which she could prevent it since Sir Henry held the trump card – the law. It seemed that for the moment he was not seeking to play it, but such was Adela's mistrust of the man, she was far from sure he would never do so.

Titus wished them to be married in the following spring, but that was only six months away. Could she, in that short time, be certain that Sir Henry would keep his word? That he would not return to his old ways? Perhaps she should suggest they delay their wedding until the early summer? In many ways, it might be better to do so, for the house Titus was having built for them on the twins' new estate would not be ready for occupation until a year hence.

Somehow the thought of residing at the parsonage as Titus planned did not lie easily in her mind, for Barnaby, too, would be living there; and despite his assurances that he was delighted that Titus had won her heart since he could not, she knew that he had not stopped loving her. She had glimpsed too often a wistful look in his eyes when she had turned her head and found him staring at her; had heard the disconsolate tone of his voice when she and Titus spoke of their future together.

Titus was convinced that Barnaby was reconciled to his betrothal to Adela; that he had already turned his attentions to Eugénie's younger sister, Marguerite. He maintained that if Barnaby were in the least saddened by events, it was only because for the first time in their lives, they would be living under separate roofs. 'When Barny marries,' Titus had said, 'I hope it will be to someone you like and admire, Addy, for it is my hope that we could all then live together on our newly acquired estate. You would not mind, my dearest?'

Loving Titus as much as she did, Adela was prepared to agree to anything that would make him happy; but until such time as Barny got over his disappointment at her rejection of him, she was not at ease in his company. Nor must her own desire to be with the man she loved interfere with her duty to her mother's memory – and to Ned.

'Well, my dear, have you reached any decision regarding your own future?' Lord Mallory prompted, for she had fallen silent at her stepfather's question as to her own movements. He turned to Sir Henry. 'We have not yet had a chance to enlighten you, but Adela has consented to become my son, Titus', wife; so whatever arrangements are made now, they will be of a temporary nature only. I trust that you, as Adela's legal guardian, will agree to this happy union?'

Sir Henry's look of pleasant surprise appeared to be genuine.

'But I am delighted! My congratulations, Adela. Young Titus, eh? I hear he and Barnaby have bought the land adjoining mine so we shall be neighbours. Titus is the elder of the twins, is he not? For my part, I can never tell one from the other! Please inform them, Mallory, that both your sons will be most welcome guests. I shall be happy to arrange some shooting for them. Higgins tells me that there is some excellent duck shooting to be had down on the marshes. Your boys are good shots, I recall!'

He turned back to Adela, his voice thickening as he said emotionally, 'You see, my dear, I have such plans for Ned's future! He shall learn all the country pursuits necessary to a squire. And I had thought I would send him to your father's public school – so much better than the one I attended, but all my poor parents could afford. The . . . er . . . the money your father left . . . it shall be spent on Ned . . . his schooling, a horse or two, some good guns. He will lack nothing he needs . . . and the parson here will see that he is properly disciplined, for I freely admit that I would find it difficult not to indulge the boy.'

He had an answer for all her doubts, Adela thought, yet she was still far from convinced he was to be trusted.

'I should like time to consider all you have said,' she told him. 'I shall be staying with Lord Mallory for the remainder of the week and if you are agreeable, I will let you know when to expect Ned after I have returned to London and spoken to my uncle.'

The muscles of Sir Henry's face, slack though they were, visibly tightened. He drew in his breath sharply and for a moment, Adela felt a chill of fear. Was he about to fly into one of his remembered rages? To threaten her with the law? Could he have her thrown into prison for kidnapping his son? Her head lifted, for she was not going to let him see her fear; nor would she ever again submit to his bullying. When her stepfather spoke, however, his voice was astonishingly humble.

'After all that has passed, it would be unreasonable of me to expect you to trust me, my dear. I have earned your scepticism. I can do no more than assure you once more that I have seen the error of my ways, and far from bearing you any ill-will, I ask only the chance to make amends.' He drew out a silk handkerchief from his pocket and dabbed his eyes before continuing in a firmer voice, 'I beg you once more to have pity on an old man and return my son to me as soon as you possibly can.'

As Lord Mallory and Adela drove back to the parsonage, Adela said doubtfully, 'I know you believe my stepfather is a reformed character, sir, and I wish I had your conviction. As he so rightly surmised, *I do not trust him*. Am I being uncharitable? Is it true he is going to die soon? He did not look to me like a man at death's door!'

'He did appear a great deal better than when I last visited him,' Lord Mallory agreed, 'but perhaps this is due to his state of mind. He is spiritually at ease now that he has confessed his sins and has reason to hope that within the month he will regain his son. It often surprises me how the mind can affect the body, for better or for worse. Many years ago, I attended a dying woman whose husband had not returned from the wars. Not only I but the physician, too, had given up all hope for her. I had even administered the last rites when suddenly her husband appeared. From that day on she began to get better and she lived a further twenty years! So you see, my dear, it is in God's hands as to whether Sir Henry will make a full recovery when he has his son home.'

'There was a time when I wished him dead!' Adela admitted as the parsonage came into sight. 'If God can be merciful, perhaps it beholds me to be so, too. But I must accompany Ned. He has forgotten his father – and perhaps Dolly, too – and will have no other familiar face but mine about him. Moreover, I myself could not sleep at night knowing he was there alone with . . . with that man!'

When Titus and Barnaby returned home, Titus at once noticed Adela's look of anxiety and took her hand in his.

'Was your visit as distressing as you had imagined, my dearest?' he asked. 'Father accompanied you, did he not? Should I, too, have gone with you?'

Adela attempted a smile.

'If I appear agitated, it is because I am still mistrustful of Sir Henry.'

'Your concerns are now mine!' Titus said, the pressure of his hand emphasizing their unity. 'Nevertheless, my dearest, it would seem that you have no choice but to relinquish to his father the responsibility you undertook for young Ned; besides which, London is no place for a boy of Ned's age to be living; and laudable though your uncle and aunt may be, they cannot wish to be permanently responsible for so young a child now their own family has grown up.'

'If Ned is unhappy at Dene Place . . . or if Sir Henry were to revert to his former behaviour,' Barnaby ventured, 'then Titus and I would be at hand to find a way to remove him.'

Titus frowned.

'But we could not take the boy back to France. Sir Henry would certainly demand his extradition.'

'If only we could have left Ned at the Château de Saint Cyrille!' Adela said sadly. 'He was happy there with Eugénie. It will not be long, I think, before she returns to her own home. Uncle Hugo says she will be in no danger now that the immediate threat to the monarchy has passed. Life has returned to normal, it seems, so she will take Kitty with her when she goes.'

In September, the French King had formally accepted the new constitution, virtually abnegating all political power but retaining his monarchy. According to a letter the Comte had received from Baron d'Anville, his former Parisian neighbour, festivities had been resumed in the city and at an appearance at the Opera, the King and Queen had even been greeted with rousing cheers. The public had enjoyed the illuminations and fireworks and drunk toasts to their monarchs.

Nevertheless Adela was aware that her uncle was not entirely without anxiety for his daughter's future safety. The Constituent Assembly had declared that there would no longer be any nobility, nor peerage, hereditary distinctions of orders, feudal regime or heredity in any public office; nor would there be any exemption for any individual from the common law of the French. Such a declaration, he reasoned, could not but have disastrous repercussions upon the nobility. He had to accept, however, that there was no immediate danger for Eugénie and he agreed reluctantly that she could return to Normandy after Christmas. Not to be gainsaid, Philippe insisted upon accompanying her.

Adela gave a deep sigh.

'Perhaps I am worrying unduly about Ned,' she said, her tone of voice without conviction.

Barnaby frowned.

'I think you should be more worried about yourself, Addy. Father and your uncle seem unconcerned by the fact that now you are back in this country, you could be apprehended at any time by the law.'

Titus shook his head.

'If Ned is safely returned to his father, I doubt Sir Henry would want to press any charges against Addy. If the matter came to court, everyone would come to learn of the events leading up to her departure from his household and it would go ill for him in society were his behaviour to become common knowledge – and he a magistrate!'

'Perhaps you are right!' Barnaby agreed. 'Perhaps that is why Sir Henry has not already taken legal steps to have you extradited from France. It explains his sudden "reformation", does it not?'

Unexpectedly, Titus smiled.

'At least we can be thankful the man is of a mind to agree to your wishes, Addy. We shall not now have to elope to Gretna Green in order to be wed – which might have been the case if he had withheld his consent. Now we can be married here, in Dene Church, as we planned, with Father giving us his blessing. Dene village will be *en fête*, as they say in France, and all Father's parishioners will be able to enjoy the celebrations.'

Glancing at Barnaby's face, Adela noticed that there was no joy in it. She understood his unhappiness for he had not only lost her, but inevitably, he would be losing some of his close ties with Titus. Somehow, she must make sure that he never felt unwanted by them; that his relationship with his twin should remain as close as it had ever been. Barnaby, however, seemed determined to leave them alone together whenever he could do so without it being too apparent to Titus.' He now excused himself on the grounds that he had promised to write some letters for his mother. Lady Mallory's eyesight was failing and the spectacles she had been wearing for the past two years no longer seemed of any benefit.

As Barnaby left the room, Titus turned and put his arms around Adela's waist, drawing her close against him.

'I cannot wait much longer for us to be wed,' he murmured huskily, then essayed a smile. 'I am hard put to refrain from touching you whenever we are in the same room. I would hold you in my arms for ever if I could. Mama would not mind, for she is very happy about our betrothal and told me she could think of no other girl she would prefer for her daughter-in-law! Father, too. It is Barny who must be considered. To tell you the truth, Addy, I cannot make up my mind if we should invite him to live in our new house with us, or if he would be happier remaining here at home with Father and Mama.'

Adela rested her head against his shoulder, her heartbeat quickening as always when he held her so close.

'I have been considering the matter of our wedding, Titus. Much as I am loath to say so, I feel it will have to be delayed until the early summer. I *must* stay at Dene Place with Ned until he becomes settled there and we can be assured Sir Henry is treating him correctly.'

Titus' arms tightened as he pressed his mouth against her hair.

'I am not sure if I can wait much longer to make you my wife! I want so much more than a mere kiss, wonderful though that is! No man ever loved a woman as greatly as I love you!'

Adela smiled.

'I dare say all lovers think the same!' she said. 'I know I do! I cannot believe I shall ever be happier than I am now, knowing how much you love me, want me.'

'We shall be happier still once we are married!' Titus said fervently. 'When we wake each morning in one another's arms; and at night . . . oh, Addy, my dearest girl, I must not allow myself to think of taking you to my bed for, if I continue to do so, I fear that I shall lose all patience and ravish you before Father or Mama can come to your rescue!'

Adela laughed happily.

'And what if I do not wish to be rescued?'

'Do not say such things, for they only incite my passions further!' Titus warned her with a mock scowl. 'Best we should talk of other things for I mean always to protect you, albeit from myself, too! Tomorrow, if the weather is kind to us, I will take you to see our land. It is good land, Addy, and the farms should prosper. Barny and I shall continue the tenancies of the farmers who are all hard-working fellows and much relieved that we wish them to stay. You must meet them, and their wives and children. Which reminds me, dearest, had you thought that when we have children, we may have twins? Father told me the other night that there have been several sets of identical twins in past generations of Mallorys! We will have twin girls, I think, looking just like you – huge green eyes and long dark lashes and . . .' he paused, a mischievous curl to his mouth as he added, 'and crooked noses!'

'It is *not* crooked!' Adela cried indignantly. 'It is only a tiny bit bent and only you have remarked upon it!'

'I like it!' Titus said as he kissed the tip. 'It reminds me of the plump little girl that you once were when you broke it falling off the stable roof . . . I remember how impressed Barny and I were because you did not cry although you hit the ground with a fearful bump!'

'I was determined to show you both that I was as brave as any boy!' Adela countered.

'As indeed you have proved, my sweeting!' Titus said, kissing her again. 'It horrifies me each time I think of you alone in London with Dolly and the children, and what dangers surrounded you! You were very brave!'

'Only because I was ignorant of the dangers awaiting me when I ran away!' Adela said truthfully. 'When we left home, Dolly and I thought that we would have enough money after we had sold Mama's jewels to live quite comfortably until you and Barny came to our rescue! We had not expected to be robbed by highwaymen even before we reached the city! And still less did we expect it would take so long for you to find us!'

The laughter left Titus' face as he said, 'That Fortescue fellow might so easily have taken advantage of you, Addy. Perhaps your extreme youth and innocence were protection of a kind. It is my belief that he intended to seduce you and, since he could not do so by any other means, he stooped to blackmail. Barny and I have often discussed what might have happened to you had Fortescue betrayed your whereabouts to Sir Henry. Child stealing is a very serious crime and you could have been imprisoned!'

Adela shivered.

'Let us not talk of it, Titus. It is long past and it would seem as if I am quite safe now; Kitty, too! I have only Ned to worry about.'

'He is a sturdy little boy,' Titus said comfortingly, 'and does not lack confidence in himself. I doubt if he will be much disturbed by his removal from his sister and the de Falences. If what Father has told me comes to pass, Sir Henry intends to give him everything a boy could want – ponies, guns, rods, toys! And he is not to be denied visits from us all. In another year or two, he will be off to school and will make many friends. No, I have no fears for young Ned!'

Adela sighed.

'Then I will inform Sir Henry that I will bring Ned to him after Christmas. I have promised Eugénie that we shall all remain together for that occasion. Then I shall return with Ned to Dene Place.' She looked up at Titus and smiled. 'Do you realize that this means I shall be living close by you again? We can see each other every day! You will come to see me often, Titus, will you not?'

Titus lifted her off the ground and swung her round as if she were still a child. She gloried in his strength almost as much as in his words as he said, 'Nothing exists in the whole wide world, my love, that would keep me away!'

CHAPTER SEVENTEEN

1792

Adela stood at her bedroom window in Dene Place and stared down into the courtyard below. She pulled her shawl more closely about her shoulders for it was bitterly cold. It lacked two hours to dawn and even when the sun rose, there was little warmth in its early April rays.

It was still pitch dark and the scene below was only discernible by the light of the lanterns carried by the servants. It was the noise of their activities which had awoken her. The men's voices were now joined by Ned's excited treble and the whining of the two dogs – Sir Henry's retriever bitch, Gem, and her yearling puppy, Prince. This dog was Ned's constant companion and of all his father's gifts to him, the most treasured.

Adela sighed as she recalled the previous day's altercation between Ned and his father. Under no circumstances, Sir Henry had declared, would he permit a dog of Prince's age to accompany them on the morrow's duck shoot. He was only partially trained and could not be relied upon to keep quiet. Ned, who was every bit as stubborn as his father, had announced that if Prince were not allowed to go, then he would not accompany his father either!

It had proved no surprise to Adela that Ned had won the day. Sir Henry doted upon the boy and could deny him nothing. If any of her earlier concerns regarding Ned's return to his father had come to pass, this over-indulgence was the only one which had emerged during the three months they had been here. Lord Mallory was not unduly worried about it for

he maintained that Sir Henry's obvious love for his son had
done much to help settle the boy in his new surroundings.

When first told of the future proposed for him, the child
had quite naturally protested, for both Dene Place and his
father were unknown to him and he was already unsettled by
his removal from France, the only country he could remember
and which he had thought of as home. For the first few days,
he was both shy and truculent; but Sir Henry's gift of the
puppy had quickly broken the ice. The white pony that had
followed marked the turning point, and now Ned had become
his father's shadow.

'If he is over-much spoiled, school will soon set him straight!'
Titus had reiterated, so Adela had held her peace. Only when
the subject of guns was raised did she protest. Ned was only
seven years old and far too young to be entrusted with so lethal
a weapon, she maintained. Sir Henry had acquiesced although
he had been hard put to restrain his anger at her interference.
She could not protest, however, when her stepfather announced
that Ned should accompany him on the shoot not as a partici-
pant but as an observer, for there was much to be learned.

Adela brought her thoughts back to the activity below. Sir
Henry was being lifted by four men into a chair which had
been bolted to the floor of one of the farm wagons. Drawn
by two strong carthorses, the wagon was to carry men, dogs
and equipment as far as the edge of the marshland. Once
there, Sir Henry would be lifted down, the chair unbolted and
two stout poles inserted through the iron rings on the sides.
The four men would then carry him along a narrow pathway
to the carefully prepared hide. It was the only way that their
master, still as obese as when Adela had first visited him, could
now enjoy his favourite sport.

There was a knock on the door and Dolly came into the
room carrying a tray. There was a wide smile on her freckled
face as she bobbed a curtsy.

'I reckoned as 'ow you'd be awake, Miss Addy,' she said,
'so I brought you a nice 'ot cup of chocolate.'

Adela took the cup from her and smiled.

'I cannot see how the killing of a dozen poor wildfowl can be worth all this pother!' she said.

Dolly grinned.

'They's good to eat all the same, Miss Addy! Master Ned was that excited I could barely get 'im to stand still whilst I dressed 'im!'

'He is certain to talk at the wrong moment!' Adela said with a sigh. 'I cannot imagine he will keep quiet for a minute, let alone an hour!'

Dolly's grin widened.

'That'll learn the Master not to take 'im next time!' She took the empty cup from Adela and touching her hand, said solicitously, 'You'm be mighty cold, Miss Addy. Best you pop back into bed. 'Twouldn't do for you to catch cold, not with so much to prepare for your wedding an' all!'

Adela allowed Dolly to lead her back to bed, but Dolly's reminder of her marriage would, she knew, prohibit any chance of going back to sleep. Her excitement was too trenchant, her longing to be Titus' wife with all that meant, too intense ever to be far from her thoughts. Whenever he and Barnaby came to visit, which was several times a week, it was all she and Titus could do to refrain from embracing one another. At such times as they discovered themselves alone for a moment, Titus would pull her into his arms and kiss her with such passion that her whole body would tremble. Whenever she glanced in his direction, he would be staring at her or smiling at her, and her heart would melt with love.

'Us'll be starting to make the spare rooms ready today!' Dolly said. 'There's two extra girls a-coming up from Dene to 'elp out with the cleaning.'

The entire de Falence family, with the exception of Eugénie and Philippe, who had returned to France with Kitty, were coming to stay for the wedding. Marguerite and Patience were to be the bridal attendants with Ned as page. Much to Adela's relief, since Sir Henry could not stand unaided, her uncle was to give her away. Barnaby, of course, was to be Titus' best man.

For the past two weeks, the tailor sent down from London by the Comtesse had been busy stitching Adela's wedding gown – a beautiful dress made of apricot-figured satin, the full, hooped panels of the skirt opening at the front to reveal a panel of silver blonde. This lace, which also trimmed the sleeves and Juliet cap, had been smuggled from France, appearing mysteriously one night with Jacques. Lady Mallory had purchased this fortuitous piece of contraband and given it to Adela as a wedding gift! The gown was almost completed and hung now in Adela's wardrobe awaiting only one last fitting.

Would Titus think her beautiful in her bridal finery? Adela asked herself as Dolly left the room. Both her bridesmaids were such pretty girls and she could not endure it if suddenly he wished he were marrying one of them! Eugénie's sister, Louise, was already married, but Marguerite . . . even Barny had come out of the doldrums and paid court to her! She was very like Eugénie – Titus' first love!

Adela snuggled more closely beneath the bedcovers for she knew she had no need to be jealous. Titus had eyes only for her. No girl could have a more adoring lover. Her marriage chest was filled with little keepsakes he was for ever giving her . . . a *Vernise Martin brisé* fan, because she had admired one like it at a Christmas ball they had attended in London; a jade archaistic vase because the colour reminded him of her eyes; a pretty, blue, heart-shaped bottle of scent only three and a half inches long – to remind her that she held his heart too, when she grasped it, he had declared.

Her own heart stirring at the memory, Adela decided that there was little point in trying to return to sleep. She would rise now, and after an early breakfast, assist the maids in making ready the rooms for her aunt and uncle and her two cousins. The chimney-sweep had come yesterday and the heavy window drapes and bed curtains had been taken down to be washed. There was still much to do. The drawers in the heavy oak chests and wardrobes must be relined with fresh paper; carpets taken down to the yard to be thoroughly beaten; windows and mirrors polished with vinegar. Then there were the menus to be given to the cook so that food could be prepared, not only for the wedding feast but for the visitors' sojourn. Despite the fact that Aunt Camille was bringing her French chef with her, who would be assisting Cook with special recipes, a great deal of food had already been prepared. Hanging in the ice-house were five turkeys, ten geese, ten quarters of veal, a quarter of beef, twenty-four ducks and several smoked hams. At Home Farm, the dairy-maids had been kept busy at their churns, and eighty pounds of yellow butter lay chilled on blocks of ice. Cook and her minions were now busy making pies, damson and greengage and quince tarts, and selecting ingredients for the Bride's Pie. In the cold store, cheeses were hanging in their cloths; and in the cellar, Unwin had stacked a shelf with home-made possets and cordials.

For days now, the kitchen-maids had been polishing the baluster glass goblets – a relic of Sir Matthew and Nadine's days; washing the pretty, hand-painted Worcester porcelain plates and dishes. Adela did not want her aunt, the Comtesse, whose own table was always so tastefully equipped, to find her housekeeping inferior!

As Adela went out on to the landing, taking her candle with her for the house was still in darkness, she wondered whether Sir Henry in his new, benign mood, might consider giving her a few of her parents' pieces of china and silver for her future use. She and Titus would be hard put to equip their new home, although as Titus had said cheerfully, they were certain to be given many useful things as wedding gifts. Not that she minded in the very least that they would be poor! Adela had told him. Poverty, in any event, was relative and compared with the conditions she had lived in in London, they would indeed be rich!

'Suppose that Mr Fortescue had ravished me,' Adela had once said, 'would you still have wanted me, Titus?'

Titus did not care to think about those days and preferred to speak instead of the love they shared. He was utterly confident that they would be wonderfully happy together. Only once had he voiced any doubts. With unaccustomed hesitancy he had said, 'Sometimes when Barny and I come to visit you, I have seen a questioning look in your eyes and realized that you were unaware which of us you were greeting. How are you so sure that it is I and not Barny who you love?'

She had been unable to give him a logical explanation for her certainty since to all intents and purposes the twins were still indistinguishable one from the other; their features, their smiles, their mannerisms, their voices, their speech were all identical; they were the same height, of the same build, and even now, in their mid-twenties, they still dressed alike.

'I cannot explain it – I just feel it when I am with you!' she had said with conviction.

'If I had never existed, would you have given your heart to Barny?' he had persisted.

She had had to tell him that she did not know the answer to that question. Love was impossible to describe or quantify or explain, she said. It was simply something she felt for him – and only for him. Could Titus himself give a logical description of 'love'? Whereupon he had shaken his head, laughed and kissed her.

Adela now fingered the ring he had given her to mark their betrothal and with a smile of pure happiness, she made her way downstairs.

As she was finishing her breakfast, some four miles distant Sir Henry's servants were depositing their heavy human load in the hide. Happy to be freed from their burden, they quickly obeyed their master's order and removed themselves back to drier ground some hundred yards away. A damp, white mist hung over the marshes and swirled about their lanterns as they squelched through the boggy ground.

Inside the hide, which had been skilfully prepared of brush-wood, reeds and grasses by Sir Henry's gamekeeper, although it was still dark Ned could discern his father's bulky frame. Sir Henry had drawn out a flask from his leather bag and was taking a quick nip of brandy. He was breathing deeply, for although he had not had to walk, the men had frequently stumbled in the darkness and he had been jolted from side to side. He gave a wry grin remembering the disapproving look on his physician's face when he had told him he was going to take Ned on a duck shoot. If the fellow had his way, he would have confined him to his sick-room, and now that he had his son back, he had no intention of becoming a bedridden invalid.

'Suppose the wildfowl heard us coming, Papa,' Ned whispered beside him. 'Suppose they saw us!'

Sir Henry put his flask back in his bag, his eyes thoughtful. Even now, three months after he had been reunited with his son, he could still not get over the pleasure it gave him to hear Ned call him 'Papa'. His love for the boy equalled only that of his hatred for his stepdaughter. But for Adela, he would not have missed these past three years of the boy's life! Ned still treated him much as he would a stranger, although he was beginning to show more affection of late and would even volunteer a kiss on receipt of a gift. The young dog had done as much to win the boy over as anything else he had given him. The animal was in the adjacent hide with Gem and the loader who would join them shortly before the duck arrived.

'The birds will not come in before dawn!' he told Ned. 'They will be flying in from their roosts to feed in the deeper water over there by those reeds.'

'How much longer must we wait?' the boy enquired. He was impatient for the action to begin. He knew that in former days, his father had gone out in a boat, which he thought would be much preferable to crouching in this sodden shelter; but now his father could no longer climb in or out of the punt because he was so fat! Ned thought him ugly and repulsive, and regretted that Sir Henry did not look more like his heroes, Uncle Titus and Uncle Barnaby. Nevertheless, his father paid him far more attention than they did – or did anyone else for that matter – and gave him everything he asked for.

If it were not for Addy, he reflected, he could do exactly as he pleased from dawn to dusk. She was very strict about his bedtime, his cleanliness, his manners; and he resented the discipline she imposed. He sensed that his father disliked her and felt allied to him because of it. Once, when he had complained to his father that Addy would not allow him to take Prince to bed with him, Sir Henry had said, 'Be patient, boy. Your sister is soon to be married and will no longer be living here!' His tone of voice had been so smug, Ned had known his father would be pleased to see her gone.

What Ned did not know was that Sir Henry fully intended to wreak his revenge upon Adela for the suffering she had caused him and the money he had been obliged to spend on his search for her. In the first place, he had no intention of advising Carstairs' executors that the girl was soon to be married. Although he, himself, could not touch the money Adela's father had put in trust for her, at least he could do his best to ensure that *she* did not receive it!

In the second place, and far more satisfying, was his intention to take Adela to law – and accuse the Mallorys of acting as her accomplices. It would please him to be rid of Lord Leonard Mallory and be free to choose a new parson for the living. The parson might deny he had helped the girl to conceal Ned from him; but there could be no doubt that she had had assistance. For one thing, some of his late wife's jewellery had been returned to him following the hanging of the highwaymen who had robbed Adela on her way to London. With no money, she could never have survived without financial support from one quarter or another.

The parson as well as the girl had outwitted him, Sir Henry had told himself bitterly, and whilst it suited him to pretend for the moment that he had forgiven them, he was merely biding his time. They might well find themselves facing the rigours of prison life before too long – and he relished the prospect, for he would then have unrestricted, unconditional care of his son.

Sir Henry was very well aware that with the law on his side, he could have reported Adela to the authorities immediately upon her return to Dene Place with Ned. That he had not done so was not for the reason others might suppose – that he was afraid of the scandal arising from a court case. It was from fear of setting the boy against him. He needed time to ingratiate himself with his son so that Ned did not look upon him as his enemy.

It was that crafty lawyer of his, Herbert Scrimgeour, who had persuaded him to curb his instincts for instant revenge and to go about achieving his aims in a more subtle fashion. Not only would it take time to obtain an order from the French courts to have Adela and the children extradited, Scrimgeour had pointed out, but such an action could only have the effect of terrorizing the boy to whom his father was a stranger. Who knew how well Adela might have succeeded in painting Ned's father as a cruel blackguard? Would it not look very unpleasant in court if the boy was screaming, trembling at the prospect of being returned to his parental home? On the other hand, if the child was clearly devoted to his father and perhaps viewing his half-sister in a less kindly light, the judge would be only too anxious to clear Sir Henry's name. Adela and the Mallorys would be seen as the guilty parties and society's sympathies would undoubtedly be with the wronged father.

The lawyer's advice, Sir Henry had decided, was excellent in every respect. Not only would his stepdaughter get her come-uppance but so, too, would the righteous parson! Mallory was revered by his parishioners who would not take kindly to his removal unless there were seen to be just cause for it. Meanwhile it served his purpose to play the penitent, and he had had little trouble convincing both Mallory and

the Comte that he deeply regretted the past. As for his son
– Ned was already half won over and was calling him 'Papa'.

His reflections were brought to a halt as he heard the sound
of boots squelching in the wet ground. His loader appeared
at the entrance.

'I've put the decoys out, sir!' he said in a low voice. 'I 'eard
a curlew call just now, so it'll not be long afore them ducks
comes in.'

From the nearby hide, came the sound of a dog whining.

'Dratted cur!' swore the loader. 'Ain't no ways 'e'll settle.'

'Prince wants to be with me!' Ned cried and was promptly
told to be quiet by his father. 'I warned you, Ned, not a sound!
Another word and I will send you back with the men!' He
glanced at the loader, frowning. 'Same goes for the dog,' he
said sharply.

'But how will Prince learn if Gem does not show him what
to do?' Ned pleaded in a whisper. 'Let me look after him,
Papa. I can keep him quiet! He is only whining because he
wants to be with me!'

Sir Henry hesitated. He needed his loader beside him and
Ned's was not such a bad idea for there was not a great deal
of space in the hide.

'Very well, but be quick, Ned. The duck will be here at any
moment and they can spot a movement a mile off!'

Ned needed no second bidding and scampered off to take
the loader's place. A moment later the dog stopped whining
and all was quiet. Sir Henry shifted his bulk, his discomfort
growing by the minute. Despite the covering of branches
laid on the ground, the cold water was seeping into his boots
and his feet were like blocks of ice. His legs, too, were
rapidly growing numb. He gritted his teeth. Come what may,
he was determined that his son should see what a fine shot
his father was. The boy must respect him. As it was, Ned
was forever bragging about the hunting in Normandy where
the Mallory boys – God rot their souls! – had effortlessly
brought down deer, boar, pheasant, quail . . . and duck!

Well, he would not go home empty-handed today; he would see to that.

Glancing out of the aperture facing the weed-covered stretch of water in front of him, Sir Henry saw the first streak of dawn light on the rim of the horizon. The faintest of breezes was stirring the tops of the rushes so that they waved gently to and fro. A few yards away to his right, he could now discern the long dark shape of the punt. It rocked gently on its mooring, the water slapping softly against the sides. Unused these past two years, it was in need of repair. It should have been mended and put away out of the rain, he thought irritably. The air smelt of the sea for although they were a long way from the coast, the river which fed these marshes was tidal.

Sir Henry was familiar with the wide stretches of landscape and although the darkness and the white mist now obscured the pollards and occasional thorn trees, he knew they were there and that he would be able to see them before long. It was a desolate place, and for those unfamiliar with the marshes and the paths that ran across it, treacherous terrain. He was aware that the paths were much used by the local smugglers but benefiting as he did from their booty, he had no quarrel with their trespassing on his land. Not Carstairs' land, but *his*, he told himself with the familiar throb of pleasure this reminder always gave him. The loader touched Sir Henry's arm and pointed skywards, putting an end to his master's reflections. The ducks were winging in in formation, dark shapes against the dawn sky. The foremost one had espied the decoys and was leading the others towards them. Sir Henry took a closer hold upon the stock of his ready-loaded gun and waiting only for the birds to come within range, he fired. With remarkable speed he took the freshly loaded gun from his servant, and less than five seconds after the first report, he fired again. As the fowl took fright and winged away, he fired a third time. Another dark shape splashed into the water some thirty yards distant. He raised his gun for a fourth shot and heard a furious barking as one of the dogs raced out of the adjoining hide and charged into the reeds.

Sir Henry's oaths mingled with Ned's shrill cry.

'Come back, Prince! Come back here this minute! Prince! *Prince!*'

'Demme if I do not shoot the brute!' Sir Henry shouted. He lifted the gun to his shoulder, his eyes following the dog's progress into the marshes. The animal deserved if not to be shot then to be thrashed within an inch of its life. It was quite old enough to know that it should not have moved until the word of command. Only for Ned's sake did he stay his finger on the trigger.

'Send Gem for the birds!' he ordered his loader. 'At least *she* knows what she is about!'

The Labrador bitch was well trained. Moreover, she knew the terrain, and her instinct kept her to the firm ground. Whilst she retrieved a feathery body, Ned remained by the hide screaming at his dog. With no clear idea of what it was supposed to do, but inbred instinct guiding it, the half-grown puppy flopped around in the water trying to reach the first of the fallen birds. Unable to get his mouth round it, he moved off the firmer ground into the reeds where the shallow water suddenly deepened. The reeds, implanted in soft silt and sand, sank beneath his weight so that he was sucked downwards.

Frantically, the dog floundered in a vain attempt to find a firm foothold. His momentum carried him still further forward. His legs impeded by the root growth beneath the surface, he was unable to swim and every minute, he sank deeper into the marsh.

'He's drowning, he's drowning!' Ned screamed. 'Get him out, Papa. Someone get Prince out – he is drowning!'

The loader looked questioningly at his master.

''E'll not get back! 'Tis a sinking bog out there. It's sucking 'im down! Best shoot 'im, sir, and put 'im out of 'is misery!'

Knowing how deeply attached to the dog his son was, Sir Henry hesitated. Ned would hold it against him if he killed the animal. On the other hand, he knew the loader was right. The brute was drowning inch by inch. He raised his gun, but that moment of hesitation was to cost him far dearer than he realized for Ned was now wading into the marsh, waving his arms and still shouting to Prince.

'Get the boy back!' Sir Henry shouted, his face white with shock. 'Get him, man, get him!'

Now it was the loader who hesitated. Even better than Sir Henry, he knew this terrain; knew that folk had disappeared here. Even the smugglers, familiar with the marshes, had been known to lose their lives crossing them!

'Get him! *Get him*!' Sir Henry cried, hitting the man a cruel blow across his back as if to push him on his way. All the time, Ned had been wading deeper and deeper into the water which was now up to his waist as he stretched out his arm towards the dog. The sky was light enough now for the scene to be vividly clear to the two men.

'The punt, sir! I'll get the punt!' the loader gasped. He was shivering violently and stood rigid as a statue as yet again, Sir Henry ordered him to go in after the boy. Then he was out of the hide and on his way to the boat before Sir Henry could stop him. His face was a greenish white and Sir Henry realized that the man was all but paralytic with fear. How could he trust such a cowardly fellow to rescue Ned? he asked himself as, with a string of oaths, he cursed the unfortunate loader.

With a superhuman effort, he dragged himself out of the hide and gasping, scrambled to his feet. Slowly, step by step, he lumbered towards the punt, shouting, 'Help me in, you idiot! Do you hear me? I am coming with you!'

When at last he lay panting inside the boat and the man had poled off from the mooring post, Sir Henry turned to look once more at the marshes. He could see no sign of the dog but Ned, thank God, was still there. The water was now up to his shoulders. Across the marsh, echoing weirdly in the mist, came the sound of the boy's screams. He was no longer calling to his dog but calling for help.

'Hurry, man, hurry!' Sir Henry shouted. With a further effort, he raised himself into a sitting position. Water was slopping round in the bottom of the boat as it lurched from side to side at his shift of weight. 'God rot your soul! Get a move on, damn you!' he cried.

Unbeknownst to himself, tears were now streaming down his face as for the first time he was gripped by a heart-stopping fear. Suppose they did not reach the boy in time? Suppose Ned, his boy, his son, were to drown before his eyes? 'Hurry, hurry!' he urged yet again, only this time, he was begging.

Yard by yard they drew nearer to Ned. Only his head and one arm were now visible. He was silent, his face white with terror, his eyes fixed upon the punt as slowly it edged its way through the reeds towards him. For moments at a time, it became stuck, the reeds and mud too thick and the water too shallow to allow its free passage. Between them, the loader and Sir Henry pushed the boat into deeper water and they made progress again.

The boy's movements were becoming increasingly frantic as he felt the water lap his chin.

'Keep still, Ned! Keep your arms flat. It will help support you!' Sir Henry shouted, his voice hoarse with desperate urgency. He turned on the man beside him. 'Damn you to hell, go faster, faster!'

They were almost within reach of the boy whose renewed screams had become choking gasps as he inhaled great gulps of muddy water. Then the punt became wedged once more amongst the reeds. As if in slow motion, the dead body of the duck that had eluded Prince floated past, its slight weight unhindered by the swampy quagmire beneath the surface. Only the boy's tousled red hair, desperate eyes and one outstretched arm were now visible.

Sir Henry grabbed the pole and leaning over the side of the punt, held it towards the child. Ned was too weak to grasp it. Believing that at long last, rescue had come, he had given way to the cold and fear, and as the muddy water filled his lungs and stifled his screams, he was unconscious of his father's struggles.

''E's going under, sir!'

The loader's voice compounded Sir Henry's own horrified realization that he had arrived too late.

'No, damn it, no!' he groaned. One more yard and he could reach down and pull Ned out, he thought. He had only been under water for a few seconds. He could be revived. He could be saved . . .

With one last mighty effort, he bent almost to the water's surface and stretched out his arm. His heavy weight on the side of the punt caused it to lurch perilously off balance. Water poured in, and as it added to the weight, the boat already low, now sank even deeper. Suddenly it tipped sideways, propelling the huge man into the marsh.

The unexpected momentum also flung the loader off-balance and he, too, was catapulted into the water. Desperate with fear for his life, he clung to the side of the punt, watching helplessly as his master sank to his waist.

'Closer, bring the boat closer!' Sir Henry screamed. He could feel himself being sucked slowly downwards and knew that his weight was against him. Why did the man not manoeuvre the boat to within his reach? What in the name of God was the fool doing? His legs were gripped by mud. His hands, searching for a firm hold, grasped only the floating reeds. It occurred to him then that if help did not reach him soon, he would be too late to save Ned. The boy had not resurfaced and he had felt no solid object.

Tears coursed down his cheeks. He opened his mouth to call uselessly, 'Ned, where are you, boy? Ned . . . Ned . . .'

As his mouth filled with water, he realized suddenly that he, too, was about to drown. He had time only to feel one last, agonizing stab of fear before a strange peace settled over him. Without Ned, life had no purpose. If the boy had gone to his Maker, he would go with him; and if he were damned to eternal hell, it would be no worse than to live without his son a second time.

'Mother of God, 'ave mercy upon 'im!' the loader whispered as the water closed over Sir Henry's head. His white wig remained upon the surface and slowly, inexorably, followed the dead body of the duck out towards the sea.

CHAPTER EIGHTEEN

1792

It was a week before the bodies of Sir Henry Nayland and his son were found and brought home for burial. Every able-bodied man in Dene, including Titus and Barnaby, had been out on the marsh day after day with grappling-irons searching for them. The loader, a gibbering wreck of a man after his ordeal, had seemed unable to locate the exact spot where the two victims had disappeared. 'It all 'appened so quick, so quick!' he kept saying, although at night, when he dreamt of the event, it had seemed like a year between the dog rushing into the water and the final moment when Sir Henry had vanished.

The Comte and Comtesse de Falence arrived two days after the accident, Jacques having ridden post-haste to London to break the news to them. They found Adela inconsolable. It was her fault little Ned had died! she reiterated. She should never have allowed him to accompany his father. She had presaged danger although she had supposed it would come from the guns rather than the marsh itself.

Now, standing between her aunt and uncle in the graveyard, her face was composed. Somehow the Comtesse and Dolly between them had managed to convince her that Ned had been his father's responsibility not hers; that she must endeavour not to think too harshly of her stepfather for at least he had died in a brave attempt to save his son.

Ironically it was a beautiful spring day when they carried the two coffins, one large, one pathetically small, from Dene Church down the mossy path and across the fresh green grass to the newly dug graves. It seemed as if every bird for miles around was singing. Primroses and daffodils had opened their buds overnight, as had the first blossoms of the wild cherry. The tops of the tall, old yew trees waved gently in a soft, balmy breeze and the grave-diggers' tame robin sat watching the procession from his perch on one of the tombstones, his red breast swelling every now and again as he burst into song.

I cannot bear it! Adela thought as, dry-eyed, she watched Ned's coffin lowered into the grave. He should be running through the fields with his dog, laughing, shouting, alive . . .

Feeling an arm go round her shoulders, she turned her head and realized that Titus had come to stand next to her. Both he and Barnaby were dressed like the Comte in sombre clothes. Their father, his white surplice fluttering in the breeze, his bewigged head bowed, intoned the familiar words of the burial service: '*In the midst of life we are in death; of whom may we seek for succour, but of Thee, O Lord, who for our sins art justly displeased?*'

Was God punishing her? Adela asked herself despairingly. Was it sinful of her ever to have removed Ned from his father? Was she wrong to have allowed him to come home? Was Lady Mallory right when she said that it was God's decision that Ned should die so young and that she, Adela, must not take it upon herself to question His will? Whatever actions she may have taken on her half-brother's behalf, Lady Mallory maintained, Adela had done so according to her conscience; and as to returning Ned to his father, she and her husband, as well as the de Falences, had all agreed that it was the right thing for Adela to do.

As her aunt stepped forward, followed by her uncle, each to cast a handful of earth upon the coffins, Adela felt Titus' hand clasp hers.

'Courage, my dearest!' he whispered. 'It will soon be over!'

At least Kitty was not here to see her brother laid to rest, Adela thought inconsequently. The child, always nervous and highly-strung, would have been distraught. But a day past,

Adela had received a letter of deepest sympathy from Eugénie with a postscript saying that Kitty was yet again confined to her bed with a fever which the physician had described as 'the ague'. She hoped Eugénie would not tell the little girl the terrible news of her brother's passing until Kitty had recovered her strength.

With Titus beside her, Adela now threw earth on to her stepfather's coffin and tried yet again to rid herself of her hatred of him. It was no easy task. Not only had he taken her father's place and virtually killed her mother, but now he had brought about Ned's death. She did not want to think of him being 'resurrected to eternal life' for, when her turn came to meet her Maker, she must meet Sir Henry again. It was only when Lord Mallory intoned the Lord's prayer that she found her heart softening. 'Forgive us our trespasses, as we forgive them that trespass against us . . .' She would try to forgive . . . perhaps even, in time, forget; although she would never, ever forget little Ned.

Two hours later, with all but the family mourners departed after their refreshment at Dene Place, the Comte withdrew to the library with Sir Henry's solicitor, Mr Herbert Scrimgeour. When he emerged to rejoin his family in the drawing-room, his expression was sombre and preoccupied.

'A singularly unsavoury gentleman!' he remarked to his wife. 'But perhaps I should have expected no less remembering the man to whom he rendered his services. However, I must not speak ill of the dead, and at least I have received some good news from the fellow.' He beckoned to Adela and the twins and bade them be seated around him. He addressed himself to Adela.

'I have known for some time, my dear, that your late step-father had no close relatives other than a distant spinster cousin residing in Canada. I understand from Mr Scrimgeour that the good lady is in her seventies and in ill health, and therefore unfit to take on the guardianship of you and Kitty. As your uncle and subsequent next-of-kin, I shall assume this role and Scrimgeour could put forward no valid reason why the courts should object to this proposal. My guardianship of you, Adela, will, of course, cease on your marriage to young Mallory. This brings me to one of the pleasanter aspects of my meeting with Scrimgeour this past hour.'

He paused to take a pinch of snuff before blowing his nose and continuing, 'The fellow revealed to me that it was your stepfather's proposal to keep secret from you the fact that on your marriage you will inherit a very worthy sum of money from your father. Sir Matthew had wisely placed this in trust for you but you were too young to be advised of its existence at the time. Your mother did mention it to me shortly before I was denied further access to her, but I have to admit that in the years that have since gone by, it had escaped my mind. Of course, had your father's executors come to learn of your marriage, the legacy would have come to light but it was not Sir Henry's intention to tell you of it.'

'*Mais ça, c'est insupportable!*' murmured the Comtesse. Her husband patted her hand.

'As things have transpired, it is of no consequence,' he said. 'Now we must take this opportunity whilst we are all gathered together here, to discuss the future. Your future, Adela . . .' he said, looking at her. 'I realize that it is only proper that you and Titus should observe a respectable period of mourning. I understand you have postponed your wedding until the autumn, so the two of you cannot take up residence here at Dene Place this summer. The house will therefore have to be closed. Scrimgeour has given me a copy of Sir Henry's will and it comes as no surprise that he has left everything to . . . er, to Ned.'

He glanced anxiously at Adela's pale face before continuing, 'As Sir Henry was predeceased by his son, his worldly goods go by law to his next-of-kin – that is to say, to Kitty! My dear wife tells me that it would be most harmful to bring Kitty back to England; that as the child looks upon Eugénie as her mother, it is best that she should stay with her. Although I shall be her guardian, I proposed to invite my daughter to be guardian of her person. Do you have any contrary suggestions to make, Adela, my dear?'

Adela bit her lip.

'No, indeed, Uncle Hugo – at least, only where Dene Place is concerned. Must the house be closed down? Could I not remain here? It is . . . it was my home—'

'My dear child!' her uncle broke in quickly. 'I had not realized that you might wish to remain here alone. Your aunt and I had supposed you would come back to London and stay with us until your marriage.'

Adela nodded.

'That is kind of you both, and Lady Mallory, too, has invited me to stay with her, but . . .' she paused as she tried to find the right words to express her feelings '. . . there will be a great deal to do here, Uncle Hugo – letters to be written, my stepfather's personal effects to be gone through; and then there are the servants, the tenants. If the house were to be closed, who will look after such things? I think you would find me well qualified to do so, for I know everyone in Dene . . . and Titus and Barnaby will be close by to assist me.'

'But you cannot remain here in this house all by yourself, *ma petite*!' the Comtesse cried. 'It would be most improper for you to live here unchaperoned – *pas du tout convenable*!'

'I will have Dolly with me. Besides . . .' she added with a faint smile '. . . for all I left Dene Place three years ago, *Tante* Camille, it *is* my family home – my father's home. It has many happy as well as sad memories for me.'

The Comte looked uneasily from Adela to his wife and back again.

'I suppose there is nothing against your staying here. In many ways, it would solve a great many problems. I do not underestimate your courage, Adela, but are you quite certain you would be happy here with no more than your maid for company? And what of the future . . . after you and Titus are married? He has had a house built for you. You still intend to live there, I presume?'

The thought had not occurred to Adela until that moment but now, with a sudden lifting of her spirits, she said, 'If Titus will agree, then I would prefer to live here, Uncle Hugo. Someone must caretake the house for Kitty. Barny might like to live in the new house. If he were to marry, he would need a home of his own.'

'What is your opinion, my dear?' the Comte enquired of his wife. 'It seems to me that if this is what Adela wishes, we should do what we can to assist her.' He cleared his throat. 'Before returning to London, I intend to go through Sir Henry's papers and take back to Scrimgeour those that require legal attention. We will need to obtain probate of the will before anything more can be done. Tomorrow, I shall arrange for a sum of money to be paid to you on a regular basis, Adela, for if you are to stay here, it will be your responsibility to pay the servants wages and settle any other household accounts for the estate. Shall I ask Lord Mallory to keep the books for you?'

Adela smiled.

'If you have no objection, Uncle, I think I am capable of managing the accounts quite adequately. It was a task my late stepfather greatly disliked and which frequently he delegated to me by way of punishment! I may have had no schooling, but Lord Mallory will tell you that I am quite proficient where mathematics are concerned.'

'You are a constant surprise to us, *chérie*!' the Comtesse said, rising from her chair and going to put an arm around Adela's shoulders. 'I cannot say, though, that I am happy that you will not return to London where I can take care of you. However, you do have your betrothed, Titus, at your side, and I have no doubt he will be a tower of strength, will you not, Titus, as will your father. I am so sad that you have had to postpone your wedding – that beautiful dress, *chérie*! – and so many other preparations already made! Your uncle and I were only saying on our way down here that we had thought our next visit to you was to be for so joyful an occasion, whereas . . .'

Tears filled her eyes, and for a moment, the two women clung together, each remembering the small boy whose voice and laughter would never be heard again. The Comtesse had not taken to her nephew to the same degree as she had to her sister's other child, Kitty – Ned had been too like his father. Yet the boy had greatly improved during his years in France. Still only seven years old there could have been many further improvements had he lived, despite his father's influence, she reflected sadly.

With an effort, the Comtesse stemmed her thoughts. As her husband had said, it did not do to think ill of the dead, and the poor unfortunate man had not died an easy death. If he had sinned against her sister-in-law, Nadine, against Adela and Kitty, then he had surely paid part of the price when he had had to watch helplessly while the only person in the world he loved, died slowly and horribly before his eyes.

'I still think you should return to London with your uncle and me next week!' she said to Adela. 'This house holds such dreadful memories for you!'

Adela nodded.

'Memories I hope one day to expunge!' she said quietly. 'You will recall, Tante Camille, how happy we were when Father and Mother were alive? If Titus agrees to live with me here after we are married, perhaps we can once more introduce a joyful ambience.'

'And why not?' the Comte said with a smile. 'Adela is very courageous, my dear, and young though she may be, she has an excellent head on her shoulders. We will make a start tomorrow, Adela, to list all that will have to be done. And let us not forget, London is only forty miles distant and we can exchange visits regularly. Meanwhile, I am sure Marguerite would love to come and stay with you, and now that spring is here, the country air would be most beneficial to her.'

Titus stood up and crossing the room, put his arm about Adela's shoulder. He said to the Comte, 'I will be very happy to assist Addy to take care of Dene Place for Kitty! As to the new house, if my brother does not wish to live there, we can find other tenants.' Despite the gravity of the occasion, he grinned disarmingly at the Comtesse as he added, 'Nothing pleases me better than that Addy should remain here in Dene for it will enable me to see far more of her than if she had chosen to go to London.'

Charmed as she always was by the Mallory twins, the Comtesse smiled.

'You know you and Barnaby are always welcome guests at our home!' she said. 'You must escort Adela to London whenever she wishes it. I promise I will not be too onerous a chaperon! Now I am sure you two young people have much to talk over, and as the weather is so mild, why do you not take a walk together in the sunshine?'

Ten minutes later, with their hands entwined, Titus and Adela strolled down the lane leading to the village.

'Your aunt is a very understanding lady,' Titus said. 'I had the feeling she realized very well how *bouleversé* I am at having to postpone our wedding.' He smiled, his mouth turning up delightfully at the corners. 'You see how Frenchified I am becoming, my sweeting? I can think of no better English word to explain my disappointment.'

Adela returned his smile.

'September is not so far away!' she murmured. Her face suddenly clouded. 'Oh, Titus, will we ever again be able to welcome the spring or look with pleasure on the marshes? Poor, darling Ned! I cannot bear to think of those last terrible moments when—'

'Hush, my dearest!' Titus interrupted. 'Barny said only this morning at breakfast that, young as Ned was, he probably had no conception of the fate awaiting him. By the way, Addy, Mother asked me to tell you, she will be calling to see you tomorrow!'

'The flowers she arranged in the church were quite beautiful!' Adela said, momentarily diverted by Titus from her sad thoughts. 'So, too, was your father's address. If there is time tomorrow, perhaps you and Barny would both accompany me on a visit I must make – to . . . to Sir Henry's loader. Dolly tells me he is quite ill. Although he was exonerated of all guilt of negligence at the inquiry, he still feels he should have done more to save them.'

Titus sighed, his eyes thoughtful.

'He could only have done so at great risk to his own life!' he said. 'We can none of us know how we would have behaved in such circumstances. Who am I to say that when given the choice, I would have the courage to risk my life for another?'

Adela looked up at him, her eyes darkening to a deeper green as she said urgently, 'Promise me you will never risk your life, Titus. I could not bear the thought of having to live without you! Promise me!'

He touched a ringlet of hair which had escaped her bonnet and said gently, 'You would not wish me branded a coward, Addy! But I will promise never to risk my life needlessly.' His tone lightened as he added, 'I can assure you that now I am about to share my life with you, I have every intention of living to a ripe old age! Life has never been more precious to me!'

He touched her lips with his own, saw the colour flood her cheeks and was newly astonished at the immensity of his love for her. Her suffering these past ten days had been his, too. Mercifully it had fallen to him to break the terrible news of Ned's death to her for one of the villagers had run to the parsonage following upon the accident, and he had been able to ride immediately to Dene Place and soften the telling before one of the servants could blurt it out in horrible detail. The sheer horror of those days had brought him and Addy even closer.

If there were one thing else which marred the joy of loving Addy and knowing himself equally loved by her, it was his awareness of his twin's distress. Although Barnaby did his best to conceal his suffering Titus was too closely attuned to his

twin not to feel it as if it were his own. He knew that Barny's
flirtation with the pretty Marguerite de Falence was but his
way of showing the world his indifference to Addy's preference
for Titus.

Adela, his mother and father, all believed Barnaby to be
genuinely interested in the pretty young girl; but Titus knew
better. He could feel the sudden tensing of his twin's body
whenever Adela's name was mentioned; detect the bitter look
in his eyes when someone spoke of their forthcoming wedding.
He had even noted a look of relief on Barnaby's face when
he heard that the marriage was, in deference to the dead, being
postponed yet again.

So disturbing was this knowledge to Titus that far more
often than he realized, he demanded assurances from Adela
that she was certain as to which of them she loved. It had
several times crossed his mind that if she harboured a single
doubt, he would step aside, no matter what the agonizing cost
to himself. It was one of the disadvantages of being an identical
twin, he thought; to be so closely linked that he felt the same
mental and physical pain as his brother.

Recently Barnaby had taken to laughing off this notion.

'Because when we were children, your wrist hurt when I
twisted mine, and I had the toothache when you did, it is no
proof of our like feelings,' he argued. 'We wanted to be the
same in all things so we imagined we felt what the other was
feeling. As to our cutting our teeth and learning to walk on
the same day, such events would be only too likely seeing that
we were born within minutes of each other. And what more
natural than that we should have measles and other such
ailments together? As to our both loving the same girl . . .
well, we have both known and loved Addy since our childhood. No, Titus, we are not two halves of the same person
even though we may often have pretended to be. Believe me,
I am very happy about your betrothal and I have quite got
over my own disappointment.'

Despite all Barnaby's protestations, Titus did not believe

him, and it hurt him to think that his present happiness should be the first thing in their lives they were unable to share.

'Your aunt and uncle are very trusting, Addy, to leave you alone with only Dolly for chaperon!' Titus said now as they resumed their walk. 'They can have no idea what thoughts keep me awake at night! How can they be sure I shall not come to your room one dark night and ravish you in your lonely bed?'

Adela smiled, although her cheeks were hot and her heart was beating fiercely as she replied, 'Perhaps you would find my bed empty since I might be on my way to find you!' she countered.

Titus drew a deep breath.

'If you say things like that to me, Addy, I swear I shall not answer for my actions. I want to take you in my arms and kiss you until you cry for mercy! I want to hold you against my heart and never, ever let you go. How shall I ever wait now until September?'

'Or I!' Adela whispered. 'Yet I am glad in a way that our wedding is not to be for a while yet. Perhaps by September, our sadness will have lessened a little. If we were to marry shortly as we had planned, we should have little Ned's ghost haunting our bridal chamber. Oh, Titus, shall I ever be able to forget?'

He brushed away the tears that were now falling slowly down her cheeks.

'No, my dearest, you will never forget the little fellow, but you will begin to remember only the happy times you shared with him. And never forget that you were the one who made these past three years so contented for him. He loved his life at the Château Saint Cyrille, and no one knows better than you what his life would have been like if you had not taken him away from here when you did. Even now when I remember what you endured at that time for his sake even more than for Kitty's or your own, it makes me shudder. Now let us talk of happier things. Did your aunt bring news of Eugénie, Philippe, Kitty and young Robert?'

Her tears drying, Adela nodded.

'There was a long letter from Eugénie. Philippe never writes for he dislikes putting pen to paper! Kitty has the ague but Eugénie's physician says she is in no great danger. Little Robert is well and walking, but poor dear old Madame Evraud died in her sleep last month. Eugénie asked me to tell you that her *belle-mère* often spoke of her pleasure at the way in which you and Barny paid court to her on your last visit – as if she were a girl again! Eugénie herself is in good health and enjoying Philippe's company, although she maintains that he broods too often about the King.'

'Surely the King is in no danger now?' Titus asked.

'No, but the power now lies in the hands of the Citizens' Assembly whose ministers are pacifists. Philippe went to Paris to meet with some of the Chevalier's friends, and it seems the King wants war with the Austrians. According to Philippe, the King is certain the Army would lose the war and that if they, the Austrians, were to win it, they might restore him to power. As you know, Titus, the Austrian King, Leopold, is Queen Marie-Antoinette's brother, so he is behind the King. *Tante* Camille told me my uncle had written to Philippe forbidding him to become involved; but as Eugénie said in her letter, Philippe is almost twenty-five years of age and old enough to form his own views and make his own decisions. She therefore doubts that even if my uncle ordered it, Philippe would return to England.'

'If I were in his shoes, I am not sure that I would do so,' Titus said thoughtfully as they turned back the way they had come. 'After all, Addy, England is not Philippe's country. The Comte told me that the situation in France worsens by the day, and that the numbers of priests and nobles who have emigrated has escalated beyond calculation. It is hardly surprising now that the Assembly has declared that those *émigrés* who did not return to France last month were guilty of conspiracy and would be sentenced to death and their property confiscated. Your uncle is deeply concerned about the fate of his estate in Normandy although all is at present quite quiet there.'

Adela nodded.

'I think Eugénie fears Philippe may try to join the army of *émigrés* some four thousand strong who have joined the Austrian-Prussian-Dutch coalition encamped on France's borders. Uncle Hugo is deeply concerned for the royal family. He says Mr Pitt is determined to keep this country neutral and that we shall not go to the King's aid.'

'To be honest, it surprised me that the Comte should have chosen to become an *émigré* when he did,' Titus said thoughtfully.

'He had *Tante* Camille and the girls to think of!' Adela replied. 'He is a very responsible man!'

'And before long, I, too, shall have responsibilities!' Titus said with a smile. 'One, at any rate. But we shall have children, shall we not, my sweeting? Many of them, I hope, to fill that large house of yours!'

'Twins, perhaps!' Adela said happily. She did not see the slight shadow that crossed Titus' face and, knowing nothing of his present concern for Barnaby, she continued, 'Identical twin sons, looking like you and Barny. I should love that.'

'As I said before, Addy, I should prefer for a start a little girl with black hair and the same beautiful green eyes as her mother! With a less fiery temper, though!'

'For gracious' sake, Titus, that is a most unjust accusation—' Adela began but broke off as she realized Titus was teasing her. The smile returned to her eyes. 'Even as a boy, you knew how to nettle me!' she said. 'I used to think it was Barny who did so, but now I am certain it was always you. Barny is too kind and gentle a person to enjoy vexing me!'

'Fiddlesticks!' Titus said emphatically. 'Barny was as often at fault as I! We loved to watch your cheeks turn pink and to see you stamp your little feet. Most of all we enjoyed it when you grew so cross you tried to butt us like one of those little goats you kept as pets.'

Adela gave a mock sigh as she smiled at the memory.

'You were both too nimble for me, I suppose because you had learned the art of feinting when you fenced. It astonishes me now to recall how much I loved you both, horrible little boys though you were!'

'We loved you, too, despite your tantrums!' Titus said, his face serious once more. 'Upon my life, Addy, I consider myself the most fortunate of men. I have so little to offer you, it surprises me that your uncle and aunt have not raised objections to our marriage.'

'Uncle Hugo is quite happy with our union for, as he said, although you are far from wealthy, you will one day have a title to offer me! As for *Tante* Camille – she has been happily married to the man she loves for the past thirty years, and she truly believes that love is far more important in a marriage than wealth. How grateful I am to Papa for leaving me a dowry to bring to our marriage, Titus!'

'It is as well I did not know of it before I proposed marriage to you, else you might have suspected that I was marrying you for your money!' Titus remarked with a grin. Adela's answering smile was, however, very brief.

'We might never have known of it if Sir Henry had lived,' she said quietly. 'I fear he was determined to punish me in one way or another.'

'I shall never forgive him for the unhappiness he brought you!' Titus replied. Determined, however, to keep Adela from brooding, he was smiling once again as he said, 'Small wonder Father says I am quite unsuited to follow his example and take Holy Orders! I fear I lack most of the Christian virtues – mercy, temperance, pudicity, forbearance—'

'And what, pray, is pudicity?' Adela broke in laughing.

'Purity, I believe!' Titus replied, his smile deepening. 'I wish I could tell you I had led an entirely chaste life, my dearest Addy, but alas, it would not be true.'

'You have loved . . . other women?' Adela asked hesitantly.

Titus' voice was serious now as he said gently, 'I have known other women, but I have never loved anyone but you, Addy, and that I can sware to upon my honour!'

The moment of jealousy and pain Adela was feeling was short-lived. Titus was almost twenty-five years of age, and it would have been unnatural for him to have led an entirely celibate life. Moreover the feelings now stirring within her whenever Titus kissed or touched her, had given her an understanding of the passions that could so easily set fire to the human body. Titus' kisses, she thought now, were no longer enough. She needed to be closer still; she needed her body to merge with his; she needed to become one with him. That inexplicable, deep yearning she had so often felt lying awake at night, sometimes when she had heard the nightingale singing to its mate in the gardens of the Château Saint Cyrille, had become crystallized when Titus first kissed her. More even than his spoken words of love; she wanted *him*, his strong, lean body; his hands . . . hands that when they touched her breasts, seemed to make them spring to life, as did her whole body. All too frequently now, she found herself remembering the horror she had felt when she had first seen men and women coupling in the darkened alleyways in London. Now she understood a little of their urgency and she longed to experience such intimacies with the man she loved.

Titus halted and placed his hands on her shoulders. His face was anxious as he stared down at her.

'Has my confession upset you, Addy? Do you love me the less because of it?'

With difficulty, Adela found her voice.

'No less, Titus! I, too, have a confession to make concerning purity. I am a virgin, yes, but . . . but my thoughts are often very far from pure!'

Titus gave a shout of laughter and regardless of who might suddenly appear round a corner of the lane, he hugged her fiercely to him.

'For that, I can but love you more, my adorable, wicked wife-to-be! And I had thought myself incapable of greater love than I already felt! Oh, Addy, my dearest, we are going to be so very happy together! I am a lusty fellow and what would I have done with a wife who did not share my pleasure in our coupling?'

His kiss – less restrained and longer-lasting than usual – banished the lingering memories in Adela's mind of the tragic deaths of Ned and Sir Henry, and the circumstances that for a while longer must keep her and Titus from consummating their love.

CHAPTER NINETEEN

1792

At the end of April, the Comte de Falence and his wife went back to London. Titus and Barnaby accompanied them and returned a few days later with Marguerite. Adela was delighted to have her cousin's companionship for, although she had thought she would not mind living alone at Dene Place, she was often lonely. In the daytime she was busy about the affairs of the household and estate, but in the evenings as it grew dark, memories of Ned's heartbreaking death would come creeping back into her mind.

Only a year older than Adela, Marguerite kept such unhappy thoughts at bay for she was a jolly, happy-natured girl with an agreeable disposition. Since childhood, she had known the Mallory twins and was not in the least shy in their presence. Both Titus and Barnaby were frequent visitors and since Titus and Adela were betrothed, she gave most of her attention to Barnaby.

Noticing how cheered Barnaby appeared by Marguerite's happy chatter and ever-ready smiles, Adela was in no doubt that he had got over his disappointment regarding herself, and she encouraged the friendship between them.

Now that the month of May had arrived, the evenings were lengthening and several times a week, Adela and Marguerite were invited to the parsonage for dinner. On such days Dolly would accompany them and Jacques would be given the afternoon off work so that they could go together to the village to make ready Nou-Nou's cottage for their married life. Jacques had finally found the courage to propose marriage and Dolly had accepted him. Their wedding was now to take place the following spring. The faithful, devoted maid had insisted upon postponing her own nuptials so that she could remain at Dene Place with her young mistress.

On one such visit to the Mallorys, however, Jacques was absent. Taking Adela to one side, Titus told her with a smile that the valet had been abroad on one of his smuggling adventures. The parson, though aware that there was hardly an able-bodied man in the village who was not involved in this illegal trade, did not feel justified in publicly condoning such illegalities. However, like so many other compassionate people, he understood that many of the participants would have been hard put to keep poverty at bay were it not for the generous wage a man might be paid for helping to off-load or conceal the smugglers' cargoes. A farm labourer at best earned no more than twelve shillings a week whereas he could be paid half a guinea for a night's work concealing the contraband brought in from the coast. Dangerous as it was, the smugglers did their utmost to protect their men and, should they be caught, to take care of their families. Lord Mallory chose, therefore, to pretend ignorance of the activities of most of his male parishioners.

The twins were in the process of accompanying Adela and Marguerite back from the parsonage to Dene Place in the family coach when Jacques came galloping after them. His clothes, face and hair were covered in dust and it was clear that he had been riding hard for his horse was heavily lathered.

'Is something amiss?' Titus enquired as he drew the four carriage horses to a halt. 'You look hotter than a smith's forge!'

'Indeed it is, Master Titus, Master Barnaby!' Jacques gasped as he fought for breath. 'We was caught in the early hours this morning on the beach. Some got away but nine of us was taken by the officers – me, George Robinson and seven others.'

He paused briefly to catch his breath before resuming his tale.

'First we was taken to The Dog and Duck and locked up. Presently we saw twenty dragoons riding up which was to escort us to the magistrate. Soon as they'd 'ad their break-fust, they fetched us outside and whilst we was in the yard awaiting to go, some of George's men as 'adn't been caught took the soldiers by surprise. Next thing, I was 'auled up behind one of 'em and as we galloped off, there was shots. Soon as I could, I found out what 'ad 'appened to the others. Two was shot, five like me got away, but they've still got George. 'Tweren't nothing to do about it for the officers knew as 'ow 'e were the leader, and four of 'em kept 'old of 'im. 'E didn't 'ave no chance. Now 'e's sore in need of 'elp if 'e ain't to 'ang.'

By the time their valet ceased talking, Titus and Barnaby had guessed why Jacques had come hot-speed home with his story. Robinson was the smuggler who had not only helped Addy on her way to London, but had later done his best to enlighten them as to her whereabouts there. At the time, they had instructed Jacques to tell the smuggler that if there were ever anything they could do to repay his kindness to Addy, he had but to ask.

'Do you know where he is being taken?' Titus asked.

'They were off to Rye to find the magistrate,' Jacques replied. He wiped his forehead with his kerchief, his face now taking on an even greater look of concern. 'Afore I were rescued, I 'eard the officer what was in command say they'd 'ave George sent to trial in Lunnon, if'n they could; that there was too many folk as were in sympathy with George in this county and 'twas certain sure the jury would be bribed if'n 'e was tried 'ere. One of the soldiers said as 'ow there were a reward for George's capture, 'e 'aving killed two riding officers; and they want 'im 'anged!'

Titus frowned.

'Is it true — that he has killed two men?'

Jacques shook his head.

'No, it ain't, Master Titus, though . . .' he added with a

shake of his head '. . . I'll not vouch for it that 'e wouldn't kill a man as threatened 'is life, no more would you nor me, sir! George be a lawless man right enough but he ain't a violent one as would kill for the pleasure of it!'

'Then we must do what we can to help him,' Titus said quietly. 'Go back to the house and get something to eat, Jacques, and tell Fred to harness our horses. You will be needing a fresh one, by the look of it. You have ridden that poor beast over hard! Be off with you now. We will be back as soon as we can.'

Adela had been listening silently whilst this interchange took place. Now, as Titus picked up the reins, she put a hand on his arm.

'If I heard correctly, you are going to attempt to rescue George Robinson, are you not?' She noted the gleam of excitement in his eyes and her own narrowed. 'Please tell me what you plan to do. You know you can trust me to be discreet.'

Titus grinned.

'The party of dragoons will not ride as swiftly as Barny, Jacques and I; and it is certain that they will not risk riding after dark. We shall discover where they are lodging with their prisoner and make our way there.'

Adela frowned.

'What you are about to undertake will be dangerous,' she said doubtfully. 'You are only three against twenty! If anything should happen to you . . .'

Titus regarded her thoughtfully.

'You do not seek to detain me, my sweeting?'

Adela's chin lifted defiantly.

'You cannot expect me to remain silent whilst you and Barnaby go riding off to rescue this outlaw and perhaps get yourselves shot in the process!' she said quietly.

'I intend no such violent confrontation. If Robinson is to be taken to London, he and his escorts will have to make many stops before they reach there. If we cannot find an easy way to relieve the officers of their burden at the first staging post, then we shall try again at the next.'

The expression on Adela's face changed from worry to excitement.

'Let me come with you!' she said. 'You know how fast I can ride, so I shall not delay you.' Seeing that both Titus and Barnaby were about to burst out with furious protests, she added quickly, 'I might well succeed in creating a diversion. No one would suspect a female of trying to rescue a smuggler! You both know that is true. I could distract the officers' attention . . . have the vapours, perhaps, or pretend a flirtation with one of them so that you, Titus, can confront him . . . suggest a duel perhaps . . . whilst Barny and Jacques do what they can to release Robinson.'

To her surprise, Titus was smiling.

'Will you ever cease to amaze me, Addy? How has such a well-thought-out scheme come into your head? Nevertheless, I cannot allow it. It would be far too dangerous.'

Adela's green eyes flashed.

'How so, with you and Barny and Jacques to protect me if the need arose? Do you doubt your ability to do so? For shame, Titus!'

'Hah! So you challenge me, do you? Well, the answer is still no. I promised your uncle I would look after you, and so I shall. I shall take you and Marguerite home this very minute, and there you shall stay!'

'And if I will not?'

'Then I shall carry you into the house by force!'

'And lock me in the cellar as Sir Henry did, I suppose!' Adela countered wickedly. 'Marguerite can stay at home with Dolly, but my mind is made up – I shall come with you.'

Barnaby, who had been listening to this spirited exchange with growing anxiety, now supported Titus' view. If anything, he was even more emphatic than his twin as he refused to allow her to accompany them.

Adela turned from one to the other, her eyes now pleading.

'Let me come with you! When we were children, you never denied me a share in your adventures. You used to say that my daring was equal to that of any boy! And have I not proved that I am no senseless female who cannot take care of herself? Besides, it is I, not the two of you, who owe Mr Robinson a favour! I give you my word that if there is a hint of danger, I will remain out of sight. Please, Barny! Please, Titus!'

The twins looked at one another anxiously. Neither was finding it easy to resist her pleas, least of all Titus who could refuse her nothing.

'Demme if we do not allow her to come with us!' he declared. 'What say you, Barny, old fellow? 'Tis true Addy could create a diversion for us and there will be three of us to see she comes to no harm. Moreover, the presence of a female would allay their fears if they are suspecting a rescue attempt.'

The officers would certainly not fire upon a woman, Barnaby told himself, and Addy would not delay them for she rode every bit as well as either of them. Nevertheless . . .

'Barny, you agree, do you not? Please say that you agree!'

Looking into Adela's eyes, Barnaby knew that he was powerless to refuse. His love for her had not lessened one jot in the months of her betrothal to Titus. If anything it had deepened with the need to conceal it. When he saw the two of them holding hands, gazing into one another's eyes, speaking of their approaching marriage, it was all he could do to stop himself from crying out so great was his pain, his sense of loss. Again and again, he would lie awake at night asking that unanswerable question: *Why does she have to love Titus? Why could it not have been me?*

He longed for the day when his love for her would fade and, hopefully, die. It might be possible were he never to see her again; but his love for Titus was as strong, if very different from his love for Adela and because of it, he could see no release from his suffering. Even to be faced with living under a different roof from his twin was wretchedness of one kind, yet he suffered in their presence and longed to leave the room when he saw them sharing a smile or a look that excluded him. It might be easier to bear if he could hate the girl Titus had chosen for a wife; but he loved Adela . . . he loved her as devotedly, as passionately, as enduringly as did Titus.

'If you come, you must promise to do exactly as we tell you!' he said, and quickly closed his eyes when, impulsively, Adela flung her arms around him and kissed his cheek.

As Adela reached the house and raced upstairs to change her clothes, leaving Dolly and Marguerite standing in the hallway, mouths agape, she had barely time to pacify them before she rejoined the twins who were waiting impatiently in the morning-room.

'You watch after Miss Addy now, Master Titus, Master Barnaby!' Dolly said, finding her voice as she stood on the doorstep to wave them goodbye. 'You tell Jacques from me that if aught 'appens to 'er, I'll not marry 'im, see?'

Their laughter was dimmed by the sound of the gravel churning beneath the horses' hooves as they set off down the drive; but there was no smile on Dolly's face as, with a sigh, she went back indoors with the disconsolate Marguerite. Close to tears of anxiety, all the French girl could do was wring her hands and repeat, '*Mon Dieu, mon Dieu!* Whatever would *Maman* and *Papa* say! *C'est une folie, une bêtise!*'

Dolly also considered it madness, but as Adela rode through the woods between the Mallory twins with Jacques safe-guarding their rear, she was too full of exhilaration to be afraid. For the most part, she enjoyed wearing pretty gowns and going to parties, especially now that she had Titus at her side; but even as a little girl she had preferred the adventure of raiding the orchards or sailing their home-made raft on the duckpond with the boys, to playing with dolls or dressing up with Patience. It was as well Patience was staying away with one of her friends, she thought as twilight began to fall,

for she would surely have told Lady Mallory what was afoot
had she known what they were about!

Despite the short cuts they were taking through the woods,
once darkness fell, they made only slow progress unable to
ride fast amongst the trees. It was therefore nearly midnight
before they reached the coaching inn at Northiam. Once there,
however, they learned from the landlord that the dragoons
had passed by with their prisoner at midday and were heading
north for Wrotham where they planned to stay the night.
George Robinson was, of course, well known to the landlord,
and although he did not recognize Adela from her brief visit
three years before, he was acquainted with Jacques.

'George knows The Bull in Wrotham!' Jacques said eagerly.
'We might get 'im out o' there, if'n we can think on a way
to do it!'

Each of the two private parlours available to gentlemen, he
recounted, had the usual big fireplaces. Inside one of them,
well known to Jacques, was an iron ladder by which a man
could ascend to the rooftop. The difficulties of using this means
of escape were threefold – one, that at this time of the year,
the fire might be lit; two, that the dragoons would for a
certainty lock their prisoner in an upstairs room; and most
important of all, that by mid-morning, when the rescue party
might expect to arrive at The Bull, both prisoner and escort
would have departed.

An hour passed before the twins and Adela devised a way
by which they might overcome these difficulties. The last was
their first concern. Titus called to the obliging landlord to
bring him paper, quill and ink, and between the three of them,
they composed a letter in as legal phraseology as they could
imagine, requesting that the dragoons keep their prisoner in
Wrotham until they received further orders from the magistrate.
With a flourish, Titus signed the name of the Rye magistrate
who had replaced Sir Henry after his death and who, by good
fortune, was an acquaintance of his father and therefore known
to him.

Jacques was then detailed to ride to Wrotham and, at dawn, present himself to the dragoon officer as the magistrate's messenger.

'We shall have to solve the other difficulties when we reach The Bull,' Titus said. 'Now for some much-needed rest for we must leave at dawn if we are to reach Wrotham by mid-morning.'

'Should we not leave now with Jacques?' Adela asked.

Titus shook his head.

''Tis better we time our arrival with one of the coaches if we are to appear as normal travellers. We must not give the soldiers any reason to connect us with Jacques.'

Barnaby nodded.

'I was thinking the same. As far as the fire is concerned, if 'tis lit, could we not demand that it be put out?'

Titus grinned.

'You and I could play the parts of two foppish Jack-a-dandies who cannot abide the smoky fumes.' He leaned forward eagerly as he warmed to Barnaby's plan. 'Adela can create a diversion and whilst you and I watch with our backs to the fireplace, Robinson will have to slip up the chimney behind us.'

''Appen it could work,' Jacques said doubtfully. 'If luck is on our side, mayhap 'e'd not be noticed. But what if they keep 'im locked in a room upstairs as landlord said 'appened 'ere?'

For a moment they were all lost in thought; then Adela said, 'The officers will be fretting at the delay and doubtless be bored with the inactivity. If we make friends with them, encourage them to drink with you, perhaps flirt a little with me, I can get them to tell me about their prisoner and request that he be brought downstairs so that I might see him – never having seen a smuggler before. Then I shall have an attack of the vapours in order to distract the soldiers, and after that, it is up to George Robinson to make his "disappearance".'

'Demme if Addy has not hit upon a most excellent scenario!' Titus said with enthusiasm.

'If we play our parts adequately, it could work!' Barnaby agreed, turning his head aside as Titus put his arm around Adela's shoulders and kissed the top of her head.

'So, to bed then!' Titus said yawning. 'Be off with you now, Jacques. We will elaborate the details of our little play on our journey tomorrow. Come, Barny, stir yourself. We will escort Addy to her room.'

Like all coaching inns, The Bull was alive with activity as shortly before midday, Adela and the twins rode into the courtyard. There was a moment of anxiety when Titus requested the private room containing the escape ladder and was informed by the landlord that it was already occupied by a worthy merchant. Titus waved both hands in the air in the most dandified of fashions.

'No matter if it costs me a king's ransom,' he drawled, 'I must have privacy, for I cannot tolerate these noisy, common travellers!' He waved a handkerchief in front of his nose. 'Pray tell the worthy merchant I will be happy to recompense him for any inconvenience if he will remove to the other room.' He tapped the landlord on the shoulder and in a confidential tone, added, 'You may think it strange, my good man, but I cannot abide to dine in a room which does not face the south!'

With an attempt to refrain from smiling, Adela said sweetly, 'M'lords will see that you are well rewarded for your trouble.'

Having made the landlord aware that Titus and Barnaby were both titled and wealthy, it was only a further five minutes before the occupants of the room they wanted had been evicted and Adela and the twins installed.

Seeing that the fire had been but newly lit, the twins were able justifiably to complain of the damage the smoke was causing their delicate lungs. Only too happy to oblige these prestigious milords, the landlord instructed the yard-boy to remove the smouldering logs forthwith whilst he departed to the cellar to fetch some of his very best French wine. As soon as the yard-boy had finished his task, Titus examined the chimney. It took only a few minutes to locate the lower rungs of the iron ladder four feet above his head.

'Robinson will have to jump for it,' he said doubtfully, 'for there is little height to be gained by standing on one of the firedogs! We must hope he is more nimble than he looked when last I saw him!'

As the landlord returned, Adela addressed herself to him.

'You appear unusually busy!' she commented. 'I thought I saw uniforms as we passed the tap-room. Do you have the Army encamped here?'

'No, m'lady, 'tis a platoon of dragoons. They have a prisoner upstairs – a smuggler – as is being took to Lunnon for trial.'

Adela clapped her hands.

'But how intriguing! Did you hear that, m'lords? The dragoons are here with a prisoner. My faith, I have not been so diverted in years. Pray invite their officer to partake of a drink with us. I would hear more of this smuggler.'

'If you insist, my dear!' Titus said in bored tones. 'Personally, I find most army fellows exceedingly boring. They talk of little else but battles and guns! So tedious, do you not agree?'

'Be good enough to do as the lady asks and invite the gentleman to join us!' Barnaby took up his cue. ''Twill pass the time whilst we await our repast. We shall expect a good one, landlord. I trust your wife is as good a cook as your wine is palatable? Be off with you now!'

Once more alone, Adela dissolved into laughter.

'I shall begin to suspect that you are both dandies at heart,' she said, 'for you play your parts most convincingly.'

'As did you, my love!' Titus said, his brown eyes alight with amusement.

With little difficulty, Adela and the twins continued with their charade. Before long the young dragoon officer was captivated by Adela's winning smiles and obvious interest in his exploits. He was delighted to be admired by so charming a young lady and wondered, privately, why she was in the company of two such effeminate aristocrats. Nevertheless, he was intrigued by their identical appearances and in the way they synchronized their movements and completed each other's sentences.

Slowly Adela brought the conversation back to the prisoner.

'I shall not leave here without setting eyes on him!' she declared prettily. 'Imagine the tale I shall have to tell my friends!' She gave an exaggerated shudder. 'Not only a smuggler but a murderer, you say? I suppose he will be hanged – a fearful but just fate, of course.'

'Perhaps I could take you to have a quick look at him, m'lady!' the officer said. 'He is handcuffed to the table so he can do you no harm.'

Adela pouted.

'But I cannot walk, sir – that is to say, not without pain. I fell from my horse whilst riding here and twisted my poor ankle.' Limping, she moved closer to the officer and rested a hand on his arm. 'Can you not bring him to me, sir?' she pleaded. 'With a strong man like you to guard me, I would have no fear.' She smiled coquettishly. 'Oh, what sport this is! I have not enjoyed such diversion in many a month. Life can be so tedious at times!'

The officer concealed a smile for he was only too ready to believe that this most feminine of young ladies would quickly tire of the company of the jack-a-dandies she was with. They had been engaged in a discussion about the new style of wigs they intended to purchase in London. One of them now looked at Adela with disapproval.

'Really, my dear, what possible interest can you have in a murderous villain? He is sure to be evil smelling and foul mouthed.'

'Not fit company for you at all, my dear!' Barnaby said, shaking his head and taking a pinch of snuff.

'But I *want* to see him!' Adela cried, pouting prettily. 'And this kind officer has agreed that I might, so why must you spoil my fun?'

Titus yawned.

'Oh, very well, my dear, if you insist!'

With an effort Adela kept her eyes averted from those of the twins as the officer departed upstairs. Her heart was beating furiously and she knew by the way Titus' fingers were drumming on the edge of the table that he, too, was tense and alert. Would George Robinson recognize her? she wondered. He would certainly recognize the twins. She held her breath.

There was little doubt that from the moment he entered the room, the smuggler recognized them all. After one quick look, he kept his eyes on the floor. Titus sauntered across the room to where Robinson stood. With a sigh of relief, he noted that there were no chains about the smuggler's ankles or wrists and that his hands were but loosely tied together with a rope. A single guard held the end of it as one might secure a dog on a leash, but its thickness was such that it could be cut with a single stroke of a sharp knife.

Titus noted with growing excitement that a carving knife lay in readiness for their repast on the sideboard, and a glance at Robinson's face revealed that he, too, had noted its presence. It remained now only for them to create an adequate diversion to allow Robinson to attempt his escape.

'Can you not make the fellow look up?' he asked the guard in a petulant tone. 'I have heard it said that one can look into a man's eyes and see at once if he is good or evil. This one looks a surly fellow right enough!'

Robinson let out an oath and spat on the floor for which he quickly received a blow to the side of his head.

''Tis the likes of you as'll come to watch me swinging in the wind!' he said with bitterness. 'But you'll drink to my eternal life, I doant doubt, in the brandy I've risked my life to bring you! And you, my fine lady, where did you buy that pretty lace jabot you're a-wearing, eh? Think on that when they puts the rope around me neck!'

Adela gave a little scream and moved closer to the officer

as if for protection. As she did so, Titus stepped forward and grabbed Robinson by the collar.

'You mind your manners, sir, when you address a lady,' he said petulantly. 'I demand an apology. Yes, an apology! Do you hear me, fellow?'

The eyes of the officer and the guard were upon the smuggler as he now sank to his knees and mouthed apologies to Adela, begging her to take pity on him and intercede on his behalf. Adela gave yet another scream.

'Why should I pity one who has robbed others of their lives?' she declared.

'Devil take you then!' Robinson said, jumping to his feet. 'May you rot in hell like me for you have no mercy in your soul!'

As Adela swayed, Barnaby took up his cue. He pushed aside the guard and caught the prisoner by his shirt collar.

'You shall be punished for this, you wicked fellow!' he cried. 'Can you not see the lady is about to faint?' He elbowed Robinson out of the way and glared at the officer and guard. 'Apologize this instant or I shall . . . I shall challenge you. Yes, that is what I shall do, I shall challenge you, sir, for allowing this young lady to be terrorized, nay insulted, in this shocking fashion!'

Adela stepped quickly forward, allowing Barnaby to move back to the fireplace beside Titus.

'You must not blame this gentleman for my carelessness, m'lord!' she reproached him. She caught hold of the officer's arm. 'Please find me a chair so that I may sit down, I beg you. Oh, dear, I feel quite faint!' She looked up appealingly at the dragoon. 'M'lord is always duelling, you see, and I cannot bear to see it . . . and really, sir, you were not in the very least to blame!'

Reaching out to grab hold of the guard's arm, she sank to the floor, her eyes closing as she did so. Titus and Barnaby were now stationed in front of the fireplace. As the guard bent simultaneously with the officer to assist Adela, he let go the end of the rope securing the smuggler. Exactly as they had hoped, Robinson slipped unnoticed into the inglenook, behind the twins, grabbing the carving knife on the way. On the second attempt, he reached the lowest rung of the ladder and within a matter of seconds, he had disappeared. But a single minute had passed since Adela's feigned collapse.

She was now making a prolonged but noisy recovery, demanding hartshorn to revive her, an arm to support her, and an explanation as to what had happened to cause her to faint. Only as she was finally helped by the dragoons into one of the chairs did the guard notice the absence of the prisoner.

''E's gone, sir, 'e's got away!' he shouted with an agonized glance at his officer.

With one accord, the two men made a dash towards the doorway into the passage. The customary noise in the inn now rose to a crescendo as the dragoons ran from room to room demanding if anyone had seen their prisoner. Four of the soldiers who had been drinking in the tap-room were despatched to the yard to ride off in pursuit of the missing man. The others continued their fruitless search of the inn. When the officer finally returned to the parlour some fifteen minutes later, his face was scarlet and his voice barely controlled as he said angrily, 'Thanks to you, m'lords, our man has escaped. 'Tis likely I shall lose my rank for this, if indeed I am not cashiered!'

Adela sobbed into her handkerchief.

'It is I who am to blame! I should never have asked to see that horrible brute!' she wept. 'I cannot tell you how distressed I am.'

Titus stepped forward.

'My dear fellow, we owe you an apology. Now do rest assured, if your men do not recapture the villain, my brother and I will speak personally to your senior commander. The blame is entirely ours, and I shall see to it that you are vindicated.'

'Influence in the right quarters, you understand?' Barnaby

said vaguely. 'Now do be seated, sir, and the landlord shall bring you a cognac. I think you are in need of it! Lud, but what a to-do!'

With a look of barely concealed contempt, the officer declined the offer of a drink and with obvious reluctance, bowed before leaving the room. He knew only too well that no matter what these two dandies might say in his defence, the fault would be laid at his door for allowing his prisoner to leave the security of his room. It was all too often that captured smugglers escaped their escorts, but nearly always such escapes followed upon an attack by well-armed bands of their confederates. Many a dragoon had lost his life in such a rescue. If they were outnumbered, there were no recriminations from their superiors; but *he* had lost his prisoner without so much as a single musket fired! Whatever their titles, these useless aristocrats would not be able to save him from disgrace, he thought bitterly. His only hope for his future career lay in finding the prisoner. At least the fellow could not have got far, and the sooner he himself joined the hunt the better.

'I almost felt sorry for him!' Adela said when eventually the last of the dragoons had left and the inn had calmed down. She turned to Titus, her eyes shining. 'It worked! I could scarce believe the soldiers would not see or hear Robinson as he scrambled up that chimney. Although my back was turned, I heard the sound of his boots against the bricks! I tried to drown the noises with my moans. Oh, Titus, Barny, do you think he got away? Will they catch him?'

The answer to her question was quickly answered. Jacques came into the room, a grin so wide upon his face that his mouth stretched from ear to ear.

'George be safe and sound in the dog kennel!' he said. 'It being so small like, they ain't thought to look there. Come dark, landlord's a-going to 'ide 'im for a day or two in the churchyard. There's a tomb there as safe an 'idy-'ole as ever there was. When all's clear, our George'll be agoin' to lie low for a bit with 'is cousin in Dover where the Excise won't be lookin' for to find 'im. 'E doant be none the worse for his nabbing and 'e said to thank you . . . you special, Miss Addy!'

Adela gave a sigh of satisfaction.

'It went so well, I am still finding it hard to credit,' she said. 'Luck was on our side, was it not? We planned our part well enough, but how did Robinson know we intended to make it possible for him to climb up that ladder in the chimney?'

'Because I tolt him!' Jacques said with yet another grin. 'As you know, Miss Addy, I ain't never learned to write, but I can draw. I drew a pitcher of the fireplace and the ladder and a clock showing twelve, and I screwed the paper up and put it in the bread 'e were getting for 'is breakfust. 'E's no fool and when 'e saw 'is chance, 'e took it right enough.'

'Oh, Jacques!' Adela exclaimed. 'You are no fool either; but suppose Robinson had swallowed your drawing?'

'That 'e did surely, Miss Addy, but 'e seed it furst!'

'Well done, Jacques!' Titus said warmly, but his face clouded momentarily as he added, 'But you, too, will have to lie low for a bit, will you not? That dragoon officer will doubtless be telling his superiors of the spurious note you delivered to him from the Rye magistrate.'

Jacques grinned.

''Tweren't me as gave it 'im, Master Titus. I axed landlord to give it 'im for me. That there officer doant know me from Adam! Now I reckon as 'ow 'tis time we went 'ome afore them soldiers cum back asking ork'ad questions.'

'But first we will partake of our meal!' Titus said. 'We do not want to appear to be leaving in a hurry. We are innocent of any complicity in Robinson's escape, remember? Thanks to Jacques' foresight, we are in no danger here.' He crossed the room and put his arm around Adela's shoulders. His voice was gruff with emotion as he said, 'I doubt we would have been successful without you, too, my love! You were matchless. You and I made a perfect team, did we not?'

As Titus kissed her cheek, neither he nor Adela noticed the desolation on Barnaby's face for he had just realized that for the first time, Titus' reference to the twosome had excluded him.

CHAPTER TWENTY

1792

Preparations for Adela's wedding to Titus were all but complete. Lady Mallory had yet to decorate the church with flowers, but she and Adela between them had already filled every available vase in Dene Place to welcome the Comte de Falence and his family who were to be Adela's guests for the two weeks prior to her marriage. Dolly, agog with excitement, had already pressed the beautiful wedding gown that had been hanging in Adela's wardrobe since the postponement in April.

It seemed as if the whole world was trying to make amends for that unhappy day, Adela thought as she awaited the arrival of her family. The farmers had had a wonderful harvest and the sun seemed to have made up its mind to shine the whole summer through.

If there were one single reason for regret, it was that Eugénie, Kitty and Philippe would not be joining them for the wedding festivities as they had planned. The political situation in France had grown even more serious. In June, a mob armed with pikes, axes, swords, muskets, roasting spits and cudgels had broken into the royal palace and confronted the King. His Majesty had been offered the choice of cockades – the white one of the old regime or the red, white and blue one of the revolution. The mob had thirteen thousand National Guards to support them and the King had placed upon his head the red bonnet signifying '*liberté*' to the mob. Eugénie had written in French:

How long will it be, before His Majesty is again challenged to accept the Rule of this rabble? The Marquis

has written to tell me that our Armies are so depleted
of their Officers – who are defecting across the Borders
– that it is not surprising the Austrians have advanced
through our Lines so swiftly. He says that the entire
Regiment of the Royal-Allemands has since defected *en
masse*.

Philippe has been recently to Paris and tells of Food
Shortages there and that the Revolutionaries are now
suspecting everyone of being Traitors to their Cause.
They all wear the bonnet *rouge* to identify what they
call the Patriots, and anyone not wishing to Risk their
wrath now wears this red hat. Needless to say, Philippe
refuses to do so!

The last part of her letter was as worrying, although for very
different reasons.

I fear I may not after all be able to come to England for
your Wedding. It breaks my heart to think I shall miss
it but I have to tell you Kitty is once again stricken with
the Ague – and more besides. She has had a bad Cough
throughout the summer and now she coughs Blood. She
has lost a great deal of Weight and although our Physician
is doing all he can, he will not even consider her travelling so long a Distance next month. He tells me it may
be many Months more before she regains her Strength.

As you know, chérie, Kitty has become as Dear to me
as my own little Robert and when I spoke of going to
your Wedding, she begged me not to leave her. I know
you, of all People, will understand that I cannot do so
however much I may Wish it. There is little Doubt she
would fall into a Decline were I to absent myself, and I
know you would not want me to take this Risk.

'I will press some of the flowers from my wedding bouquet
and send them to poor little Kitty!' Adela said to Dolly as

they put the finishing touches to the big bedchamber that had once been her parents' room and was soon to be hers and Titus'. They had just hung the new linen curtains round the large tent bed and Dolly was grinning as she stood back to admire it.

'I reckon as 'ow you and Master Titus'll be snug as two bugs in a rug in there and noways wanting to be up with the larks!'

Well aware of Dolly's meaning, Adela felt her cheeks grow hot for she, too, had been imagining how it would feel to lie in this secret cavern in Titus' embrace. These past weeks the tension between them had increased to the point where they could hardly bear to part when evening came; and must be forever touching one another's hand or arm. When their eyes met, they held one another's gaze and the blood would race through Adela's body with the need for his arms around her, his lips on hers, his strong firm body to be pressed against her own. At night she lay wakeful, restless, unfulfilled and knew that he did so, too, for he had told her so. Was it possible, she asked herself now, that Dolly – her round-faced, freckled, cheerful little maid – harboured the same consuming passion for her Jacques? She could not believe it possible, for the twins' valet was over forty years of age, and yet Dolly was eagerly awaiting her own wedding date.

'No one has ever loved another as dearly as I love you!' Titus had declared, his voice deep and urgent, his brown eyes bright with fervour. 'I shall love you till I die – and into the life hereafter. Swear to me that if I were to die, you will never marry another – as your mother did! One should not speak ill of the dead, yet when I remember how Sir Henry treated your mama . . . Promise me you will never marry if, God forbid, I am taken from you?'

How easy it had been to give that promise, for she could not imagine ever again feeling as she did about Titus . . . and this even before their marriage.

At the sound of coach wheels crunching over the gravelled driveway, Dolly hurried across to the window to stare down into the courtyard below.

''Tis them, Miss Addy! They's 'ere!' she cried. 'I rekondize the de Falence crest on the carriage door. Oooh, Miss Addy, you should see your aunt's travelling cloak! 'Tis ever so smart! And the coachmen are in new green-and-silver liveries!'

Smiling, Adela removed her apron and handing it to Dolly, ran downstairs to greet her relatives. In the hallway behind them, the de Falence servants were depositing numerous boxes and parcels.

'Wedding presents, *chérie*!' the Comtesse said as she embraced her niece. 'Since we had room in our second carriage, we thought it practical to bring them with us rather than entrust them to a carrier! Now let me look at you. *Ma foi*, how pretty you are, child! No wonder your Titus is in love with you!'

'He and Barnaby will be joining us for dinner!' Adela said as she returned her aunt's kiss and enjoyed her uncle's customary bear hug. 'And tomorrow, Lady Mallory and Patience are calling to pay their respects. Lord Mallory is performing a christening in Udimore but has asked me to convey his good wishes and to say he is looking forward to renewing your acquaintance at the wedding!'

'We must hope this fine weather continues!' the Comte said jovially. 'Happy the bride the sun shines on, eh?'

The fine weather was, indeed, quite perfect on Adela's wedding day. The tiny village church in Dene was full to capacity as Titus' father performed the service. Only those of the villagers who were sick and infirm failed to be present in the churchyard to strew flowers, herbs and rushes before the happy couple as they emerged from the shadowy interior into the bright morning sunlight that beat down upon them. If some remembered that day not twenty weeks past when they had similarly attended the double funeral of Sir Henry Nayland and little Ned, they, like Adela and Titus, pushed such memories aside, intent upon enjoying this happy event. Many of the older men and women had known and loved Sir Matthew Carstairs and were happy to see his daughter marrying the son of their own loved and respected parson. An ox was to be roasted on the village green and as much ale, cordial and ginger wine as could be consumed awaited the local population for their celebrations. They cheered heartily as the carriages of the gentry departed one after the other to the big house, and it was time for them to begin their own feasting.

Alone for a brief five minutes whilst they were driven from the church to Dene Place, Titus took Adela in his arms.

'At last – at long last, you are my wife!' he said. 'And soon, my beloved, I shall make you truly mine!' He kissed her passionately before adding, 'No bride ever looked more beautiful! And how charming Patience and Marguerite looked in their attendant's gowns. I think Barny noticed them, too. Would it not be splendid if Barny were to fall in love with your cousin? Now that I am a married man, I am most anxious that he should be as happy as I! Look, my dearest, what wedding token he gave me last night!'

He produced from an inner pocket of his pale grey velvet coat, a gold watch chain fashioned from two linked strands twisted around one another.

''Tis intended to remind me of our close brotherhood, Barny said, and that he would always be close by if I needed him! He had it fashioned especially by the goldsmith.'

'What a lovely thought!' Adela remarked as she returned the chain to him. 'Was he pleased with the snuff-box you gave him?'

Titus grinned.

'I think he was touched by the entwining of his initials with mine,' he replied. 'He knows I am not as a rule given to sentimentality but I did want to reassure him that my marriage to you in no way diminishes my closeness to him. Now I know the same idea was in his mind!'

Yet how could their relationship remain unchanged? Adela wondered as later that night, she lay in Titus' arms. In sealing the bonds of their marriage, she and Titus had experienced moments of joy, passion, tenderness and love that could never be shared with another. She knew without asking that Titus would never speak of their love-making to Barnaby, for it was theirs alone and their happiness indescribable. If Titus had proved insatiable during those long hours of darkness, then so, too, had she. After the first brief moments of pain, she had felt her body respond with a desire she could never have imagined. It was truly as if she and Titus had become one entity and that only as one, could they have reached such heights of happiness.

Much as Adela loved her aunt and uncle and her cousins, she was nevertheless guiltily pleased to see their carriages departing the following morning, for it meant that she and Titus could be alone together once more. Dolly had been right, Titus remarked with a smile, when she had foretold that they would be loath to leave the privacy of their bedchamber! Nevertheless, they took time on the second day of their married life, to walk to the village so that they could thank all the people who had presented them with unexpected gifts – a lucky horseshoe from Dodds, the smithy; a corn dolly from Quincey, the thatcher; a beautifully carved wooden cheese scoop from Coombes, the carpenter; a cask of brandy from the landlord of The Shepherd's Arms. 'Undoubtedly contributed by George Robinson and his cronies!' Titus had said, laughing, when it had been delivered to Dene Place.

Arm in arm, he and Adela called in to drink a cup of Hyson tea with his mother. Barnaby was out riding with Jacques, Lady Mallory told them, omitting to add that he had opted to be out when they called. In her motherly way, Frances Mallory was well aware how acutely this second son of hers was suffering, not only in the separation from his twin, but in the finality of Titus' marriage to the girl he, himself, still loved. Time would soften the pain, she prayed and, God willing, Barnaby would find some other young woman who would make him as happy as her dear Adela was making Titus. How well matched they were, she told her husband later, for both looked radiant with their new-found unity.

It was a happiness that was not to last beyond their third day and night together. As they breakfasted on the following morning, one of the Comte's servants arrived from London with an urgent letter for Titus. The Comte had written:

I hate to be the sender of Bad Tidings at such a time, but my Wife and I returned home to find a Letter awaiting us from our dearest Eugénie.

It is with the deepest Regret that I have to inform you of the Death of our little Grandson, Robert. Eugénie tells us that the poor Child escaped the vigilance of his *Nourrice* and wandered over to the Folly where he disturbed a Viper. Had a Ligature been applied immediately it might have been Possible to save his Life, but by the time the *Nourrice* found him and realized that the Serpent had bitten the Boy, the lethal venom had infiltrated his Body and he was beyond Saving.

Please break this News gently to Adela for I know she will be Heartbroken on Eugénie's behalf at this needless Loss of Life. My Wife wished to travel at once to France to comfort our Daughter but I have had to Forbid such an undertaking for the following Reason.

Unbeknownst to us, Eugénie has been giving sanctuary to the local Cleric this past month. Two weeks ago, Philippe arrived back at the Château from Paris bringing with him an Abbé who had, with his help, escaped Death at the hands of a rabble of Revolutionaries. Our Son's part in the Rescue was observed and he can now only enter Paris in disguise. Eugénie says it is imperative that the Curé, Monsieur l'Abbé and Philippe should be smuggled back to England at the Earliest Opportunity. She suggests that Jacques will know a way of effecting this as the fugitives could not hope to travel by packet since the Ports are now watched for *Emigrés*.

I have given the matter much thought and have decided I cannot request that you, Titus, should leave your Bride so soon after your Wedding. However, perhaps you could suggest to Barnaby that he accompany Jacques on this dangerous Mission. I know that Eugénie would not have written for assistance were she able to call upon the help of any of her servants, many of whom, I suspect, are not to be trusted; and those that are would be too easily recognized by any local People loyal to the Assembly.

My dear wife is distraught both with concern for Eugénie's bereavement and with anxiety for Philippe's safety. I must confess that whilst I applaud his Courage, he cannot be allowed to continue with these dangerous activities. Barnaby, should he go to Normandy, must ensure that our Son returns with him. Eugénie does not think that Barnaby will be in any immediate Danger, but he must, of course, consult with Lord Mallory before undertaking the Journey. Barnaby has not previously been involved with the uprising in France and in any event, is of English nationality. Moreover, although France may be at war with Russia and Austria, they have not yet declared war on England!

Our fondest love to my dear Niece, Adela, who will, I do not doubt, be as devastated as we are by the Tragic and unseemly Death of our Grandson. At least she can look forward to the return of her Half-Sister, Kitty, in the near future for I am writing Today to Eugénie to insist that she travels to London as soon as the little girl can undertake the Journey.

As Titus read the letter to her, Adela watched his face across the breakfast table. Her cheeks had paled at the news of little

Robert's death. Poor darling Eugénie, she thought, to lose first her husband and now her only child! Not only this but her life as well as Philippe's might now be in danger. Without any indication from Titus, she knew that he wanted to be part of this plan to bring the refugees back to England. Nevertheless, as he met her eyes, he said quickly, 'Of course, I shall not suggest I go with Barny. As your uncle says, it would not be fair of me to leave you so soon after our wedding.' He attempted a smile.

With an effort, Adela kept her voice steady.

'We are too close-knit now for there to be pretence between us!' she said quietly. 'Just as you know how I am feeling, so I, too, know what you are thinking. At this moment you would like to be free to go where you will, without a wife's restraining hand. If you do not go, it will be only from consideration for me. Tell me truthfully, Titus, is that not so?'

His expression was rueful – almost guilty – and so like that of a small boy with his prank unmasked that Adela almost smiled.

'I know you do not want to be parted from me – any more than I can endure the thought of being parted from you,' she continued. 'Nevertheless, I realize that you could not be happy allowing Barny and Jacques to go without you. Seeing you unhappy would make me so – and I should feel guilty for being the cause. Go if you must, my love. I'll not seek to detain you!'

Titus hurried from his chair to hers and drawing her to her feet, he put his arms around her.

'You are as generous in your thinking as in your loving!' he whispered against her hair. 'But I will not leave you. In any event, Jacques will have to make two journeys. The cutter will only take four people – perhaps five. With Eugénie and Kitty, Philippe, the Abbé, the Curé, Jacques and Barny, the rescue cannot be accomplished in one sailing. Perhaps I might go on the second crossing!'

It was a compromise solution which Adela would have been more than happy to accept had she not seen Titus' expression

when he returned from his ride to the parsonage. Barnaby and
Jacques were hoping to sail on the night tide, he informed her,
trying to keep the envy from his voice as he elaborated their
hastily convened plans. Their father had readily given his
consent to this mission of mercy, and provided Jacques could
provision the cutter and have it made ready in time, by morning
they should be nearing the Normandy coast.

'I know Mr Titus longs to go with them!' Adela bemoaned
as later she recounted the day's events to Dolly who was
helping her to change into one of her new afternoon gowns.
'I told him once more that I would not demur if he leaves
me; but he is too kind-hearted and will not do so.'

Dolly bit her lower lip as she frowned in concentration.

'I've a good idea, Miss Addy . . .' She sucked in her breath
and then let it out in an excited gabble. 'Mr Titus doant leave
you on your ownsome, Miss Addy, *you goes with 'im.* You
ain't sea-sick like wot I am and you'd be a right comfort to
Miss Eugénie; an' you'd see Miss Kitty; and if'n Miss Kitty
ain't well enough to come 'ome directly, then you and Mr
Titus could stay on at that there château together.'

By the time Dolly paused to draw breath, Adela's face was
as excited as her maid's.

''Tis a splendid idea, Dolly!' she cried, but then her smile
vanished. 'But will Titus agree to it? Oh, Dolly, he must, he
must! He'll say there will be danger, but I do not care about
that if I am with him. He would take care of me . . . and . . .'

She broke off to hug Dolly before rushing away downstairs
to find Titus. He was in the gunroom, cleaning his pistols. He
looked up guiltily as she burst into the room.

'It is only in case I should need them at some future date!'
he said.

Adela laughed.

'Which may be sooner than you think!' she cried. 'Titus,
listen, and do not interrupt me, I beg you, until you have
heard me out.' Choosing her words with care, she outlined
Dolly's 'good idea'. 'It is a far better compromise than yours,

my love,' she ended, 'for we shall neither of us be obliged to sacrifice our wishes for the other.'

Slowly, Titus put down the pistol he was holding. His face was sterner than she had ever seen it.

'I will not allow you to risk your life!' he said flatly. 'And it could come to that, I do not doubt. Obviously you have not stopped to consider quite how dear you are to me. How can you imagine that I would permit you to accompany me on such a dangerous mission? We intend to spirit away two wanted clergymen from beneath the very noses of the revolutionaries. We could be shot for spies. No, my love, I will not allow you to take such risks!'

Adela's head shot up and her eyes flashed a brilliant green as temper replaced disappointment.

'Are you not as dear to me as I appear to be to you? Am I not to care that *you* risk *your* life? What difference is there between your feelings and mine, Titus Mallory? None – but that I am a female. Eugénie needs me – I have no doubt of it.'

'I cannot allow you to risk your life for no better reason than that you wish to accompany me,' Titus repeated quietly. He put out his hand, but she turned away from him, her body rigid.

'I have loved you for a long, long time, Titus!' she said. 'When first I knew it, I think I was six years old. I had fallen out of a tree and when I did not cry, you turned to Barny and said, "Our Addy has a courage equal to that of any boy!" And I loved you because you respected me as an equal. Well, I have not changed since then, but *you* have. You treat me now as someone who must be cosseted and coddled as if I were some stupid girl given to the vapours! I could be of equal use to you as . . . as Barny!'

'That is not true, Addy, and you know it.'

Addy's chin lifted.

'I can speak French as a native and since I am half French by birth, I could pass as a Frenchwoman if the need arose. I could pretend Philippe was my servant; or the Curé could be disguised as such.'

Although Titus was silenced by the truth of this suggestion, he remained unmoved. Much as he longed to put an end to this – their first marital dispute – he could not bring himself to agree to her wishes.

'I have told you I shall not go with Barny and Jacques. What more do you want of me?' he asked, his voice cool.

'I do not want your sacrifice, though you make it on my behalf. Eugénie needs help; Philippe, too, and it is your duty to assist them whether you wish to do so or not. Let us not argue further on the matter; if you are going, I shall go with you. My mind is made up on this point. I assume that it is not your intention to lock me in the cellar – as did my step-father – to prevent me doing as I wish?'

'Devil take it, Addy, you know I would never do such a thing!' Titus began indignantly, but seeing the hint of a smile touching the corners of her mouth, he too smiled.

'Despite your vow to "Obey" as well as to "Honour" and "Love" me, I should know better than to expect obedience from you, of all people, my love!' he said. 'What can have possessed me to take such a wilful female to wife? I should have chosen a gentle, sweet-opinioned girl like Eugénie!'

'And so you might, had she not been bespoke to another!' Adela said. 'I was once so jealous of the love you had for her!'

'A boy's adoration, no more!' Titus insisted, moving to put his arm around her. 'You are my only true love and ever will be!'

'Then you will take me to Normandy with you?'

The smile left Titus' face.

'It seems I have little choice in the matter!' he said, sighing. 'But upon one condition, Addy – that you will give me your word to obey me without question. I meant it when I said we could be in great danger, and I will need my wits about me which they would not be were I to be worrying as to what you were about.'

'I promise, I promise!' Adela cried as she covered his face with kisses. 'And I swear I will not be a burden to you. If need be, I can disguise myself as a French peasant. I have a natural ear for language and I can speak the Normandy dialect as well as Parisian French. And do not forget that I learned to live like the poor in the squalid quarters Dolly and I shared in London. I know how they speak! How they think! How they behave! And I am well accustomed to cold, hunger, hardship—'

'Enough!' Titus broke in. 'It is not my intention that you shall endure any such privations. God willing, we shall travel from Rye to the Normandy coast without interruption; and if the weather favours us, we shall make the crossing to the cove they call Anse Goéland without difficulty. Now it is time we both made ready. You must take only the bare necessity of clothing for there will be no room for baggage. A warm cloak; stout shoes; gloves . . . indeed, I have a mind to lend you a pair of my breeches since Jacques, Barny and I will be clothed as fishermen. Were it not for those long black tresses of yours, you could be our cabin-boy and would attract less attention when we reach France.'

'Have no worry on that score!' Adela cried, her eyes brilliant with excitement. 'I shall pin up my hair and tuck it beneath a woollen cap. I will even go barefoot if it please you, Cap'n!'

Despite his inner concern, Titus smiled as she touched her finger to her forehead in a passable imitation of a young tar.

'I realize you are joshing, Addy, but this is no game! It could be that lives are at stake.'

'I know, Titus!' Adela said, her voice now serious. 'That is why I must go with you. If anything were to happen to you . . . well, I would want it to happen to me, too, for I could not live without you . . . not now. I love you so very much. Nothing matters to me now except that we are together.'

Titus' kiss was no less ardent than Adela's voice, but even as they left the gunroom, arms around each other, the deep

frown of worry still creased his forehead. He knew without
question that Barnaby would condemn him for his weakness
in allowing Adela to accompany them . . . and others would,
too – the Comte and Comtesse, his parents, perhaps even
Eugénie. If anything were to happen to his beloved Addy, it
would be his fault for giving way to her persuasions. Had he
done so simply to please her or because it allowed him to go
with Barny on this particular adventure with a clear conscience?
To have left Addy so soon after their wedding would have
been cruel – or at least heartless. And she *could* be of assistance! None knew better than he how cool she was in a crisis;
how resourceful; how courageous; how daring. There lay the
trouble, for Adela had little thought for her own safety when
her spirit ran high. Barnaby knew all this, and the more he,
Titus, considered it, the more likely he thought it that his twin
would refuse adamantly to set sail with Adela aboard; that
he would insist she return home alone with the coachman.
Would he then feel obliged to abandon his own desires and
go home with her?

'I have been thinking these past few minutes, Addy!' he
said as they reached their bedchamber. 'Perhaps you should
travel in disguise – at least until we are well out into the
English Channel. Barny might not be as easily persuaded as
you have found me, and I very much doubt if Jacques, either,
will be in favour of you going. You can keep in the shadows
whilst we are preparing to embark and conceal yourself in
the little cabin when Barny and Jacques are busy about their
business. What say you, my love?'

Adela's eyes shone as she regarded him.

'A moment ago, I would have sworn on my life that I could
not love you more than at that moment. Now I know I was
wrong. We think as one now, Titus, for that same idea was
already in my mind as you spoke. We are both afraid that
Barny will forbid my going!'

'And not unreasonably!' Titus admitted ruefully as Adela
hugged him. 'It will be your task to mollify him when he

discovers the truth for I fear he will be very angry with me. Although he pretends otherwise, I am in little doubt that his devotion to you still runs deep, albeit he denies it. He will berate me as surely as I would berate him were I in his shoes.'

'He will forgive you later if not sooner!' Adela said. 'When must we leave, Titus? Will you send word to the parsonage that you are to accompany them after all? What carriage shall we take? Will we eat on the way to Rye or shall I ask Dolly to get the servants to prepare food for us to take with us? And I must ask her to bring me coffee to stain my face and hands. My skin is too fair for me to pass as a cabin-boy.'

Titus was watching her as she paced the room, his eyes following the lithe young figure which curved so temptingly that he could think of little but his growing desire for her. He glanced at his timepiece and saw that it was not yet three o'clock. They were not departing until sunset and there was time enough for loving.

As Adela passed by, still chattering excitedly, he caught her by her arm and drew her to him.

'Do not call your precious Dolly yet awhile!' he said in a low voice. 'If you agree, I can think of more urgent business to attend to than making ready for our journey. Addy, my love, my sweeting, my wife . . .'

They fell upon the bedcover and impatient with the impediment of their clothing, their hands reached out to touch and to hold one another. The excitement of their proposed adventure added still further to the passion which now flamed between them. Three days of marriage to Titus had dispelled all inhibitions Adela might have had, and now she could give herself to him and take from him with an ardour which matched his own. There was no time to draw the bed-curtains, no time to remove all their clothing; no time even to turn the key in the door. They were conscious only of each other; of the need to be close, closer, moving as one until at last they could cry out in shared release from their hunger for harmony and unity.

When at last she could draw breath and speak, Adela looked up at Titus' flushed face and with a smile, whispered, 'We should quarrel more often, my love, if this is to be the outcome! If it were not for the tragic news of little Robert, I would be so happy I could die of it!'

'Do not speak of death,' Titus said quickly, covering her face with kisses, 'lest you remind me of the dangers and I change my mind. I had always believed myself decisive and yet . . . do you understand my dilemma, Addy? I want you with me, always, always, always, and at the same time, I want to go to Philippe's and Eugénie's aid. I should not take you with me, but I cannot bring myself to leave you. What spell is this you have cast upon me, my dearest girl? Is it not strange that once I believed I could not be happy without Barny beside me? Yet now I know it is you who makes me feel most fully myself.'

'Poor Barny!' Adela said softly as she traced the outline of Titus' lips with her finger. 'We have so much – and he has lost so much in that he must live his life without you beside him. We must not allow him to feel too alone, Titus. At least he will be happy you are journeying with him, will he not?'

'Indeed he will – until he discovers you aboard!' Titus said with a wry smile. 'Come now, my dearest, 'tis time we began our preparations. I will send a message to Barny to await my arrival. Meanwhile, let us see this miracle of your transformation, for to tell you the truth, I cannot conceive how you will turn such a truly delectable female body into an urchin's image.'

'You will see!' Adela said as reluctantly she disentangled herself from Titus' embrace. 'I did not spend two months in Mr Fortescue's theatre with my eyes blindfolded. There were many times when I took costumes to and from the cast's dressing-room and saw how skilfully they applied their paints and powders.'

So well was Adela disguised that not only Titus but Fisher, Sir Henry's coachman, failed to recognize Adela when three hours later she approached the carriage from the servants' quarters. Brusquely, the coachman ordered the 'boy' to get up on the back with the Master's valise and be sharp about it if 'he' did not want to feel the whip about 'his' skinny little legs.

CHAPTER TWENTY-ONE

1792

'I am so very happy to see you both!' Eugénie cried as she embraced each of the twins in turn. Her cheeks were pale and there were deep shadows beneath her eyes as she looked from one to the other. 'I have never been in greater need of assistance,' she said in a low voice, 'and just to see you gives me fresh courage!'

She smiled briefly at Jacques.

'It is good to see you, too, Jacques!' she remarked. 'You must be hungry, tired. You and the boy will find plenty of accommodation . . . many of our servants have left, you see.' With a frown, her glance turned again to the lad standing quietly at Jacques' side. 'You have been here before?' she questioned. 'Your face is familiar, boy, but your name escapes me . . .'

'I had thought that you of all people would have recognized me at once!' Adela said as she ran forward to hug her cousin. She was a little shocked but not altogether surprised by the pallor of Eugénie's cheeks. It was after all but a few weeks since she had lost her only child. This was not the moment, Adela sensed, to offer her condolences.

'You must find me some proper clothes for I have brought nothing with me,' she said brightly, adding with a smile, 'although I must confess, I have become quite attached to these breeches. They are so much easier to manage than our skirts and petticoats! Do you know that when we rode here on our hired nags, I had no need of a side-saddle? It reminded me of my childhood when Papa allowed me to sit astride the farm horses.'

'Adela, you are *nonpareille*!' Eugénie cried. 'But why the disguise? No one questioned you, did they? You are not suspected?'

'I will explain everything later!' Adela said quickly with a sideways glance at Barnaby. His face was unsmiling and she knew that he had still not forgiven Titus for permitting her to practise the deception upon him. When he had discovered her at sea an hour from the English coast, he had been white with anger. Nothing that she or Titus said could placate him and but for the bare necessities of speech, he had not addressed either of them since that first outburst.

'He will get over it!' Titus had said reassuringly; but so far, Barnaby had given no indication of doing so.

'How is Philippe?' she asked, as much to change the conversation as from a genuine desire to know that her cousin was safe and well.

Eugénie's expression deepened to one of grave concern.

'In great danger!' she said in a low voice, glancing about her to ensure that none of her servants was within earshot. 'He is in hiding with the Abbé and our Curé. When it is safe, I will take you to see them. First you must wash off the dust of your journey and then eat. Your old rooms are made ready for you. If you will come with me to my room, *chérie*, I will find you a gown, and then you will wish to see Kitty!'

'How is she?' Adela asked eagerly. '*Tante* Camille is most anxious about her, as, indeed, are we all. We were so sad the two of you could not be at our wedding.'

'Ah, yes, the wedding!' Eugénie said sighing. 'My felicitations to you both. I so longed to be there, but I am sorry to have to tell you that Kitty is no better. The physician has said that there is nothing more he can do to aid her recovery. She has lost so much weight and is so weak! But you will see her for yourself. *Viens avec moi, chérie!* We will see you presently!' she added with a quick glance at the twins as she led Adela from the room.

As they mounted the stairs to the first-floor landing, Eugénie took Adela's hand.

'It grieves me beyond belief to have to say this to you, *chérie*, but it is better you know how serious the situation is before you see the child. She has fallen into a decline and although she does not appear to be in any pain, it is as if she has given up the fight to live. Our physician – in whom I have the utmost faith – is doubtful if she will survive the coming winter. I have grown to love her as if she were my own, and it breaks my heart to have to contemplate such an outcome. To lose her so soon after losing my poor darling Robert . . . it is more than I can bear!'

Adela's eyes as well as Eugénie's filled with tears as they embraced one another. In heartbroken tones, Eugénie described the dreadful circumstances of her little son's death.

'Perhaps I could have accepted it more readily if it had truly been an accident,' she said finally, 'but it was not, Adela. It was negligence!'

With difficulty, Adela pieced together the facts. Berthe, the *nourrice*, had, it seemed, finally admitted beneath Philippe's questioning that she had had a little too much *vin du pays* at the midday meal and had been unable to prevent herself dozing off in the afternoon sunshine. She had been instantly dismissed without a character by Eugénie; sent back to her home in Saint Cyrille and told never to set foot on the Evraud estate again. Such punishment, however, could not bring little Robert back, Eugénie wept, and her heart had been newly broken when she had had to impart the dreadful news to Kitty. Now Kitty, too, was close to death.

'I had been so certain she would have recovered enough to return to England with us!' Adela said sadly. 'Are you certain she could not undertake the journey? Once we reached home—'

'No, dearest, do not speak further of this for when you have seen her, you will realize that such a thing is impossible . . . would be so even were we able to travel in the greatest comfort. The child is too weak even to leave her bed.'

'I will go to her at once . . .' Adela began but with a gentle gesture Eugénie detained her.

'First you must change your attire. *Grâce à Dieu*, Kitty has no knowledge of the recent happenings in this country or of the danger we are all in. I have sought to protect her from fear and were she to see you in such garb, she would suspect something was afoot. This way, your advent will come as a truly delightful surprise and, of course, you will pretend that you have come on an ordinary visit with the twins.'

With Kitty foremost in their minds, the two young women did not indulge in merriment as Adela tried on various gowns in an attempt to find one to fit her. Eugénie's figure had become much fuller after the birth of her son and they had finally to make use of a broad sash to pull in the folds of a dress to the tiny circle of Adela's waist. With the dust-streaked stains of coffee washed from her face and hands, her hair brushed up into curls and powdered, Adela looked like any other girl of her age and circumstances.

'I shall take you to Kitty's room now,' Eugénie said, satisfied with her efforts. 'Marriage suits you, *chérie*, for I have never seen you look prettier!'

'And but for your tragic circumstances, I could not be happier!' Adela said softly. 'Titus is the most wonderful husband, Eugénie!'

'And Barnaby?' Eugénie enquired as they made their way upstairs to the nursery quarters. 'Is he reconciled to your marriage?'

'I think so!' Adela replied with a sigh. 'But he is angry with Titus for permitting me to accompany them on this journey. Eugénie, is it true that Philippe is in real danger? And the Abbé? The Curé? Surely no one would dare harm men of the cloth?'

Eugénie's mouth tightened.

'You can have no idea of the horrors that are now perpetrated in the name of the people. It seems they have gone quite mad! I do understand that the ordinary citizens wish – need

– to improve their lives; but they are trying to do so without regard to the law; to common humanities. They are attacking any who stand in their way and even those who seek to argue with their methods of achieving their aims.'

She drew a long sigh before adding in sombre tones, 'They have resorted to murdering those who are no more than suspected of resisting their demands; those who will not actively support them. Of a hundred and fifty priests imprisoned in the Carmelite convent in Paris, only Monsieur l'Abbé and some forty others survived the massacre and not all of them were able to escape. Everyone is now in fear of everyone else, for people are spying upon each other. Even in this household we cannot be sure the few remaining servants are to be trusted. You remember Gustave – Robert's old valet? He, at least, is dependable and it is he who sees to the needs of our fugitives. They are concealed in the little dressing-room adjoining Robert's bedchamber. As you will remember, we locked these rooms when my poor Robert passed away, so no one goes there.'

'But Philippe – surely he has no need to hide in his sister's home?'

Eugénie shook her head.

'He is a marked man, *chérie*, his identity well known to the Commune. The last time he was in Paris he went to the aid of a royalist friend of his who had drawn his sword in defence of the Queen's good name. Although Philippe was disguised as a *sansculotte* and wore the *bonnet rouge*, he was armed. As it happened he and his friend were greatly outnumbered and had no alternative but to make such escape as they could. His friend called out to him, "Flee for your life, de Falence!" and the name was noted by one of their attackers. They suspected that Philippe would make for his family home, the Château de Falence. It was searched from cellar to roof, and when they did not find him there, they came here to question me. I pretended I believed my brother to be in England, and since none of the servants had noted Philippe's arrival by night, they all bore out my story that he was not here. I was warned that if I harboured him, I would be called to account for aiding an enemy of the people, and then, *grâce à Dieu*, they left, taking no more than the jewellery I was wearing to "compensate" them for "the trouble" my brother had caused.'

Adela's eyes were wide with horror at the thought of the danger her cousin had been in – and, by all accounts, was not free of yet.

'You must come home to England, Eugénie!' she said, momentarily forgetting Kitty. But by now they had reached the door of the child's room and as Eugénie opened it, Adela saw for the first time in twelve months, the tiny, skeletal figure of her nine-year-old half-sister. As she approached the bed, she tried to conceal her shock and forced a smile to her lips.

'It is I, Addy!' she said. 'I have come to pay you a surprise visit, my darling!'

Kitty's blue eyes lit in a delighted smile.

'Oh, but how wonderful! I am not dreaming, am I, *Tante* Eugénie? Why did you not tell me Addy was coming to see me?'

'Because she did not know of my intention, my love!' Adela said as she bent to embrace the little girl. 'And your two favourite uncles are here too, and will visit you presently.'

'Uncle Titus? Uncle Barnaby? I long to see them . . . and Addy, I want to hear all about your wedding. I was so sad I could not be there to see it! Did you look very beautiful in your bridal gown? *Tante* Eugénie described it to me for you had told her about it in a letter. And did the sun shine? Were there flowers in the church? And did you and Uncle Titus put flowers on Ned's grave?'

'Indeed we did, my sweeting!' Adela said as she sat beside the child, her face averted so that Kitty could not see that her eyes were full of tears. 'I will tell you all about it, but first I want to know how you are. It is important to me that you try to get well as quickly as you can. You see, I want to have you home with me. Dolly, too, is longing to see you.'

The excitement had left Kitty's face. Her eyes were thoughtful as she sought for words to express herself.

'I would like to see my home again,' she said tentatively. 'I would like to visit Ned's grave . . . I never really said goodbye to him, you see. But I am so tired, Addy, and it is such a long, long way to England, is it not? I like it here in this room where it is quiet. I can see the sky from my window and I watch the birds and the sunsets which are so pretty! Sometimes I long to be well again and to go out into the garden to play; but it makes my head and my legs and arms ache if I try to stand up. I am quite content to lie here. *Tante* Eugénie reads to me and sometimes we tell each other stories whilst she does her tapestry work; and a lot of the time, I sleep. Sometimes, Addy, I dream of you and Ned and Mama and although you may think me foolish, when I wake up I think I have been in heaven for a little while and I am sad that I cannot stay there.'

Adela could not speak for the emotion she felt but Eugénie, accustomed as she was to the child's condition, said lightly, 'God will take you to His side in His own good time! It is not something for you to think about, *chérie*. Now it is time you rested a little after this excitement. Adela will return when you wake, and, if you are a good girl and eat all your supper, perhaps she will bring Uncle Titus and Uncle Barny to see you.'

'Oh, yes, please!' Kitty said, her eyes bright once more. She reached out her arms and wound them round Adela's neck. 'I am so happy you came!' she whispered. 'Once or twice I have been afraid I might not see you again. Was that not silly of me?'

'Very silly, my dearest!' Adela said huskily.

'And you will stay now for a long, long visit?'

'For as long as I possibly can!' Adela answered. But as she left the room, her eyes were once more full of tears for she knew that it could not be more than a few days at most before she must go home. Titus would never agree to leave her here – unless she could persuade him to stay with her? She did not need Eugénie or the physician to tell her now that her little sister was not long for this world. There was an ethereal look about the child which she knew instinctively was a presentiment of death. She had seen that same transparent pallor in Nou-Nou's face during her last weeks of life; had never forgotten it in those of her beloved parents during the weeks before they died.

Titus was not yet down when Adela walked back into the big *salon*. Only Barnaby was there standing motionless as he stared out into the garden. With no more than token courtesy, he bowed as she entered the room, but he did not speak.

Adela bit her lip.

'Oh, Barny, please do not continue to be so vexed with me . . .' She hesitated as her voice began to tremble on the verge of tears. 'If you had seen Kitty as I have just done . . . I fear she is not long for this world and had I not come here – albeit for different reasons – I might never have seen her again before she . . . she . . .'

The tautness of Barnaby's face and body dissolved instantly as he realized the extent of Adela's distress. Hurrying to her side, he put his arm around her shoulder with great tenderness and said, 'I am very sorry to hear such news. Please do not cry, Addy. I am sorry if I have been churlish, but Titus should never have permitted you to come with us. Has he really so little regard for your life?' His eyes were bitter as he added, 'For as long as we have lived, he and I have shared our thoughts. Indeed, we thought as one person. He *knew* I would never agree to your involvement, and I cannot forgive him for deceiving me.'

Recognizing the justification for his bitterness, Adela said quickly, 'It was I who persuaded him! I knew he wanted more than anything in the world to go with you and Jacques but he felt it unfair to leave me so . . . so soon after our marriage. I begged him to solve the dilemma by allowing me to go with him. You must not be angry with him, Barny. I cannot bear the thought that I have inadvertently come between you.'

Even as she spoke the words, she knew that by marrying Titus she *had* come between them. Even if Barny lived with them, she and Titus would be intimate in ways Barny could never know; united in experiences, memories of their shared loving.

As similar thoughts went through Barnaby's mind, he knew that nothing could be done to alter matters for the better. Loving both Titus and Adela as he did, his jealousy, his sense of exclusion, must somehow be quelled, he told himself, and he must reconcile himself to their closeness. Of all people in the world, it must not be he who dimmed their joy in each other.

'What you have told me about Kitty's condition does greatly alter my feelings,' he said awkwardly. 'I am so sorry, Addy. I do not see how we are going to resolve the problem of Eugénie's escape to England for it would seem that she cannot leave the child. Perhaps it would be best if I were to remain here to protect them both until . . . until Kitty's health improves or . . . or when the inevitable happens, bring Eugénie home alone. I will discuss the matter with Titus. You must promise me, though, that you will go back with him.'

'Alternatively, Titus could remain here with me!' Adela said tentatively. 'Eugénie will need my support if . . . when . . .' She broke off, unable to voice the words that spelt death for her little sister. Titus' arrival with Eugénie put a timely end to the conversation, for Eugénie was waiting to take them to see the fugitives.

Both Titus and Barnaby were shocked to discover how old and frail the Abbé was. The Chevalier's dressing-room was only just large enough to accommodate a bed, two armchairs, a *prie-dieu* and a table. The Abbé sat propped by pillows on the single bed. His bald pate fringed with white hair glistened for the room was warm and stuffy. His face, creased by the wrinkles of old age, was thin and drawn; his wrists, protruding from his habit, were painfully thin and veined. Beside him on the bedcover lay his grey scapular and a mound of books and sheets of manuscript which, he told them later, he had been able to save during the attack on the convent.

The Curé, Père Jérôme, rose from his chair, his faded blue eyes peering anxiously at the visitors through thick spectacles. His soutane was green and shabby and his once plump face looked drawn and grey. There was an unmistakable aura of fear about him – not misplaced, perhaps, in view of the fact that he had come close to being lynched by a posse of patriots who had come upon him preaching a pro-royalist sermon to his parishioners. But for Philippe's timely intervention, he would certainly not have escaped with his life.

Philippe was now greeting his cousin and the Mallory twins. With a beaming smile, he kissed Adela on either cheek.

'How charming you look, Cousin Adela!' he said, and turned to the twins. 'I had no doubt you would come to our aid!' He bowed to each in turn as if this were a normal social occasion. 'Now, allow me to introduce you to my fellow "prisoners" – for that is what we are since my dear sister will not permit us to leave this room.' He gestured towards the Abbé. 'Monsieur l'Abbé, this is my sweet cousin, Adela, wife to my good friends here, les Messieurs Titus and Barnaby Mallory. Gentlemen, Adela, may I present Monsieur le Curé, Pére Jérôme, who I believe you already know.'

A bottle of wine and some goblets stood on the single small table by the window.

'I think we should drink to this occasion!' Philippe added when the courtesies had been exchanged. 'With your permission, Monsieur l'Abbé?'

The Abbé smiled.

'But first we will thank le bon Dieu for bringing these brave people to our aid. May God bless you, mes enfants!' He lifted the heavy silver crucifix lying on his chest and kissing it, made the sign of the cross before each of the four visitors. Philippe now distributed the wine and then turned eagerly to the twins, his voice deepening as he said seriously, 'Eugénie informed us you would almost certainly be smuggling us back to England in your cutter. But first we must get to the coast. What plans have you, *mes amis*? I am impatient to be gone, for our presence here places Eugénie and Kitty in great danger. Every day Gustave has to make a secret raid upon the kitchens to find food for us, and sooner or later the cook or the pantry-maid will notice that the stores are unreasonably depleted. We require water as well as food, and there are the slops to be carried away. So far we have remained undetected, but for how long will our luck hold?'

'I had thought we might go as we came – on horseback through le Forêt d'Eu,' Titus said, 'but it is a long and arduous ride and we must endeavour to find a better way.'

Philippe nodded.

'I have already given the matter a great deal of thought!' he said. His blue eyes, so like Eugénie's, brightened with excitement. 'As you know, I am familiar with every part of this countryside having spent my childhood here. We could go by the river. You will be embarking from Anse Goéland, the cove near Le Tréport, I imagine? That being the rendezvous of our friend, Jacques, with his French compatriots if I am not mistaken,' he added with a smile. 'Gustave says he can arrange for a barge to be available. He has a cousin who owns such a vessel and uses it to transport grain to his brother who is miller in Aumale. He returns with barrels of fresh fish and for a consideration, would permit us to go with him. He is a religious man and although many of his sympathies are with the revolutionaries, he does not countenance harm to men of the cloth and fears God's wrath on those who perpetrate these outrages. If we can reach Aumale – disguised, of course – we should be able to travel the short distance to the coast by wagon or other means.'

'We will discuss this excellent plan later when the servants are abed!' Titus said with an anxious glance at Adela's white face. Although she had borne the hardships of the journey from England without complaint, it had been arduous and tiring even for the men. They had spent one night at sea where sleep had been well nigh impossible; and a second night in a derelict forester's hut. The thatched roof had fallen in, allowing the cold autumn air to chill their tired bodies, but they had not dared to light a fire for fear of detection. As a consequence, sleep had once more eluded them and now, after many more hours on horseback, it was nearing the end of the day, and they were all exhausted.

'My wife must lie down before the evening meal!' he said firmly. 'You and I also, Barny, for we shall not think clearly whilst our brains are befuddled with fatigue. If you will excuse us, Monsieur l'Abbé, Monsieur le Curé, Philippe, we will leave you now and return after dinner.'

'But I had promised to return to Kitty's bedside,' Adela protested as Titus led her from the room. 'I cannot disappoint her!'

'Barny and I will go in your place!' Titus said gently. 'You shall sit with her later this evening for there is no need for you to be present when we draw up our plan of escape.'

Too tired to argue, Adela did as she was told and retired to her bedchamber. Two hours later she was woken by Eugénie and a young maid carrying a tray of food.

'I had not the heart to disturb you in time for dinner!' she said. 'It was perhaps as well, for the twins were engaging in a heated argument concerning you. Now there is no need to look so alarmed,' she continued as Adela sat upright with a look of deep anxiety. 'Barnaby was proposing that he stay behind with me since the cutter will not carry all of you at one time. Titus was insisting that he be the one to stay – with you, *chérie*; and that Jacques could return for you both. Barny was determined upon you being sent home and Titus was doing his best to explain that if *he* did not go, *you* would not!'

'And Titus was right!' Adela cried. 'I cannot go home yet, Eugénie. I want to spend at least a little time with you and

Kitty. Unlike you all, I am surely not in danger. You spoke up for me, did you not?'

Eugénie sighed.

'I have to agree with Barnaby that it would be safer for you to go home now. However, I understand your reluctance to depart so soon and I told the twins they must appreciate the fact that you might never see your little sister again. They finally agreed that having escorted the Abbé, Philippe and Père Jérôme safely to the French coast, they would then *both* return so that there would be two of them to safeguard us.'

She leaned forward so that her lips were close to Adela's ear.

'You must promise not tell them, Adela, if I pass on a secret to you. Will you give me your word? Were they to know what I will tell you, they would never permit you to stay!'

'Then I give my word!' Adela said instantly. 'Although I do not like to begin my marriage with secrets withheld from my husband!'

'You will understand presently why it is necessary,' Eugénie said. 'You shall impart the information when they return. It is that Philippe has told his most trusted friends that if they are in danger of their lives, I will conceal them here, just as I have concealed the Abbé and the Curé. Others like them may arrive, and I cannot refuse them sanctuary. Philippe had hoped to be here to assist me, but now that he has been exposed, were he to stay he would only increase the dangers for those trying to leave the country.'

'But Eugénie, if you were discovered . . .' Adela gasped.

'I try not to think of the consequences; but even were I to be arrested, imprisoned, at least I shall feel that I have achieved something worthwhile in my life. Without my dear Robert and my poor baby – and soon I shall not even have my adopted daughter, Kitty – what purpose does my life have? It is different for you, *chérie*. You have Titus . . . and you will have children, a family who need you.'

'But your papa, *Tante* Camille, your sisters, Philippe . . .'

'Their lives are fulfilled without me!' Eugénie said quietly.

'As you know, I have never been a very courageous person. Unlike your own, my dearest, my life has always been protected. Robert's death was my first experience of horror. When my little boy died I was inconsolable and felt unable to face the future. Then I remembered how you had had to come to terms with Ned's drowning and I realized that your life had been far harder than mine. Philippe's activities have given me the opportunity to prove to myself that I, too, have a little of your courage. If you are truthful, you, too, would harbour these fugitives and do what you could to save their lives were the choice and the opportunity yours.'

That was indeed true, Adela thought as she imagined how empty her life would be were anything to happen to Titus. Had Eugénie's child lived, perhaps she would not be so ready to put her life at risk.

'Are matters here in France really as terrible as are reported in England?' she asked.

'Philippe says they are far worse than we can imagine. Our beautiful capital is in torment! Is it known in England that our King and Queen are in prison without friends or servants? Even Her Majesty's friend and comforter, the Princess de Lamballe, has been taken from her and, horror of horrors, Philippe heard that she had been hacked to death not ten days ago! Her head was put on a pike and paraded in front of the Temple prison so that their Majesties could see it.'

Eugénie covered her eyes with her hands as if by doing so, she could erase the image her words had evoked.

'It is wicked what they are doing! They have arrested good and holy men and women and are using the monasteries and convents as prisons. *Quel sacrilege!* One such man – a priest – is well known to us, and my Robert often sent money to him for he looked after and taught beggar children and deaf-mutes. He was their saviour and unquestionably a saint! Now he, too, has been executed. *C'est incroyable!* The rabble seem to take delight in arresting the scholars, editors, printers, legal men – even judges – anyone who might speak out against their atrocities. The National Guard are worse than beasts! They stormed the prisons, hacked to death the convicts – even the children, as well as many of our friends – some fourteen hundred people or more. Our dear friend, Charles de Valfons, the Archbishop of Ailes, the bishops of Saintes and Beauvais – all have been butchered with axes, sabres, pikes following what can only be called a grotesque pretence of a trial.'

Adela's face had paled at this inconceivable story. As if sensing her disbelief, Eugénie said, 'I have heard all this at first hand from Philippe, and from others who have escaped. They have taken sanctuary here and recounted their experiences. One man saw the carts carrying the bodies of the dead, stripped naked, to a pit where they were thrown like so much refuse. Cart after cart passed by him and the crowds stood watching as though this were a new form of entertainment offering them the sight and smell of blood! Who can say how long their Majesties will survive this terrible lust for killing? No one seems to know where the Dauphin is – poor little boy. They have taken him from his mother and hidden him somewhere. Could anything be more cruel!'

Adela's face was grave.

'If Uncle Hugo knows even part of this, he said nothing of it when he came to Dene for our wedding. He spoke only of his knowledge that his estates had been appropriated by the people; and of his concern for your safety, Eugénie. He said that if the Republic can appropriate his home – the de Falence birthright – in so lawless a fashion, how long will it be before they attempt to take this estate? And if they could imprison so important a personage as the King of France, would they be likely to spare you? Kitty? Now it is known that your brother has been aiding the royalists; that your own family are *émigrés*, how can you be so calm?'

Eugénie gave a wan smile.

'I am aware of the risks, *chérie*. Fortunately, my Robert was much loved by the local people and Gustave has told me that only a few dissidents speak against me. He does not believe the majority would allow me to be harmed.'

'Yet the Curé was threatened by your own peasants! A man of God, Eugénie! It is inconceivable!'

'Père Jérôme is a good man, but unworldly, and he was unwise enough to condemn from the pulpit the National Convention; their incitement to take France into war; Danton and his revolutionary tribunals; the cruelty; the spilling of innocent blood. One may applaud his courageous adherence to his principles, but whilst not condoning the behaviour of the revolutionaries, a wiser man would have remained silent upon matters of politics. Even Philippe had learned not openly to declare his royalist sympathies, and wore *le bonnet rouge*. It was a tragedy that his friend unmasked him for he had already saved many lives and might well have saved others. It is his work I hope to continue.'

She sat down on the end of Adela's bed, her face now animated as she declared, 'If Jacques and the twins will assist me as they are now doing, who knows how many more we may help to escape to England? But for your approaching wedding, *chérie*, Philippe would have asked for their help two months ago! I would not allow him to do so, for no one knew better than I what store you set upon your marriage to Titus. Even now I am unsure if I have the right to ask your beloved husband to put his life at risk with further journeys to this unhappy country! I am all too well aware of what it is like to lose the husband you love, and before I speak to Titus, I have to ask how you yourself feel about this.'

The gravity of her cousin's words were not lost upon Adela. If Titus were to die . . . but to think of it was to put her own happiness before the lives of others. As for Titus, he would not hesitate unless it be on her account, and she loved him far too much to wish to be a burden to him. He himself would not want her widowed and would take no unnecessary risks.

'I had no doubt you would reach such a decision,' Eugénie

said quietly when Adela had expressed her views, 'for you are both brave and unselfish. I can now tell Philippe he may speak openly to Titus and Barnaby of our future plans. Titus will be happy to learn they have your approval! I will go and speak to Philippe whilst you sit with Kitty for a little while. She naps so frequently in the daytime, she does not sleep well at night, and she will welcome your company in place of the elderly *nourrice* who sits with her until morning.'

Adela made her way to Kitty's bedchamber. Her concerns were quickly forgotten when she saw the child's eyes widen with pleasure as she approached the bed.

'I was afraid you might have gone home to England already!' she said as Adela embraced her.

'Whatever gave you that notion?' Adela asked, forcing a smile to her lips. 'I shall be here for quite a little while, my darling.'

'Uncle Titus came to see me with Uncle Barny. They told me you would be going home tomorrow or the next day.'

Adela shook her head.

'No, dearest, you have misunderstood. It is they who will be leaving – just for a little while. They will be coming back and you will see them both again before they take me home.'

Kitty drew a deep sigh.

'I expect I dreamt you were going, Addy!' she murmured. 'Sometimes I do become confused between my dreams and reality. I have such lovely dreams! I am well again and can run and play with Ned; and sometimes *Tante* Eugénie allows me to hold little Robert's hand whilst we walk in the garden. I wish then that I need never wake up, for on waking, I am obliged to remember that they have both gone to Jesus.' She drew a deep sigh. 'Everyone is very kind to me, and I know *Tante* Eugénie loves me, but I am tired of lying here in my bed. I wish I could go home with you tomorrow, Addy. I wish you were never going away!'

'But my darling, I am not going anywhere. You must indeed have been dreaming if you heard your uncles tell you so. Now show me that pretty smile of yours. You have no cause to fear I shall leave you.'

Adela could not have spoken so convincingly had she been present in the *salon* where plans for the escape had not long been finalized. Despite the satisfaction both Titus and Barnaby felt at the arrangements agreed upon, their faces wore identical expressions of anxiety.

'I very much doubt if you will succeed in persuading Addy to do as you wish, Titus!' Barnaby said. 'Now she knows that this could be the last time she sees that poor child alive, she will resist any attempt to make her leave with the others!'

Titus' face looked even more worried than his twin's.

'She gave me her word she would obey my orders if I agreed to her joining us on the journey here!' he muttered.

'So you have said; but it is my belief she will feel the circumstances are such that you will release her from that promise. The child is Addy's sister; her last link with her mother. Moreover, she will be aware now of the danger Eugénie is in and feel it is her duty to remain with Kitty until . . . well, until the worst happens.'

Earlier, at their conference with the Abbé and the Curé, Philippe had left both young men in little doubt of the risks they all incurred. Even with Titus and Barnaby returning to safeguard the two women and the child, there could be no guarantee that they could protect them should a mob descend upon them, he had reiterated. Two men and perhaps a few servants against a mob? Adela's presence could only add to their problems.

Titus knew that Philippe was right; knew, too, that he should have withstood Addy's pleas to go to France with him. He did not need Barnaby to tell him he had been weak, for he knew his twin was justified in the accusations he was making. He, too, blamed himself.

'I agree that Addy must be made to go back with the others!' he said quietly. 'And if she will not agree, then I shall be obliged to use force.'

For the first time, Barnaby smiled.

'If I know Addy, you will need to give her a dose of laudanum first!' he said.

'And so I will if the need arises!' Titus replied with an answering smile.

The earlier tension between the brothers had vanished, and now that they were agreed upon their actions, they were in total accord once more. Their movements became simultaneous again as each stood up and firmly sealed their decision with a mutual clasp of their hands.

CHAPTER TWENTY-TWO

1792

It was after ten o'clock on the following morning when Adela awoke. Eugénie was standing by the window.

'Titus left me with instructions not to awaken you until you were fully rested,' she said. 'He and Barnaby have gone down to the river!'

Rubbing her eyes as she sat up, Adela looked at the empty space in the bed beside her. The indentation of Titus' head was still in the pillow. How was it possible, she wondered, that he had risen without waking her? She felt a moment of dismay for this was the first morning since their wedding that she had not opened her eyes to find his arms around her, his eyes smiling into her own. A faint blush stole into her cheeks as she recalled their love-making the previous night. Despite his fatigue – and indeed, her own – they had been unwilling to sleep without kisses and embraces and inevitably, their desire for one another had swept them into further intimacies, their travel weariness forgotten.

'If I live to be a hundred, I shall never cease to want you, my own sweet wife!' Titus had said. 'I shall miss you infernally when you are gone.'

'Gone? Gone where, Titus?' she had asked. Surely he could not have been thinking of her death?

He had parried her question with further kisses and murmured that tomorrow would be time enough for talking. Now they must both sleep, he said, for tomorrow, if their plans went well, he and Barnaby would be on their way with Philippe and the fugitives to the coast.

Her eyes now went to Eugénie's in sudden anxiety.

'They have not yet gone . . . to the coast, I mean?' She could not bear it if Titus had left without bidding her farewell.

Eugénie smiled.

'No, of course not, *chérie*. There is much to be done before they can go, and it is unlikely they will do so before nightfall. I must leave you now, for one of my tasks is to find suitable disguises for the Abbé and the Curé. It has been decided that they will wear female attire. If they are stopped and questioned, the Abbé will be less recognizable as an old peasant woman, and Pére Jérôme, his "daughter", will be a deaf-mute so that he neither understands the questions nor is obliged to speak. Until they are all well clear of Saint Cyrille, the Curé is in great danger of recognition for there is scarcely a family whose members he has not married or buried; whose children he has not christened.'

'And Philippe?' Adela enquired as Eugénie drew the curtains back and opened the shutters to reveal a beautiful sunny autumn day.

Eugénie sighed.

'He is well used to playing the part of a common citizen, and has adequate clothing. As for the twins, they will travel as they came – in sailors' garb. Now, my dearest, I will send Marie to you to help you dress and after you have had *le petit déjeuner*, you will want to sit with Kitty. She is awake and greatly looking forward to seeing you.'

Having successfully diverted Adela from further questioning, Eugénie hurried downstairs to find Gustave's wife from whom she hoped to borrow the necessary rough-spun clothes for the *religieux*. During breakfast with the twins, she had been present at their discussion concerning her own safety. If both young men were to escort Adela and the fugitives to the coast, she and Kitty would be left unguarded until their return – a matter of perhaps six days; therefore one should remain with her, they insisted; but she would not allow it.

She was in no immediate danger, she had told them, and since neither Adela nor the elderly Abbé nor the Curé were in a position to defend themselves should they be apprehended, and Jacques would need Philippe's assistance to handle the boat, both Titus and Barnaby might be required to defend the party against any interference.

Eugénie had not added to all their worries by expressing her own concerning Adela. Knowing what was to happen to her cousin, she could well imagine Adela's feelings when she discovered that she had been drugged in order for her to be sent home. She would be heartbroken when she became aware that she would never see Kitty again, for the child's condition worsened every day. Eugénie could but hope that this enforcement of the twins' wishes would not cause a rift between the newly-weds for Adela would be unlikely to forgive the twins their deception. Meanwhile, they had sworn her, Eugénie, to secrecy.

By good fortune, she was still sitting alone in the *petit salon* when the twins returned with Jacques from their visit to the river. All three faces wore identical expressions of concern as they announced that their plans had been balked. Gustave's cousin, the bargee, had been forbidden by the municipal council to make further deliveries to Aumale. In future he must take grain to Paris, he had been instructed, for it was in the capital that the citizens had the greatest need. The harvest everywhere had been meagre and poor folk in the city were starving.

'We shall have to travel by wagon!' Titus announced. 'It will not be easy through the forest – as we discovered on our way here. There are no roads and even the pathways are overgrown. Twice we became lost in the density of the trees and at night we saw several packs of wolves. Barnaby and I must ride guard. Jacques will have to drive the wagon. If we meet anyone, we shall pass ourselves off as woodcutters. The "women" can have accompanied us to collect beechmasts.'

'We can devise no better plan,' Barnaby said uneasily. 'What think you, Eugénie?'

'If Philippe is of the same mind, it would seem the only alternative,' she replied, although she was apprehensive at the thought of the frail, elderly Abbé being jolted and bumped about in a wagon for several days. On the other hand, she could think of no better way of transporting the refugees to the coast.

'It might be possible to obtain a sack or two of beechmasts from the village to lend credence to our disguises. The women and children collect them for they have many uses hereabouts. They grind the kernels into flour, press them to extract cooking oil and feed the *marc* to cattle and poultry. The beechmasts are only just now ripening so you may encounter others in the forest eager to collect the first fruits.'

Philippe was in favour of this revised plan and Gustave was sent to the village to collect any beechmasts he could persuade their harvesters to sell. When he returned he reported that there was a band of citizen-patriots on the road into the village who were stopping all-comers from the direction of Paris.

'The citizen-patriots are armed with National Guard muskets and are questioning everyone!' he announced with a worried frown. They were demanding papers which, needless to say, few could present, for since the peasants could neither read nor write, they were not aware that they must have these pieces of paper identifying themselves!

'It was as well for us that so many were gathered arguing the sense of it,' Jacques now said with a worried frown, 'for in the mêlée, we was able to slip past the taxing 'ouse unnoticed. The men 'ad orders to check each name against a list they was carrying, and like as not, that of Monsieur le Curé and perhaps Monsieur Philippe are on it.'

'Although on whose authority they were acting, we do not know!' Philippe broke in. 'We were told they are seeking to apprehend "traitors" and "immigrants", and on no more than a suspicion, are taking those without papers straight to the nearest prison.'

'Are they likely to come asking questions here at the château?' Titus enquired anxiously.

'Not yet awhile, Master Titus!' Jacques replied with a grin. 'They 'ave too much to pucker 'em with the villagers.'

'Nevertheless I suggest that it would be as well if we can be away by nightfall,' Philippe said quickly. 'By then, I fancy, many will be as drunk as lords and their so-called justice distributed in even more haphazard a fashion!'

'I have food and clothing ready,' Eugénie said, 'and Gustave can arrange now with our *sous-intendant* for a wagon to be prepared with two of our stoutest horses to pull it.'

'It is to be hoped your bailiff is to be trusted, Eugénie,' Barnaby said doubtfully. 'If he were to alert these citizen-patriots—'

'You may trust him with your life, Barnaby!' Eugénie interrupted him with a smile. 'His father was *sous-intendant* here before him, and Robert gave him a cottage and land of his own when he retired. Even if his son's loyalty were in question, he can have no grudge against us. Have no fear!'

'So we have only our darling Addy to worry about!' Titus said ruefully. 'You will administer the laudanum, Eugénie? She must remain asleep at least until we are well clear of the château lest she attempts to return here. I would not put it past her to steal one of our horses and try such madness. From everything she said last night, I do not believe she can ever be persuaded to leave Kitty of her own accord.'

'I will see to it,' Eugénie said quietly. 'Adela's safety is more important to me than her goodwill for I fear she will hate me when she discovers what part I have played in this. Adela will be very angry with you, too, Titus!'

'I know that only too well, but I think she loves me enough to forgive me.'

'You would do better not to take her forgiveness too much for granted, Titus,' Barnaby said in a low voice. 'You know how headstrong she can be!'

'Hush now, she is coming!' Eugénie whispered, her quick

ear having detected Adela's footfall outside the door of the *salon*.

Unsuspecting of their plans for her, Adela came forward with a smile on her lips.

'So you are safely back!' she said as Titus bent to kiss her hand. 'Is all well?'

She listened quietly whilst Titus explained the change in their proposed method of travel and the necessity for it. Then she nodded her head. Her eyes met those of Titus as she said, 'It will take longer to travel this way. You and Barny will be as quick as you can, dearest, will you not? Eugénie and I will be watching for your safe return.'

To her surprise, not one of the three replied to this remark. Misunderstanding their silence, she added, 'Although you need have no fear for us. If we are questioned by this mob Jacques speaks of, we shall know nothing of your movements. If you have been seen here at the château, we shall say you have been visiting and gone hunting for boar in the forest.'

'How did you find Kitty this morning?' Eugénie said quickly, once again diverting Adela's train of thought. 'I think she has rallied a little since your arrival.'

Adela's face clouded.

'I had thought so too, but gradually as the morning passed, she became less animated and I could see that she was exhausted. It broke my heart to hear her talking of poor little Ned. She was devoted to him . . . and to your little Robert, Eugénie. She told me that last night, she dreamt once again of playing with them in heaven and how much she looked forward to the reality which she hoped would be soon.' Adela's eyes filled with tears and Titus hurried forward to put his arm around her.

'Can you remember, my love, telling me how your mother longed for the day she would be reunited with your father? You were only a child at the time, but you said you understood her feelings. Now you must quench your grief for Kitty since she herself is not afraid of what is to come.'

'But she is so young!' Adela cried. 'Only nine years old!'

'My Robert was only two!' Eugénie added wistfully. 'But this is no time for grieving, *chérie*. We have much to do. First we will eat *le déjeuner* and then we must complete the preparations.'

Twilight had fallen and Kitty was almost asleep as Adela sat by her bedside reading to her her favourite story, a French translation of the life of St Francis of Assisi. Not only his love of all living creatures appealed to the child but his affinity with the sun, the moon, the wind and the water, which he called 'brother' or 'sister'. In her whimsical way, Kitty liked to think of them as her brothers and sisters, too.

'I will finish the story tomorrow, my darling!' Adela promised as Eugénie came into the room bearing a tray with two cups of hot chocolate on a dainty, embroidered cloth.

'I thought you would share Kitty's bedtime drink with her, *chérie*!' Eugénie said with apparent casualness to Adela. 'We will see which of you is the first to drink it all up, shall we?'

Believing that Eugénie was attempting to persuade the child to take this nourishment, Adela readily took her cup from her cousin.

'I am not very thirsty, *Tante* Eugénie!' Kitty said sleepily.

'No, *mignonne*, but you will not allow Addy to win the race, will you? Take a sip or two just to please me, *non*?'

As Kitty drank, so, too, did Adela. The brownish-red colour of the opiate was undetectable in the chocolate, but the strong odour of opium was more difficult to mask. Eugénie had added sugar to the mixture but Adela was hard put to empty her cup. Kitty had replaced her own cup of unwanted beverage in its saucer after drinking no more than a third.

'I do not wonder your patient refuses it!' Adela said now, wrinkling her nose. 'Your cook has made it too strong, Eugénie. Tomorrow I shall make it myself and then Kitty will drink it, will you not, my sweeting?'

She drew the bedclothes over the thin, emaciated arms and bent to kiss the child.

'Thank you for reading to me, Addy!' Kitty said, her eyes half closing in sleep. 'Perhaps I shall dream of St Francis and the birds, and Ned and I will be allowed to feed them with him.'

As the night-time *nourrice* came into the room, Adela stood up.

'Sleep well, dearest!' she said, bending to give Kitty a last kiss; but the child's eyes had already closed. Feeling surprisingly cheerful and filled with unexpected energy, Adela followed Eugénie as she led the way to the bedchamber she shared with Titus. Only now did she realize that in a matter of an hour or two, Titus would be leaving and it might be a week or more before she saw him again.

'Where is Titus?' she asked Eugénie who was fumbling meaninglessly with the bed curtains.

'He will be here directly, *chérie*!' Eugénie said for she knew that it was not Titus' intention to parody a farewell to Adela. 'He wanted me to tell you to lie down for a little while and rest. He will join you as soon as he can.'

'But I am not in the least tired, Eugénie!' Adela protested. 'Is there not something I can do?'

'No, nothing, *chérie*! All is prepared and the twins are even now escorting Monsieur l'Abbé to the stables. Afterwards they will collect Père Jérôme and then Philippe.'

'But I have not bade them adieu!' Adela protested yet again. 'I am so confused. I thought they were not leaving for a further hour?'

'Titus will come and say goodbye presently,' Eugénie said reassuringly as she turned down Adela's bedcovers. 'See, it is only seven o'clock. There will be an hour or more before . . . before they depart!'

Adela sat down on the edge of the bed for, to her surprise, she was suddenly feeling quite dizzy. Her thoughts were tumbling about her head, racing one against the other in confusion.

'Perhaps I have read too long from that book!' she murmured as she lay back on the pillows. 'The print was very small. Would you fetch me a glass of water, dearest? I have such a horrid taste in my mouth – that chocolate you gave me – no wonder Kitty did not drink it!'

Yawning, she allowed her eyelids to drop for without warning they had become unbearably heavy. If only Titus would come, she might sleep, she thought as she struggled against the desire to do so. If he were to leave without holding her, kissing her, telling her that he loved her, one last time . . .

She had succumbed to the laudanum by the time Titus came into the room. He looked questioningly at Eugénie, and as she nodded, he turned his gaze to Adela. Her breathing seemed to him to be unnaturally slow. He looked anxiously once more at Eugénie.

'You are certain that you administered the correct dosage?' he asked. 'I have heard that too much of this compound can be very dangerous!'

'The physician was quite clear as to the amount Adela should have,' Eugénie said reassuringly. 'But he has warned that when she wakens, she will almost certainly have a head-ache and may feel nauseous. She will not thank us for this, Titus!'

'Perhaps not!' he agreed as he bent to stroke a ringlet of dark hair from Adela's forehead. 'But I love her far too dearly to allow her to remain here as she wishes. I understand why you cannot leave now whilst the child is so ill; but you must come home too, Eugénie, as soon as possible. Barny and I will be back at the earliest opportunity. I wish we could feel more certain of your safety here. Despite all you say, we still feel it wrong that we should both be leaving tonight.'

'No more of this, Titus!' Eugénie said firmly. 'Gustave will see I come to no harm . . . and I will be without Monsieur l'Abbé, Philippe or Monsieur le Curé. If any of these so-called patriotic citizens come to search my home, they will find only a defenceless woman and a dying child.'

'You are none the less an aristocrat and Philippe tells me that now all "aristos" are suspect!' Titus argued.

'We are wasting time,' Eugénie said dismissively. 'We must change Adela's clothes before you carry her downstairs. *Grâce à Dieu*, she knows nothing of this! My poor Adela. Take care of her, Titus, for she is as dear to me as my sisters.'

Five minutes later, with great ease and even greater tenderness, Titus gathered Adela's sleeping form into his arms; and having ascertained that there were no prying servants' eyes in the passage, he carried her down to the *salon* where Barnaby was waiting.

'So, we are ready to go!' he greeted Titus. He looked relieved that Adela was unconscious and could make no argument about her unceremonious departure. Although he had forgiven Titus for permitting her ever to come to France, his confidence in his twin had been undermined. He feared that Titus' love for Adela had clouded his judgement and that all too easily she might persuade him to her will again. Loving Adela as *he* did, Barnaby knew he would not be happy until he saw her safely aboard their boat.

They had been travelling for three hours before the effects of the laudanum slowly wore off and Adela became conscious of her surroundings. She was lying on a heap of clean straw, the floor beneath her swaying, as were the shadowy figures of two women seated opposite her, their backs against a wooden wall. She could hear the jangling of harness and the rattle of wheels and realized that she and her companions were in a farm cart – a wagon roofed by a big tar-covered canvas sheet. The severe ache in her head was momentarily intensified as the wheels of the cart jolted over a deep rut and she was flung roughly against the side.

Easing herself into a sitting position she saw that she was no longer dressed in Eugénie's pretty flowered muslin gown but was clad in a drab, brown, home-spun dress and coarse woollen cloak. There was a black cotton scarf tied over her head, and on her feet were a pair of wooden *sabots*.

Certain that she was dreaming, Adela now became aware

of the sound of hoof-beats outside the wagon, and the muffled voices of their riders. Such dim light as there was inside the cart was filtering through the flaps of the canvas and, she now saw, came from a bright, nearly full moon. Her arm brushed against a small mound of sacks which had been piled close to the opening. As she reached out a hand to discover the contents, a voice said, 'You are awake, my child. Are you thirsty? Would you care for a little wine?'

'No – no thank you!' Adela said quickly for she was conscious now of a feeling of nausea. Hurriedly, she eased herself nearer to the opening so that she could breathe in the sharpness of the cold night air. Its freshness seemed to clear her mind a little, and she peered at her two female companions. The voice which had addressed her had been that of an educated man, clear, resonant like that of a clergyman speaking from his pulpit.

'My appearance has confused you, Madame Mallory! I am wearing the garb of a peasant woman and the gentleman here beside me is Monsieur le Curé, Père Jérôme, whom you have already had the pleasure of meeting in your dear cousin's house.'

With a gasp, Adela realized that she was being addressed by the Abbé and now at last she guessed what was happening. They were on their way to the Normandy coast in a farm wagon – as planned by Titus and Barnaby – but why, *why* was she with them? Had there been a change of plan? And how could she have slept through their departure?

Her thoughts were arrested as suddenly the wagon jolted to a halt. It was now possible to identify Jacques' voice as he spoke soothingly to the horses pulling the wagon. A moment later Titus dismounted from his horse and appeared at the canvas opening.

'Titus!' Adela said in relief. 'What is happening? Why am I here? Where are we?'

He was regarding her anxiously, his face close to hers in the semi-darkness.

'You are not unwell? Eugénie said that when the laudanum wore off, you—'

'Laudanum! So that is why I slept so soundly!' Adela interrupted. 'But I do not understand what this is about? Why was I put to sleep? Why am I here? I was in our bedchamber waiting for you to come and bid me farewell and then . . . then I remember nothing.'

'Let me help you to alight!' Titus said, taking her arm in a firm grip. 'The night air will clear your head. Come, my love!'

Still confused but with a deepening feeling of unease, Adela allowed Titus to lift her down from the wagon. She could now see Barnaby and Philippe still astride their horses, silhouetted against the shaft of moonlight pouring through the beech trees. They seemed to be in a clearing, for the huge trees were less dense and the undergrowth on either side of the rutted track had been trodden down. There were signs of recent charcoal burning although no hut or shelter was visible.

Clinging to Titus' arm for she still felt dizzy, Adela allowed him to lead her to the edge of the clearing. He was attired in the clothes of a woodman but in place of an axe, he had a pistol tucked into the thick leather belt about his waist. His blond curls were, like Barnaby's, concealed beneath a black felt hat.

He took off his long leather jerkin and spread it on the ground which was strewn with the husks of the beechnuts. Squirrels had already been busy harvesting the fruit, Adela thought irrelevantly. An owl hooted from one of the big trees and another answered from near by. She shivered and Titus quickly put an arm around her shoulders.

'I owe you an explanation, my dearest,' he said softly, 'and an apology for having deceived you in this fashion; but I had to take these measures, Addy. You would never have agreed to leave Kitty, and we were all determined that you must be made to go home.'

As understanding filled her mind, Adela twisted free of his embrace, her eyes brilliant with anger as she stared up at him. 'You had no right to force me against my will, Titus. Have you not understood anything at all? Kitty, my little sister, is dying – dying, Titus, and you expect me to leave her at such a time? When she might be in danger? We discussed it, and you agreed – yes, *agreed* – that I should stay with Eugénie and Kitty and that you and Barnaby would return to the château when you have seen Monsieur l'Abbé and the others safely on board.'

'That was before I realized quite how serious the situation was here in France!' Titus said. 'Both Barny and I had supposed that the violence, the killings, the bloodshed were taking place for the most part in Paris. We did not appreciate that it could be happening here in the country, in Normandy. I love you too much to allow you to risk your life unnecessarily, my dearest!'

Adela's mouth tightened. Despite the thrumming in her head, she beat her hands against his chest in frustration.

'I do not call that love!' she said bitterly. 'I had made clear to you where *I* felt my duty lay, yet you put your peace of mind before my wishes. As to my "risking my life unnecessarily" – can you really call the comfort I could bring to a dying child "unnecessary"?'

The scorn in her voice was like a knife wound and Titus flinched from it, but he would not alter his standpoint.

'You are my wife now, Addy, and I freely admit that your safe keeping is of greater importance to me than your sister's happiness. In any event, Eugénie loves her and will care for her without your assistance as she has done for the past year.'

'It is precisely because I have spent so little time with Kitty this last year that I wished now to share with her what time is left. I shall go back, Titus. You shall not prevent me.'

As she tried to rise to her feet, Titus took hold once more of her arm.

'We have been travelling four hours or more, Addy. You cannot go back. For one thing there is no one to escort you. You know very well that we *must* get Philippe and the others away from France as quickly as we can. Three lives are at stake!'

'I do not ask for an escort!' Adela cried furiously. 'I will go on my own. One of you can ride in the wagon and I will take his horse.'

'Calm yourself, my love! You know you could never find your way!' Titus said gently. 'Even with Philippe to assist us, we have twice taken the wrong track. In places, there are no tracks at all! And the wolves . . . even I, an armed man, would not venture at night alone in this benighted forest!'

That Titus' words were entirely logical and could brook no reasonable argument, only increased Adela's frustration which was mingled in equal parts with grief at her unwitting parting from Kitty. Where a short while ago she had imagined it impossible for any woman to love a man as much as she loved Titus, now she felt only anger and hatred towards him.

'You deceived me . . . cheated . . . lied!' she flared. 'Eugénie would never have given me that opiate had you not obliged her to do so. I know why you have done this – Barny made you do it. He was never in agreement that I should come to Normandy in the first place. You do as *he* wants rather than as *I* want. Your twin is more important to you than your wife and I suppose it is time I woke up to the fact. You would do anything for each other, would you not? You would die for him – yet you would not even put my wishes before your own. I hate you, Titus Mallory. I hate you – and I wish I had never married you!'

'Addy – enough!' Titus said sharply. 'I told you I was sorry I was forced to deceive you. I think my behaviour was justified – the more so now I realize that Barny was right – you would never have left of your own free will. Well, like it or not, you *are* my wife and as your husband, I shall decide what is best for you.'

Despite her attempts to resist him, he pulled her to her feet and started back towards the wagon. Philippe and Barnaby had dismounted and were talking quietly together. Philippe looked up anxiously as Titus approached.

'I think we should move on as quickly as we can!' he said in a low voice. 'We must be far deeper into the forest before dawn. I heard a church clock strike midnight not long back so we cannot be far from a town or village. I fear we have been travelling round in a circle this past hour!'

With a feeling of helplessness mixed with a desire to retain her dignity, Adela twisted free of Titus' restraining hand and walked stiffly back to the wagon. It was Barnaby who hurried forward to assist her.

'It is for the best, Addy, believe me!' he said as, with a stony face, she accepted his help. 'You must not be angry with Titus!'

Ignoring him, she let the canvas flaps fall to behind her.

The old Abbé and the Curé had, in her absence, fallen asleep. The grey wig Eugénic had provided for the elderly man had slipped sideways and his mouth had fallen open as he snored. Beside him, the Curé's head had sunk on to his chest, his bonnet tipped at a grotesque angle over his pointed features. So ridiculous did they both look that for a moment, Adela was hard put to remind herself that they were men of God, men whose faith in God was immutable.

How, she asked herself as the tears stung her eyes, could they reconcile this Heavenly Being with a God who refused to save the life of the innocent nine-year-old Kitty? With a God who ordained that Ned – and then little Robert – should die in so horrifying a fashion? Would a merciful deity condemn a fine, good, kind man like her father to be paralysed for so many years of his life? How could they worship a God who allowed his Catholic subjects to torture, butcher their clerics – men like this Abbé and the simple Père Jérôme? Did the beautiful Princess Lamballe keep *her* faith as her head was struck from her body?

As the tears poured down Adela's cheeks, she remembered the depths of love she and Titus had so recently shared, and questioned how such God-given beauty and passion could so easily be turned to resentment and hate.

CHAPTER TWENTY-THREE

1792

For the fifth time in the space of an hour, the three young men were obliged to dismount as the wagon ground to a halt. Twice, fallen branches lay across the only clear passage through the beech trees and had to be dragged aside; twice the rough track petered out and they were forced to retrace their passage and take an alternative route; once, one of the wagon wheels had dipped so deeply into a rut that even with Jacques' and the Curé's assistance, the three young men had been hard put to drag the cart clear.

'The progress we are making is all but negligible!' Titus said as, yet again, they found themselves unable to make headway through the undergrowth. 'If we are ever to reach the coast, we shall have to risk detection upon the roads. What say you, Philippe, Barny?'

His companions looked anxiously at the wagon. Despite its covering, the cold night air had penetrated the interior and on their last inspection, they had observed all three occupants shivering beneath their cloaks. The Abbé looked exhausted although he protested that he had no need of sleep but was merely a little stiff from the jolting of the cart. Adela, mercifully, had succumbed once more to the after-effects of the laudanum and was curled up on the straw oblivious to the problems.

Titus looked up through the trees, some of which were approaching one hundred feet in height. No moonlight filtered through the branches now and he could see no sign of any stars. He pulled a compass from his pocket.

'Let us go on in as easterly a direction as we can,' he suggested. 'There must be country lanes leading north in the direction of Abbeville. How many leagues would you think we have travelled, Philippe?'

'No more than ten at most!' Philippe muttered. 'Perhaps less!'

'It would seem as if even the weather is turning to our disadvantage!' Barnaby said for he had felt the spattering of raindrops on his face.

The slight protection that the canopy of leaves had briefly afforded them now ceased to be effective as the storm broke. Within minutes, they were all drenched. Their mounts and the two cart-horses stood patiently with heads drooping as the water dripped off their steaming flanks. The dusty track turned inexorably into a quagmire.

'We must get out of this forest afore we carnt shift the wagon no more!' Jacques' voice sounded calm but authoritative as he came to stand beside them. 'I saw one of them shrines to St Christophe not a league back, an' if I'm not much mistook, Aubépine village ain't far from there.'

'I had forgot that you roamed these woods as a boy!' Titus said with a lightening of his spirits. 'We must be close to the de Falence estate then, Jacques?'

The man grinned.

'I reckon as 'ow it were the de Falence village church we 'eard a-striking not long since.'

'Devil take it, man, you should have spoken sooner!' Philippe said uneasily for his keen ear had detected the distant rumble of thunder. 'En avant, mes amis, before we are drowned like rats!'

Dawn was breaking when at last the trees began to thin out and the wagon drew to yet another halt. The violence of the storm had abated but evidence of its effects were all too obvious as the travellers surveyed one another. They were besmattered with mud from head to toe, as were the horses and the wagon. The tarred canvas had not withstood the downpour and although the occupants were not mud covered, they were wet through. Adela was shivering with cold as she emerged to stand beside Philippe. Titus hurried to her side but still furiously angry with him, she ignored both him and Barnaby as simultaneously, they removed their jerkins and offered them to her.

'Where are we? What is happening?' she asked, trying unsuccessfully to keep her teeth from chattering.

'We are close by the village d'Aubépine, cousin!' Philippe said as he put an arm protectively about her shoulders. 'See down there, beyond that large oak tree? You can just make out the roofs of the cottages.'

'And smoke coming from some of them, Miss Addy!' Jacques said, his voice tinged with anxiety. 'We cannot be sure 'tis safe to go any nearer. I think we should see if we can find shelter in the castle ruins. Over there on that 'illtop there was once a Roman military camp what was built on in the twelfth century, Master tolt me. 'Tis said the ruins be 'aunted by the ghosts of the *Seigneur* and his family what owned the castle and was all murdered there a 'undred years ago. No one ain't lived there since, and no local man, woman or child will venture there.'

'Then it will be ideal for us!' Titus said eagerly. 'We will rest there during the day and travel on at nightfall.'

He made as if to assist Adela back into the wagon, but she turned quickly away from him, and with as much dignity as she could manage in the circumstances, climbed in unaided. Philippe grinned but Barnaby could see how upset and angry Titus was and, as he swung himself back into the saddle, he said quietly to his brother, 'Give her time, Titus! It is not in Addy's nature to remain angry for long.'

As Adela relayed the latest plan to the Abbé and the Curé, she was not so much angry as determined. As soon as she could, she would return to the Château de Saint Cyrille, she had decided. There was no going back for the present; but after Titus and Barnaby had seen the three men safely on to the cutter with Jacques, she intended to return to Eugénie with the twins. For one thing, Philippe's horse would be available for her use. If Titus tried once again to persuade her or force her to board with the Abbé and the Curé, she would gallop off without him! She might even find an opportunity to do so before they reached Anse Goéland, the cove where the boat had been concealed in one of the many huge caves bordering the beach.

Adela had but one thought in her mind now, and that was to return to Kitty's bedside and remain there for as long as there was reason to do so. She considered it unlikely the citizen-patriots would know of her cousinly relationship to Philippe, whereas it was common knowledge that Eugénie was his sister; thus Eugénie was in far greater danger than herself, more especially if one of the servants betrayed their mistress and revealed that she had been hiding *émigrés* in her home.

By the time the tired horses pulled the creaking wagon over the rotting boards of the drawbridge into the inner courtyard of the castle, dawn had broken. There the tall, crumbling masonry of the keep sheltered them from the chilling wind and concealed them from the village which had now come to life. Sounds reached them from across the fields – the crowing of cockerels, the noise of hammer on anvil, the shout of the goatherd as he shepherded his animals into the rough pastures on the hillside. A dog was barking furiously in a farmyard, the sound intermingling with the loud cackle of geese from the village pond. The figure of a woman, diminished by the distance, could be seen working the pump handle, sending bright streams of water into her pail. The scene was one of peace and normality. Nevertheless, Titus said, 'We dare not risk lighting a fire. I regret that I cannot offer you greater comfort, Monsieur l'Abbé, Monsieur le Curé. A little cognac perhaps will restore some warmth to our veins.'

The old man allowed himself to be lifted down from the wagon. He stumbled as his clogged feet touched the ground and shook his head apologetically as Titus and Philippe helped him to prop himself in a sitting position against one of the moss-covered walls.

'I fear I am a burden to you all, my children!' he said in a weak voice. 'But for my frailties, you could have reached the coast on horseback by now.'

'And been obliged to forgo all the comforts with which my dear cousin has provided us!' Adela said quickly. 'We shall not go short of food for she has supplied us with a big hamper that will surely last us a week or more! There is a cask of ale; cognac; fruit, and she has even thought of oats for the horses so that we shall not need to risk them being seen grazing.'

'May *le bon Dieu* reward Madame for her goodness,' the Abbé said sighing. 'My books and parchments are safe, my daughter?'

'I wrapped them in oilskin to protect them!' Adela said reassuringly. 'Now I will prepare the meal and then you must try to sleep, Monsieur l'Abbé, for I fear you had little rest last night.'

It seemed as if the fates were being kinder to them on this new day for the storm had passed and now a pale autumn sun was giving them warmth as well as the comfort of blue skies and larks singing high above the ruined castle tower.

Having dispensed the food, Adela sat between the Abbé and the Curé so that Titus had no chance to talk to her privately. She was very well aware of his proximity as with long legs stretched out before him, he laughed and joked with Barnaby and Philippe, seemingly unaware of her presence. He looked, as did Barnaby, astonishingly handsome despite their lowly peasant garb. Wigless, their fair hair curling about their faces, their appearance reminded her of the two youths of her childhood whom she had loved so dearly.

With an effort, Adela steeled herself against the longing to forgive the twins for deceiving her, for she wanted nothing more than to be sitting near to Titus, his arm around her, his body close to hers. She knew that she had but to make a move towards him and they would be instantly reconciled; but she dared not do so lest he use her weakness as a reason to renew his demands that she go back to England. It was far easier to resist him whilst she could nurture her resentment and keep him physically at a distance.

By the time they had finished eating and the Abbé had led them in prayers for their safe-keeping, for Kitty, for Eugénie and for all those in peril during his country's turmoil, the long night's exigencies were taking their toll, and one by one each member of the party fell asleep. The sun was already moving to the west when Adela was awoken by the touch of a hand on her shoulder. Her brain still befuddled with sleep, she forgot her anger and held out her arms to the man she believed to be Titus. It was, however, Barnaby, who quickly identified himself as he helped her to her feet. Adela tried to conceal her disappointment as, with his finger to his lips, he beckoned her to follow him to a spot some distance away where they would be beyond the earshot of the others.

'Forgive me for disturbing your slumbers, Addy!' he said. 'I wanted to talk to you alone.'

He was frowning as he spoke and did not meet Adela's questioning gaze.

'I felt I should enlighten you as to . . . as to Titus' feelings,' he said awkwardly. 'He is wretchedly disquieted, Addy . . . about the quarrel you and he had last night.'

Adela's voice was icy-cold as she said forcefully, 'May I ask why your brother, *my husband*, has not the courage to speak for himself? Is he so frightened of a mere female that he must send an emissary to speak for him? For shame, Barny, you do him no service!'

Barnaby's cheeks were flushed as at last he looked into Adela's eyes.

'Titus did not ask me to speak for him, Addy. I took it upon myself. I know how he is feeling at this moment. He loves you dearly . . . and to be at crossed swords with you must be tormenting him.'

Adela's green eyes flashed.

'It would not seem so, Barny, for he sleeps like a child! I think you are mistaken in attributing your feelings to him.'

As tears filled her eyes, Barnaby's face whitened. 'Titus is only doing his duty by seeking to protect you, and if you have any real love for him, you would not seek to countermand his wishes.'

It was so unlike Barnaby to speak harshly to her that Adela's tears were arrested. Her mouth tightened.

'I had hoped that *you* would understand, Barny. I suppose I should have known that you would side with Titus no matter what. Both of you speak as if my life might be forfeit if I remained at the château, but if you are sincere in your belief that there is real danger of an attack by that wretched mob of bloodthirsty villains, then you had no right to leave Eugénie alone. Why did not one of you remain with her? You would only be gone three days, you said, but we are nowhere near the coast and at the rate we are travelling, it could be three days yet before we reach it.'

Barnaby was effectively silenced, for it was true that they were taking far longer to cover each league than they had estimated. Should he, perhaps, return to take care of Eugénie and the child?

They were standing thus, silent, each deep in their own thoughts when they became aware that Jacques had joined them. His brow was creased in a worried frown.

''Tis the 'orses, Master Barnaby. I cannot stop them from neighing. The grey mare is the worst . . . the one they call Fleur. 'Tis my guess she's 'eard one of them farm 'orses in the field yonder and is inviting 'im to visit 'er. Could be she's ready for 'orsing . . .' He glanced apologetically at Adela and said, 'In season, Miss Addy!'

'I will inform Titus!' Barnaby said immediately. 'Perhaps we should move back into the woods.'

Titus wakened at a touch and his face clouded as he listened to what his twin had to say. He peered through one of the apertures in the walls and as he did so, he saw the farm horses turn their heads as Fleur gave a shrill whinny. It was impossible to tell at such a distance if the farmer, too, looked towards the castle, but as Titus watched, the man drew his horses to a halt and climbed down from his cart. Abandoning his animals, he made off across the beet field towards the village.

'Could be he fears an attack by robbers and has gone to seek assistance,' Titus said.

'Perhaps he thinks there are horses amongst the castle ghosts?' Barnaby suggested with a wry grin.

'Or he suspects someone is in hiding here and is going to alert the citizen-patriots who are almost certainly in authority in the village.'

'Maybe I should ride down on Fleur and put 'is mind at rest!' Jacques said thoughtfully. 'I could pretend I'd stolen 'er from the farm of an *aristo* but 'ad lost my way in the forest.'

'A brave notion,' Titus said warmly, 'but not a practical one, Jacques. For one thing, you have no papers and you would certainly be taken for questioning. Who knows that you would not be arrested on suspicion of heaven-knows-what? If you were not able to return to us, who would sail the cutter back to England?'

'They might take Fleur, too, and one horse alone could not draw the wagon,' Barnaby added. 'It is too risky, Jacques.'

Adela now spoke for the first time.

'Could we not wait to see what happens? The farmer knows no more than that there is a horse somewhere up here.'

'An animal valuable as a beast of burden or as food!' Titus pointed out. 'It is my opinion that the wagon should be moved immediately before the man returns. Philippe can stay with it whilst Barny and I remain concealed on the edge of the forest. If it seems that our presence here has prompted an investigation, we can cause a diversion by allowing ourselves to be seen and then riding off in the opposite direction. What say you, Barny?'

'Agreed!' Barnaby said instantly. Titus now turned his attention to Adela.

'I shall be relying on you to see that Monsieur l'Abbé and Monsieur le Curé are kept as comfortable as possible!' he said. 'Philippe will need to keep his eyes and ears alert for unwelcome visitors and Jacques will have his hands full with the horses. If Barny and I are forced in the opposite direction, we will turn about at the earliest opportunity and rejoin you.'

It was on the tip of Adela's tongue to protest, but even with her own plans to the forefront of her mind, she recognized the need for an urgent departure. With a nod, she hurried away to assist the two clerics who, ignorant of this new possible danger, were still dozing against the castle wall.

Some time elapsed before the hamper, the flagons, nosebags, tankards and cushions had been stacked inside the wagon, and Jacques had put both horses back in the shafts. As they drove once more over the thick planks of the drawbridge, the wheels of the wagon and hooves of the horses echoing in the empty moat beneath, Adela peered anxiously in the direction of the village. With a hurriedly beating heart, she saw that a group of people on foot were heading towards the beet fields. Titus and Barnaby must have seen them too, for she could hear them calling to Jacques to hurry the horses without regard to the jolting of the occupants of the cart.

'Make speed, make speed!' they shouted in unison.

'Keep as near to the north-west as you can!' Titus added a last instruction to Philippe as they approached the first sparse cluster of trees. 'We will wait here, and if they approach, we will ride off to the south. May God go with you!'

He leaned down from his horse so that his face was but a yard from Adela's.

'Take great care of yourself, my dearest!' he said in a low, urgent voice. 'I shall be with you again soon but meanwhile, remember that I love you with all my heart. *A bientôt!*'

As he and Barnaby rode away, Adela felt her own heart constrict. 'I shall be with you again soon!' he had said, but how long would it really be before she could tell him that *she* loved *him*; that she was frightened not for herself but for his safe keeping. Titus was already beyond earshot, his tall, straight back erect in the saddle as he rode beside his brother. She knew it was nonsensical to fear that their separation might prove to last far longer than an hour or two; that Titus was in any real danger. Even if they intended harm which was not yet proven, the approaching men were on foot and Titus and Barnaby were mounted. Why then should she feel as if an icy wind were blowing against the back of her neck? It was not simply that the evening shadows were falling and that the air had suddenly cooled; nor that behind her the Abbé was intoning the twenty-third psalm. It was a presentiment stronger than a dream; more tenacious than a nightmare.

The tilting of the wagon as it hit a raised tree root swung Adela off balance. Her head thudded heavily against an iron hinge, and with one single cry of pain, she lost consciousness. A full half-hour passed before she once more became aware of her surroundings. Père Jérôme was kneeling beside her, holding a cold wet kerchief against her forehead.

'Titus? My husband . . .? What has happened?' she asked as she struggled to a sitting position. 'Where are we?'

'Quite safe, my child!' said the Curé. 'We have been sorely anxious about you. You hit your head, you see. Fortunately, I could feel no serious damage though I fear you may be bruised.'

'But Titus – Mr Mallory!' Adela said weakly. 'Have he and his brother rejoined us?'

'Not yet, but I am certain they will do so shortly. Events transpired as your husband had anticipated, and he and his brother were obliged to ride south. We did hear the distant sound of a musket shot . . . perhaps two . . . but . . . I am sure we have no occasion to worry. The good Lord will be with them both.'

Despite the throbbing of her head, Adela was now fully conscious.

'How can you be so certain, Père Jérôme? You said you heard two musket shots—'

'We must put our trust in God, my daughter!' the Abbé broke in in his high, quavering voice. 'Your husband and his brother are good Christians and the good Lord will protect them!'

'As He protected the Princess Lamballe? Your own monks? All those other "good Christians" who have been murdered?' Adela cried, too disturbed to remember that she was addressing so august a personage as the Abbé.

'His will be done!' the Abbé said. 'Now let us say the Lord's prayer!'

It was not a prayer Adela desired at that moment, nor indeed that matters should be left to the will of God. She wanted Titus safely back where she could see him, hear his voice, tell him that she was deeply sorry for having lost her temper with him; that she could never, ever hate him; that she loved him more than life itself. Two musket shots! The words hammered in her brain, drowning the words of the Abbé; stifling the sound of the creaking wagon, the horses' hooves. Two musket shots – and Titus and Barny carried only pistols.

'Please, God,' she whispered, 'do not let Titus – or Barny – be harmed.'

Despite her protest to the Abbé, Adela prayed.

It was close on half an hour before the search party was near enough to the fringe of the forest for Titus and Barnaby to assess whether they were in any danger, or if it were no more than curiosity that had brought the group of men to investigate. However, their fears were justified. One of the men was wearing a red cap and tricoloured cockade; he was armed with a musket and sabre, and was mounted on horseback. The remainder were peasants, poorly clad with straw twisted around their legs and thatched over their shoulders to protect them from the rain now driving down in cold spears. They, too, were armed – but with pitchforks, iron bars and hatchets. There could be little doubt as to the outcome were they to find their quarry.

Waiting only until they could be sighted, Titus and Barnaby spurred their horses and set off at speed towards the cover of the trees deeper in the forest. Hunched over his saddle, Titus heard the sound of a musket shot followed shortly after by another. He could also hear the loud cries of their pursuers one to another. He turned to Barnaby with a grin of satisfaction for he knew now that they had succeeded in diverting the men's attention from the track the wagon had taken and which would now be out of sight. To his astonishment, he saw that his twin had allowed his reins to fall slack and that he was holding his left hand against his right shoulder. Moreover, Barnaby's horse was following his own and was in danger of tripping over the slackened rein.

Hurriedly Titus drew his mount to a halt and reaching over, grabbed Barnaby's bridle. His brother's face was deathly white and twisted in pain. Realizing that Barnaby had been hit, Titus vaulted from his horse and ran to his twin's side.

'The second shot . . . glanced off my shoulder . . .' Barnaby managed to gasp before his body slumped in the saddle. But for Titus' support, he would have fallen heavily to the ground.

'God's teeth!' Titus expostulated as he struggled to manoeuvre Barnaby's body from his horse to a nearby tree. Propping him into a sitting position, he asked urgently, 'Is the pain bad? Say something – anything!'

He could almost feel the agony Barnaby was suffering now that the first numbness had worn off. Attempting a smile Barnaby muttered, 'Cannot move my right hand! Better in moment, God willing!'

Titus pulled the rough cotton neckcloth from around his throat and as gently as he could, tried to staunch the flow of blood from the wound. He saw at once that the musketball had not entered the shoulder but had grazed it deeply enough to expose the muscle and blade-bone. He realized then that the wound needed expert attention. A more superficial injury he could have seared with a hot iron – a remedy he knew Jacques had successfully employed on cuts to horses' legs to safeguard the animals from poisoning of the blood – for both he and Barnaby carried tinderboxes with which to light a fire.

The rain now falling steadily through the tree branches was diluting the stream of blood from Barnaby's wound and his shirt was stained a vivid pink. Without thought for the cold, Titus removed his jerkin and pulled his shirt over his head. With steady hands, he tore off strips of cotton to make a bandage and with the remaining rags, formed a pad which he placed gently over the wound. Barnaby's gasp of pain as he performed these tasks ate into his very soul.

'Beg pardon, old fellow! Not cut out for a bone-setter, I fear!' he said with an attempt at humour. Barnaby's parody of a smile only added to his distress. As he worked to staunch the wound, he realized that there was no question now that they could catch up with Philippe, Adela and the wagon. Barnaby was in no condition to sit upon his horse and even were Titus to hold him astride his own nag, the animal would be over-weighted and move far too slowly with its double load. However slowly the wagon was travelling, an hour at least must have passed since they departed in opposite directions and the distance between them was lengthening with every passing minute.

Barnaby had been following his twin's train of thought.

'You should go without me, Titus,' he said. 'I will rest here awhile and when I am stronger, I will make my way back to Saint Cyrille. Eugénie will tend my wound.'

''Pon my soul, brother, 'tis not only your arm which is disabled but your thinking, too! You'd not make the distance in your condition. Now lie still whilst I seek some shelter for us. We cannot spend the night in this accursed rain!'

'But Addy, the others—' Barnaby protested weakly.

Titus interrupted him, the firmness of his tone belying his unease as he said, 'They have Philippe and Jacques to protect them. Tomorrow, when you are recovered a little, I shall accompany you back to the château and . . .' He broke off, putting his finger to his lips. 'Hush, I can hear voices!' he cautioned.

'They are searching for us. Pray God those confounded nags of ours keep silent!'

The muffled shouts of their pursuers came from some distance away. Gradually, they came closer and Titus held his breath as the breaking of twigs and the sound of their voices finally reached him from but a dozen yards away.

'We have been searching long enough, citizens . . .'

'. . . our duty to the Republic . . .'

'. . . traitors, I tell you; traitors who seek to 'ide from the justice of the people . . .'

'This rain is wetting me to the bone. I say we've searched long enough . . .'

There was a moment or two's silence followed by a trampling of the undergrowth and then with agonizing slowness, the rough, guttural voices died away.

'Demme if the dolts have not abandoned their search!' Titus whispered softly in relief. He turned to Barnaby, the eagerness of his expression quickly fading as with a stab of fear he saw that his twin's head had fallen sideways on to his chest, and his fair curls were stained scarlet by the blood now seeping from the thickly padded wound.

CHAPTER TWENTY-FOUR

1792

Every nerve in Adela's body was screaming in protest as Jacques drew the wagon to a halt behind a cluster of wind-swept trees. They were at the summit of a footpath but a few leagues distant from the port of le Tréport, leading down the cliff face to the cove where the cutter lay hidden. From here she could see the wide expanse of grey water which was the English Channel.

But for Jacques and Philippe, she thought, she would not be here. It was Philippe who had finally persuaded her that if she were to remain in France, far from being of assistance to the twins, she would of a certainty be a burden. Moreover, it was now two days since they had parted company, and even she accepted that it was madness to expect she could find them. The dangers besetting a young woman alone on horseback in the vast expanse of the forest were immense, Philippe had reiterated. There were hungry packs of wolves, outlaws, criminals whom the patriots had released from the gaols, even peasants sympathetic to the causes of the Republic, all of whom would be ready to attack her. It was not even as if she could find her way unaided to Saint Cyrille.

Jacques had added his own persuasions.

'Even if you was lucky enough to meet up with the young masters, Miss Addy, they would 'ave to be watching after your safety 'stead of looking to their own. You doant need worry about them none – they can tek care o' theirselves. 'Sides which . . .' he had added with a quick glance at Philippe, '. . . Monsieur de Falence tolt me he ain't much of a sailor, 'e 'aving no stomach for it; Monsieur l'Abbé ain't fit and I doubt as 'ow Monsieur le Curé knows the bow from the stern, let alone a mainsa'l from a jib! Like as not, I am a-going to need your 'elp, Miss Addy.'

Beside herself with anxiety for Titus, Adela had pleaded for a delay to their sailing in case the twins should yet arrive; but Philippe would not hear of it. When he reminded her that he had promised Eugénie they would get the two clerics safely to England, she was obliged to abandon any further thought of taking his horse and going in search of the twins. Jacques had assured her that as soon as the passengers were safely landed, he would return to France without delay to ascertain their well-being. Although neither he nor Philippe were yet aware of it, she had every intention of accompanying Jacques.

She glanced now at the Abbé and saw at once that Jacques was right to have suggested that they must leave the wagon here and carry the old man down the cliff path. After two days and nights of travel, the elderly abbot was far too weak to stand, and during the night, his mind had begun to wander. Privately she doubted if he would ever reach England alive.

Between them Jacques and Philippe struggled down the narrow rocky path with their burden. Seagulls screeched above their heads and Adela, who was leading the way, was hit frequently by small stones and rocks dislodged by the men behind her. A stiff breeze tore into the cliff face and tossed back the hood of her cloak so that her hair blew blindingly across her face making the descent even more perilous.

Close behind her was the Curé, like herself clutching a parcel of the Abbé's books and documents between his hands. Adela could see the terror on his face as he struggled to keep his balance on the steep incline. If one of his muttered prayers had been answered by the Almighty, she told herself wryly, it was that they saw no sign of human activity other than that of two fishing boats out to sea. Nor, as Jacques had feared, was there sign of a French naval vessel patrolling the coastline in an attempt to arrest any *émigrés* they might espy.

The path came to an abrupt halt some thirty feet above the sea. From then on it was a matter of trying to keep a foothold on the jagged rocks. They sloped sharply down and now she could see the twins' cutter rocking at its mooring in the deep inlet into the cliff where it had been hidden from view. So cleverly had it been concealed, it was impossible for anyone to see it from above where the outcrop of rocks over-hung the cove; or from the sea where a large spur of rock jutted out at an angle across the entrance.

It would be no easy matter steering the boat past this rock and out to sea, Adela thought uneasily as she stared down at the cuts and grazes on her hands. Père Jérôme was doing likewise, his thin face deathly pale and heavily lined as he stared at the boat.

'It is so small!' he muttered apprehensively. 'Perhaps . . . if we are too many for the boat . . . I should remain here?'

Adela realized with some surprise that the Curé was now trembling with naked fear which he was trying unsuccessfully to conceal.

'We shall manage!' she said firmly. 'I can assure you, Père Jérôme, that Jacques is an excellent sailor!'

Nevertheless she was very well aware that the tiny cuddy had been built to shelter no more than two. The Abbé would have to be lain full length on the single bunk, and such floor space as remained would be cramped and uncomfortable if two more were to shelter there.

Jacques and Philippe had now reached the rock where Adela was standing. They were gasping for breath as they laid down their burden. Adela bent down to the old man. His breathing was shallow, his skin an unhealthy parchment colour, his eyes closed. From time to time, he muttered a word or two and she was able to understand that his mind was concerned with one thing only – his life's work.

'Your books and documents are quite safe, Monsieur L'Abbé,' she reassured him. 'I give you my word we shall not leave them behind.'

He appeared to lapse into unconsciousness then, which was as well for it proved no easy matter to carry him aboard the cutter. The boat rocked wildly, threatening to tip them all over the gunnel. Jacques now took command. As soon as the Abbé and the Curé were settled in the cuddy, he called to Philippe to hoist the jib whilst he dealt with the mainsail.

'You take the tiller, Miss Addy, whilst I am busy! Keep 'er steady on the rock until I tek over.'

Obediently Adela eased herself in the stern sheets and tucked the tiller under her arm. As soon as the sails came up, the boat began to move and she tightened her hold on the tiller. Keeping her eyes firmly fixed on the rock guarding the entrance to the cove, she saw the white water as the waves broke against the base on the outgoing tide. Jacques scrambled aft and took the tiller from her. Casting an anxious look ahead of him, he said, 'Think we might be in for some dirty weather, Miss Addy!'

She followed his gaze and for the first time, noticed the spume blowing off the crests of the waves quite far out to sea. As they cleared the shelter of the land, the wind billowed in great gusts under her cloak and once more blew the hood from about her head.

Without warning, both sails suddenly filled out and the little boat heeled dangerously.

'See to the jib, Miss Addy!' Jacques said authoritatively. He raised his voice and beckoned furiously to Philippe. 'Come aft, Monsieur Philippe, over here!' he shouted. As Philippe staggered precariously towards him edging awkwardly past Adela, she saw that her cousin's face had lost every vestige of colour. It was clear that the motion of the boat was already having its effect and that there would not be much assistance forthcoming from him. It was a mercy, she thought, that she had paid proper attention during those long hours at sea when Titus, Barnaby and Jacques had initiated her into the mysteries of seamanship. Obedient to Jacques' command, she reached for the rope wound round the cleat.

The coarse wet hemp chafed her hands as she hauled the jib in and wound it back round the cleat. It was a very long time since she had subjected her hands to such rough treatment and if it continued, they would quickly blister, she realized with dismay.

With Philippe now hanging weakly to the side of the boat, it returned to a more even keel. He cast an apologetic smile at Jacques, and was about to speak when he was obliged to give way to violent retching.

As the light strengthened, Adela could see the outline of the French coast fading rapidly. She felt a wave of renewed anxiety for Titus as they sailed further and further north. Where was he? Which of the twins, if either, had been shot? There had been two shots. Was it possible that both had been wounded? Killed? If they had been unharmed as Jacques and Philippe had assured her, why had they not caught up with the wagon during these past two days? Although she had hated Philippe for reminding her, she knew he was right when he said that if Titus and Barnaby could be asked, they would have insisted that the wagon was not delayed in order to wait for them.

Fortunately she was allowed no time for further deliberations. Jacques was calling to her once more for help.

'We've shipped a fair bit of water, Miss Addy. Can you take the tiller for a moment whilst I bail?'

He produced a bailing-tin from beneath his seat and as she took the tiller from him, he began scooping up the dirty water now slopping from side to side in the bottom of the boat. Looking down at her feet, Adela realized that her shoes and stockings were soaking wet. It was several minutes before Jacques, grinning cheerfully, returned to her side to take the tiller from her.

'Carnt see the French coast no more. We should be safe enough now, lessen we meet up with a Frenchie patrol boat. You'm looking larmentable cold, Miss Addy. Now the wind's dropped, it'll be safe enough for you to go in to the cuddy. Ain't much room in there but it'll be a sight warmer, surely!'

Over the years, Jacques' native accent had become more and more peppered with Sussex dialect and at times, except for a slight rolling of his r's, it was hard to tell he was not reared in that county. He was a good man, Adela thought as she made her way with difficulty to the tiny cabin. Small wonder that Dolly was willing to marry him despite the difference in their ages; and that the twins looked upon him more as a friend than a servant. His loyalty was absolute and she took comfort from the fact that he would appear more deeply worried if he really believed harm had come to either of them.

The rise in Adela's spirits lasted only until she was crouched within the cuddy where she found Père Jérôme kneeling beside the bunk on which lay the Abbé. The Curé was praying, intoning the Latin words in a soft keening tone as he gave his superior the Last Rites. One look at the Abbé's face confirmed Adela's fears – the man they had risked so much to rescue was dying. That the old man would pass away before they could reach the safe haven of England was a bitter realization. Eugénie had warned her that he was ill – too ill really to make such a long and perilous journey. None the less there had been no alternative, for to remain could only mean certain death for him at the hands of his persecutors. At least the poor man seemed in no pain, the slow rise and fall of his chest indicating that his heart was beating ever more slowly until finally it must stop.

As she knelt down beside Père Jérôme, Adela tried to keep her thoughts upon his prayers; but the boat's noises distracted her – the slapping of the waves, the hissing of the water as they cut their way through it, the clapping of the sails, the creaking of the hull. The sounds evoked memories of the journey out from England and distracted her mind. When Jacques and Barnaby had crewed, she and Titus had lain locked together on the tiny bunk, the warmth of their bodies permeating their clothes as they had kissed and embraced one another. With a wicked gleam in his eyes, Titus had suggested they remove their clothes and laughed at Adela's protest that Jacques or Barnaby might come in whilst they were taking their pleasure of each other.

'One day, we will go sailing together – just the two of us!' he had said. 'Then we shall wait until we are becalmed and I shall make love to you, here on this bunk. I wonder sometimes if you have even a tiny notion of how desirable you are, my dearest. If only your mama had had a dozen more like you, then other men could have enjoyed the same pleasure you give me!'

Adela had not thought of it at the time but now, remembering, she wondered if he had really meant 'a dozen'; or had he wished that she, too, had been an identical twin so that poor Barnaby could be as happy as he was?

'Monsieur l'Abbé is in God's hands!'

Père Jérôme's voice broke in on Adela's thoughts, and she looked at him guiltily.

'I am so very sorry,' she said. 'Should I tell Monsieur de Falence?'

Pale-faced, the Curé nodded.

'Monsieur l'Abbé has many Brothers in your country. They will wish to conduct an appropriate burial service for him, so we must not bury him at sea.'

Philippe, however, was unable to feel any concern for the Abbé's passing. He was suffering so badly from *mal de mer* that Adela did not doubt him when he groaned that he, too, wished to die!

'Best leave the reverend gen'leman's corpse where 'tis, Miss Addy!' Jacques called over to her. 'We doant 'ave no canvas to bury 'im in and it wouldn't be fittin' just to put 'im over the side. Like Monsieur le Curé said, 'e can be buried proper when we gets ashore.'

Adela nodded.

'Perhaps you would feel a little better if you were to lie down, Philippe,' she suggested, fearful now that he was so weakened by nausea that he might fall overboard. 'If Père

Jérôme will come out, you can stretch out on the floor. Perhaps you might sleep!'

'*Sacrebleu!*' Philippe gasped. 'I thought I could not feel worse than I did on the packets, but this . . .'

When he had recovered from yet another bout of retching, Adela took the tiller once more from Jacques who half carried the sufferer into the cuddy. The Curé emerged, his face whiter than ever.

'Did your servant say how long this journey will be, madame?' he enquired. 'You will think me unworthy of my cloth for admitting it, but I am far more frightened here on this tiny boat than ever I was in Madame la Chevalière's home! I have never even seen the sea before, you understand, and this vessel seems so small!'

Adela did what she could to reassure him.

'We should reach land before nightfall tomorrow,' she told him. 'With a following wind, we could make even better speed. As to our size, we shall be less easily seen if a French patrol is near by. Jacques is a very experienced sailor and I can only repeat that we may leave matters safely in his hands.'

The Curé sighed.

'We are in God's hands!' he intoned. He glanced shyly at Adela. 'You are very courageous, madame!' he said. 'Your husband and his brother likewise; and but for the intervention of Monsieur de Falence, Monsieur l'Abbé and I would most certainly have met with brutal deaths. What is happening now in our country is beyond reason – and I can see no end to it! I am comforted only by the thought that those who desert God cannot prosper.'

'There are those who would say God has deserted the believers,' Adela replied quietly. 'Now that your King has been murdered, methinks 'tis the Devil who rules France!'

Their conversation ended as Jacques reappeared without Philippe; he was carrying a small tin chest.

'There are a few ship's biscuits and some dried fruit in 'ere, Miss Addy,' he told her. 'You and Monsieur le Curé should eat a little whilst you can. Fortunately I'd left these few stores in the locker lest any of us was obliged to return 'ome without provisions.'

Unappetizing as the fare was, Adela took Jacques' advice and urged the Curé to do likewise, for she knew it would be many hours yet before they could eat a proper meal and already they were weakened by exhaustion after so many days on the road. Despite the generous hamper of food Eugénie had prepared for them, with first seven and then five of them to consume it, they had finished the last stick of bread and round of cheese whilst awaiting their dawn descent to the cove.

'There is water and a small cask of wine in the cuddy!' Jacques told her. 'Enough to last us, Miss Addy, if we's careful.'

He glanced down at the compass he had attached round his neck on a cord, and frowned.

'Wind 'as changed!' he muttered. 'We be too far to the west!' He made the necessary adjustment to the tiller and bade Adela tighten on the jib.

With Philippe stretched out upon the floor, mercifully asleep, and the Abbé's body on the bunk, there was no room for Adela to return to the cabin even had she wished to take shelter in the presence of a corpse. Sitting beside Jacques, she gazed at the vast, grey expanse of the sea, the horizon clearly delineated now that the apricot dawn sky had turned a brilliant blue, and was comforted by the thought that the bad weather Jacques' had feared had not been forthcoming. The bow was rising and dipping with soothing regularity and with the wind, they appeared to be making good speed. Every once in a while, a cloud of spray showered her face, hair, clothes, rousing her momentarily from the torpor that had overtaken her. She was growing colder as the hours passed, and to restore her circulation, she paid several visits to the cuddy to see if Philippe was feeling a little better. He was still asleep and she did not try to rouse him.

On her return from one such visit, a sudden gust of wind sent the boat tilting to one side, and as it slanted, she was obliged to cling to the side to avoid being thrown overboard. The mast was leaning over at an acute angle and Jacques shouted to her to reef the sail. It was no easy task slackening the ropes and somewhat to her surprise, Père Jérôme came to assist her. Between them, they managed somehow to secure them as the boat returned once more to an even keel.

Seeing that the Curé's cloak had been drenched with water, she suggested it would be drier if he went to sit in the shelter of the cuddy. She herself returned to Jacques' side and took the tiller from him.

'Time you had a rest and something to eat and drink!' she said to him. 'If we are set on the right course, I think I can hold her steady.'

Jacques grinned as he moved to let her take his place.

'Doant know as 'ow I'd be managing wi'out you, Miss Addy!' he said with a sideways glance at the Curé who was leaning dejectedly against the door of the cuddy with his hands folded. 'Sir Matthew, God bless 'im, would've been that proud of you. 'E were right when 'e said as 'ow you should've been 'is son, not 'is daughter.'

Adela smiled, her spirits lifting.

'My father would certainly be pleased to know that Mr Titus and I are living at Dene Place. Do you ever think of the years Sir Henry had possession of Papa's home, Jacques? Already it seems a long time ago since . . . since . . . he died and yet—'

'Nobbut six months, Miss Addy. Us'll not forget young Master Ned, but Sir 'Enry – 'e were better forgot, I'm thinking.'

As day turned to evening and then to night, the wind freshened and blew steadily from the north-east. Jacques was again in charge of the tiller and was having difficulty in keeping on course. They were travelling at four or five knots and Philippe was once more racked by sickness. He was now so weak that the Curé was obliged to hold him steady as he leaned over the side. The water was flying over the bow and despite her blistered hands, Adela set to with the bailer. The task seemed endless, for as fast as she tipped the tins of water into the ocean, more poured in.

The sky became studded with stars but there was no moon to light the sea. The white crested waves could no longer be seen. The world had closed in around them. Aching in every limb and soaked to the skin, Adela felt more and more miserable. They seemed to have been at sea for weeks although it was not yet a full day since they had set sail, she thought. As exhaustion took hold of her, she found herself dozing off, and her grip on the bailer slackened. Her immobility brought a shout from Jacques.

'You all right, Miss Addy?' he asked, regarding her anxiously. 'What you need is a bit o' sleep. You go into the cuddy and I'll call you if'n I need you.'

Despite her chilled bones and her intense fatigue, Adela shook her head. She could not bring herself to go and lie beside the Abbé's corpse. She knew she would feel even more fearful in the presence of death. Of late they had all been too close to the Life Hereafter and she did not wish this grim reminder of how quickly a life could be extinguished. She wanted to live; to love; to be happy for evermore with Titus. She wanted to be able to reach out and touch his warm, vibrant body – not to be reminded of the dreadful sound of those musket shots.

Whilst Adela's thoughts had been wandering, Jacques, guessing at the cause of her reluctance to follow his suggestion, went to stand beside the Curé. They spoke quietly together for a few minutes and then the Curé nodded his head. Jacques now approached Philippe.

'If'n you can manage it, monsieur, I think we should put . . . put the . . . er, corpse overboard. Miss Addy needs to rest and we is overloaded. We'll make faster speed, as I'm sure you'll be wanting, sir,' he added pointedly.

It was clear that Philippe felt too ill to care what happened, and when Jacques told him that the Curé had reluctantly agreed with this suggestion, he gathered what little strength remained to him and assisted the valet in bringing the Abbé's body out of the cuddy.

'I have never done this before – buried a man at sea!' the Curé said helplessly. 'I think there may be special prayers!'

'For the love of God, get on with it, Père Jérôme!' Philippe said impatiently. 'There is no time for a proper service. Let us say the Lord's prayer and be done with it!'

Although the Curé looked deeply shocked, he obeyed Philippe's instruction and stood back as the two men lifted the body over the side. As if in a dream, Adela saw the dark shape hit the water and disappear quickly in the darkness as the boat sped past it. Automatically she murmured the familiar words of the prayer, but her mind was now wandering.

As Adela hovered between waking and sleeping, the spectacle she had witnessed had no reality. Although she had grown quite fond of the old man during their journey to the coast, she felt no sense of pity, no sadness, as she recalled his body disappearing from sight. Later, she told herself, later I will think about it, pray for him. She heard Jacques' voice, 'Adone-do, Miss Addy! You're to sleep now.'

He took the tiller from her frozen hands and fastened the loose end of rope round a cleat.

'That'll do for the moment!' he muttered as he put his arm around her and half carried her into the cuddy. By the time she was stretched out on the bunk, her eyes had closed and she was no longer aware of her surroundings. Jacques covered her with the Abbé's dry cloak, crossed himself and hurried back outside.

CHAPTER TWENTY-FIVE

1792

Throughout the night, Titus trudged step by weary step along the road. With one hand, he held his horse's reins; with the other he supported Barnaby's limp body which he had secured to the saddle by means of his belt. Barnaby's horse followed behind, attached to the leader by its reins. Titus had skirted the village beneath the castle and in the hope that news had not yet reached the neighbouring town of their presence in the forest, was making his way there as speedily as he dared.

He was in no doubt that on reaching the gates of the town he would be stopped and questioned; that both he and Barnaby would be in great danger of arrest. Equally he was in no doubt that if Barnaby's wound was not stitched, he would bleed to death. He had tightened the bandage around it which seemed to have lessened the bleeding, but as the hours passed the cloth had once more become soaked. Not even his concern for Adela's safety could divert his fears for his twin for more than a few minutes at a time.

Mercifully the rain had eased and was now only a light drizzle. Twice he thought he heard the sound of someone or something approaching and dragged the horses quickly to the side of the road, hoping that the darkness would conceal him from any nocturnal traveller. Each time it was a false alarm – on one occasion a badger snuffling its way from one ditch to another; on the second, a terror-stricken bull-calf which had doubtless become separated from its mother, perhaps by the pack of wolves he had heard howling in the forest.

At least the protracted walk had given him time to invent

a plausible story to tell his questioners, he thought, as a dog barked not a league distant and he knew he was reaching his destination. He would tell his interrogators that he and Barnaby were players, magicians, who, unable to find work in their own country, had come to France in the hope of finding a troupe who would engage their services. Since neither he nor Barnaby were in fact able to perform any wizardry to substantiate such a tale, he would explain that their identical looks enabled them to trick their audiences. As boys they had enjoyed practising this dupery on their parents' new acquaintances, one climbing into a trunk which their sister, Patience, duly locked; the other appearing upon the wave of a wand from behind the nearest window drape. Such a trick could only be performed on virtual strangers who were unaware of the boys' extraordinary similarity. This subterfuge might serve them well now, Titus had decided.

At the *barrière* guarding the entrance to the town, Titus made no attempt to conceal himself or try to slip past the two sleeping sentinels.

'Ho, there, citizens!' he said boldly. 'Your assistance, if you please!'

The watchmen rubbed their eyes and reaching for their muskets, stumbled to their feet.

'Who are you? Name yourself! What is your purpose here?'

Titus did not resist as his arm was gripped in a firm hold by one of the guards.

'A traveller in need of help, *mes amis*!' he said calmly. 'I would not have awoken you had the matter not been one of great urgency. My brother needs the ministrations of a physician. I have money to pay for his services!'

The second guard ambled over to Titus' horses and regarded Barnaby's inert body and blood-soaked clothing with interest.

'On that we are agreed!' he said cheerfully. 'However, we have no physician here. The monks at the *abbaye* once ministered to our sick and dying but they . . .' he spat on the ground '. . . traitors all, they have gone where they deserve – to the nearest prison; those as weren't shot or better still, disembowelled!' he added with a coarse laugh.

With an effort, Titus controlled the angry protest which had risen to his lips. He forced another smile.

'They are in good company, then, for I have heard that many illustrious personages have suffered similar fates! Nevertheless, I could wish you had spared but one with knowledge enough to see to my brother.'

'Who are you? You have your papers? Show them to me, stranger. How do I know you are not an emigrant? You talk like an aristocrat – though your speech sounds strange to my ears.'

'An aristocrat? Me?' Titus said jovially. 'Do I look like one? See my hands, *mon ami*.' They were indeed filthy, scratched by brambles and covered with caked blood. 'I am a foreigner, as you so cleverly surmised from my accent.'

The man's grip on Titus' arm had not slackened and now he tightened his hold.

'An Austrian, God rot all their souls? A Russian? More like an escaping prisoner!' he said accusingly. He jerked his head in Barnaby's direction. 'Wounded by one of our brave soldiers, was he?'

With well-assumed mirth, Titus threw back his head and laughed.

'Would I be asking your help, my good fellow, if I were your enemy? My brother and I come from the Scandinavian countries.' He pulled off his round hat and pointed to his head. 'See how fair my hair is? Such is the colouring of our race!'

The second man now drew closer and peered with curiosity at Titus' curls. Even in the pre-dawn darkness, they gleamed a bright gold.

'You say you have money!' he said, spitting to one side. 'How came you by it if you are without a means of livelihood?'

Titus shrugged his shoulders and smiled.

'Stole it from one of those cursed *aristos*!' he said conspiratorially. 'My brother and I happened upon a lady and gentleman in a carriage not ten leagues back. They were making for Dieppe in the hope of escaping their just deserts. When they refused us money, we decided to help ourselves, but the gentleman was uncommonly handy with his pistol and my poor brother caught the worst of it as we were fleeing.'

'Not empty-handed, though!' the man replied. There was a greedy look in his eyes as he added, 'Since you say you are a friend of our Republic, you'll know our watchword – "Liberty, Equality, Fraternity!" – and since you are rich and we are poor, you'll be wanting to share your wealth with your brothers, no?'

Well aware that these armed men could take what money he had by force if they wished, Titus chose not to argue the point.

'Not wealthy, my friends, but I am more than happy that you should partake of our booty.' He withdrew two *livres* and watched as each man's eyes glistened at the sight of the coins. 'I have kept one or two for myself and my brother,' he said casually, 'for I shall need to pay for the services my brother needs. Can you not assist me? Is there no one who can see to his wounds?'

No longer suspicious of this stranger come so fortuitously into their hands, the guards consulted with one another in whispers. After a moment, they turned to him, their eyes sly and filled with cunning.

'There is a prisoner in the guardhouse – an *apothicaire*. You give us a *livre* to encourage him and doubtless he will tend your brother!'

Titus did not doubt for one moment that the guards would keep the *livre* for themselves, but he decided not to argue the point. Barnaby was still unconscious and if the bleeding were not soon stopped . . .

'Forward, my good friends!' he said. 'Let us meet this apothecary prisoner of yours!'

Leaving one guard at the gate, the other led Titus to the guardhouse which, because of the time of night, had none of the customary medley of people, carts, horses and traffickers waiting outside to be permitted to pass the *barrière*. Inside the guardhouse, a mixed group of soldiers and citizen-patriots sat round a table in various attitudes of drunken slumber. The room stank of tobacco and wine, of unwashed bodies and of smoke from the oil-lamps. With some difficulty, Titus' guard woke the officer, and drawing him to one side, explained his mission. Titus pretended unconcern as from time to time, both men glanced in his direction. After what seemed to him an unconscionably long time, his guard produced the *livre* and the officer, pocketing it, nodded his head.

'You may release the prisoner to attend to the injured man – but under guard, you understand? He is not to be let out of your sight!' He glanced once more at Titus and revealing tobacco-stained teeth as he yawned, he rose to his feet. 'Let us see this brother of yours who you say is so much to your own likeness that no one can tell you apart!'

'Most certainly,' Titus said agreeably, 'but bear in mind that his suffering these past few hours have taken their toll upon his countenance. If you are agreed, I would prefer to wait until he has recovered and we shall then be pleased to entertain you with our act. To see him now would be to spoil the surprise.'

And delay the attention Barny so sorely needed, he thought as he waited impatiently for the guard to bring forth the unhappy prisoner from his place of captivity.

One glance at the prisoner as he was dragged into the room told Titus that the grey-haired man, if not a gentleman of noble birth, was none the less superior to the ruffians guarding him. The shabbiness of his waistcoat and breeches, the fraying of the ruffles of his linen shirt could not hide their excellent quality; the gaunt face had the expression of intelligence. He bowed to Titus and introduced himself.

'Etienne Delarge, at your service, sir!'

It was only with a great effort of self-control that Titus forbore from returning this courteous greeting.

'You are wasting precious time, citizen!' he said sharply. 'Has your guard not told you that my brother is outside and needs urgent attention?'

The apothecary's eyes lost their expression of hope and his shoulders drooped as the guard prodded him roughly with the butt of his musket.

'Outside, traitor!' he ordered, jabbing the prisoner brutally in the back.

When they reached the gate, the second watchman greeted them with relief. Jerking his head in Barnaby's direction, he said, 'Not long for this world, I'd say. Been groaning like a farrowing sow!'

Titus hurried to Barnaby's side. Seeing that his eyes were open, he murmured in a low voice, 'Take heart, old fellow. Help is at hand!'

'Allow me, sir!' the apothecary said, gently easing Titus aside. One look at Barnaby's shoulder was sufficient for him to announce, 'I cannot treat this gentleman here in the road. A bed must be found for him immediately; and I shall want hot water, bandages, access to my medicaments. I need ointments, salves, opiates . . .'

Titus looked anxiously at the guards who shrugged their shoulders.

'His shop were pillaged when he were arrested!' one said. ''Twas only right to share the traitor's ill-gotten gains amongst the citizens of the Republic!'

The old man drew himself upright, his eyes scornful as he said bitterly, 'And who amongst these worthy citizens would know what is the proper dosage of pilocarpine, hemlock and potash, pareira root, thorn apple . . .?' He broke off to shrug his shoulders, and turned back to Titus. 'I cannot save your brother, sir, without the means to do so!'

Titus looked quickly at the guards.

'Another *livre* for your pains if you can retrieve what the apothecary needs,' he said. 'My brother would not begrudge you his share of the *aristo's* booty if it will save his life!'

Both guards spoke at once.

'Perhaps my wife could . . .'

'And my son . . . they can search!'

'But it will take time!' Titus pointed out. 'Whilst they are looking, we must have accommodation – a nearby *auberge*, perhaps?'

'My house is nearer, *monsieur*!' the apothecary said quickly. 'If it has not been ransacked, I have a few medicaments stored there.'

By now Barnaby had lapsed into complete unconsciousness. Tying the horses to a nearby post, Titus and the guard who was to accompany them, carried him to the house of M. Etienne Delarge.

'I am a widower,' he informed Titus as he led the way to his own bedroom, 'so all is not as it should be. Nevertheless, if they have not been stolen, you will find clean sheets, towels, covers, over there in the marriage chest.'

Fear of theft by the woman who had cleaned for him before his arrest had prompted the apothecary to put a heavy lock on the hinged linen coffer, the key to which still hung on a nail concealed beneath the washstand. He lifted his hands – which were still manacled together by a chain – to indicate his inability to put them now to good use.

'With you to guard the door, citizen, the prisoner cannot possibly escape,' Titus said to the guard. 'Release his chain like a good fellow so that we may put him to work!'

The guard grinned as he obeyed Titus' friendly suggestion. He was conversant with the reason the apothecary had been arrested, for it was well known in the town. Delarge had on an occasion two years' past given a farmer's wife a cure for a mushroom poisoning of the stomach. The good woman had died none the less and the farmer, believing the apothecary to have cheated him out of his money, had borne a grudge ever since. When it became known that the Republic welcomed information from true patriots that would warrant the arrest and imprisonment of traitors, the farmer had named Monsieur Etienne Delarge. The man had, of course, protested his innocence. It was the farmer's own fault his wife had died, he had declared as he was dragged off to the guardhouse, there to await transportation to prison after his trial, for when the cure had not immediately proved effective and the woman had cried out in pain, the farmer had doubled the dose and thereby poisoned her.

It was doubtful if anyone would believe his story, the apothecary knew, since the self-appointed band of men who were to try him were neither lawyers nor literates and incapable of distinguishing between one medicament and another. He therefore believed himself destined to incarceration in prison, if not death.

In the meanwhile the guard could think of no good reason why the prisoner should not do a little work for the foreigner who seemed an honest and generous fellow.

The bed was quickly made and Barnaby laid on a clean sheet, a towel beneath him to protect the mattress from the blood still seeping ominously through the soaked bandages.

'I will do my best for him!' the old man said to Titus as he inspected the wound. 'It will not be easy!'

A cold feeling of despair gripped Titus' heart as he stared down at his twin. If Barnaby were to die . . . The thought was one he had steadfastly put to the back of his mind until this moment; but now, the look on the apothecary's face was such that he could no longer pretend to himself that such an eventuality was impossible.

'I will help in any way I can!' he said. 'My brother is as dear to me as anyone in the world could be!'

As he spoke the words, memories of Adela surged into his mind. He loved her, too – and with all his heart. During those brief days and nights after their wedding, he had barely given a thought to Barnaby. Yet dear as his beloved Addy was to him, his twin was a part of his very being. To lose him would be to lose a part of himself.

'Save him, good sir, and I will do what I can to save you!' he murmured in a voice so low the guard who stood in the doorway could not hear him.

'Who are you?' his companion whispered back. 'The guard said you were a travelling player, a magician, but your speech is that of a gentleman. You did not learn our language in the streets, I wager!'

'My father is an English *milord* – a parson!' Titus replied. 'My brother and I are here in your country at the request of my wife's French cousins. We were assisting them to escape to England when we became separated and my brother was wounded.'

As with gentle hands, M. Delarge cleansed Barnaby's wound so that he could better estimate what could be done to staunch the bleeding and assist its healing, he continued to talk as he bent over his patient.

'The guardhouse where I am imprisoned is ill-attended,' he told Titus. 'At night, the officer in charge as well as the soldiers are nearly always drunk. Like all of us these days, they have little to eat and it takes but a small amount of wine to befuddle their brains. If I am still imprisoned there when your brother has recovered—'

'You have my word that I will do what I can!' Titus broke in quickly. 'For a start I can request that you are kept near to hand whilst your patient has need of you. I have money with which to bribe these rogues.'

'Then guard it carefully, sir!' the apothecary said urgently. 'There is no law left these days. Since no one goes to church, to Confession, it no longer troubles those who lie, steal, even kill. God has deserted them, and they are like wild animals, lusting for blood.'

M. Delarge's fear was unmistakable, and his hands trembled as he reached for the box now brought to them by a peasant woman whose surly manner was equalled only by her look of intense curiosity. When the apothecary's shop had been pillaged, she had purloined the box but discovering nothing of saleable value within, had pushed it beneath her bed. By good fortune, her husband was one of M. Delarge's guards, and he, knowing its whereabouts, had instructed her to present it to the apothecary and claim the promised reward.

Titus withdrew a handful of *sous* from the flapped pocket of his jerkin and dropped them into her outstretched hand.

Twice during the apothecary's ministrations, Barnaby regained consciousness. He was now feverish and when he cried out, it was in English. Titus could make little sense of his words although he distinguished Adela's name and once again, his fear for her safety mingled with fear for his twin. M. Delarge was silent now as, having stitched the wound as best he could, he applied salves and anodynes to lessen the pain.

He reached once more into his box and produced a packet of white powder.

'Ergotin, to reduce the bleeding!' he told Titus. 'Two to five grains – no more, you understand? Meanwhile, you and your brother may make use of such clean clothing as will fit you which you will find in the marriage chest.'

'I am indebted to you, sir,' Titus said in an undertone. He turned to the guard.

'You may have your prisoner back now, citizen, and the reward I promised you. However, I do have a request – namely that this unworthy fellow be brought back to me this evening. I shall require his services again.'

He held the coin tantalizingly before the guard's eyes.

'I will do what I can. It is the officer who makes such directives,' the man said as eagerly he grasped the *livre* Titus dropped into his palm. He glanced at the bed where Barnaby now appeared to be in a restless sleep. 'I'll send a boy to take your horses to the stables at the *auberge*,' he proffered, anxious to keep in Titus' good offices. 'The landlord of the *auberge* across the road will serve you well. He is a good citizen and sits on the Municipal Council.'

Titus forced a laugh.

'Then I must persuade him not to call this traitor for trial and have him despatched to prison before I have done with him!' he said jovially. He turned and stared deeply into the apothecary's eyes. 'I shall guard your box of magic potions, my good man. Who knows but you might poison yourself and cheat the good citizens of this town of their just right to punish you? You shall have your medicines back this evening, and since by the look of you, you do not seem inclined to trust me, I tell you before this witness, *I am a man of my word*!'

His meaning was unmistakable to the prisoner who acknowledged his understanding by no more than a flicker of his eyelids.

'Having no use yourself for your house, I shall appropriate it,' Titus continued, 'for it is clear my brother should not be moved. Since you are a traitor to your country, you are in no position to demand payment for our lodging.' He turned to the guard who was regarding him approvingly. 'Be so good as to remove this fellow, citizen, for I am growing tired of his ugly face!'

The guard's laughter at this cruel sally was all the reassurance Titus needed that he was looked upon now as a sympathetic friend to the people's unholy Republic.

It was now daylight and the *auberge* across the street had become a hive of activity as Titus, having seen the prisoner and his guard on their way, went over to the inn to supervise the arrangements for his horses' stabling. Realizing his hunger, he partook of a good French breakfast and ordered a chicken broth to be brought over to the apothecary's house for Barnaby. Sitting by his twin's bedside, listening anxiously to Barnaby's laboured breathing, he felt himself relaxing for the first time since their pursuers had fired their ill-fated shots. There was nothing more that he could do for his brother's safety, he realized, nor, indeed, his own. For the present no one had doubted his false identity and, even if word reached the town that fugitives were possibly heading this way, their pursuers had not come close enough in the forest to identify him or Barnaby, nor observe their likeness to one another.

If only he could be certain of his twin's recovery, he told himself as fatigue overcame him! If only he could be certain that Adela and Philippe and their party had safely reached the coast, he might sleep peacefully! Hopefully his mind would be more alert after he had rested, for there awaited fresh problems to be solved – the freeing of the unfortunate apothecary being not the least of them. Was the old man capable of riding a horse? he wondered. And how long would it be before Barny, weakened by his wounds, could ride again? With so many bribes yet to be paid, would he have money enough left to purchase a small cart? He did not regret his promise to the old man to assist in his escape even though his presence would greatly add to their danger. He would make the same promise again to any man, good or evil, who saved his twin's life.

As exhaustion overcame him, Titus stretched out on the big feather bed beside his brother and ceasing his anxious pondering, he fell into a deep sleep.

For the next three days, Barnaby tossed and turned as his body was racked by a fearsome fever. M. Delarge did what he could to alleviate it but was hampered by the loss of many of his precious powders. Terrified that his twin might be on the point of death, Titus gave larger and larger bribes to the officers and guards to ensure that the apothecary could remain at his patient's bedside.

On the fourth day Titus realized that if he were to retain money enough to ensure they reached the comparative safety of the Château Saint Cyrille, there to await Jacques' return, he could afford no more privileges. By now he had managed to secure a small handcart, for it was obvious that Barnaby would be in no condition to ride. He was, he knew, being asked to render double the cost of his horses' keep but he dared not risk any controversy for fear of arousing the land-lord's antagonism.

Barnaby regained his senses in the middle of the fifth night. His voice, weakened by his ordeal, woke Titus none the less. Hurriedly he lit the candle and stared with growing joy at his twin's face.

'Are we safely home?' Barnaby asked. 'Is everyone safe? Addy? The others?'

'Are you feeling better at last?' Titus asked, avoiding Barnaby's questions. 'Are you hungry? Could you eat something?'

'Thirsty!' Barnaby answered. 'Where are we, Titus? Why the candle? I thought a while back that we were at sea. I could feel the cutter lifting and dipping. I fear I have not been much help to you all. Is Addy here?'

Realizing that he could no longer prevaricate, Titus gently related the events of the past week. He could see by the expression on Barnaby's face that he was gradually remembering some of the facts for himself.

'You have been close to death, old fellow!' Titus said finally. 'But for Monsieur Delarge, I believe you would not have survived. As soon as you are well enough, we must get him away from here.'

Barnaby nodded weakly, but his thoughts were elsewhere.

'What think you of the others' chances?' he asked urgently. 'Are you not concerned for Addy? You should have left me to fend for myself, Titus, and gone after them!'

'Then you would most certainly have died!' Titus said with an attempted smile. 'And then how could I have faced my darling Addy? You know how devoted to you she is and—'

'But it is you she loves!' Barnaby broke in. 'And once you were safely home with her—'

'It is done and I am here!' Titus interrupted. 'Even had you, not I, been wed to Addy, you would have done the same as I; so let us not speak of it further. Pray God Addy is now safely home at Dene Place and Philippe is with the Comte and Comtesse. Jacques may well be on his return to France by now and he will be deeply concerned if we are not at the Château Saint Cyrille on his arrival.'

'As will Eugénie,' Barnaby agreed, 'for she can know nothing of our adventures!'

'So we will leave as soon as you have recovered your strength, Barny. Now try to eat. I have a bowl of calves'-foot jelly here – every bit as good as Mama used to make us when we were sickly as children, remember?'

Barnaby obediently partook of a few mouthfuls before he lay back on his pillows.

'Tell me again what part I have to play – a magician, you say? And what names have you given us? You will need to be patient with me for my head is far from clear!'

It was an unavoidable misfortune, Titus thought as he ministered to his convalescent brother over the next two days, that word had spread through the town of 'the foreigners with identical looks who could perform magical tricks that would astound ordinary folk'. From time to time, a man, woman, or child would stand beneath the window of the apothecary's house hoping to catch a glimpse of this curiosity. For Titus to move anywhere without a group of villagers following him was an impossibility. Moreover, those citizens who had taken charge of the town were demanding that as soon as Barnaby had recovered, the twins must perform their act for the towns- folk. It seemed that no one had seen identical twins in their lifetime, Titus told Barnaby, although one woman professed to have heard her grandmother speak of two such children in a nearby village where she had been born; but they had died in infancy.

Titus smiled.

'Have you forgotten those simple tricks we performed as children for Addy's amusement?' he said. They had pretended to read each other's thoughts, he reminded Titus. One pointed to an object unknown to them which had been chosen by one of the onlookers and enquired, 'Is it this? No? Then how about this? Or that?' to which the reply was always 'no' until the enquirer demanded, 'Can it be this?' The single word 'can' was the key for the other twin to reply in the affirmative. Would the townsfolk be as easily duped as the four-year-old Adela?

They recalled two other simple tricks before Titus realized that Barnaby was quickly tiring. They would discuss their act further in the morning, he said. For the first time in many days, he slept soundly without fear that he might wake to find that, despite all his and the apothecary's care, his twin had passed away.

For ten days the twins remained in the town – long enough for Barnaby to make a partial recovery; and as he took his first faltering steps outside, long enough for the inhabitants to have become accustomed to their identical appearances and bored by the few simple tricks they were able to perform. It was time to leave, Titus realized, although Barnaby was not yet strong enough to ride the distance to Saint Cyrille. Having decided to continue in the present successful guise of travelling players, both he and Barnaby agreed that they would travel openly by road. Since they would have no money left after they had settled their final account with the landlord of the *auberge*, they hoped to receive a *sou* here and there from whatever audience they could muster in the villages *en route*.

There remained only the problem of how to free the apothecary. Since neither could produce a better plan, they opted for the simplest of all their varied suggestions – for Titus to distract the guard's attention whilst M. Delarge was dressing Barnaby's wound. Having previously emptied the vast linen chest, the apothecary must conceal himself inside, at which juncture they would shout to the guard outside the door that his prisoner had escaped through the open window.

The plan worked perfectly. When the hue and cry finally died down, the unfortunate guard was arrested by the officer for his negligence. Titus and Barnaby – who had joined in the search for the prisoner – retired to their bedchamber where they released the old man. M. Delarge remained hidden in the room for a further day until they were certain that no suspicion was being cast upon them. Once the night was all but ended, they hid the apothecary beneath the straw in their cart, and as soon as it was dawn, they sauntered over to the *auberge* to bid the landlord a final farewell, making an open display of their departure. Followed by hearty shouts wishing them safe journey, they drove slowly out of the town, Titus mounted on his own horse and Barnaby holding the reins of the cart-horse he had exchanged for his own more valuable beast.

Not until they were well advanced upon the road did the apothecary emerge from beneath his straw covering to breathe the delights of fresh air and, even more important, of freedom.

The old man's gratitude to his rescuers was piteous in its intensity for he had fully expected to spend his few remaining years in prison. In a quavering voice, he related, ''Tis said that in Paris the mobs can no longer be controlled; that they have on occasions stormed the prisons, released the prisoners and hacked them to death – even women and children.' He shuddered. 'Only yesterday, one of my guards told me almost with pride that even scrubbing the streets and courtyards with vinegar had failed to remove the bloodstains; that if I was sent to the city, I might suffer the same fate as those other poor souls.'

'You are safe for the present, my friend!' Titus said reassuringly, but he knew they were far from free of danger yet.

Nevertheless they passed through several villages and towns without suspicion, and reached the village of Saint Cyrille without being apprehended. Luck was with them, it seemed, for as the weary horses clattered over the cobblestones on the outskirts of the village, Titus caught sight of Jean Dupois, the nephew of Eugénie's manservant, Gustave. At first the man pretended not to hear Titus as he hailed him with the obligatory greeting.

'Good day to you, Citizen!' Titus called a second time.

With a furtive look, the man crossed the road to Titus' side.

'Go back, *monsieur*!' the man whispered in a voice hoarse with urgency. 'Make haste, I beg you, before you are seen! *Allez-vous en, messieurs, vites, je vous en prie!*'

He was glancing behind him as he spoke with quick, nervous movements of his head. He made no attempt to disguise his fear.

'Come now, Jean, calm yourself!' Barnaby said soothingly. 'Are there soldiers in the village? What cause have you for such warnings?'

The man nodded his head frantically, his eyes rolling as he stammered, 'Soldiers, yes! They and some of the citizen-patriots have ransacked the château. May God have mercy upon Madame la Chevalière!'

Titus grabbed the trembling man by his arm.

'Madame has been arrested? And the child? What have they done with the little girl?'

The man's mouth fell open in surprise.

'You do not know, *monsieur*? The child died ten days ago! As for Madame Evraud, I cannot say. Maybe she, too, is dead. They have arrested some of the servants. Let me go now, *monsieur*, for I cannot be seen talking to you. My family and I are already under suspicion for having relatives working for Madame la Chevalière.'

As Titus released him, he darted back across the road and scuttled off in the direction of the river like a rabbit fleeing from a fox.

Barnaby's eyes met those of his twin.

'The forest!' he gasped. 'We must take cover there until dark.'

'And only then make our way to the château!' Titus agreed at once. 'Can you ride, Barny? It would be quicker on horseback. M. Delarge can ride behind you.'

When Barnaby nodded, Titus hurriedly unhitched the carthorse. Without the cart, he estimated that they could cut across the fields and reach the trees more speedily.

It was several minutes before all three were remounted and a further ten before they were safely out of sight of the village, the tall beech trees affording them the cover they needed. Only then as they regained their breath did the twins dare voice their fears for Eugénie. Saddened though they were by the news of Kitty's passing, it was not unexpected; but that Eugénie's life was endangered – and perhaps also that of Jacques – had shocked them deeply.

'We can do nothing until darkness falls,' Titus said. 'At least Jean has heard nothing of Eugénie's arrest. She may still be at the château, and if she is not, someone there will inform us of her whereabouts.'

Having rested the two horses, they made use of the remaining daylight to approach as closely as they could the boundaries of the Saint Cyrille estate. Here the twins waited until dark before setting off on foot across the fields, leaving M. Delarge with the horses to await their return.

Titus was the first to smell smoke; Barnaby to see the glow of flames. As they hurried forward cursing at their frequent stumbles in the darkness, each was consumed by the same fear. The château, a dark shadow looming beyond the red glow of the fire, appeared untouched – and deserted. It was the barn which had been set ablaze.

They reached the kitchen wall without reason for alarm. Peering through the window, all appeared shrouded and empty. With growing confidence, they moved over the terrace to the windows of the *salon*. To their relief, the shutters had not been closed. Titus reached out to touch Barnaby's hand and place a finger to his lips as he saw the glow from within. Finding a chink in the heavy curtains, neither could restrain a gasp at the sight now exposed to their horrified gaze.

A group of some eight or ten men were sprawled on the sofas and chairs. Their heavy sabots, covered in mud, were propped up on the priceless lavender brocade cushions and coverings. All around them lay the evidence of their debauchery – empty flagons of wine, wooden casks of brandy, broken remnants of the Chevalier's priceless crystal goblets. Poultry bones lay strewn on the pale-blue Aubusson carpets; guttering candles were spilling hot wax on to the surface of the giltwood console table, the satinwood *guéridon*, the inlaid rosewood cabinet. A giltwood pier-glass lay on the floor, its glass shattered, the bevelled scrolled border splintered. Wine dripped from the surface of Eugénie's treasured harpsichord, staining the keys red. The room appeared to have been stripped of all its portable ornaments and paintings.

That they had heard no sound from this sordid band of vandals was not surprising for they all appeared to be the worse for drink and were in a stupor. One, however, was more alert than his companions. As Barnaby's foot collided in the darkness with a stone flower-urn and sent it crashing on to its side, he jumped to his feet and grabbed one of the muskets propped up in the empty fireplace.

Exchanging a horrified glance with Barnaby, Titus whispered, 'Run for it – same way we came!'

Barnaby stumbled off into the darkness. He had still not fully recovered from his wounding, and Titus, realizing that his twin would move slower than he, paused momentarily to cover his retreat. As he stood poised for flight, the good luck they had welcomed these past weeks now deserted them. The clouds which until this moment had shrouded the moon, drifted away and the gardens of the château were bathed in a pale, misty light.

Realizing the new danger this posed, Titus waited no longer but sped across the terrace and joined Barnaby at the far end of the flower borders. By now they could hear shouts from the terrace behind them and turning his head, Titus saw the men, silhouetted against the light streaming from the windows of the *salon*. They were gazing in his direction. He could see, too, that they had their muskets to their shoulders and were taking aim.

Grabbing Barnaby's arm, he sped forward once more. The

moonlight, whilst aiding their flight, also made them clearly visible to their pursuers and they had travelled but twenty paces further when a fusillade of shots shattered the silence. Simultaneously they toppled and fell, one across the other, on to the ground.

CHAPTER TWENTY-SIX

1792

When Adela awoke it was pitch dark. Every limb was cold and cramped and her hands felt swollen and painful. She could taste salt on her lips. As full consciousness returned, she realized where she was and what it was that had awoken her. The boat's motion had become violent, the bow rising and falling as it rolled from side to side. The noise of the wind in the canvas and the creaking of the mast was deafening; and louder still was an ominous rumble of thunder. It was followed not long after by another, and another. Turning her head she could now see rain lashing against the small porthole.

Hurriedly she sprang off the bunk and gasped as she knocked her knee against the side. She was vaguely aware that she must have bruised it earlier for the pain was acute. Biting her lip she found the tinderbox she knew would be within reach on the ledge above her, and lit the lantern. Seeing a rough thickset jacket lying on the floor, she pulled it on over her dress. Long enough to cover a man's hips, it reached almost to her ankles, and despite her urgency she almost smiled as she tied a thin strand of rope around the waist to keep the garment secure in the wind outside the cuddy.

She needed all her strength to force open the door. The rain slashed into her face, blinding her. Within seconds, her hair was streaming with water and she cursed herself for not having looked for a cap. Dark shadows loomed in the wet murk in front of her. One man, small and thin who she guessed to be Père Jérôme, was clinging to the tiller. Jacques and Philippe were struggling with the billowing sails. The noise was now truly deafening.

Clinging to any support she could find, Adela edged her way over to Jacques.

'What shall I do?' she shouted, her voice carrying away on the wind. There was a blinding flash of lightning followed quickly by a crack of thunder so loud that it struck an icy chord of fear in her heart. Their frail craft, she realized, was in the very teeth of the storm. She saw Jacques pointing but could not hear his words as the thunder followed almost immediately upon yet another brilliant flash of lightning.

She clambered closer to Jacques grabbing whatever part of the heaving boat she could as a handhold, and in the next brilliant streak of lightning, saw the look on his face. Only then did she understand the degree of danger they were in for his expression was one of naked despair.

'The sheet! The sheet! Loosen the sheets!' he screamed at her.

She turned to do his bidding, and at that moment, there was an ear-splitting noise as the mainsail ripped apart. The supporting stays sagged and the great sheath of canvas collapsed. Part fell in sodden folds into the boat, but the greater portion trailed over the side. The cutter now listed so heavily that it was in real danger of turning turtle.

Adela's horrified gaze returned to Jacques. He had pulled a knife from his belt and was shouting to Philippe to help him cut the sail adrift. Realizing the urgency, she hurried over to the Curé. He appeared numb with shock.

'Quickly, help them!' she gasped, pulling him to his feet. 'You are stronger than I am. They have got to get the sail overboard. For the love of God, *mon père*, hurry!'

The Curé blinked, shook his head like a dog, and then squared his shoulders. He had been in little doubt this past five minutes that he was shortly to follow his superior to his Maker. Since he must die anyway, he told himself now, he might as well make one last effort to set aside his fear and try and save the brave men and woman who had tried so hard to save him!

'My *poignard*!' Philippe called to him. 'In the cuddy – quick!'

The Curé lurched across the sloping deck into the cuddy and with surprising speed, emerged with Philippe's dagger. With a twisted grin of triumph, he raised it above his head and began hacking wildly at the tangle of ropes and canvas. It was no easy task, for only in the flashes of lightning could he see where to strike. As he misaimed one of his strikes, the leather protecting the handle of the dagger was wrenched off. He was breathing fiercely but with a glorious feeling of freedom as all traces of fear left him. He could hear himself laughing triumphantly as a huge wave surged over him and all but washed him overboard. The crash of thunder and the incandescent flashes of lightning, once terrifying, now seemed to him to be an entirely appropriate setting for this life-and-death struggle for survival.

Adela was too engrossed in her own activities to marvel at this transformation of the timid little cleric. The tiller was shuddering in her hands and she could not understand what had happened to it. Once – it seemed a life-time ago – Titus or Barnaby had explained to her how the tiller worked. She searched her memory – '*the tiller is a horizontal bar attached to the rudder-head . . . the pintle is the bolt . . .*' Suddenly she understood what was wrong – the pintle had broken and without this precious bolt to secure it, the rudder flapped from side to side and no longer guided the vessel in one direction. It had been rendered useless.

As Adela turned to relay this desperate news to Jacques, the lightning forked again and the sky above seemed to shiver with the loudest thunderclap she had yet heard. Before she could even draw breath, there was a further brilliant flash and she saw Père Jérôme standing with his mouth agape in a maniacal laugh as he raised the poniard for yet another blow. Mingled with the attendant clap of thunder, the Curé's laugh turned to a high-pitched, agonized scream as the poniard became a white-hot spear. The black-clad figure of the doomed man was thrown into the air and his body was catapulted into the sea.

Speechless with fear, Adela saw the unfortunate Curé's garments torn from his body before she turned her head away. One of his boots landed with a thud near her feet. The brief incandescent light vanished and the world about her became black once more. Too stunned with horror to cry out or move, Adela remained glued to her seat, her hands gripping hard on the useless tiller as sea water poured over the side. The boat, weighted down by the sodden canvas, was now all but horizontal. Without knowing it, she held her breath as she waited for the next flash. It came very quickly. By its light, she saw two other bodies lying in the heaving boat.

'Mother of God!' she cried out. 'Jacques! Philippe!'

Their names burst from her lips in a terrified scream. Releasing her grip on the tiller, she scrambled forward on her hands and knees, and bent over the prone bodies.

Jacques was the first to recover from the stunning blow he had suffered when the lightning had struck the Curé. Too weak as yet to get to his feet, he lifted his head and gazed stupidly at Adela.

'Push the sail overboard!' he gasped. 'Quickly, Miss Addy! Never mind 'im!' he added as she bent over Philippe.

The urgency of his tone galvanized Adela into action. She grabbed hold of as much of the sodden sailcloth as she could and, oblivious to her blistered hands and aching back, heaved it over the side. It took three more such attempts before the mainsail was free of the boat. Relieved of the weight, the cutter rolled back into an upright position; but now it lay deep in the water, the waves lapping within inches of the gunnel.

'The bailer!' Jacques shouted. He was struggling to his feet. 'I'll get another. Quick now, Miss Addy!'

As she reached for the bailing-tin, Adela saw blood seeping

from her palms and between her fingers. She was not aware
of any pain, only curiosity at the sight of the bright red colour
of her blood. She was aware, too, that there had been no more
lightning and the thunder had become but a faint rumble in
the distance.

A faint hint of light on the eastern horizon heralded the
first glimmer of dawn as Adela started the seemingly impossible task of emptying hundreds of tins of sea water over the
side. Jacques must have lost his reason, she thought, if he
imagined she could ever complete the task he had set her!
Then she saw that he, too, was bailing and that gradually the
level of water in the boat was dropping. Philippe's body was
no longer rocking from side to side.

Was her cousin dead? she asked herself. Had Philippe too
been struck by that dreadful bolt of forked lightning, and if
so, why had he not been thrown into the air like poor Père
Jérôme? The Curé's black boot drifted past her, its progress
arrested as it bumped against Jacques' legs. He picked it up
and flung it over the side. The wind had dropped now and
the sea was strangely calm. Overhead, she saw the brilliant
white glow of the evening star. In this living hell, it looked to
her astonishingly beautiful.

A groaning noise followed by a violent retching interrupted
her half-conscious reverie. Glancing towards Philippe, she saw
that he had moved – was now on all fours like a dog as he
tried to rid himself of the sea water in his lungs.

'*Grâce à Dieu!*' Jacques said beside her. 'Monsieur Philippe
is alive!'

His look of relief was immensely comforting to Adela and
she smiled back at him.

'We are safe now, are we not, Jacques?' she asked him.
Jacques shook his head.

'Gale's over – worst I ever been in, but we ain't safe yet,
Miss Addy. Sail's gorn, rudder's gorn and we be an unaccountable long ways from 'ome.'

Only now did Adela realize how shockingly close to death

she had been – and, according to Jacques, still was. She felt a swift primeval surge of longing for survival. To have come through such dangers only to die would be a terrible injustice . . . one that had already been inflicted on the Abbé and the Curé. The memory of what she had witnessed now filled her mind, and hurriedly, she crossed herself. No man should suffer such a terrible death as Père Jérôme's. She knew it must have been all but instantaneous, but this made it none the less horrifying. Strangely, just before he died, he had looked happy. It was hard to understand for he had not struck her previously as a man of courage. Thank the Lord, she thought, that Philippe had been spared! He was lying quietly now and looked so weak and ill, she knew she and Jacques must get him into the cuddy as soon as they had finished bailing. She doubted very much if he could walk, and she herself was so tired – so very tired! Her hair and every stitch of clothing was drenched, stiffening in the slight breeze as the salt dried and crusted on her outer garments. Her face was stinging and her hands . . .

'I cannot go on!' she whispered when for the first time, she became aware of the agonizing pain of the blisters which had punctured, leaving her skin raw. They stung with the salt water, and tears of self-pity rolled down her cheeks. As she held her hands out to Jacques, he regarded them with horror and concern.

'You be a right valiant-'earted sailor, Miss Addy, that's for sure. There's a flask of oak-bark lotion in the locker – might ease the soreness a bit. There weren't room for no more ointments and such, what with the food and clothes and all and nowhere else to put 'em!'

Adela managed a smile.

'I will be all right, Jacques! Can we get Monsieur Philippe into the cuddy now?'

Jacques nodded.

'Furst we see to them 'ands of yourn. 'Appen we'll be needing a bit of that petticoat to bind 'em up, Miss Addy!'

He gave her an impish grin as he added, 'No disrespect, but reckon as 'ow this'll be the furst time you'm glad you wear 'em, Miss Addy, and not them breeches like a man! T'ain't fair, you used to say when you was little and Master Titus an' Master Barnaby were shinning up them there trees. T'ain't fair, you allus said, and them two young varmints kept a-telling you it wus your own fault for being born a lass!'

'Oh, Jacques,' Adela whispered, halfway to tears, 'if only . . . if only they were here to tease me now!'

Only too well aware of how close to exhaustion Adela was, Jacques felt this was not the moment to add to her ordeal by expressing his relief that the twins were *not* aboard. With the mainsail gone, the jib damaged and the rudder useless, the occupants were at the mercy of the sea, and without steerage he could not hope to direct their landfall or even be certain that they would ever see the English coast.

Whilst tending Adela's hands, he attempted to make some calculations. They had left the coast of France with a fresh southerly wind behind them and had been making good time. The tide had been flooding up the Channel and they must have been midway across when it started to ebb. He had hoped to reach Rye on a flooding tide and had been making a good course towards Bullock Bank some ten miles south of Dungeness, when the storm had broken. They had now been at sea close on fourteen hours, and a glance at his compass had shown him that they were drifting to the north.

Leaving Adela to find some dry clothing, he went out to Philippe. The young Frenchman was sitting in shocked silence in the sternsheets, his arms clasping his aching ribs and stomach, his head bent. As Jacques approached, he looked up with an apologetic smile.

'I fear I have been of little help to you, Jacques!' he said weakly. 'How is Miss Adela? And how is Monsieur le Curé? Are they in the cuddy recovering?'

So Monsieur Philippe had not seen the unfortunate Curé, struck by the lightning bolt! Jacques realized. Omitting the worst of the detail, he related the circumstances of the wretched man's death. Philippe groaned.

'And Miss Adela saw this happen?' he muttered. 'It must have been a fiendish shock to her. That poor girl! What a terrible experience for a young female. Will she be all right, do you suppose?'

''Tis to be 'oped so, Monsieur Philippe. I tolt 'er to try to get some sleep. 'Twill be a long while afore daylight and we mun save our strength for I reckons we may be many days adrift at sea.'

Since Philippe seemed so much stronger, he explained the dire straits they were in.

'We ain't sailing no longer, *monsieur*, we be drifting!' he ended his account. Glancing up at the sky which had cleared of all but a few dark clouds, he added, 'Northwards at the moment, so if our luck 'olds, we may yet 'it land.'

'*Grâce à Dieu!*' Philippe said, crossing himself. 'At least I am feeling a little better and can be of help to you, perhaps? Do we have water enough? I am very thirsty!'

Jacques grinned.

'*Une goutte de cognac* would do you better, sir! Best eat summat too, if'n you think you can keep it down, but . . .' he added in a serious tone '. . . no more'n a bite or two. We doant know 'ow long them vittals 'as got to last us!'

As the hours passed, the cutter began to drift north-east on the spring tide. Jacques estimated that they were moving at around three knots. Slowly the wind shifted to the south-east and when Adela came out of the cuddy, he was able to tell her that they were being pushed towards the coast. As much to occupy her than with any real hope of results, he suggested she keep a look-out for the new Dungeness lighthouse, for if they were to see the beam of the oil lamp, he would have a better idea of their possible landfall.

When Philippe came out from the cuddy after a brief rest, Jacques took his place on the bunk. He had not slept for twenty-four hours and was on the point of total exhaustion.

'Do not worry, Jacques!' Adela said reassuringly. 'Monsieur Philippe and I will keep watch and we will call you instantly if there is anything whatever to report.'

Jacques had been asleep for little less than two hours when Adela became aware that the wind was freshening. By the time she and Philippe realized that they could no longer delay waking him, the speed of the boat had increased alarmingly. The green sea was rushing past the bows, and white-topped waves, whipped up by the wind, were slapping against the sides of the cutter, showering Philippe and herself with cascades of bitterly cold water.

Jacques' weather-beaten face was lined with concern as he stumbled out of the cuddy. Even in the few minutes it had taken to rouse him, the wind strength had increased and he was obliged to brace himself against it. It must be all of thirty – perhaps forty knots – he estimated. Although dawn had broken, the dark storm clouds racing across the sky gave an ominous illusion of twilight. There was no sign of the coastline, but he now feared to see it for there could be little hope of survival for them if they were blown ashore in this gale.

Adela and Philippe were looking at him for guidance, and he shook his head in an attempt to wake himself more fully. Ropes! he thought. They must secure themselves with ropes, for if the cutter turned turtle, even the strongest swimmer would not stay afloat more than a few minutes in this sea. Roped to the boat, at least they could cling to the sides.

Philippe edged his way over to assist him. He wanted Adela to shelter in the cuddy but Jacques would not allow it; she could be drowned in there like a rat in a trap, he cautioned. Despite the bitterly cold wind, now gusting at fifty knots and slowly freezing their very bones, they must remain outside, he insisted.

Adela did not need Jacques to tell her how dangerous their situation was. The very fact that he had asked her earlier to look out for the lighthouse was proof that they were nearing the coast . . . and she was perfectly familiar with the coastline.

Lord Mallory had taken her with Patience and the twins to the Sussex coast one summer and walked with them along the top of the white, chalk cliffs, from where, with the aid of a telescope he had told them, they could see Calais. Far, far down below her, Adela had seen angry white waves crashing against the ugly rocks at the base of the cliffs. She knew now that there were harbours, in the jagged coastline, but what chance did they have of being blown into the safe haven of one of them?

Tied to the bow thwart, huddled into the protective covering Jacques had given her which he had ripped from a piece of sailcloth, Adela felt strangely calm. If she were now to die, who would there be other than Titus and Dolly, to mourn her? Barnaby, too, would be saddened by her death, she thought, but with their whole lives ahead of them, it would not be long before the twins recovered from their grief. Titus would find some other girl to love and when she, Adela, was little more than a memory, he would marry again and his new wife would bear his children.

The route Adela's imagination had taken her did not please her one bit. Tightening her mouth, she braced herself. She was not going to die! She would not allow any other woman to take Titus from her or him to forget her! *She and no one else would bear his children when the time came!* To be frightened – as indeed she was at the howling wind and mountainous seas – was something she could not help; but she would not give in to that fear. She glanced across at Philippe who, with Jacques, was wearily bailing water from the bottom of the boat. Her cousin was no sailor and quite possibly did not realize the danger they were in. Jacques would know – but if there was one man in the world who could save them, it was he. Titus and Barnaby had always declared him to be the best sailor they had ever come across and held his seamanship in the highest regard.

Adela's thoughts were interrupted as Jacques stood up and shouted to her. She could not make out his words against the noise of the wind but she saw his finger pointing behind her. Turning her head, she understood. Away to their left were the dark, ugly, unmistakable shapes of rocks. She gripped the side of the boat more tightly and held her breath as they drew nearer. Below her seat the level of water was rising rapidly. Jacques and Philippe had stopped bailing, for the little they threw out was useless against the quantity coming in. The sea around them was now a boiling white cauldron. She could see great fountains of spray as the waves hit the rocks ahead.

Philippe and Jacques, their arms entwined, made their way towards her and secured their ropes to the stern thwart. Seconds later a huge dark wall of water, topped by white spume, surged towards them, breaking against the side of the cutter which listed dangerously. Another followed; then another.

'Here comes the seventh wave!' Philippe shouted ominously.

As it surged relentlessly towards them, the three occupants of the boat stared in horrified anticipation, and then the wave hit them. In the split second that followed, the boat listed, righted itself and was propelled in a furious forward move-ment which carried them directly on to the jagged outcrop of rocks. There was a deafening explosion of noise as the cutter hit solid ground. There followed a high-pitched grating as the momentum of the wave swept the boat still further forward and the planks splintered and were wrenched apart.

Adela gulped for breath as she surfaced, and was briefly aware of an agonizing pain in her upper body. Dimly she realized that she was being dragged backwards by a savage undertow. A piece of planking swept past her, missing her face by inches. Fighting for breath, she saw a thwart to her right and realized that the rope around her waist was attached to it. Reaching out for this only handhold, she discovered that her left arm was refusing to obey her commands. Gasping she clung to the lifeline as best she could with her right hand.

There was no sign of Jacques or Philippe, but the sight of another huge wave bearing down on her put all other thoughts from Adela's mind. Powerless to control her direction, she felt herself being carried forward. A searing pain stabbed her as a submerged rock cut through her clothing and tore a deep cut in her leg. As she cried out, she felt herself tumbling forward, her lungs filling rapidly with sea water, her limbs twisting grotesquely like those of a rag doll tossed in the air.

Mercifully Adela was no longer conscious as the wave receded, leaving her limp body, still attached to the splintered plank, wedged in a cleft between the dark-green seaweed-covered rocks.

CHAPTER TWENTY-SEVEN

1792

For two weeks, Adela lay in her bed forbidden by the physician to move. She was in considerable pain from a dislocated shoulder, and the rest of her body was badly bruised. Dolly applied opium liniment and refilled countless warming-pans in an attempt to relieve her mistress' suffering. The physician had assured the Comtesse de Falence that with rest and care, Adela should in time make a complete recovery. It was not, however, until the sixteenth day, when she was finally able to move her arm without too much discomfort, that the faithful Dolly believed there were no broken bones.

By then Adela was familiar with the facts of her rescue. The cutter had foundered on the rocky foreshore some seven miles west-southwest of Dover. It had been shortly after seven o'clock when the lookout aboard a fishing boat seeking shelter in the little harbour of Kingston, had seen that the cutter was in trouble and realized that it was being blown inshore. When the fishing smack docked, the coastguard had been alerted and a rescue party sent out to seek for survivors of the boat now seen to be wrecked. None had been expected and it was deemed something of a miracle that all were found alive.

Philippe and Jacques had been far more fortunate than Adela. Their ropes had been attached to a section of wooden planking which, as the cutter broke up, had formed a raft-like structure. This was flung on to a rocky ledge whose surface, thick with seaweed, had caused the raft to slide over the top at such an angle as to resist the strong pull by the backwash of the sea. Both men were able to drag themselves up by the ropes securing them to the raft, and had scrambled on to the comparative safety of the ledge. With no sound footing, they had been drenched by every incoming wave, but the planks had remained firmly wedged in the rocks and their hold upon them had prevented them being swept back out to sea.

By the time the rescue party had reached them, they were barely conscious but, apart from Adela, had suffered no worse than cuts to the exposed parts of their bodies and severe bruising. Lodgings were found for all of them in Folkestone, and the Comtesse de Falence had arrived with Dolly to nurse the survivors back to health. Within a week, Philippe and Jacques were sufficiently recovered, Philippe to travel on to London and Jacques to set about buying a new cutter which the Comte was to pay for. The dauntless little valet was anxious to go back to France as speedily as possible, hopefully to bring Eugénie and the twins home with him.

By the end of the second week, Adela's confused mutterings were once again making sense and it was no longer necessary for Dolly to apply cold cloths to her forehead and give her constant purgatives in an attempt to calm her restless agitation.

It was in all three weeks before the physician would allow Adela to be taken home. The thirty-mile journey had been a long and painful one, for her dislocated shoulder had hurt quite unbearably with every jolt over the rutted roads. Consequently, it had taken them three days to reach Dene Place and by the time they had done so, Adela's condition had relapsed. Heavily dosed with laudanum to ease her pain, she had been only half conscious as they carried her upstairs and finally laid her down in her own bed.

A further week passed before Adela was permitted to leave her bedchamber. The Comtesse wanted to take her back to London to complete her convalescence, but Adela would not hear of it. Titus and Barnaby might return at any moment, she explained, and she must be at home to greet them. Aware that her aunt wanted to return to her husband and family, she insisted that with Dolly to nurse her so devotedly, there was now no need for the Comtesse to remain; her full recovery was only a matter of time and once she was reunited with Titus and could set aside her fears for his safety, she would cease to be an invalid! Before leaving for France, Jacques had attempted to reassure her with his own conviction that the twins would long since have made their way back to the château where, almost certainly, they would be awaiting him; that he would be seeing them very shortly for he should be in Normandy within the week as the new cutter was far bigger and faster than the wrecked boat. He departed the week before the Comtesse left in her carriage for London, and now Adela had little to distract her as she waited impatiently for his return, perhaps with the twins or at least with news of them.

During the long days and nights while she had been confined to her sick-bed, Adela had been plagued by unhappy memories of the storm and the tragic deaths of the Abbé and the Curé. But for Jacques' bravery, she told Dolly over and over again, both she and Philippe would have died, too.

Dolly managed with difficulty to conceal her own fears for Jacques. She had grown to love the devoted, steadfast Frenchman and worried lest his loyalty to his young masters might jeopardize his own safety in France. It was, therefore, with a great cry of relief that ten days after the Comtesse de Falence had left, she saw Jacques turn into the courtyard driving a coach and pair. Adela, who was entertaining the parson and Lady Mallory in the drawing-room, was unaware of the arrival of the carriage.

Peering through the kitchen window, Dolly could see no sign of the twins and only Madame la Chevalière de Saint Cyrille alighted from the coach. She hurried out to meet her, her sharp mind anticipating the shock it would be to Miss Addy and the young masters' parents to hear that Master Titus and Master Barnaby were not yet safely home.

There was no way, however, that Eugénie could soften the terrible news she quickly imparted to Dolly – that Kitty was dead and that one of the twins had been mortally wounded; the other arrested.

As Dolly let out a small cry of distress, Eugénie took her arm.

'You had best come with me to break the news, Dolly, for it will be distressing for all of them.'

'And my poor Miss Addy not long out of her sick-bed!' Dolly wailed. ''Twill be the death of 'er!'

'Pull yourself together, girl,' Eugénie said sharply, 'for I shall doubtless need your help if this proves too much for her.'

As Adela rose to greet her cousin, one look at Eugénie's face was sufficient to warn her that all was far from well. Giving Eugénie no time to greet the Mallorys, she ran forward and grasped her hands.

'The twins are not with you? What has happened, Eugénie? For pity's sake, tell me I am mistaken, and that there is some good reason why they are not here.'

The parson stepped forward and bowed to Eugénie.

'Please forgive our impatience, Madame Evraud. Do please be seated and then, if you will, tell us what news you have of our sons. The uncertainty is very distressing – as I am sure you will understand.'

Eugénie hesitated only a moment longer before gaining the courage she needed to tell these poor parents the unhappy tidings – that one of their sons was dead; that the other had been arrested. She could not meet Adela's agonized eyes as she murmured that Kitty, too, had passed away.

Unnoticed by Adela, Lady Mallory slipped from her chair to the floor in a faint. Clinging to Eugénie's hands, Adela whispered, '*Which one*, Eugénie? Which of the twins was killed? Tell me . . . *I have to know* . . . was it Titus?'

Her voice was tortured, but Eugénie could do nothing to lessen the pain. She put her arms round Adela's shoulders.

'I do not know, dearest; really, I do not! It was so dark . . . and Jacques and I were at some distance . . .' She broke off and turned to assist Dolly who was endeavouring to help Lady

Mallory back into her chair. 'I am so sorry to be the bearer of this dreadful news,' she murmured as the poor woman moaned uncontrollably.

Lord Mallory had been standing like a statue, too shocked to speak or move. Now at last he addressed Eugénie. In a voice which shook with emotion, he said, 'Will you repeat the facts, dear lady? I am somewhat confused . . .'

With an anxious glance at Adela's ashen face, Eugénie drew her cousin down beside her on the settee, and held tightly to her hand as she replied to the desperate father's request.

'I will relate everything as it happened,' she told the parson gently. 'Our poor little Kitty passed away not three days after Adela, Philippe, the twins and the clerics had departed. Since there was no Curé to conduct the burial and we dared not go to the church, Gustave and I laid the child to rest in the garden, close by the little statue of the boy with his dog outside the Temple to Nature she so loved. I thought *la petite* could lie in peace there until these dreadful times have passed and we could remove her body to consecrated ground.' Eugénie turned to face Adela. 'Kitty died in her sleep without pain or suffering, so you must try not to grieve for her, *chérie*.'

She paused, her expression deeply concerned as she glanced once more at the twins' parents. Lady Mallory had recovered her senses and was clinging to her husband's hand.

'Soon after this sad little ceremony, I began to receive visits from some horrifying men,' Eugénie continued. 'They called themselves citizen-patriots and they accused me of being a traitor and threatened me with arrest in the name of the Republic if I did not tell them where Philippe was.' She glanced despairingly at Adela. 'You see, Berthe, little Robert's *nourrice*, had denounced me. Doubtless both she and her parents were bitter because I had dismissed her without a character, and welcomed this opportunity to take their revenge.'

Her eyes were bitter as she added, 'It is not unusual for such things to happen these days, and so the questioning by the citizen-patriots continued for several days, their tempers and threats worsening each time they visited. They searched the château from attics to cellars but could find no proof to substantiate Berthe's suspicions. Gustave, you see, had removed all evidence of the fugitives from Robert's dressing-room. Afterwards, they ransacked my home, taking away any small *objets d'art* they could carry. I feared then that it would be only a few more days at most before they arrested me. Then Jacques arrived and told me what had happened to you and Philippe on the way to the coast and how you had all become separated from Titus and Barnaby. Since there had been no sign of the twins at the château, nor any word from them, Jacques pleaded with me not to await them any longer, but to depart that very night. He convinced me that it would have been their wish that he took me to safety whilst it was still possible and assured me he would return for them at a later date.'

She drew a deep sigh, tears spilling from her eyes as she said, 'I cannot tell you how I felt at the prospect of leaving my home, my possessions, all the mementoes of my beloved husband, of my baby, of Kitty . . . and having to say farewell to those loyal servants who remained to who-knew-what fate. But I could see the urgency for myself for that afternoon, some soldiers had amused themselves by setting fire to that big barn near the pigsties. Such wantonness, *non*? And who could say if they would not fire my home next?'

She gave a long, trembling sigh before continuing, 'I packed only clothes and food for the sea journey and waited for nightfall. At dusk I went with Jacques to the Temple of Nature for the last time to put flowers on Kitty's grave. I dared not go to the churchyard to bid farewell to my little son. It was whilst Jacques and I were at the Temple that we saw soldiers marching up the drive and into my home. They were armed, and by the noise they made, we judged them to be very drunk. As a consequence, we decided it would be too dangerous for me to return to the château to collect my belongings.'

As she paused once more, Adela leaned forward and white-faced, urged her to continue.

'Jacques bade me wait in the Temple whilst he attempted to reach the stables where the horses had been prepared for our journey. It was whilst he was gone that I glimpsed two shadowy figures making their way across the garden. I supposed at first that one of them was Jacques, the other possibly one of our servants. I saw them go to the kitchen window and peer inside the casement. Then they disappeared round the west wall. I had the notion that it was their intention next to see into the windows of the *salon*. Then I heard a noise – as of masonry falling – followed by shouts. I was very frightened but the more so when at that moment, the moon appeared from behind a cloud and I saw quite clearly the same two men running swiftly away across the terrace and on to the lawn leading to the forest.'

She covered her face with her hands as if she could hide the memory of what was to follow.

'A moment later, Jacques appeared at my side,' she continued. 'Before he could speak, shots rang out and . . . and both men fell. One rose to his feet, and as further shots sounded he tried to lift the injured man – as if he intended to carry him, *tu comprends*? I can but suppose it was too heavy a load but he made no attempt to run for the cover of the trees. By now the soldiers were close by. There was another shot and he fell a second time. He can only have been slightly wounded for by now a third man appeared from the forest in total disregard for his own safety; helped the wounded one to his feet. The soldiers were now upon them.'

'You are suggesting those two men you first saw were . . . were our sons, *madame*?' The parson's voice was filled with apprehension. His wife was now weeping uncontrollably.

'But it was dark . . . you were some distance away,' Adela cried. 'You could not be sure who they were.'

When Eugénie could speak once more, her voice was husky with tears.

'Jacques was nearer to them than I, concealed beneath the wall of the kitchen gardens. He is in no doubt of their identity.

The moon was shining and . . . well, he confirmed my fears. I have to say that Jacques is quite adamant that he was not mistaken, as he will tell you himself in due course. I do not have to tell you that he would have gone to the twins' aid had there been even a remote chance of saving them; but he was some distance away and unarmed, and would have been the easiest of targets for the soldiers had he tried to reach them.'

She drew a long, trembling sigh. 'Jacques is a brave man, Adela, and you know how devoted he has always been to Titus and Barnaby! I have no doubt that had it not been for me, he would have risked his life – as that third man did – however impossible the odds. As it was, Jacques knew I could not reach England without him and, moreover, that the twins would not have allowed him to abandon me to my fate. You must not allow Jacques to think he acted wrongly for he truly believed he was carrying out their wishes.'

Shocked – and fearful beyond belief for Titus – Adela said weakly, 'I understand that Jacques could not tell which . . . which of the twins . . . was wounded; which of the two . . . fell; but what of the third man who came to their assistance?'

'He was far shorter and his movements were those of an old man. He was quickly arrested.'

Her hopes fading, Adela nevertheless clung to one last hope. 'How can you be so certain that the first to be shot was . . . was killed? Can he not have been too badly wounded to rise? Maybe he is not dead . . .'

Eugénie's eyes were full of pity as she looked from Adela to the two despairing parents.

'Both Jacques and I heard his voice – that of the one who survived – as the soldiers dragged him back to the château. Two of them were carrying the . . . the body, and the wounded twin was shouting in English, "You black-hearted villains! You murderous dogs, you have killed my brother! May you rot in hell! May your souls be damned to eternity!" He was beside himself with grief and hatred, and struggling with such violence to strike his guards that he was only silenced by the butts of the soldiers' muskets. I was so sickened by what I had seen and heard that I fainted. When I came to, Jacques was trying to lift me on to my horse, and the next thing I remember, we were in the forest.'

Lady Mallory was sobbing quietly, her husband doing his best to comfort her although his eyes, too, were full of tears. Only Adela remained dry-eyed. She was appalled by the thoughts racing through her head for she could think of only one thing – that she wanted it to be Barnaby who had died! Oh God, she prayed silently, You can take Barnaby if You must, but not Titus, not *Titus*! I love him! I need him! I want him back with me! Even if it was Titus You took, You can change Your mind. No one can tell them apart. Take Barnaby, but not the man I love.

Another thought followed. Even if God answered her prayer, it would still mean Titus had been wounded; arrested by the soldiers; suffering some unthinkable fate at the hands of those vile men. They were only too ready to shoot spies!

The grief Adela might have felt on learning of Kitty's death was diminished by her overriding concern for Titus. In the days following Eugénie's arrival, she alternated between hope and despair. Eugénie went home to her family who were longing to see her. Like the Comtesse before her, she begged Adela to accompany her, but Adela would not leave Dene Place. Jacques returned once more to France in the hope of finding out if the wounded twin had survived, and Adela found it increasingly difficult to wait for any news he might bring back to her.

Fully recovered now from her injuries, she walked each day to the parsonage to visit her in-laws. Lady Mallory was inconsolable at the death of one of her sons and the possible fate of the other, and unable to offer any comfort to Adela. The parson had escaped into a private world of his own, saying that the fate of his sons lay in the hands of God to

Whom, when his clerical duties permitted, he spent his time offering innumerable prayers. Only to Dolly could Adela express her fears and her despair that she might never see Titus again.

During the long, sleepless nights, she lay awake remembering how for so short a time they had slept in each other's arms; recalling each embrace, each kiss, each touch. She knew this to be folly for such memories only added a physical longing for him to those in her heart.

Titus cannot be dead, he cannot! she kept telling herself, for if he were, she would surely know it. Sometimes her thoughts wandered and she let herself believe that she and Titus would be happily reunited; but she could not bring herself to imagine *his* suffering at the loss of his twin. If only she had him back, she would help him to overcome his sorrow, she told herself. She would give him so much love that he did not miss Barnaby's affection. She would give him children – a son whom they might name after poor Barnaby. She would make Titus happy – *if only he returned home*!

Philippe came down to see her. It was not an easy reunion for he was guiltily aware that his attempt to rescue the Abbé and Père Jérôme had been primarily responsible if not for *their* deaths, then in all likelihood, those of the twins. Although he had intended to comfort her as best he could, it was she who spent their days together trying to reassure him.

The situation in France was worsening every day, he told her. News of the shocking execution of the King had reached London, all efforts to retain a reprieve after his trial on 15 January having failed. The Prime Minister, Mr Pitt, had denounced it as 'the foulest and most atrocious act the world had ever seen', he related, unaware that Adela was too preoccupied with her concern for the fate of the twins to be more than mildly disquieted.

'I do not see how this country of yours can continue its policy of neutrality!' Philippe remarked bitterly. 'I dread to think what will now be done with our imprisoned Queen. It seems that the little Dauphin is "missing", whatever that may mean.'

Try as she might, Adela could not feel any emotion beyond that of a casual pity for the French royal family or take any interest in the country's politics. Her whole being was concentrated on one single hope – that Titus should be alive.

In February, Jacques returned – but alone. Nevertheless he did have some news to impart. He had learned that on the night he and Eugénie had made their escape, the soldiers had remained for some time at the château celebrating their capture of a French traitor and, more interestingly, of the English 'spy'! One of the kitchen-maids had managed to slip out of the building and had escaped the subsequent arrests of all the remaining servants. Hiding in her parents' farmhouse, she had witnessed the soldiers escorting the prisoners a few days later along the road leading from Saint Cyrille to their headquarters at Rouen, there, doubtless, to be further interrogated. Amongst the prisoners was the faithful Gustave. He was supporting a wounded man whom she had recognized as being one of the young English milords.

As they had passed alongside the river, a man, who appeared to be an imbecile, had jumped out from behind a bush and caused the horses pulling the cartload of prisoners to bolt. In the mêlée that ensued, some of the prisoners had been thrown into the road and, by the time order had been restored and the prisoners counted, it was seen that Gustave and the English milord were missing. For an hour or more the soldiers had searched the surroundings, including the farmhouse where the maid was in hiding; but with no success. They had continued upon their way, cursing roundly.

Later the kitchen-maid had discovered that the man she had thought to be the village idiot was in reality Josef, the bargee. Everyone in the village had been aware that those prisoners still alive in the château were to be taken on the following day to Rouen. Josef had managed to get word to Gustave by the good offices of a cousin who was one of the men guarding the prisoners. Blood had proved thicker than water, Jacques commented wryly. Warned in advance of Josef's plan, Gustave and the Englishman had been able to take advantage of the diversion. Jacques knew no more than that Josef had not returned to the village, but as far as Jacques had been able to ascertain, no bodies had been found in or near the locality. There was, therefore, every reason to hope that both the prisoners had made a successful escape.

'I searched the forest best I could, Miss Addy!' Jacques said with a sympathetic look at Adela's white, drawn face. 'As you know, 'tis so vast that 'twould 'ave been a miracle 'ad I come upon 'em. I went twice to Anse Goéland to see if the boat had gone, but it were there, concealed be'ind the rocks as I'd left 'er, so I knowed they 'adn't gone to the cove.'

'You think they will try to make their way home?' Adela asked. 'Could Titus – or Barnaby – sail the boat without you?'

'If Josef is with them, 'e would 'elp. 'E were a cabin-boy on a merchant ship when 'e were a lad. 'Twas not 'til his father died and left 'im the barge that 'e gave up 'is life at sea. Anyroad, I left the cutter where it was, Miss Addy, and got me a passage back with George Robinson in his boat. I hope I did right to leave 'er there all this time. If someone 'appens to come upon 'er, she could be stolen and—'

'No, no, you did exactly right, Jacques!' Adela interrupted. 'But what hope have we after all this time that the boat will be needed? It is over three months now since . . . since . . .'

Her voice broke as she struggled against the engulfing tears.

'Now, now, Miss Addy! There's a number o' reasons why they ain't come 'ome as yet. Remember, they don't 'ave no 'orses; and like as not, no money neither. 'Tis a good long walk from Saint Cyrille to the coast, fifteen leagues or more. Gustave ain't a youngster and – if the girl were right and it were Master Titus or Master Barnaby as were one o' the prisoners – 'e'd been wounded. That would slow 'em. Then there's the weather . . . mayhap they done decided to shelter in one of them there game-keepers' cottages 'til the worst of the cold is be'ind 'em.'

'You think they could survive for so long? Perhaps without food?' Adela said huskily.

Jacques' weather-beaten face creased into a reassuring grin.

'Plenty o' game in the forest for them as can catch it!' he said. 'I'll warrant Josef 'as done a fair bit of poaching in 'is time same as any villager does, though 'twould not do for Miss Eugénie to hear of it, seeing 'e'd 'ave been poaching on Monsieur le Chevalier's land! Josef 'ud know well enough 'ow to snare a rabbit, a young boar even. 'E'd not need a firearm to catch a bit of game for theirselves.'

Adela's spirits rose.

'And there are beechmasts!' she cried. 'The wild pigs and squirrels cannot have taken them all! Oh, Jacques, thank you for giving me this new hope! Go now to Dolly, for she has been as anxious as I for your safe return.'

At least Dolly could be happy if only for a little while, Adela told herself as she hurried down to the parsonage to relate the news to her in-laws, for with his master's permission, Jacques intended to return yet again to France to search for the fugitives. Having left the cutter over there, he must wait seven days until the smugglers made yet another secret foray to Normandy. Now that the two countries were at war, these smuggling escapades had become far more dangerous, and the smugglers were considering abandoning them.

As the weather improved, Adela attempted to renew the duties that had once been such a large part of her mother's daily life. She called upon every family in Dene village, listening carefully to the names of all the children; sending comforts to the sick. Although none spoke of it to her, every man and woman knew that her husband might be dead and their sympathy was evident in their gentle voices and concern for her well-being. She knew that she had lost a great deal of weight, and each time Dolly admonished her for her lack of appetite, she struggled to eat more of the tempting dishes sent in by the cook. But worry and sleeplessness had taken their toll and her clothes hung on her as if they had once belonged to another person.

She made frequent visits to the churchyard and put fresh spring flowers on Ned's grave and at the family vault. It would have been hypocritical, she thought, for her to do the same for Sir Henry; and she would hurry past the bleak granite headstone which marked the resting place of the man who had tried so hard to destroy her life. How long ago the tragedy of Ned's death now seemed, she remarked to Dolly who always accompanied her on such sorties. She would think sadly of Kitty's grave and how lonely the little girl must be, buried so far from home and those who loved her. The parson's insistence that Kitty would now be reunited with her brother only revived sad memories of Kitty's last days when she had spoken of her dreams of seeing Ned again in heaven.

Eugénie came to stay bringing with her her sister, Marguerite, who was now married to the captain of a naval vessel presently at sea. Happy though Adela was to have her cousins' company, she found it very difficult to avoid asking Eugénie to repeat again and again her story of the events as she had observed them that night in the gardens of the château. As they walked together along the leafy lane to Dene village and back, she plied her cousin with questions to which she knew in her heart there were no answers. Was Eugénie really unable to identify which of the twins had survived? she begged, knowing that even in full daylight it was impossible to distinguish one from the other. Was Titus' voice a little deeper, perhaps? Could Eugénie not tell which of the two had cursed the soldiers who had killed his beloved twin?

'I am so sorry, *chérie*, but it would be quite wrong of me to pretend I have even a suspicion of the truth,' Eugénie replied. 'The men were but shadows at first and then, later . . . it all happened so fast and I was so frightened! Believe me, dearest, I have relived that night many times, both waking and in my dreams; but I am none the wiser. I do realize how much you want it to be Titus who survived, but I cannot lie to you!'

'You must think I have no love at all for Barny!' Adela said apologetically as they paused to allow Marguerite to pick some violets and primroses from the hedgerows. 'At one time, when we were all children, I loved the twins equally; and at that tender age, I was determined to marry one or the other. I cannot say at what moment I knew it was Titus I truly loved – as a woman must love the man she is to marry. I think it was on that journey back from London when I drove down to the coast alone with Titus. He and I dined together at a posting inn, and as I sat looking at him, he smiled at me and . . . I think I knew then.'

As Marguerite rejoined them, Eugénie linked her arm in Adela's, her eyes sympathetic as she waited for her to continue. Having lost both husband and child, she understood Adela's suffering better than her sister.

'When Barnaby proposed marriage to me in your garden,' Adela continued, 'I found myself wishing beyond anything that it was Titus telling me he loved me. I was quite devastated by jealousy when he flirted with those pretty girls you invited to your home. When finally Titus asked me to marry him, it was the happiest day of my life – until we were married, for only then did I understand how blissful life could be between true lovers!'

'Perhaps Titus will come safely home!' Marguerite said comfortingly. 'At least we know that one of them survived; that he escaped from his guards.'

'You must not give up hope, *chérie*,' Eugénie said gently as they reached the house and made their way upstairs to ready themselves for dinner.

'It will be the anniversary of our engagement tomorrow!' Adela said with a deep sigh. 'Will you accompany me to church? My father-in-law will say special prayers for us. Do you recall how brightly the sun shone at our wedding, Marguerite? It was such a beautiful day, and we were so happy. We supposed we had a whole lifetime ahead of us. Even Barnaby was happy. We thought then that he was enamoured of you!'

'You were quite taken with him, were you not, dearest?'

Eugénie said with a smile. 'But when he did not visit you in London, your handsome young naval officer appeared on the scene and . . . well, poor Barnaby was forgotten.'

'I believed then that he was still in love with you, Adela,' Marguerite said, adding thoughtfully, 'I suppose being so alike, perhaps it was inevitable that the twins should both fall in love with the same girl!'

'It is so difficult to explain why Titus rather than Barnaby stole my heart,' Adela admitted. 'One could not tell them apart – yet I detected a difference . . . not in their looks, but in their natures. Titus has become the stronger of the two. I have always known I could twist Barnaby round my little finger, but Titus . . .' she broke off with a little shrug of her shoulders as she smiled wistfully at her cousins. 'If only both could come safely home,' she murmured, knowing – as did her cousins – that this could never happen now.

As Eugénie and Marguerite departed once more to London having failed yet again to persuade their cousin to go with them, Adela did her best to occupy herself so fully each day that she did not have time on her hands to think, to worry. The spring-cleaning began at her instigation and she was kept busy supervising the servants as they turned the house inside out from attic to cellar. She left untouched some of the wedding presents she and Titus had received, as yet unused, for it seemed like tempting Fate to do otherwise.

April gave way to May and Adela's spirits were fading as fast as the new spring blossoms were burgeoning. Now in the evenings, she sat alone with Dolly in the drawing-room either in silence or, as they bent over their embroidery, talking on any subject that did not involve the twins. Jacques was once more in France, and knowing that it could be weeks before they saw him again, there could be no hope of news.

News arrived, however, late one night after they had retired to bed. Adela opened her eyes to see Dolly standing by her bedside, her round face glowing in the light of her candle as she urged her mistress to rouse herself.

''Tis a messenger come, Miss Addy – one of George Robinson's lads. 'E's got word for us . . . important, 'e says, as to do with Mr Mallory.'

Now wide awake, Adela sprang out of bed and slipped her arms quickly into the sleeves of her wrapper. Her heart was beating furiously as she mouthed the question, 'Which one, Dolly? Mr Titus, or Mr Barnaby? *Which one?*'

''E didn't say, Miss Addy – only as he was to speak to you personal like, and I was to get you quick as a weaver's shuttle else you'd be too late.'

'Too late for what?' Adela asked excitedly, but Dolly could give no answer.

'For the next tide, mistress!' the messenger boy replied when a few minutes later, Adela asked him the same question. 'Mr Robinson said to tell you as 'ow 'e'd 'ave the gentleman aboard and you was to come an' fetch 'im. Mr Mallory were ailing, Mr Robinson said, and I wus to tek you near as we could get to the landing-beach.' He paused only to catch his breath before adding, 'I'se to tell 'ee to tek caution we ain't followed else Mr Robinson'd be swinging on the gallows like as not! And you wus to come on your ownsome, mistress, if'n Jack wusn't 'ere, as 'e doant trust no one else!'

'Dear God!' Adela whispered, her hand covering her mouth as she tried to take in the meaning of the boy's message. One thought only was clouding all others – which of the twins had the smugglers brought home? Which one would she find at the landing-beach?

'The coach!' she gasped, turning to Dolly. 'Have it made ready at once whilst I dress . . . no, no, the whiskey. I will drive myself – the whiskey will be quicker and less likely to be spotted than the coach.'

Her mind had now cleared, and when Dolly returned to her bedchamber to help her complete her dressing, she gave quick, clear instructions.

'A warm travelling rug, Dolly, and a flask of brandy; and money . . . I will need to reward the smugglers; a fresh horse for the messenger; and I may need Mama's medicine chest – the small one she always used for travelling. And Dolly, whilst I am away, put warming-pans in the bed in the guest-room and light the fires. And rouse Cook and tell her to make some broth and prepare a meal.'

'You be careful now, Miss Addy!' Dolly muttered as she handed Adela her old, fur-lined pelisse. 'You be that incited, you ain't thinking 'bout them Excise men as'll be watching the beaches like as not. Jacques said as 'ow they've been known to shoot first and ask questions arter if'n they sees the lads coming ashore.'

Adela gave her a quick hug, her green eyes sparkling with nervous intensity as she bade her farewell.

'Pray for me . . . pray that I shall be home again soon . . . with Master Titus!' she murmured and with Dolly following anxiously behind her, she ran down the stairs.

The sky was clear of clouds and bright with stars as the carriage horse followed in the hoofprints of the messenger boy's chestnut pony. She supposed the lad to be about fifteen or sixteen years of age for he had a sensible head on his shoulders and was keeping his mount to a pace suitable for the whiskey to be travelling fast but at a safe speed. The road, so often flooded during the winter months, was reasonably dry and a light mist clung to the trees and hedgerows which swayed eerily as they swept past. Occasionally a vixen darted into the hedge ahead of them, out searching for food for her new cubs, Adela thought, for at this time of the year, all the wild animals were giving birth to new life. If Titus were to come home, perhaps next spring she, too, would be bringing a new life into the world! Her heartbeat quickened as she considered the possibility. But she set such imaginings aside for fear that she might be tempting Fate, reminding herself that *it might not be Titus coming home.*

They halted twice to give the horses a brief rest and then hurried on their way. They were nearing Rye when dawn broke. As they reached a crossroads, the boy turned westward into a rough country lane. The ruts in the road now forced them to a slower pace and Adela's body began to ache with the jolting as the whiskey lurched from side to side. The countryside was wakening now; cocks were crowing and the occasional farm cart or labourer could be seen in the fields. The mist cleared as the sun rose, and the air was tangy with the salt carried in from the sea. From a rise in the land, Adela could see the grey outline of Camber Castle, the fields around it white with flocks of sheep and their lambs. Their high bleating was audible despite the steady drumming of the horses' hooves on the hard chalky surface of the track.

Suddenly, as they came over the rise of the hill, Adela saw the grey waters of the English Channel. Seagulls soared overhead, dipping with their high, shrill cries into the white wavecrests and over the tops of the masts of fishing boats lying offshore outside Rye harbour. Tired though she was, Adela's heartbeats quickened once more with excitement as she realized they had almost reached their destination.

The messenger boy seemed to know his direction, for he chose the route with unerring accuracy. He turned once more down an even narrower lane and as the chalky soil gave way to grass and sand, he drew his pony to a halt.

'Carnt go no further, mistress!' he said, tying the chestnut's reins to a wind-bent thorn bush. ''Tis but a short walk from 'ere.' He secured her horse and helped her down from the whiskey. 'Best keep quiet now!' he murmured. 'I'll go forrard and see if 'tis safe to go down!'

Without waiting for her reply, he scrambled up the side of a steep sand dune and lay atop on his stomach, his body invisible in the clumps of grass concealing him. After a moment or two he slid down the bank and grinned, 'Tide's in!' he announced cheerfully. 'They saw me signal and they's lowering the dinghy.'

'Will no one see them?' Adela asked anxiously. She had supposed that the smugglers always unloaded their booty at night.

'So what if they does, mistress?' the boy replied grinning. 'They got the cargo off long afore dawn. Now they is trawling, like any honest fishermen. Come evening, they'll tek the boat into 'arbour and sell the catch – mayhap to an Excise man 'isself!' he added with an impish chuckle.

Unable to sustain her patience, Adela struggled up the side of the dune until she could lie beside the boy, straining her eyes to make out the occupants of the little dinghy. Two men were rowing. The third was immobile, leaning against the stern; but even as the boat grazed the sandy shore, she could still not make out his identity. Despite the woollen cap he was wearing, Adela guessed that the man now being helped on to the beach was one of the twins. He was stooped, and stumbled like an inebriate as, supported by his fellows, the group started moving towards her.

Forgetting the possibility of danger, and shaking free of the boy's detaining hand on her arm, Adela scrambled to her feet and slipping and sliding down the sandy bank, she ran towards them. So great was her anticipation that she could scarcely breathe as she reached them. The man's head was drooped on his chest.

'Titus? Titus?' she asked. 'Titus, my dearest, my love, is it you?'

The man's head lifted and she gazed into eyes she had feared she might never see again. As she spoke his name a third time, recognition pierced the stupor to which privation and illness had reduced him, and he smiled.

'Addy! Oh, Addy!' he murmured before his senses left him and, but for the men gripping his arms, he would have fallen to the ground at Adela's feet.

CHAPTER TWENTY-EIGHT

1793

'You are looking so much better, Titus, my love!' Adela said tenderly as she gazed down at the frail figure stretched out on the day-bed which had once been so well-used by her father. Dolly had brought it down from the attic and cleaned it thoroughly before it had been taken out on to the sunny terrace for the invalid's convalescence. Despite the physician's admonitions, Adela had insisted that Titus would never recover from his melancholy whilst lying in the darkened bedchamber.

'The May sunshine will do you so much good, dearest!' she had urged persuasively, and he had finally agreed to be carried downstairs and out into the garden.

'I must admit that I do feel better!' he said now as he watched the gardener staking the delphiniums in the border on the far side of the lawn.

'You are sleeping better now, are you not, Titus?' Adela enquired softly, taking his hand in her own and stroking it gently. She loved to touch him even in so insignificant a fashion, for although almost a month had passed since his return, she still found it hard to believe that he was really and truly safely home. He had been very ill. For several weeks after his escape from the prison cart, he had lain in a derelict forester's hut, tended by Josef and Gustave as the poison from the wounding he had sustained at the château spread all over his emaciated body. Such fevers raged through him that his companions had been convinced he would die.

Further weeks had gone by before he was well enough to make the long slow journey, which they must travel on foot, to the coast. Such was the invalid's lack of strength that he had been obliged to rest every few leagues; and all the time they had feared detection by the frequent patrols out searching for *émigrés*.

When finally they had reached the cove where Jacques had hidden the cutter, the fever had once more taken hold of his body and there was no possibility that Josef could have sailed the boat without his assistance. For a week they lived in one of the big caves, feeding from raw crab meat, prawns and shrimps which Gustave and Josef managed to catch during the limited hours of darkness. When Robinson and his fellow smugglers had sailed their boat into the cove one night, it had seemed like a miracle. Which indeed it was, Adela maintained when she learned how he had travelled back to England without further mishap, leaving Gustave and his cousin to seek sanctuary with relations in Aumale whilst her beloved husband returned to her.

But it was not this story of survival of which Titus dreamed, Adela told Dolly, but his recurrent nightmare. As she sat by his bedside, bathing his forehead as the sweat poured from him, he would call out, '*Murderous dogs, you have killed my brother! Black-hearted villains, may you rot in hell! You have killed him . . . my brother . . . my brother . .*.' It was always the same nightmare as again and again he relived the moment outside the château when he had witnessed the death of his beloved twin. Adela had wept, too, knowing that there was nothing she could do to prevent these nightmares, nor to console him.

Soon, she thought now, he would be well enough to leave the guest chamber which had been turned into a sick-room, and return to their bed. Then, once she and Titus resumed their love-making, if the nightmares still recurred she could wake him and make him forget Barnaby – if only for a little while.

Sometimes as she stared down into those pale, gaunt features, Adela felt such a surge of love that it was all she

could do to restrain the desires of her body; reduce them to
a gentle kiss on his lips. It was weakness, she knew, that
prevented him from wanting a more passionate embrace. She
had noticed that of late, his eyes followed her each time she
left his side; and if she had been gazing down at a book as
she read aloud to him, she would look up to find his eyes
fixed upon her. His expression was one of deepest love, of
passionate desire. Her heart would start racing and her body
incline towards him; but then, inexplicably, he would turn
away and invite her to continue reading.

'Of what are you thinking, my dearest?' she had asked the
first time this had happened; but the look of love and longing
in his eyes had changed to one of such sadness, she was certain
that he was once again remembering poor Barny; that he was
wondering if he had the right to be happy, to fulfil his life,
when his twin was dead. She had never questioned him again.

'*Tante* Camille and Uncle Hugo are bringing Eugénie to
visit you tomorrow, Titus!' she said now as she tucked the
rug more securely about his legs. 'They will be staying only
the one night, so I hope their visit will not over-tire you!'

'Oh, Addy, you take such good care of me!' he answered,
sighing. 'Do you not sometimes weary of sitting at my side?
You should be enjoying the company of others; go to parties,
balls, the theatre. Why do you not return to London with
Eugénie and allow your aunt and uncle to spoil you a little
as you spoil me? You could order some new clothes and—'

Adela stared down at him aghast as she broke in, 'Leave you?
Have you lost your wits again, Titus? How could I even think
of leaving you when you have only just come back to me?'

He gave a wry smile.

'You are so beautiful when you are angry, Addy! Your eyes
look twice as large and your cheeks grow pinker and your
chin lifts! Is it possible that any man could love you as much
as I do?'

Adela sprang from her chair and threw her arms around
him.

'I love you, too!' she said, kissing his lips, his forehead, his cheeks. 'When I thought it was you who had been killed, I wanted to die, too. I love you, Titus, with all my heart. You are my life!'

'I know, dearest, I know!' he said. 'I sometimes wonder if it is for the best – that two people love one another as much as we do.'

Adela's eyes flashed anew as she said reprovingly, 'How can you doubt it, Titus? You frighten me. It is almost as if you . . . you wished our love a lesser thing!'

'Perhaps!' he murmured. 'When you spoke just now of death . . .'

Adela's face softened as she reproached herself for not choosing her words more carefully. No one knew better than she that Barnaby was never far from Titus' thoughts and the least little thing reminded him of his twin. Hurriedly, she changed the conversation.

'Your mother will be here presently,' she said as she rose to her feet. 'Had you forgotten that she is coming to see us? I must go and tidy my hair.' She essayed a smile. 'I expect dear Lady Mallory will chide me for not feeding you well enough, my love. You must try to eat more lest she start wishing she had a different daughter-in-law!'

Lady Mallory, however, was quite pleased with the obvious improvement in her son's health.

'Titus looks so much better!' she said as Adela went with her to the door when it was time for her to leave. She drew a deep sigh. 'It is not his physical health that concerns his father and me,' she confided. 'The physician has assured us Titus is out of danger and that it is only a matter of time now before he fully recovers his strength. No, my dear, it is his state of mind. He is so changed . . . so downcast!'

'I know!' Adela replied. 'I try very hard to keep his mind from . . . from the dreadful things that happened, but he seems unable to come to terms with a life without Barnaby.'

Frances Mallory nodded.

'It must be difficult for you to understand, my dear, but before you and Titus were married, the boys had never been apart. As you know, they lived their lives as one person. Their father and I always thought of them as linked together for life – inseparable – like the silver links that form the bracelet my dear husband gave me the day they were born. When Titus told us he had fallen in love with you and hoped to marry you, we did wonder how Barny would cope with their separation.' Her eyes filled with tears. 'We shall never know now if he, too, could have found someone to love; but Titus . . . he has you now, and we hoped that this would make it easier for him to be without his brother.'

'I, too, had the same hope!' Adela admitted. 'But perhaps we both expect too much too soon. Time must surely help and the memory of what happened fade a little as his strength returns.'

Lady Mallory nodded.

'Perhaps if you were to have a child, Adela?' she said hesitantly. 'You must forgive me for making such a suggestion. If I have offended you—'

'No, no, of course not!' Adela interrupted. 'I have had the same thought. I know Titus would welcome a son . . . he told me so on our wedding night, but . . . in a little while, perhaps . . . when he is better?'

Lady Mallory put her arms around Adela and kissed her warmly on both cheeks.

'I am so happy Titus has you to love and to love him, my dear!' she said. 'We – Lord Mallory and I – both love you as a daughter and if ever we can help in any way . . .' She drew a deep sigh. 'We know Titus is suffering just as we are; more, perhaps; but he will not speak of it to us. The twins used to be very close to their father, but now it is as if Titus wishes to put a barrier between them. My husband wanted to discuss a memorial plaque to Barnaby to go in the church, but Titus refused to do so. Some other time, he said; perhaps later, when he was fully recovered . . .'

Adela nodded.

'Please tell Lord Mallory not to be distressed. I believe the only reason why Titus will not share his grief with you, is because he cannot bring himself to accept, as we do, that Barny has passed away; that if we do not speak of it, he can pretend to himself that it never happened.'

'Yet he was the one who witnessed that dreadful event! My poor darling Barnaby! My husband believes with you that we must give Titus more time; but it is so hard for us to . . . to behave as if nothing had happened. We would have liked to give our son a proper burial service; to have knelt in God's house and commend his spirit to his Maker. Titus will not agree . . . not even that his father should hold a memorial service for him. Naturally my husband could do so if he wishes, but in the light of Titus' health and state of mind since his return, his father does not want to distress him further.'

'I am glad you told me about this, Lady Mallory!' Adela said. 'If I am able to find a suitable occasion, I will myself raise the matter of a memorial service with Titus. Meanwhile you will visit again very soon, will you not? I am certain Titus loves to have you here even if he . . . he does not converse very freely.'

Lady Mallory nodded.

'I am his mother, my dear, so I am as concerned as you for his well-being. Nevertheless, it is not easy for me—' her voice broke as she said huskily, 'They are so alike . . . to see Titus even in ill health . . . is to see my poor, dear Barnaby. Perhaps Titus looks at himself in the mirror and is reminded as I am – as we all are! Now I must go, for it will soon be time for Evensong and the parson becomes quite cross with me if I am late.' She essayed a smile. 'It sets a bad example, he says, and of course, he is quite right!'

That evening, as had become her custom, Adela played chess with the invalid. Because he seemed unable to concentrate for very long, Adela usually won the games; but on this occasion, he seemed quite like his old self as he made a determined effort to be the one to call 'check-mate'. When after two long hours he was able to do so, his face was wreathed in a boyish smile as he said triumphantly, 'You should have guarded your queen better, Addy! That was really most enjoyable!'

'I shall try to take my revenge tomorrow!' Adela said, returning his smile. She reached out and covered his hand with her own as he made to collect the pieces. 'It makes me very happy, my dearest, to see you so much improved. It shows you are getting better. Your mama said so, too.'

As he let fall the pieces and imprisoned her hand between his own, she caught her breath before, taking her courage in her hands, she said softly, 'Shall we retire now, Titus? If you are no longer to be an invalid, will you return to our bed? It is such a long, long time since I last slept in your arms!'

For a moment there could be no mistaking the look of eager acceptance in his eyes; but then he began to pick up the chess pieces once more and she was unable to read his expression as he said, 'I do not sleep well, as you know, Addy. I fear I might disturb you!'

'Oh, Titus,' Adela cried, 'can you really believe I would mind if you woke me? Waking or sleeping, I want to be close to you. I do not care which!'

He paused only a moment before looking up once more.

'If you are quite certain that is what you wish . . .' he said quietly. 'I want nothing more than to make you happy. That is my sole purpose in life. During these past weeks when I was so ill – so near to death – I think it was your voice telling me that you could not bear to go on living without me which . . . which made me want to live. You were so determined . . . and loving you as I do, I knew that somehow I must recover so that you . . . oh, Addy, my love, my only love!'

He rose slowly to his feet and took her in his arms. His lips were against her forehead, and then her mouth. Adela cupped his face in her hands, her heart soaring with joy as she realized she had broken through the barrier of melancholy at last and that, for the moment the death of Titus' twin was forgotten.

'Come, my darling, my dearest!' she said, her arm now going about his waist to support him as they turned towards the door. She knew instinctively that she must not give him time for reflection, for he might start remembering Barnaby once more and change his mind.

At last she was undressed and lying beneath the coverlets, her hair spread out on the pillow, only one candle sending a small golden circle of light by the bedside. With growing unease, she waited. Were her intuitive fears about to be justified? she asked herself. Was Titus finding himself unable to set aside his grief? It was a further fifteen minutes before the door of his dressing-room opened and he approached the bed. His face was haggard; his eyes tormented.

'I am afraid I was delayed, Addy. I was looking at the moon – a full moon. Once I had thought her beautiful – but as I stood at the window, it occurred to me that had she not shown her face that night at the château, we might both have escaped undetected. It was Shakespeare, was it not, who called her "inconstant"? I call her "betrayer"!'

The bitterness in his voice struck at her heart. How was she to remove the guilt he felt when at moments like this he recalled the death of his twin?

'Oh, Titus, my love!' she said. 'You cannot live in the past. Memories will not alter the circumstances and remorse cannot bring back to us those who have gone. I grieve for my parents, for Kitty, and not least for poor little Ned. If I allowed myself to dwell on the manner of his passing . . . no, we *must* live for the years to come, Titus. It is the only way.'

Her arms were held out to him and slowly, as a drowning man might do, he reached out and caught hold of them. His voice was barely audible as she drew him towards her.

'Is it enough, Addy? Is it enough that I love you? With all my heart I do love you . . . as a husband should love his wife. *Is it enough?*'

'It is everything!' Adela whispered back before pressing her mouth to his. 'I want a child, Titus . . . our child. I will give you a son to love and cherish. He will comfort your parents; comfort you; he will be our future!'

With simple abandon, she lay back on the pillows, her body arching towards him as his hands moved to cover her breasts. His breathing had quickened and she could feel his heart pulsating against her own as now he reached beneath her nightgown. She felt his fingertips tracing the line of her body slowly from her waist to her hips and then linger between her thighs. It was as if he were exploring her for the first time, she thought, as on their wedding night. How wonderful had been their discovery of one another! His caresses now were becoming more urgent and with a fierce hunger, she parted her legs and felt him move atop her.

'I love you . . . so much . . . too much!' he cried out. 'Oh, Addy, forgive me . . . forgive me . . . may God forgive me, but I cannot . . .'

As these cries were wrung from him, he was struggling to prove his manhood, his body at fever heat as Adela strived to let him know how ready she was to receive him.

With one last cry, he tore himself from her arms and moved quickly to his own side of the bed. He lay there with his back towards her, his breath coming in short, uneven gasps.

Adela stifled her own cry of dismay as she tried to find words to comfort him.

'It is of no import, Titus, truly it is not. It was my fault for . . . for asking something of you when you are not yet well enough. Please forgive me!'

For a moment, he did not reply. Then he said, 'I could not bear it if you thought I loved you less than . . .' He broke off and began again. 'I wanted you, Addy. I wanted you so much; but I could not . . . I . . .'

Adela moved quickly to his side and pressing her soft warm body against his back, she kissed the damp curls at the back of his neck.

'Shhsh . . . shssh!' she crooned. 'I know you love me, Titus. How could I doubt it? I love you, too, with all my heart. I have always loved you and I always will. Now sleep, my darling. We are both tired. Sleep now, my love. All will be well, I promise you!'

It was some long time before she felt his body losing its tenseness. Only then did she cease to think of his unhappy frustrations and admit her own. Every nerve-end seemed alive, sensitive to each part of him that was touching her breasts, her stomach, her legs. She had not realized until this moment, how starved she had been of this aspect of her married life. It was strange, she thought now, that until Titus had awakened her to these new, unimagined pleasures, she had not given much thought to them, for who could tell a blind man what a colour looked like or describe to a deaf man the sound of music?

Whilst Titus had been missing, she had not dared to allow herself to remember too often the few beautiful nights they had shared here in their home, or at the château. Since he had started to recover his health and strength, it had become increasingly difficult not to anticipate his full recovery; and this night . . . when he had kissed her, caressed her so ardently, she had been aroused as magically as before. There had been a difference, of course; but she understood why this must be so. In the past, Titus had been filled with strength and vigour; dominant, masterful, commanding and yet never less than gentle. This night, when he was still a convalescent, had been very different, as if he needed her to be in command.

Gradually her heartbeat slowed and her body cooled. As her mind regained control, she convinced herself that time and renewed good health would cure this trouble, and finally she fell asleep.

When Adela awoke, the sun was pouring through the curtains which Dolly was drawing apart.

'Master Titus said as 'ow you was to 'ave breakfast in your bed, Miss Addy,' she said cheerfully, 'and I was to tell you 'e thought best not to wake you and 'e 'as gorn down to the garden, it being such purty weather!'

Adela's immediate feeling of disappointment that it was
Dolly and not her husband who stood beside the bed,
compounded the pain in her head which had begun to throb.
Without understanding the reason, she wanted to weep. She
turned her head aside so that Dolly should not see the tears
which were stinging the backs of her eyes. Although she took
the breakfast tray on to her lap and pretended to eat, she gave
up the pretence as soon as Dolly left and, pushing the tray
aside, climbed out of bed and went to the window.

Down below she could see a lone figure pacing the terrace
with the aid of a walking-stick. Titus seemed to be testing his
strength, she thought, and she caught her breath as he stumbled. Dolly had opened the casement at her request and now
she leaned out, her eyes anxious as the man below stumbled
a second time. Did he not know he was not yet strong enough
to go at such a pace?

'Titus! Titus, take care!' she called.

He did not turn his head and she called his name again
more loudly. This time he stopped abruptly and looked up
towards her window.

'Let Unwin take your arm until I come down!' Adela called.
'Please, Titus! I will not be long!'

She could see his mouth open as if he were about to reply;
but without a word, he turned away and limped slowly towards
the daybed. Watching him as he lowered himself on to it and
dropped his stick to the ground, Adela was pierced with a
fear so intense that it left her shivering despite the warm
sunlight in which she was bathed. Something was wrong with
Titus . . . very wrong! He must have heard her call, for he
was well within earshot, yet he had been so lost to the world
– in thought? in his grief? in memories of Barny? – that he
had been oblivious to the sound of her voice. Had his mind
been affected in some way by the privations he had endured?
And why, when he had looked up and seen her, had he not
smiled at her, or at least acknowledged her call with a wave?

Slowly she sat down on the edge of the bed and put her

hands to her cheeks. How, she asked herself, was she to help him get well if she did not know what was wrong with him? Could illness, deprivation, grief, change someone so much that at times they seemed a different person? The physician had assured her that he was quite out of danger and, but for the limp and the need to put on weight, was 'in very good shape'. Such had been his words – yet they took no account of Titus' state of mind, she told herself. His parents, too, were concerned about his sensibility. Would it be better if they were all to speak openly of Barnaby so that Titus could not continue to live in a make-believe world where his twin had not died? Was *this* what was wrong with him?

That night, without request from her, he came once more to their room. They had played their game of chess and because he had made some careless errors, Adela had won easily. He was unnaturally quiet and it had fallen to her to keep the conversation going. Climbing stiffly into bed beside her, he extinguished the candle and turning to her with a roughness of which she would not have believed him capable, tried without preamble to make love to her. On this occasion, as on subsequent nights, Adela felt no frustration, for her instinct warned her that he would not succeed. She was unhappily aware that he was no longer trying to take her with love but was attempting to prove to himself that he was not impotent.

After five such unsuccessful efforts, Adela waited until he had put out the candle on the sixth night before telling him that she did not wish him to approach her again.

'We should wait a while, Titus,' she said gently. 'You do not have to prove yourself to me, dearest. I know that you love me, and that is enough.'

'But not for me!' he replied harshly, his voice full of pain. 'The least a husband can do is to get his wife with child!'

'But Titus! I am in no great hurry for a child,' Adela protested. 'I only spoke of it because I hoped to cheer you! You are my husband and I love you!'

'How can you say that when I am not the man you married . . . I am different . . . I . . . have changed. Can you deny it?'

His voice was taut, challenging, almost despairing. She wanted to lie to him, to tell him it was not so; but she could not bring herself to do so. He *had* changed. The differences were indefinable, yet they existed. He knew it – and she did, too. How was it possible, she asked herself, that two people who loved each other as much as they did, could arrive at this state of unhappiness? for that was the only way she could truthfully describe their situation. He was unhappy; and because he could feel no joy in life, nor could she.

He did not press her for a reply, her silence being all the answer he needed, but with a long, trembling sigh, he turned away from her. Although she wished it, he did not reopen the conversation. As was now customary he fell asleep before she did, and it was long past midnight before suddenly, Adela awoke. Opening her eyes, she saw that moonlight was flooding the room, and turning her head, realized that the space beside her was empty. Silhouetted against the window was a lone figure seated in a chair, his profile just discernible against the bright nocturnal sky.

Her heart jolted and her skin broke out in a cold sweat as she stared at the shadowy form by the window. Just for a moment . . . for one single instant . . . she had thought it was Barnaby.

No, she told herself, this was no apparition! Ghosts belonged to fairy tales, to Shakespeare's plays. It was Titus, her husband, who sat there, so still, so quiet that he might have been a statue.

'Titus!' she whispered. 'Titus!'

Her need to see him move, to hurry to her side so that she could feel his touch, feel that he was warm, alive, no statue, no ghost, was paramount.

The figure at the window did not move.

'Titus?' This time, her voice was a question. It remained unanswered. 'Please answer me. Are you remembering Barny?'

At the mention of Barnaby's name, he did turn, so suddenly that Adela was horrified at the thought that this evoked – *Titus had not answered to his own name, but he had reacted instantly to that of his twin.* No, she told herself sharply, this is madness! I am dreaming. I know that this is Titus . . . yes, a changed, different Titus to the man I left in France, but he has been very, very ill; he has lost his twin, his identical twin . . . the brother so like him that neither of his parents have ever been able to tell them apart. I would know! When he held me in his arms, I would have known if it were not Titus!

The words were unspoken but seemed to scream inside her skull.

I would have known when he kissed me, she thought, her body rigid as she fought her fears. But those kisses, embraces – they, too, have changed. But only because he has been so weak, so ill, argued that second voice inside her head. This man is my husband, the man I love. It *is* Titus!

Unable to bear her thoughts a second longer, Adela sprang out of bed and ran to stand beside him. His back was once more towards her, but she thrust herself between him and the window. As if to compound her fears, a cloud drifted across the face of the moon, plunging the room into semi-darkness.

'Titus, look at me! What is happening to us? You have to talk to me, tell me, *what is wrong?*' she begged.

When still he did not speak, she reached out her hands and touched his face. Horrified and terribly afraid, she felt his cheeks and realized that they were wet with tears.

CHAPTER TWENTY-NINE

1793

Adela was shivering with a combination of cold and fear as she took an involuntary step backwards. Her mouth was dry and her heart thudded in her chest. She stared in shocked silence at the man in front of her.

'Now you know the truth, Addy!'

His voice was so quiet and strained – as if the words were dredged from deep within him – that she barely heard him.

'No! No I do *not* understand. What are you trying to tell me? That you are not . . . not Titus? That . . .'

She could not bring herself to express her fears and she fell silent again. It seemed as if the whole room was holding its breath as she waited for him to speak.

'Yes, Addy, yes! I deceived you. *I am Barnaby!*'

As she swayed, he rose slowly to his feet. His face was no more than a dark shadow, the expression in his eyes hidden from her as he continued in a tone of despair, 'When Titus was killed – shot – he lived just long enough to speak your name and to urge me to escape whilst I still could. He insisted – and I would have said the same to him – that at least one of us must survive to take care of you.' His voice was sharp with pain. '*It was what he wanted, Addy.* He had been shot in the chest and he knew he was dying. He wanted me to go – to get back to England to – to comfort you as best I could. They were the last words he spoke before the soldiers came and took me away and . . . and I never saw him again.'

Adela caught her breath. Her body was trembling uncontrollably as she said in a cold, hard voice, 'Titus wanted you to comfort me! Yes, Barny, but *not to take his place*. How could you have done such a thing? Did you really believe I would never discover the truth? Or did you just want what you could never have by rights?'

Barnaby held out his hands in a gesture of supplication.

'Please try to understand. I know you must hate me, but upon my solemn word of honour, it was not my intention to deceive you. That morning when you ran to greet me on the beach and asked if I was Titus, I would have told you the truth had I not lost consciousness. When I regained my senses here in the guest-chamber bed, I realized that you thought I was Titus. You kept telling me that if only one of us was to survive, how thankful you were it was he, my brother. I wanted so much to tell you the truth but I could not bring myself to do so, knowing how much it would hurt you. Each day that followed when I awoke, I promised myself I would speak out; each day passed without my finding the courage to destroy your happiness. *I loved you too much, Addy!* Can you not understand?'

Adela turned away and walked across to the bed. Gathering up her night-robe, she put it round her shoulders and then paused in the action of lighting the candle. No, she thought, it is better the room should remain in darkness for I cannot bear to look at Barny. Oh, Titus, Titus, my dearest love, just when I thought you had come back to me I have learned that I will never see you again!

She rocked to and fro, keening softly, too shocked to weep as the full understanding of her bereavement wiped out for the moment the enormity of Barnaby's duplicity.

Barnaby took a step towards Adela and then halted, knowing that he must not touch her. She could not hate him more at this minute than he was hating himself. If only it could have been he, not Titus, who had lost his life! How many times these past weeks had he wished that he had been the one to die!

The silence had become all but unbearable when finally

Adela spoke. Her voice was harsh with bitterness as she said, 'I suppose you thought that the end justified the means! That I could be happy sharing my life – my bed – with you! Who knows if one day that might have been so, Barny, *if you had been honest with me*. Now I shall always hate you. You let me go on living in a false world and I will never forgive you . . . never!'

She heard the sharp intake of his breath and knew that her blow had struck home. She was glad; she wanted to hurt him, to make him suffer the same pain she felt.

'You have every right to call me a cheat, a coward. I hate myself,' Barnaby said in a low voice. 'If Titus were alive he too would condemn me . . . but at least you do now know the truth.'

'Oh, yes, and I understand now so much that has been concerning me. I understand why you could not make love to me; why so often you would not look at me when I took your hand; why you turned your head away when I told you how much I loved you. You *were* different from the Titus I had known in many ways, but, fool that I was, I assumed it was because you had been so very ill. Then, when you began to recover . . .'

She broke off, covering her mouth with her hand as her mind recalled in sharp, clear, horrifying detail how she had urged him to become her lover again. Had this been the one step up a mountain of deception that he could not bring himself to take? Was it guilt that had made him impotent?

'I wanted you to be happy!' Barnaby's voice was a plea for understanding. 'I loved you. I still do. I would do anything in the world to ensure your happiness. I allowed myself to hope – believe – that I could do so; but by the time I realized that I could never replace Titus . . . I could not find a way to tell you. I do not expect you to forgive me, but please, please, Addy, try to understand. It was never my intention to deceive you.'

Tears were now threatening to engulf Adela. She barely

heard Barnaby's words, for the full force of her loss was slowly submerging her as if she were once again drowning in the dark, cold waters of the sea. Why had she not died during that fearsome storm? She would be happier dead than living the rest of her life without Titus.

'I will rouse one of the servants and have a chaise made ready,' Barnaby muttered in a low voice of resignation. 'Perhaps one day in the future, I shall see you again; but in the meantime, I will not burden you with my presence. I can only say again how . . . how sorry I am; and that I love you and always will. Goodbye, Addy, and please try to understand.'

Barnaby reached the door before the meaning of his words penetrated Adela's consciousness.

'You are going away?' she asked sharply. 'Where? Why? You cannot leave in this fashion, Barnaby. You are still not well and . . . besides, what reason can you give your parents? They will be no better able to understand or bear this than I! They have been so worried about you . . .'

Not only worried but confused, Adela thought. No wonder Barnaby did not want his father to hold a memorial service for him when it should be held for Titus! They would no more be able to understand how Barnaby could have taken his twin's identity than was she – perhaps less so. If Barnaby returned home to live with them, questions would be asked and they would be obliged to reveal his deception to everyone – friends, neighbours, the parishioners. How could the parson justify such sinful behaviour to his congregation? It was unthinkable.

'You cannot leave, Barny!' she cried impulsively. 'There is no easy undoing of this mischief! To confess the truth now would be to destroy your parents!'

'It was not my intention to return to their house,' he replied. 'I was going to remove myself somewhere far away . . . where none of you need ever see me again.'

'Run away?' Adela's voice was sharp with scorn. 'That would be an easy way out for you, Barny, but not for those of us you left behind. Am I to tell everyone that my husband has deserted me? You started this and however hard it might prove for us both, we must continue as we are.'

'Continue?' Barnaby repeated in shocked tones. 'You mean, you want me to remain here, in this house? To go on pretending that . . . that I am Titus?'

Adela had spoken without prior thought but now as she considered the options, she was certain that this must be the only way to protect her in-laws. As for herself, she would prefer not to see him again. At the same time, she was beginning to realize that she was not entirely free of complicity. Had she not put an impossible burden on Barnaby's shoulders when she told him how grateful she was that God had spared Titus rather than his twin? Had she not *willed* Barnaby to be Titus?

'Why not continue with the pretence? You have succeeded very well so far.' Adela was unable to keep the bitterness from her voice. 'I am the only one who suspected something might be wrong – although I did not dream *how* wrong! Oh, your mother and father were worried about you – not your bodily health but the state of your mind – they feared that your brother's death had unhinged you. Nevertheless, they still took your word for it that it was Titus and not you who had survived. Who knows how long I might have gone on thinking the same if . . .' She broke off, her cheeks colouring as she recalled his inability to perform as a lover as well as a husband.

Barnaby's head drooped. His hands hung helplessly at his sides.

'I will do anything you ask, Addy. Whatever you think best,' he muttered.

With an effort, Adela drew herself upright. Her voice gained conviction as she said firmly, 'I think it best that we continue our life together as we have done ever since your return – except, of course, that you will in future keep to your own bedchamber. As to how we behave towards one another in front of others – we must maintain a polite affection. I do not want your mother to suspect that we are not . . . not as devoted as . . . as she believes us to be. Nor must Jacques ever know the truth, still less Dolly lest you lose their respect. Titus would not wish his beloved twin to be regarded with anything less, and they would despise you, as I do, were they to know the truth.'

In the darkness, she could not see him flinch at this cruel barb, but in her own agony of mind, she would not have retracted it even had she seen how painfully it had struck home.

'Addy!' The single word was an appeal. 'To go on living with you – as if you were my wife – knowing all the time that you hate me . . . *I cannot do it* . . . not even for you!'

'Then do it for Titus!' Adela retorted instantly. 'You owe him that much, do you not? He wanted you to take care of me – not to make me the laughing-stock of the village and the object of pity to our relations, friends, servants! Do it for your parents who have suffered enough already at the loss of a son.'

Only as Barnaby left the room closing the door quietly behind him, did she give way to the storm of tears that had been threatening to choke her. Throwing herself on the bed, Adela buried her face in the pillow and sobbed broken-heartedly for the husband she knew now she would never see again.

Slowly, inexorably, the long summer days passed. Each hour Barnaby and Adela spent in each other's company widened the unbreachable rift between them. Whenever possible they avoided one another's eyes, for in Adela's there was only reproach; in Barnaby's guilt and an unquenchable sorrow. As his health improved, neighbours began to call and then to invite them to dinner; to play cards, or be entertained with music or poetry reading. They travelled to London in the early summer and stayed with the de Falence family for a month, during which time they attended a masked ball, a reception at Carlton House and visited Ranelagh Gardens and the Opera.

On such occasions Adela pretended a false gaiety, smiled coquettishly at the young men who, attracted by her extraordinary beauty, invariably gathered around her, flirting with and complimenting her. She had not regained the weight she had lost during those days at sea and her face was now perfectly heart-shaped, her eyes seeming larger and more luminous than ever. Despite the laughter, the upward tilt of her chin, the brave carriage of her head, there was an indefinable *tristesse* about Adela which intrigued her admirers who felt that there was some hidden mystery deep within her demanding to be unveiled.

Those of their friends and relations who considered her husband to be greatly changed and unnaturally quiet and reserved, were reassured by Adela's oft-repeated explanation – that he had never fully come to terms with the death of his twin. Although she had been grateful for the pleasurable diversion, Adela was relieved when they returned to the comparative solitude of Dene Place.

At the end of October Jacques returned home from France where he had learned that on the day following upon the shooting, the soldiers had boasted of having buried all the dead prisoners in the grounds of the château. Only the female servants had been left alive to wait upon the soldiers. These women were subsequently branded as spies and traitors, and it had been only a matter of weeks before they, too, were arrested, after which the château had been ransacked and then burned to the ground. The blackened ruins of the masonry still remained to mark where the beautiful Evraud family seat had once graced the countryside.

Jacques had been up to the estate and tried to locate the graves; but so many *sabots* – belonging to the hordes who had pillaged the house of its contents – had flattened the paths, lawns and flowerbeds, that he had been unable to find them. Those peasants in the village who had previously denounced the Revolution in the privacy of their homes, were too afraid to talk of the atrocities that had taken place; or, indeed, of the aristocratic members of the Evraud family to whom they had once been loyal. Like the citizens of Paris, they were demanding the destruction of the nobility as well as the clergy.

In grim tones, Jacques described a new contraption called the guillotine, which had been set up in Paris and was now in use for exacting the death penalty upon the ever-growing number of 'traitors'. A merchant from Paris, whom he had encountered by chance in Saint Cyrille, told him of the existence of an assembly of some score of self-appointed men who gathered in a dank, evil-smelling coffee-room named the Cheval Borgneto, to denounce whomsoever they pleased as enemies of the people. In hushed tones, the man had described how they sat on upturned empty wine-barrels at trestle-tables roughly erected from old deal boards, enjoying to the full their newly acquired powers. So irresponsible and depraved were they that they had even resorted to denouncing one another.

All over France, men and women were now spying upon one another and reporting their neighbours for contravening the new edicts of the Revolution, often without just cause but because of a grudge, an unpaid bill, an illegitimate child, a short measure of grain or the purchase of a fowl that would not lay.

''E tolt me it was like Judgement Day in 'ell! They've gone mad!' Jacques said, tapping his forehead. 'No one is safe in their beds now – or even supping a tankard of ale in the village inn in Saint Cyrille. One evening I saw a dispute between a farmer and Dupois, the son of Gustave's brother, who 'e said 'ad sold 'im short. The next morning the farmer was arrested as a traitor – and 'e'd been one of the first to wear the tricolor! May God have mercy on them, for those who send these innocents to their deaths must surely be condemned to 'ell!'

On hearing that Jacques had not found their son's resting place, Lord and Lady Mallory raised yet again the subject of a memorial plaque for him to be erected in the church. This time, Adela, aware of the reasons for Barnaby's objections to their wishes, supported his request that this should not be done.

'He is trying so hard to forget the death of his twin,' she said weakly, muttering the only excuse that occurred to her. 'He feels that a plaque would only serve as yet another reminder of his brother's death.'

Lady Mallory was distressed.

'It is a year since we lost my poor Barny,' she said with tears in her eyes as her daughter-in-law accompanied her one cold October morning to place flowers in Dene church. 'I am beginning to fear that Titus will never be himself again. Have you considered, Adela, my dear, that you and he should go to live elsewhere? Perhaps there are too many memories for him here in Dene.'

Adela's mouth tightened and her hands clenched around the stems of the yellow and bronze chrysanthemums she was holding.

'I do not necessarily think that it is right that he . . . that any of us should try to forget!' she said with difficulty. 'I am sure you would agree Lady Mallory, that we would be wrong to run away from life's problems. Perhaps in time, Titus will come to terms with his loss – as I am trying to do.'

Hurriedly, Lady Mallory put her arm around Adela's shoulders.

'My dear child, in my concern for Titus I forgot how many of your nearest and dearest have passed away – your poor mother, your papa, your little brother and sister! You are so brave, Adela, that you put me to shame. I am sure you are right – Titus must never be allowed to forget his brother but should remember him with gladness. Perhaps, as you say, given time, and . . .' she added with a wistful smile '. . . that grand-child you promised me?'

Adela bit her lip. She hated deceiving this good, kindly woman whose suffering at the loss of her son she knew to be equal to her own. Yet if she and Barnaby were to continue to protect Lady Mallory and her husband from the lie they were perpetrating, how could she tell her mother-in-law that there would *never* be a grandchild for her to hold in her arms?

Although a little of Adela's anger towards Barnaby had by now given way to a measure of pity, she knew she could never feel the same affection for him as before. His likeness to Titus no longer disturbed her. He had grown much thinner and his features more angular. Even his hair had lost its golden lights, and here and there she could detect a strand of grey. His posture was no longer upright but slightly stooped, his shoulders hunched. When she looked up suddenly and saw him approaching, she no longer saw Titus.

The time had come, Adela decided, when she must insist that Dolly put Jacques' need of her before her own. Their wedding had been too long postponed. It was nearly three years since Nou-Nou had died and Jacques had long since made ready their little cottage in the village in preparation for their marriage. Moreover, she would be relieved not to have Dolly's watchful eye upon her. Since Adela had known the truth about Barnaby and they had agreed to continue to enact the parts of husband and wife, Dolly was the one person Adela feared would suspect something was amiss. She promptly selected one of the parlour-maids to become her personal maid, and although after her wedding, Dolly still insisted upon coming up to Dene Place to supervise the care of Adela's clothes, she was too preoccupied with her own new domestic duties to pay the same attention to Adela's well-being.

There were to be no more visits to France by Jacques as there was no further need for him to go there. The route of escape had ceased to exist with Eugénie's and Philippe's departures from Saint Cyrille and the demise of the château, beside which there was the danger now that anyone might be arrested on any pretext. He therefore resumed his employment as Barnaby's valet but at Dene Place.

Dolly's wedding in Dene Church had brought back painful memories to Adela of her own wedding but little more than a year ago. She and Titus had stood side by side in the same place, listening to the same parson delivering the same words. Tears filled her eyes as Jacques kissed Dolly's round, red-cheeked, glowing face, for as she regarded these two faithful servants, Adela had almost felt the touch of Titus' lips on her own; heard his whispered words as he had said, 'My wife!'

Beside her in the pew, Barnaby had stood motionless, staring not at the bridal couple but at the stained-glass window behind the altar. Was he, too, remembering? Adela wondered.

Somehow, in the ensuing days, they learned to live together in seeming harmony; like any other happily married couple. Each morning, they planned the day across the breakfast table. Side by side, they drove out in the chaise to call upon their neighbours; greeted guests; discussed improvements to the house, the gardens, the farms, the staff. Together they would visit the Mallorys or entertain them at Dene Place; but they were never at ease in one another's company.

Eugénie came on a prolonged sojourn and Adela was able to escape Barnaby's company and go with her cousin to the circulating library or to the mantua-maker, to choose materials for new clothes, new hangings. Eugénie seemed reconciled to her widowhood and to have settled happily to being a companion to her mother, the Comtesse. She could have married again had she wished, she told Adela, for she had received a proposal from Sir Percival Tuke, a charming man who had a beautiful home in Ireland to offer her and a ready-made family, for he, too, had been widowed.

'But I could not accept him, *chérie*!' Eugénie confided. '*Maman* does not understand, but I am sure that you do. I was so very much in love with Robert, you see, and I could not bring myself to accept anyone else in his place. I am sure if, God forbid, you were ever to lose Titus, you would feel the same! Married life is so intimate, is it not? To share my bed with another man, however charming . . . no, I could not do it.'

Adela understood only too well. She sometimes marvelled – albeit with a sense of horror – at the urgency with which she had awaited Barnaby's recovery after his return from France so that they could relive the pleasures she had enjoyed so briefly with Titus. She had sat by his bedside, happy to be able to reach out a hand to touch him; to lean over and kiss him; to lay her cheek against his . . . but only because she had thought him to be Titus. Now, whilst she longed for her husband, her body no longer desired the identical body of his twin.

By unspoken agreement, neither ever referred to the night when Barnaby had confessed the truth. It lay between them, an invisible, impassable barrier. When they were obliged in public to touch, each stiffened involuntarily as their mouths spoke casual endearments. It was strange, she thought, how she could say the word 'dearest' without it having any meaning other than to misguide those who heard it. When Barnaby called her 'my wife', both knew that of all the women in the world, she was the least likely to belong to him as a true wife should.

They were helped in their deception by Barnaby's long-lasting convalescence. No one questioned the fact that they had separate bedchambers for even after he had recovered physically, Barnaby still suffered from horrifying dreams and would wake in the night. On such occasions, he would ask his servant to light the candles and to bring him a toddy; and when the autumn nights became colder, to rekindle the fire. Then he would sit in his chair reading until his mind had quietened. During the preceding summer, he had put on his clothes and walked in the garden until his restlessness had left him. Adela had made Lady Mallory aware of these disturbances and trusted that her mother-in-law took them as reason enough why a couple so newly wed should choose to sleep apart.

Somehow she and Barnaby contrived never to spend much time alone in one another's company. Philippe had given her a deer-hound which had proved too energetic for life in London, and Barnaby had appropriated it. He would take the dog with him on long rides in the countryside and the animal became devoted to him, sleeping on his bed and at his feet beneath a table or by his chair. He had changed its name to 'Gloucester' he told Adela. Seeing the question in her eyes, he had given her a wry smile not untinged with bitterness, as he explained, 'You will recall that King Richard III, Duke of Gloucester, was a usurper? Now that the dog has become my shadow, the name seems suitable, do you not agree?'

The look of sadness, despair, guilt that had been on Barnaby's face when he had spoken those words, came into Adela's mind as late one autumn afternoon she sat by the fire in her bedchamber, her embroidery idle in her hands as she stared into the flames. Barnaby had gone down to see the tenant of the home farm taking the dog with him, and she preferred the comparative homeliness of her own room to the solitude of the empty drawing-room downstairs. Despite the devotion of the animal, Barnaby must be even lonelier than I am! she thought. Although they shared their home and their lives, they each lived in their own private world. Had she imposed too harsh a punishment? she asked herself. Would it have been fairer to everyone, including the Mallorys, if she had allowed Barnaby to confess the truth when first she discovered it? The secret she and Barnaby now shared was slowly destroying them both. Poor Barny was suffering even more than was she, and she had no right to force him to continue living a lie.

With an effort, she diverted her thoughts to the news in the letter from Eugénie which Dolly had brought to her but an hour ago.

Father has just learned that our poor misguided Queen has been put to Death! It is hard to believe that this terrible Murder could have been committed in the name of France. If they desired to Punish her was it not enough that they took first her little Marie Thérèse and then the Dauphin from her? Had she not suffered enough at the Death of her Husband? And such terrible Accusations were made against her at her Trial! I cannot bear to imagine what horrible Pressures must have been put upon her poor little Son for him to have signed a Testimony saying that she had corrupted him in so depraved a Manner! Could they have thought of a worse or more horrible Crime with which to blacken her Name than Incest?

As you can imagine, *Chérie*, it has been all Papa and *Maman* can do to prevent Philippe returning to Paris to kill those who perpetrated these terrible Lies. Even now we cannot believe this has happened. There is still no news of the Whereabouts of the Dauphin, but at least we can assume the poor Child is still alive since they have obtained his Signature to his mother's Death Warrant. What will happen to him now that he has been made a Ward of the Republic we dare not imagine . . .

'I've brought you a nice 'ot cup of chocolate, Miss Addy!' Dolly announced as she came into the room. 'We're clean out of tea, and Cook says 'tis the same all over the village.' She put the cup down on the sewing-table beside Adela's chair and went to throw another log on the fire. 'It's that cold out, Miss Addy, for all we ain't into November yet. Jacques said as 'ow 'e reckons it'll be a larmentable raw winter.' She turned and grinned cheerfully at her mistress. ''E said as 'ow we'd like as not be getting fresh supplies of tea in shortly – that there George being gorn to France this past week!'

Glad to have her mind diverted from the shocking news of Marie Antoinette and her children, Adela took the hot drink gratefully.

'Did Jacques not tell us that it had become too dangerous these days for the smugglers to continue their trading?' she asked.

Dolly nodded.

''Deed 'e did, Miss Addy, but that ain't stopped George none. There's a deal more money to be made these days ferrying them poor Frenchie ladies and gentlemen back to England than ever there were carting brandy and the like! Not that George doant bring a cask or two along with 'im. As good be 'anged for an old sheep as a young lamb, 'e says, and 'e ain't got caught yet. Right sharp 'e be, and a right good friend to my Jacques!'

'God keep him, then!' Adela said, her thoughts turning yet again as Dolly went across the room to draw the curtains. 'Is Mr Titus back yet, Dolly?' she asked. ''Tis growing dark already.'

''E'll be back presently, surely!' Dolly replied, drawing the curtains against the deepening shadows outside. The smile had left her face as she regarded Adela's pallor, an expression of anxiety on her own.

'You'd no ought to be sitting up 'ere on your ownsome, Miss Addy. It doant do no one no good to think too much – about wot's past, I mean. You be only twenty year old, and times is you look like you 'as the cares of the world on your shoulders!'

Adela put down her empty cup and assayed a smile.

'Are you trying to tell me that I look like an old woman, Dolly?' she asked. She put her hand on the maid's arm and gave it an affectionate squeeze. 'You and I have lived through some difficult times together, have we not?' she said. 'How long is it since you first came to Dene to look after me? Ten, eleven years? It seems a life-time ago.'

'Nor won't I never leave you, Miss Addy!' Dolly said quickly. 'Not even if Jacques ordered me to!'

Now Adela was able to laugh.

'It was only the other day that you promised to love, honour and *obey* your husband!' she chided.

'Yes, well I didn't 'ave no choice about it, did I?' Dolly countered with a frown. Then her face cleared. 'Jacques won't never leave you neither, Miss Addy, not seeing as 'ow you be married to one of 'is young masters! Them two always was like family to 'im, same as you 'is to me, Miss Addy!'

An uneasy silence fell between them, for Dolly had brought Titus once more to Adela's mind. She bit her lip, determined not to give way to tears, although it was at moments like these that her loss was most poignant, most heart-wrenching.

'I can 'ear that there dog barking!' Dolly said into the silence. "Appen 'tis Mr Titus back, Miss Addy. 'E'll be chilled through, like as not. Jacques says 'e doant tek no care of 'isself!'

Perhaps *I* should take better care of Barnaby, Adela thought guiltily. It was true that he neglected himself. He was a constant disappointment to the cook, for he ate very little. She, Adela, must list a number of his favourite dishes and insist that Cook included one or other of them in the menus she prepared. He would return from one of his long walks or rides with Gloucester and slump in a chair in front of the fire in clothes that were often soaked by rain. It was Jacques, not she, who persuaded him upstairs with the promise of a hot bath to revive him.

As she went to greet him, Adela's eyes were thoughtful. Perhaps, she told herself, she had been unwarrantably unkind to Barnaby, showing him only a cold indifference. That he had deceived her so cruelly was no justification for such punishment; and had she not really been punishing him for being himself, not Titus; for being the one to live? If Titus had lived to discover that Barnaby had taken his place would *he* have forgiven him? His love for his twin had been so absolute, she supposed now that he would have understood; would have excused Barnaby on the grounds that his motives had been for the best.

Barnaby was in the drawing-room, kneeling before the fire, his back towards her. He looked round as she approached and she saw that his face was drawn with worry. His hand was lying on the outstretched body of the deer-hound.

'I think Gloucester must have picked up some poison!' he said in a low voice. 'I have told that gamekeeper a dozen times he may snare the foxes but is *never* to put down poison. I was afraid something like this would happen. Gloucester is very ill. He . . . he may be dying!'

Quickly, Adela knelt down and looked more closely at the unfortunate animal. The dog had been vomiting and was clearly in pain; his tongue which hung from the half-open mouth was a silvery white. Arsenic! Once when she had been out riding, she had come upon a fox similarly poisoned, and her groom had pointed out the colour of its tongue when he identified the cause of its recent death.

'I have sent Jacques down to the village to fetch Dodds. If anyone can save Gloucester, he can!'

Adela felt a glimmer of hope. Although Dodds, the blacksmith, was now in his eighties and his son had taken over the village forge, people still came to him for advice even from long distances if their horses, cattle or sheepdogs were ill, or if their sows were having trouble farrowing. He was never without a remedy for whatever malady was apparent. Barnaby's distress was painful to watch as he tried to soothe the animal with reassurances that help would soon be to hand.

The old man, battered felt hat in hand, apologized for his muddy boots but lost no time examining the big hound. He immediately confirmed Adela's fears. He would give Gloucester 'summat to mek 'im vomit' he told Barnaby, and then turning to Adela, added, 'Beg pardon, Mrs Mallory, but if'n you can get 'olt of some 'ot, greasy water with a deal o' salt innit, it 'ud save precious time. And I'll be needin' some plain 'ot water besides. Now if'n you'll lend me an 'and, sir, we'll carry 'im out to the stables.'

The blacksmith was clearly shocked when Adela and Barnaby said in unison that he could attend to the dog here in the warmth of the drawing-room. Nevertheless, he made no protest for he knew even better than did they the need for urgency.

With no more ado, as soon as the footman arrived with

the salted water, he emptied the dog's stomach. He then concocted an infusion of glasswort and a preparation which he described simply as 'steel' which he proceeded to strain through a kerchief before diluting it with hot water. With Barnaby's eager assistance, he proceeded to pour this down the dog's throat until he could take no more.

'Give 'im barley-water, and the white of egg in water and linseed tea, sir!' Dodds said as he rose with difficulty to his feet. 'Keep 'im warm and feed 'im reg'lar doses of castoreum.'

'He is not going to die then?' Barnaby enquired, his voice taut as he waited for the smith's reply.

'Carnt say as yet, sir, but I seen worse afore now. I saved a goat once and that were a sight more awk'ard, it 'aving four stomachs like. Mind 'e, sir, that weren't arsenic – that were parson's laurel bush she'd taken a mind to.'

Now that he had done all he could for the dog, the old man seemed eager to embark on reminiscences of his past triumphs. Knowing how many there might be, Adela ushered him to the door. Telling Jacques to pay him and be sure to arrange for him to return in the morning, she went back to the drawing-room. Barnaby was crouching on the floor, the deer-hound's head on his lap.

'I did not realize how attached to the brute I had become!' he said with a catch in his voice. 'He has been such a splendid companion, I . . . I do not know what I would do if—'

'You must not give up hope, Barny!' Adela interrupted quickly. 'Dodds seemed to think there was every chance Gloucester would get better.' She glanced at the dog's prostrate form and added, 'He cannot have much of the poison left inside him, and he is young and strong. I will ring for someone to come and clear up the mess and make up the fire.'

Barnaby regarded her gratefully.

'You do not mind him staying here? The rugs—'

'They can be cleaned!' Adela broke in. 'I expect you will wish to sit up with Gloucester tonight. I will have the day-bed brought in for you. Try not to worry too much!'

'You are very kind, Addy! I am grateful! Silly as it must sound, Gloucester means more to me than a mere dog – he has become a friend.'

Sympathetic was the least she could be, Adela thought as she went to the kitchen to make sure that Cook was preparing the tonics the dog was, hopefully, going to need. Barnaby would be devastated if he were to lose his faithful companion. From now on, she decided, she herself would try to be more of a companion to him for it had compounded her feeling of guilt when he had indicated how dependent he had become upon the animal's company.

She was returning across the hall to the drawing-room carrying the jugs of freshly made barley-water and diluted egg-white when Jacques came hurrying through the garden door.

'I was a-looking for you, Miss Addy,' he said, his voice breathless as if he had been riding hard. 'When I was tekking old Dodds 'ome, I ran into George – George Robinson. 'E were newly back from France.'

'He has brought with him a fresh consignment of tea?' Adela asked hopefully.

Jacques shook his head.

''Tain't that, Miss Addy.' He glanced around the empty hallway as if to ensure that they were alone. Then he said in a low voice, 'George 'ad one of 'is special passengers aboard, a Frenchie as were on 'is way to Lunnon. It were a gen'leman, Miss Addy, as 'ad escaped from the prison in Saint Cyrille.'

'In Saint Cyrille?' Adela repeated stupidly. 'Was this Frenchman someone I know, Jacques?'

'No, Miss Addy, but 'e knows you. That's to say, 'e'd been in prison with someone as you and me knows. The Frenchie gen'leman as called 'isself Monsieur Vermond thought as 'ow 'e ought to come and tell you about 'im 'isself, but George said as 'ow 'e'd be coming this way this very night and seeing as 'ow 'e knowed you, personal like, e'd be 'appy to get a letter to you if the gen'leman cared to write, 'e being in a 'urry to get 'isself to Lunnon.'

'What is it that you are trying to tell me, Jacques? That there is a letter for me? For pity's sake, explain yourself more slowly. *What is this news?*'

Her heart was hammering as she waited for Jacques to reply . . . beating with a mad irrational hope that she dared not admit.

CHAPTER THIRTY

1793

Jacques looked anxiously at Adela's face. It was chalk-white. Her eyes were enormous.

'Best sit down a moment, Miss Addy,' he said, but ignoring his suggestion, she stepped forward and gripped his arm.

'I must know!' she cried. 'Good news or bad, Jacques you must tell me. I beg you not to keep me in suspense any longer!'

Jacques' face did not lose its look of concern although he said quickly, 'Reckon as 'ow it be good news, Miss Addy. George tolt me the Frenchie said there were other prisoners alongside him; Frenchies mostly, but there was one other – an English gen'leman, all of six foot tall and with fair hair and brown eyes. 'E said 'is name were—'

'Titus! Titus Mallory! Titus!'

Jacques nodded, his eyes misty as he handed her an envelope addressed to 'Mrs Titus Mallory', and marked 'Personal'.

''Appen I should've given it you afore, Miss Addy, but thinking as 'ow it 'ud come as a shock an' all, I thought 'twould be best to let you come to it gentle like.'

For a moment Adela stood holding the letter in trembling hands as if she were afraid it might burn her. There were two feverish patches of colour on both cheeks and her eyes were wide as she stared back at Jacques' anxious countenance. Much as she longed to tear open the envelope and read the contents, she was afraid to do so, for Monsieur Vermond's words might well destroy all her hopes. Yet she had to know . . .

Taking her courage in both hands, she broke the seal.

Feverishly now, her eyes scanned the first paragraph before she turned to Jacques with a cry of joy.

'He is alive!' she cried, her face radiant. 'Titus is alive. He is in Saint Cyrille prison – *but he is alive!*'

'If'n the Frenchie gen'leman escaped, 'appen we can get Master Titus out, too!' Jacques said grinning.

Adela's eyes were now brilliant with excitement as she clasped her hands together, saying, 'Oh, Jacques, it must be Titus! It must. You will go to France and find him, will you not? You will leave at once? Now? Tonight?'

Jacques nodded, but his smile gave way to a frown as he added, 'Reckon as 'ow Master Barnaby'll be wanting to come along with me! But I be none too certain if'n 'e'll not be more an 'indrance – 'im being English and one of the enemy like. Will you speak to Master Barnaby, Miss Addy?'

'It will be best if I see him alone,' Adela said thoughtfully as the fever of excitement in her blood cooled, 'for he will be even more shocked than I; but we will be wanting to see you later, Jacques, to make arrangements for your journey.'

Adela's excitement had been so intense that it was only now that the thought struck her – if Jacques believed Titus had been found, he must know that Barnaby had taken his place here at home. She stared at him aghast.

'You . . . you asked me to break the news to . . . to Master Barnaby . . .' She faltered as Jacques put a gentle hand on her arm.

'Ain't no need to fret, Miss Addy!' he said quietly. 'I knowed from the furst – well, almost the furst – that it weren't Master Titus as 'ad come back. 'Tis the way Master Barnaby sits on 'is horse, you see. 'E always did like his stirrups shorter'n Master Titus.'

Adela's eyes were wide with astonishment.

'But you never said anything!' she gasped.

Jacques drew a long sigh.

''Tweren't none of my business, Miss Addy, and anyroad, I couldn't see no 'arm in it for no one, 'cepting maybe your ownselfs. 'Tweren't as if Master Titus were ever coming back – leastways, so we all reckoned; and if'n 'e were dead same as we thought, it weren't doing 'im no 'arm. Mind you, Miss Addy, from what Dolly's tolt me, it ain't made you and Master Barnaby no 'appier – if'n you'll pardon me saying so!'

'You mean . . . Dolly knows the truth too?'

Jacques shook his head.

'No, I ain't never tolt her! But she's been that worrit about you – says as 'ow you doant live no more like 'usband and wife, and you doant eat proper and doant sleep so well neither.'

Tears filled Adela's eyes.

'How could I – knowing my husband was never coming back?' she cried.

''Appen he will now, Miss Addy, if'n 'tis really 'im wot the Frenchie gen'leman knowed, and if we can get 'im out of that there prison.'

'We must waste no more time, Jacques. I will go now and talk to Master Barnaby. Will you find Dolly and tell her you might be going away again?'

Jacques grinned.

'She won't like it none but she'll unnerstand!' he said, and departed in the direction of the kitchen to search for his wife.

As Jacques disappeared, Adela paused, gripping the handle of the drawing-room door as she tried to steady herself, for although she could foresee the need to break the news gently to Barnaby, she was filled with impatience to read the rest of the Frenchman's letter.

Although it was addressed to her, she felt that Titus' twin had as much right to news of Titus' fate as she did.

As she opened the door, she saw that Barnaby was still seated on the floor by his dog. Momentarily Adela had forgotten about the animal's collapse. Barnaby glanced up at her briefly, saying, 'Poor old Gloucester! He is still in great pain. If only I could be sure he will survive the night!'

Adela drew a deep breath.

'Barny, will you leave him just for a moment? I have

something of the greatest importance to tell you – to share with you; something far, far more important even than Gloucester's life. Will you sit here beside me?'

Reluctantly he left the dog's side and went to sit next to Adela on the settee. He was frowning in puzzlement for she had shown such concern for Gloucester, her remark had seemed almost cruel.

'Well?' he prompted. 'What is it, Addy?'

'Jacques has brought news of . . . of Titus. It is wonderful news, Barny. It seems that after all our suffering, we have every reason to think that Titus may be alive!' Her voice barely contained her excitement as she went on to explain how she had come by the news. Only then did she show him the letter.

'I have read only the beginning,' she said gently, 'Shall I translate it for you? It is written in French.'

Barnaby's face, which had paled with shock, was now flushed with eagerness as wordless, he nodded. Hurriedly Adela perused the closely written pages. Consumed with impatience, Barnaby waited. Her eyes were shining as she turned to him saying, 'Monsieur Vermond writes that he was incarcerated in Saint Cyrille prison with Titus for three months before Titus was confined to a single cell because he had been inciting the other prisoners to organize an escape. Is that not just like him, Barny?'

Her voice was husky with emotion. Not waiting for his reply, she continued, 'Monsieur Vermond describes Titus as "a very brave man". He says that conditions in the gaol are appalling. All the prisoners are chained, and their guards are drunken oafs who make no distinction between noblemen and common criminals. All are treated like animals, men and women together. Few know why they are there and who will be next to be taken away for trial. Even fewer return from these so-called trials. If a new prisoner arrives with money in his pockets, he can buy food but it is quickly stolen by the rogues with whom he and Titus were closeted. They had only straw, dirty and verminous, to lie on.'

Adela shuddered as she paused to draw breath.

'And this Monsieur Vermond – how did he escape?' Barnaby asked eagerly.

Adela glanced down once more at the delicate script.

'It happened on the night when news reached the village that Marie Antoinette had been guillotined. The gaolers were celebrating the despatch of the "widow Capet" as they called the French Queen. Some were calling her "harlot", "*Autrichienne*", "the new Agrippina!" Oh, Barny, it is wrong of me, I know, but I cannot concern myself now with that poor woman's death! Nevertheless, we do have her to thank for Monsieur Vermond's escape.'

She smiled briefly at Barny before the expression of impatience on his face urged her to continue. She glanced yet again at the letter.

'Monsieur Vermond says that he had been busy for some time ingratiating himself with one of the gaolers, pretending sympathy for the new regime. On this night of celebration, realizing that his gaolers were the worse for wine, he seized his opportunity. Being a musician by profession who could play any tune he pleased on his flute, he persuaded his guards to permit him to entertain them. For this purpose, he insisted, he must have his chains removed. When the jollifications were at their height and his gaolers stupefied with liquor and their patriotic songs were drowning the sound of his flute, he grabbed the opportunity to slip out of the guard house.'

As Adela paused once more for breath, Barnaby could see that she was momentarily overcome by emotion. Gently he took the remaining pages of the letter from her and not without difficulty he read on. Weakened though Monsieur Vermond was by lack of food and exercise, he had managed to walk to Anse Goéland where Titus had told him the French smugglers often supplied George Robinson with contraband. Two days after Monsieur Vermond reached the cove, hearing the English voices of the smugglers, he revealed himself from his hiding place and obtained passage to England. On the journey home, in the course of regaling stories of his imprisonment to George Robinson, he had spoken of the Englishman who had befriended him in the gaol, mentioning him by name. At Robinson's suggestion, Monsieur Vermond had penned the letter for the smuggler to take to Adela as he wished to make all speed to London without having to divert his journey unnecessarily to Dene.

Adela's eyes were wet as Barnaby put down the pages and turned to look at her. Happiness was engulfing her. She reached out and took Barnaby's hands in hers.

'Thank God! Oh, Barny, Titus is alive! It is hard to believe, is it not? We believed there was no hope, and now a miracle has happened!'

Barnaby's expression of joy had become one of bewilderment.

'It is beyond my understanding. I saw with my own eyes that Titus was mortally wounded. He had been hit in the chest and his shirt front was soaked with blood. He . . . he was still conscious and he himself told me he was dying. He begged me to leave him – to save my life – to come home to look after you, Addy.' He covered his face with his hands as the memory of the horror of the scene returned as it did so often in his nightmares. 'No, this is beyond my understanding. We must pray that this Monsieur Vermond has not been mistaken.'

'How can you doubt it?' Adela burst out. She did not want to be obliged to consider that a mistake could have been made. 'Monsieur Vermond knew Titus – was imprisoned with him for three months!' she added indignantly. 'He addressed his letter to me – to Madame Titus Mallory!'

Barnaby shook his head as if to clear his mind.

'His account contravenes everything we know. Had you forgotten that Jacques returned to Saint Cyrille last February and questioned everyone he could think of? If Titus had not, as I believed, been mortally wounded and had been taken to the village gaol, someone must have known of his presence there and would have told Jacques. Jacques is well liked in

Saint Cyrille – and more importantly, he is trusted by the peasants. Titus' gaolers would of a certainty have gossiped about an English gentleman they held in their prison for he could never have passed himself off as a Frenchman; his accent is little better than my own. Villagers love to gossip, and Jacques must surely have learned of Titus' arrest.'

He was trembling violently and Adela withdrew her hands and gripped him by the shoulders.

'It does not matter how he came to be in that prison, Barny. Can you not see, *it does not matter*! M. Vermond is quite explicit about the name and nationality of the prisoner. They became friends!'

Barnaby's look of bewilderment was unchanged.

'Have you forgotten we are at war with France? Titus is known to be an Englishman, so why has he not been shot? Those soldiers caught us spying upon the château and must surely have connected us with Philippe's activities, with the disappearance of the Curé? They murdered nearly all of Eugénie's servants and they suspected me of being a spy. Why would they spare his life? They even shot that poor apothecary who saved my life because he would not reveal my identity!'

Adela frowned, for Barnaby's words raised terrible doubts in her mind. But she would not allow them the upper hand.

'Titus will explain everything when he returns,' she said sharply. 'We are wasting time with this speculation, Barny. Titus is alive – imprisoned – and we have to think how we can help him escape. Jacques has said he will leave for France tonight. He said you will want to go with him, but he believes it will be too dangerous for you to set foot on French soil.'

Barnaby jumped to his feet, his eyes flashing as he said harshly, 'Have you lost your wits? Of course I must go! Do you really think I could remain here while my brother lies rotting in a filthy gaol, perhaps destined to die tomorrow? Where is Jacques? He will not sail the cutter without me – and you, you of all people, Addy, must understand why I *have* to go.'

Aware of her own desperate desire to go to Titus' aid, Adela could not protest. Throughout these long, difficult months, she had never doubted Barnaby's love for his brother. It surmounted even his love for her, and despite his assumption of his twin's identity, he had done so only in the hope of alleviating her sorrow and brought nothing but pain and despair upon himself.

'You will take care, will you not, Barnaby!' she said at last. 'I . . . I want you both back.'

Barnaby's mouth twisted.

'Do you, Addy? You told me once that you hated me – and I do not blame you for it.'

'I have never truly hated *you*, Barny,' Adela said softly, 'only what you did – and I know you meant it well. It has been hard for us both, this pretence, and perhaps I was wrong ever to have insisted upon continuing it. Nor were we as successful as we supposed, for Jacques guessed the truth almost from the first. But it is in the past now, and we must think only of the future. Let me send for Jacques and, whilst you and he make plans for your journey, I will arrange for food, clothing, horses.' Her eyes caught the slight movement of the deer-hound as it shifted its weight. 'I will take care of Gloucester. Dolly will help me.'

Barnaby gave her a grateful look as he bent to pat the dog's head.

'God willing, I will be back soon, old fellow!' he murmured as Adela went past him to summon Jacques with an urgent pull on the bell-rope. As soon as the valet arrived, she left the room to hurry upstairs to her bedchamber. She withdrew a small casket from her wardrobe and took from it a quantity of *livres* and a handful of *sous*. Eugénie had given her these when she left Normandy. She had no further use for them, she said, and Adela might pass them on to Jacques who could perhaps purchase a length of lace or silk for Adela's use. At the time, Adela had planned to have a pretty night-gown made for Titus' return; but events had taken place so quickly, she had forgotten the existence of the money until now.

'These might serve to bribe the guards!' she said, handing the purse to Barnaby when she went back downstairs. Barnaby was now attired as a French *matelot*. Nevertheless his bright gold hair, even dulled though it was by the occasional strand of grey, was arresting. Regarding him thoughtfully, she said, 'You will be less noticeable if you wear Jacques' woollen cap. You must disguise your hands and face too, for they are very pale. Dolly shall bring you a sack of the walnuts we gathered last month. Hopefully you can darken your skin whilst in Rye awaiting the next tide for there is no time now.'

For the first time in many months, she saw a boyish grin spread over Barnaby's face. He was once again the Barnaby she remembered – her childhood friend. How could she ever have thought she hated him?

Whilst they awaited Jacques in silence, Adela's thoughts were racing. If all their hopes were justified and Titus were to escape, what would Barny tell him? The truth? Suppose Titus were never to forgive Barny for impersonating him? Or far, far worse, never forgive *her* for permitting it. The thought struck a chill of fear in her heart. How would any husband feel, returning from the dead to discover that his brother and the woman he had married had been living as man and wife? It was a sobering conjecture. Would she be able to make him understand how it had come about? And would he believe that she and Barnaby had never taken advantage of their 'married' state?

If it had been possible, Adela would have set aside such fearful anxieties until Titus was safely home; but she realized they could not so simply be postponed. When he and Barny met, Titus would be desperate for news of her and Barnaby would somehow have to explain.

'No! I want to be the one to do so!'

Without knowing it, Adela had spoken aloud. Barnaby

looked at her anxiously. She was very pale, and for the past few moments, had seemed oblivious to his company.

'What is it, Addy? You are not seeking a way to prevent my going . . .?'

Biting her lip, Adela shook her head.

'I know that would be an impossibility,' she said. 'But I am afraid . . . afraid Titus may not understand when he discovers that you . . . we . . .'

She broke off, unable to speak the words. Barnaby was in no need of an explanation for the same fear had been passing through his mind.

'I shall have to tell him the truth however much he is hurt by it,' he said thoughtfully. 'But it might be simpler, kinder, if you will say nothing for the time being to our parents – or to anyone else.'

Adela's eyes widened and her mouth fell open as she considered his remark.

'Do you not see, Addy?' he persisted. 'Everyone believes it was I, not Titus, who was killed. I, Barnaby, will be the one who everyone will question on our return about *my* imprisonment and I can say it was so disagreeable I do not wish to speak of it. Titus will simply resume his rightful place here as your husband and I shall return to my parents.'

Adela covered her mouth with her hands.

'I am at a loss for words!' she muttered. 'It would mean our perpetuating the deceit! Perhaps that should be our punishment! Oh, Barny, we need more time to think about this, and there is no time. Dolly will be here at any moment and . . . oh, if only I could be certain Titus will understand, forgive us! I could not bear it if he hated me . . . not now when . . . Barny, promise me you will not tell him – at least until he is safely home and I can welcome him without fear of his rejection. Perhaps we need never tell him the truth, but meanwhile, *promise me you will remain silent*. Please, Barny?'

'It will not be easy!' Barny muttered. 'But since you ask it, I give you my word. You should know by now that I will do anything in the world to make you happy, Addy, even though my last attempt has had such terrible consequences. I know you never believed that I only took Titus' place for your sake; that you will never forgive me for doing so.'

'Barny, listen to me, please. Although I was deeply shocked and miserably unhappy when I discovered that you were not Titus, I could not go on hating you. I do not think I ever really did; and I do believe it was never your intention to advance your own interests. It would have been quite contrary to your nature. Titus will know that, too.'

The sound of Jacques' and Dolly's voices outside the door brought an abrupt end to their conversation. Unwilling to let Barnaby leave on so incomplete a reconciliation, Adela reached up impulsively and kissed his cheek.

'Godspeed!' she whispered. 'And a safe crossing! I want you both home, for I love you, too, Barny, if not as a husband, then as a very dear friend.'

It was no more than the truth, she realized, for if he were not to return from this mission, she would mourn him almost as much as she had mourned Titus.

Within the hour, Barnaby and Jacques had gone. Adela sat on by the fire, stopping occasionally to spoon more barley-water into the deer-hound's mouth. Dolly insisted upon remaining with her and, for a while, they sat in silence. Then Dolly spoke.

'Jacques tolt me it were *Master Titus* in that French prison and that it were *Master Barnaby* as were going to 'elp get 'im out! It ain't none of my business, Miss Addy, but . . . but it ain't like my Jacques to get his head in a muddle.'

Adela's hesitation was very brief. Of all the people in the world, she knew Dolly was to be trusted. Moreover, when – if – Barnaby brought Titus safely home, she might need Dolly's connivance if the twins were to change places again.

Dolly listened quietly to Adela's confession and then with surprising pragmatism, she said, 'I reckoned as 'ow something were amiss, though I didn't say aught to Jacques. Master

Barnaby should've known it couldn't never 'ave worked, Miss Addy, leastways, not for long. Them two young men might be as like as two peas in a pod, but they ain't 'dentical for all that. I remembers Master Titus was often as not more forceful like – first up on his pony; first up a tree; first to think up a prank and a way to get out of trouble if'n they was caught!'

Adela smiled.

'I suppose he was always the leader – or almost always – but I attributed the change in his behaviour to the fact that he was ill; and that he had seen his twin killed in so horrible a manner. Oh, Dolly, I have been unspeakably miserable and now I am filled with joy – yet I dare not allow myself to be so happy. Suppose Jacques and Barny arrive too late to help Titus escape? Suppose they cannot find a way to release him from prison? Suppose the prisoner is not my Titus after all?'

'Hush, now, Miss Addy! You be forgetting the Frenchie gentleman was locked up aside of Master Titus. 'E'd not be mistook in knowing 'is name, now would 'e?'

Adela's spirits lifted once more and she leaned over and hugged Dolly.

'When I was little, I often heard Mama say, "*L'espoir est ma force*" – hope is my strength. It is an old French proverb which I did not understand then, but I do now. I feel as if I can brave the world again. When I believed Titus was lost to me for ever, even the smallest difficulty seemed insurmountable. Now nothing can daunt me for I have hope – hope of holding him in my arms again.'

'Reckon Master Barnaby feels the same way you does, Miss Addy!' Dolly said cheerfully. ''E looked that lightsome when 'e went riding off with my Jacques!'

Adela smiled.

'And earlier this evening he had been so downhearted with poor Gloucester being so ill. We must take good care of the dog, Dolly, for it would be poor reward for Master Barnaby to come home and find no Gloucester waiting for him.'

Momentarily Adela's euphoria deserted her as she remembered that, whilst Barnaby had promised he would not tell Titus of their deception, she would have to find the courage to do so. If, God willing, Titus were to be returned to her, at least she could give him a joyous welcome! Closing her eyes, she could almost feel his arms around her; his kisses on her lips. She could see the same love shining in his eyes as would be in her own. They would love each other as on their wedding eve! At least she would be able to tell him that she had never been unfaithful, in mind or body!

With a renewed surge of joy in her heart, Adela refused to think further of the difficulties which might lie ahead. Hope had been renewed when she had thought it gone for ever, and she cared for nothing but the one glorious fact – Titus might yet come home to her, resurrected from the dead.

It was bitterly cold in the barn loft where Barnaby and Jacques had been concealing themselves for the past two days. Fortunately the abandoned farm building was still filled with straw, and they had been able to stuff most of the cracks in the wooden boards of the walls and thatching to keep out the icy draughts of the November winds.

Barnaby shivered as he opened the trapdoor to allow Jacques into the loft.

'I have not been warm since we left England – a week ago today, was it not, Jacques?'

The valet nodded, his attention on the bundle he had been carrying. He let it fall to the floor and assisted Barnaby as he hauled up the ladder and closed the trap door.

'You are looking in good heart!' Barnaby said as Jacques began to untie the corners of the sack he had brought with him from the village. 'Did you get what you wanted?'

Jacques nodded as he withdrew from the sack a white cavalry officer's coat with a high-standing, gold-braided collar and gold buttons, a pair of white cashmere breeches and a wide, white-and-gold sash with a deep gold-braid fringe. Black top-boots, gloves, a short fur-trimmed cape and tricorn hat with a blue curled feather joined the heap on the dusty floor.

'That I did, surely!' he replied with a grin of satisfaction. ''Appen you'll not credit it, Master Barnaby, but them's more what we be needing than I'd dared 'ope to find. I bought 'em off a Romany passing through the village. 'E were perched up on that there caravan of 'is wearing that very coat. Old-fashioned, mind you, but just about what the late Monsieur le Chevalier de Saint Cyrille might've worn. "Any more of them?" I axed 'im and jingled a few coins in my pocket; so it weren't but a moment afore his wife comes up with the rest of 'em. Stolen they was for sure, but not 'ereabouts, from what I could make out. We couldn't 'ave asked for no better, Master Barnaby, sir!'

Barnaby drew a great sigh of relief. Jacques' plan to rescue Titus from the village gaol was an excellent one, but for the past two days they could think of no way to obtain the disguise they needed. He, Barnaby, was to 'haunt' the ruins of the Château de Saint Cyrille. Jacques would spread word in the village that the ghost of the late Chevalier had been seen riding near the ruins of his estate. Barnaby would then allow himself to be glimpsed to give credence to the story. He and Jacques were trusting that peasant curiosity being what it was, the villagers would be tempted to verify the ghost's existence; that those who saw the apparition would challenge any doubters to see for themselves.

The plot had been hatched during the many long hours Barnaby and Jacques had spent together as they had made their way inland on their two hired horses. Piece by piece, they had filled in the details of their plan. The 'haunting' must continue to the point where curiosity was at its height, they had decided. Jacques would then approach the prison gaolers and announce that he had himself seen the Chevalier's ghost, now haunting the churchyard at the far end of the village.

Jacques had now established that there were seldom more than two men on guard at night. If he could distract one, he would have an excellent chance of taking the other by surprise and overpowering him, Barnaby having meanwhile taken a wide circle round the outside of the village where he would be waiting at the end of the road with the horses. They had only two – the thin, scrawny nags they had hired in the coastal town of Eu – for to have demanded better mounts would have been to arouse suspicion that they might not be the simple sailors on shore leave they had professed to be. However, in his recent sorties to Saint Cyrille, Jacques had espied a mule in an unlocked shed near the old *presbytère*, and had little doubt that he could steal the animal and ride it saddleless.

'You are to be congratulated, Jacques!' Barnaby said warmly as he folded the garments and settled back as comfortably as he could on the straw. 'You were not detected returning here?'

Jacques grinned.

'If'n you'd been as long as I 'ave in the smuggling trade, sir, you'd know well as I does 'ow best to make yerself scarce!'

Barnaby returned the valet's smile, but he quickly became serious once more as he added, 'And you have no doubt whatever that it is my brother in the gaol?'

'I be certain sure, Master Barnaby!' Jacques' face widened into a vast grin. 'Like we planned, I made friends with one of the guards which were off duty. I treated 'im to a drink or two in *Le Cheval Blanc* and loosened 'is tongue, you might say! Seems Master Titus ain't been there all that long. 'E were brought in last May by some soldiers wot 'ad found 'im chained up in a farm not two leagues from 'ere. No one in the village seemed to know where 'e'd come from nor 'ow 'e came to be there. The gaoler tolt me the prisoner 'ad come close to being shot as a spy, but 'e claimed to be an American wot 'ated the English and 'ad crossed the seas so's 'e could kill some of 'em. 'E said his family 'ad been wiped out in that war for Independence wot Miss Addy's pa fought in, and he wanted revenge.'

'That was clever of Master Titus, for no one could disprove such a story!' Barnaby commented.

'Seems 'e's been forgot by them as fixes the prisoners' trials in Rouen. The guards like 'im well enough, for 'e's pretended 'e's a magician by trade and does tricks for 'em.'

Barnaby gave a shout of laughter.

'That is Titus, for sure!' he said. 'Remember how we used to practise those tricks as boys, Jacques? Mother used to get us to perform them for the village children at their Christmas party.'

Jacques nodded, his tanned face still further wrinkled with smiles.

'And that ain't all the good news, Master Barnaby. Tomorrow evening, when my good friend is on duty again, 'e'll let me 'ave a look at the prisoner; says if'n I tek 'im an apple or a bit o' cheese, 'e'll mek 'im do a trick or two for me.'

Barnaby's eyes were glowing.

'So we can get a message to my brother? Let him know what we plan to do and to be ready for us? We can conceal it in the food you take in to him!'

Jacques' smile turned to a look of concern.

'The prisoners doant get much to eat, Master Barnaby. We must 'ope Master Titus ain't so 'ungry 'e wolfs down the message afore 'e's read it!'

Barnaby patted him on the shoulder.

'Titus will recognize you at once, Jacques! He will guess there is a plan afoot, so stop fretting! Now if I am to begin my "haunting" tonight, I had best try on these clothes!'

They were over-large but fitted well enough for their purpose. Jacques stayed long enough to watch Barnaby circling the ruins of the château after dark on horseback before returning to the village to announce his first sighting of the ghost of the Chevalier de Saint Cyrille. The occupants of the village inn were at first sceptical; but seeing that Jacques was not the worse for wine, they began to regard one another uneasily. Had not Monsieur le Chevalier's family home been ransacked and burned to the ground? Had he returned from the dead to seek revenge? What of his widow who disappeared without trace, never to be seen

again? Had not her brother, Monsieur de Falence, done likewise?
Père Jérôme, too? Could the ghost have aided their escape? And
what had become of Gustave and his nephew, Josef? They too
had mysteriously disappeared!

Jacques encouraged such speculation and suggested that
those few who professed not to believe in ghosts might care
to go up to the château and see the apparition for themselves.
He promised a free drink to anyone with the courage to prove
he was not a liar, and the more courageous of the men began
daring one another to accept the challenge. It was finally
decided that four of them would go together – there being
safety in numbers – on the following evening. Jacques, they
insisted, should accompany them.

There were few in the village who had not heard of the
wave of executions now taking place in Paris. Rumours
abounded of streets running in blood; of the numbers losing
their heads to 'Madame Guillotine'; of the wholesale destruction of the aristocracy and nobility of France. Deaths, violence,
brutality were common enough even in their own village to
be no strangers; but ghosts – they *were* uncommon, and those
who had abandoned their religion harboured secret fears about
their unconfessed sins. If ghosts belonged in another world,
who knew but they were God's henchmen sent to exact judgement upon the guilty?

'The men were frightened, but curious!' Jacques related to
Barnaby, who was well aware what effect Jacques' story might
have on the simple, uneducated peasants whose knowledge of
the world went little beyond the boundaries of their village.
By morning everyone would have heard of the ghost of the
Chevalier de Saint Cyrille, and the women would keep their
children well away from the ruins of the château and probably
even from the fields surrounding it.

'Would that I could go with you tomorrow to see my
brother!' Barnaby said wistfully. 'Until you have actually
looked upon him, Jacques, I shall not be wholly reassured that
he is still alive.'

Not to Jacques, still less to Adela, or to anyone in the world, could he describe the pictures that more than ever here in France still tormented his dreams – of Titus lying on the wet ground, gasping for breath as he bid him, Barnaby, to escape so that he could take care of Adela for him. He would never forget the sight of the blood pouring from his brother's wound, staining his white shirt an unforgettable red; nor cease to hear the voice of the apothecary telling him that Titus was beyond human aid.

CHAPTER THIRTY-ONE

1793

The chains around Titus' wrists rattled as he attempted to shuffle the greasy, dog-eared pack of cards he was holding. Tossing the long fair hair which hung to his shoulders, he looked up at the gaoler standing in the doorway of his cell.

'You know very well I cannot perform my magic with these on!' he said wearily, displaying his chains. 'Remove them and I will oblige you, Citizen Greuze!'

They had gone through this ritual so many times that he wondered why the oaf who stood before him even hesitated. Nevertheless it was a relief to be without the manacles even for a quarter of an hour, and he was prepared to go through the motions for this brief illusion of freedom and for the more important reason, that his card tricks kept his gaolers in good temper. From time to time they made concessions – a bucket of water so that he could wash himself; clean straw to lie on; a quill, ink and paper on which he could write. But he had never yet persuaded them to remove the chains from around his ankles.

One day, he hoped, they would do so – and then he might escape. It was this hope alone which kept his spirits up. For the past six months, he had not known whether he would be dragged out for trial like so many other of the unfortunate captives in the main prison cell adjoining his solitary one; had not been certain if he would live to see another day, for none ever returned after their trials. It would be all too easy since he had been confined to this tiny cell, eight feet by four, to allow despair to gain the upper hand. At least he had had company in the main prison room, and for those first few weeks after his capture, he had enjoyed the conversation of the well-educated musician, Vermond, and a bibliographer from Bordeaux. Unlike himself, Vermond had had a little money which entitled him to buy food and this he had happily shared with Titus, providing a most welcome alternative to the pig-swill they were obliged to eat. Often the prison fare consisted of dry vegetables full of hair, mud and worms. Occasionally there was some rotten pork mixed in with fermented cabbage. Only to avoid starvation did the prisoners eat it. He and Vermond had kept one another's spirits up making plans to escape.

With no more than two turnkeys at any time to look after a hundred or so prisoners, it should not be so difficult to overpower them, he had pointed out to Vermond. But one of the common criminals with whom they were incarcerated, in the hope of gaining a reprieve for himself, had betrayed him. It was Titus, the traitor had told the guards, who was the instigator of a plan for all the prisoners to riot and overpower their gaolers. Since then, Titus had been in solitary confinement.

'Well now, *Monsieur le Magicien*,' Greuze said as he unlocked the heavy chains around Titus' wrists, 'have you something new to tell me today, eh?'

Titus had long since exhausted the tricks he knew and the ones he had invented. He had therefore aroused his gaolers' interest in fortune-telling. It was an excellent diversion, he had decided, for there need be no end to the 'fortunes' he invented. He spread the cards on the wooden planks that served both as his bed and table.

'Devil take it if I do not see money here!' he announced cheerfully, for he well knew how avaricious his gaoler was. 'It should come to you shortly – not tomorrow, though . . .' he cautioned quickly '. . . but in the future.'

'Near or far?' asked the turnkey eagerly.

''Tis difficult to say!' Titus prevaricated. 'But I can assure you, citizen, that there are benefits coming. Yes, indeed . . . this card indicates a messenger carrying excellent news.'

'A messenger?' the man repeated. 'How shall I know him? Will he seek me out?'

'All in good time!' Titus replied. 'He may be here in the village already – but for reasons of his own, is not yet willing for you to recognize him.'

Greuze removed his *bonnet rouge* and scratched his head. 'If this fellow is the bringer of good tidings, why should 'e not reveal 'isself?' he asked with a peasant's quick cunning.

In order to give himself time to think of a logical reply to this somewhat awkward question, Titus reshuffled the cards.

'Egad, but 'tis clearer now!' he muttered. 'I see why he disguises himself. Only he knows where this money which is rightfully yours is concealed, and he is trying to think of a way to keep it for himself!'

'I'll 'ave 'is life first!' the turnkey said, tightening his hold upon his musket.

'But not before he has revealed where this money is concealed!' Titus suggested, enjoying himself. 'Perhaps next time I read the cards, the whole matter will become clearer to me. At the moment I am too weak from lack of food to see this messenger sufficiently well to describe him to you. For the present, he is but a wraith!'

'I will bring you some bread when next I be on duty!' Greuze said eagerly. He was always prepared to supply Titus with food in exchange for good news. 'Look at the cards again, I beg you. Are you sure you cannot see 'im now?'

Titus made pretence of further study and after a suitable interval during which he could hear his gaoler's deep anxious breaths, he looked up at the simpleton with a sigh.

'He is still there, but it is as if I see him through a mist.'

The man's mouth fell open and he gaped fearfully at Titus.

'Like . . . like an apparition?' he gasped, his eyes wide with awe.

'Certainly, like an apparition!' Titus agreed for want of any better reason than to take advantage of his gaoler's credulity.

'In uniform? In the uniform of a French cavalry officer?'

'Possibly!' Titus said, yawning. 'I cannot say!'

Then it could be him!

The tone of Greuze's voice caused Titus to look at him with sudden interest.

'Him? Of whom do you speak, citizen?'

'The apparition wot was seen near the château! There were a fellow in *Le Cheval Blanc* sharing a glass of cider with me last Monday wot 'ad seen the ghost. 'E swore it on 'is life. 'Twas thought by some it might be that of the late Chevalier de Saint Cyrille – the *aristo* wot once lived there. 'E were wearing a cavalry officer's coat and breeches and were about his 'eight and shape.'

Hurriedly the turnkey crossed himself. Only last week the belfry had been defaced and the Holy Water basins and Baptismal font removed from the church by order of the national agent; but the habit was too engrained to have been erased from the man's subconsciousness by the popular hatred for anything theological.

'And you believe this fellow's story?' Titus enquired with some amusement which he took pains not to show.

'No reason to doubt 'im!' his guard replied. ''E be a simple, common man same as myself; not one as you'd think was given to fancy tales. I seed 'im several times these past few days. Comes from Rouen, 'e says, where 'e's employed by masters making touchpapers from nitre – gets it from animal urine and lime, 'e tolt me. 'E were born in these parts but don't live 'ere no more and comes back now and agin to visit 'is family. I've promised 'im 'e can come and tek a look at you tomorrow – 'e being a curious-minded fellow and not never 'aving seen a magician afore.'

Disinterested now in his gaoler's new acquaintance and his unlikely story, Titus was nevertheless quite cheered by the thought of seeing another face. He had observed none other but those of his two gaolers and an occasional soldier these past fourteen weeks. It was now six months and two days since he had been brought under guard from the farm to Saint Cyrille. He had marked each day with a scratch on the sides of one of his wooden *sabots*, determined as he was to keep some awareness of life and not be reduced to the mindless vegetable state of some of the prisoners. Despite his rough, peasant attire, Titus had lost neither his dignity nor his courage and had never lost hope of an eventual escape.

There were days, however, when he was dispirited. Now, as his guard left him alone once more, he knew he was unlikely to see another face before morning. Gregarious by nature, he chafed against his solitary confinement. At this very moment he felt too downhearted even to write his long daily letter to Adela. 'Speaking' to her with his pen somehow brought her closer, and he was the happier for being able to express – if only by the written word – the intensity of his love for her. He knew she might never receive his letters, but he lived in the hope that if ever she did read them, she would know that not a day or night passed without him thinking of her; of their brief marriage; of their shared passion; of the days of their childhood which one by one he recalled in the greatest detail. His quill was now his single, most treasured possession of which he took the utmost care.

At the farmstead where he had lived for the six months prior to his recapture, he had had no such luxury – nor indeed any of the normal creature comforts to which he had once been accustomed. He was deprived of everything other than the means of survival – yet he did not blame the farmer who was responsible, for he owed him his life. He knew that the man's behaviour sprang from fear and ignorance, and bore him no grudge.

After his gaoler had departed, locking the door behind him, Titus lay back on his straw palliasse and once more gave thanks to God for the miracle which had saved his life. Immediately after the soldiers at the Château de Saint Cyrille had shot him, he had been in no doubt that he was dying. Barely conscious, he was aware of Barnaby leaning over him; of the apothecary slipping a phial of laudanum into his hand. Memories of the moments that followed were confused. He remembered feeling no pain and wondering why M. Delarge had thought he needed the opiate; remembered his own anxiety lest Barny did not escape in time and the urgent need for his twin to get back to England to take care of Addy. When the soldiers had approached and dragged Barnaby and the apothecary away, he had heard dimly the sound of his brother's voice shouting, 'You've killed him!' Then, believing himself to be drawing his last breath, he had been conscious of one thought only – that Barnaby was in terrible danger – before darkness had closed in on him. When he had regained consciousness, it was to find himself in one of the cellars of the château, the upper half of his body splinted and heavily bandaged, his hands folded in front of him like a corpse prepared for burial.

He had drifted once more into unconsciousness and could not afterwards be sure when he had regained his senses sufficiently to recognize Blanche, one of the Saint Cyrille maidservants, leaning over him. 'I have told the soldiers you died last night!' she whispered. 'They had been hoping that if I treated your wound, you might recover long enough for them to question you about Madame la Chevalière. The other prisoners wouldn't say nothing although they was beaten. You must feign death, *monsieur*, for my life now depends upon it. You must try not to cry out or move when they come for you. I discovered a phial of laudanum on you last night and I will give you some of this. One of the soldiers told me you were to be buried in the ditch where they had flung the bodies of the menservants after they had shot them. All the soldiers are already very drunk and the two corporals detailed to bury you will, hopefully, not realize that your body is still warm! As soon as you are covered with earth – even before if we can manage it – Lisette will tempt the soldiers into the wood whilst I remove you. Do you understand what I am saying, *monsieur*?'

Although racked with pain and near to fainting with loss of blood, Titus' mind had been surprisingly clear. He could remember now how he had considered Blanche's plan and believed that this brave attempt by the Saint Cyrille servants to save his life must surely be in vain since he would of a certainty die of his wound anyway. He could recall, now, his protest that the pretty Lisette – Eugénie's personal maid – should not risk herself on his behalf, for the soldiers would undoubtedly take advantage of her seeming willingness to satisfy their lust. He was in great pain and but for the maid-servant's timely administration of the laudanum when the soldiers came for his body, he might well have cried out when he was moved.

That this courageous plan had actually succeeded could be no less than a miracle, he had written to Adela. He recalled nothing of his burial, nor of the speed with which Blanche had dug him up. Somehow the two girls had managed to take him in a handcart to a farm some three leagues distant from the château. There they had bribed the farmer with money taken from Titus' pocket to take care of him and promised an even greater reward if he survived.

Titus could remember very little of the subsequent weeks when he had hovered between life and death. The farmer's daughter, Giselle, was given the task of nursing him back to health. Having no knowledge of medical matters, she had used the same remedies as she used on the farm animals. She had been no less rough in her handling of his wounds than was her custom with the animals, and Titus was often in great pain.

As he grew stronger and his broken ribs knit, the wound in his chest had finally healed. But for his ever-present fears for Barnaby's fate, he had all but recovered his health and spirits, as a consequence of which Giselle's father demanded that he be put to work for his living since neither Blanche nor Lisette had ever returned to the farm with the promised reward. Giselle thought it likely that the two maids had been arrested, for when she had gone to the market, she had heard it said that all the Saint Cyrille servants were either dead or imprisoned.

The news might have saddened Titus even more had the girl not also related the gossip circulating in the market place that two prisoners – an English milord and the servant, Gustave, from the Château de Saint Cyrille – had escaped from the soldiers escorting them to Rouen.

Titus had never doubted that Barnaby was the 'milord' and, convinced now that his twin was alive and perhaps already safely home in England, his complete recovery had been but a matter of days. Bolstered by this conviction he had worked contentedly enough for several weeks until word reached Giselle's father that England was now at war with France.

He was intent upon going at once to the village to denounce Titus, for to keep him at the farm would be to risk arrest for concealing an enemy spy beneath his roof. It was Giselle who had argued that it was not in her father's best interest to get rid of Titus now that he was well enough to help around the farm. They were behind with nearly every task that needed to be done, she pointed out, for her three brothers had – in defiance of their irascible father's orders – volunteered to fight the Austrians and had left home.

They had argued Titus' fate long into the night until finally, with his own interests foremost in his mind, the farmer had determined that his need for Titus' assistance outweighed his patriotism. Titus should be permitted to remain, he announced, but must be chained in the stable whenever he was not at work in the fields. Thus they could prevent him escaping, if such was his intention; and at the same time, he would be safely out of sight of anyone who might come to the farmhouse.

Country born and bred, Titus had not been discontented with those months on the farm, despite the long hours of unrelenting toil that was the lot of any farm labourer. The work he undertook strengthened his body and he loved the hours when he could be out in the fields, but he had missed intellectual company, not least the sharing of his thoughts and activities with Barnaby. He had, *faute de mieux*, adopted one of the sheepdog puppies which became his constant companion and always curled up beside him in the stable where, at night, tired as he was from his labours, he had always slept soundly. He had named the dog Foster, although what had caused him to choose this name, he had never been able to fathom.

This tolerable existence, however, had not continued for long. One bright, sunny day in May, a posse of soldiers from the National Guard had come to the farm to check if there were men available for service in the Army. Unaware of their presence in the house, Titus had gone into the yard with a sack of beetroot he had dug up for the family's larder. The soldiers had promptly demanded to know who he was. Although he had no love for the farmer, he had every reason to wish to protect Giselle and he did not, therefore, dispute the farmer's story that the vagrant had wandered into the farm a day or two earlier; that it was his intention to take Titus in to town to hand him over to the authorities but had not yet had time to do so. Meanwhile he had kept the prisoner in chains, the frightened farmer assured the soldiers, which, if they wished, they could go and see for themselves. As to the prisoner's name, nationality or from whence he had come, he had no knowledge.

For no better reason than in the hope of saving his own life, on the way to the guardhouse Titus had adopted a new nationality. He was a magician by profession and an American by birth, he had told his captors, so under no circumstances could he be an English spy. Since he carried no papers, his story could not be disproved and whilst enquiries were to be made about him, he was locked up in the Saint Cyrille gaol.

Titus now drew a deep sigh which he instantly regretted, for his ribs still ached and the scar on his chest wound still pained him at times, though less with each day that passed.

But for the few strands of grey in his hair and a loss of weight, he told himself wryly, Adela would see little outward change in him – *if* she were ever to set eyes on him again. For the thousandth time since he had seen her ride off with the Abbé and the Curé, he wondered what had become of them all; what Adela was doing, thinking, feeling; whether Barnaby, too, had reached home safely. He had no doubt that his twin was alive for he was certain he would have known it deep inside himself if Barnaby had died. Meanwhile Barnaby knew nothing of his, Titus', fate, and in all probability thought him dead! Had he not himself believed he was dying? And Adela – she, too, must think he was never coming back to her.

He tried now to distract his mind, for thoughts of his beautiful young wife conjured up images of her which could only torment him. She haunted his dreams, which were all too often erotic, and only left him the more frustrated. Notching up the end of another long, tedious day on the heel of his *sabot*, Titus switched his thoughts elsewhere. With so little to distract him, he recalled his fortune-telling session with the turnkey. How easy it was to flummox the fellow, he told himself with a smile. And how fortuitous his invention of a mist to delay the giving of a description of his fictitious 'bearer of good tidings'! It did not surprise him in the least that someone had purported to see the ghost of Eugénie's husband. Villagers were notoriously superstitious, and since most had at one time been the Chevalier's tenants, doubtless it lay on their consciences that they had hounded his wife and burned down his home. The château had been in the Evraud family for centuries and it was only too likely that one of its members would return from the Life Hereafter to complain about the desecration of their home!

It was not without a genuine curiosity that he awaited the next visit from his credulous turnkey and, with less interest, the visit of the touchpaper-maker who claimed to have seen the apparition.

With Adela momentarily forgotten, it was with a slight smile on his face that Titus drifted finally into sleep.

Jacques could scarcely contain his excitement when he returned the following evening to the barn where Barnaby was impatiently awaiting him.

"Twas him, 'isself, Master Barnaby. I seed Master Titus with my own eyes – plain as I see you! And I gived 'im the *billet* when the turnkey weren't looking.'

He gave an excited grin. 'I might have been looking at you, Master Barnaby, for Master Titus be a deal skinnier nor 'e used to be, same as you be.'

Barnaby's eyes glowed.

'Did he recognize you, Jacques?'

The valet's grin widened.

'That 'e did, and right feared I was 'e'd open 'is mouth and let the turnkey know it! Caught 'isself just in time, and the turnkey must 'ave tolt 'im what you've been about, for Master Titus said to me, "So you are the fellow who saw the ghost of the Chevalier de Saint Cyrille up at the château!" and I said I were but there was none but me as 'ad the courage to go and see for theirselves and 'twas being said as I'd been dreaming – or in my cups!'

'And then . . .?' Barnaby prompted eagerly as Jacques paused for breath.

'I reckon as 'ow Master Titus guessed then I was up to something and 'e played along real smart. "Ho, Citizen Greuze, my fine fellow," 'e says to the turnkey, "can it be true that the men of Saint Cyrille, good citizens of the Republic, are cowards? Shame on you!" he says, and the turnkey looked sheepish, so I says to 'im, "P'raps *they* doant mind none being called cowards but *I'm* not one as is willing to be called a liar. See 'ere, citizen," I says, "I ain't a rich man but I ain't a poor one neither, and I'll give two *livres* to the furst man as sets eyes on that there ghost and can verify I'm a man 'o my word!" There weren't no doubting 'e were int'rested in the money. 'E looked at Master Titus and said something about me being "the messenger as 'e'd seen in the cards" which made no sense to me. Then the turnkey made me show him the coins wot I'd promised the furst man as seed the ghost. You should've seen the gaoler's face, sir!'

Barnaby clapped him over the shoulder.

'This is splendid news. Well done, Jacques! Now I have but to don the officer's uniform once more and ride round the ruins whilst you go back to the village and tell the simpleton you have seen me a second time.'

''Tis a good enough plan, Master Barnaby, but we'd best wait till the morrow to rescue Master Titus, surely. The turnkey ain't on guard again until tomorrow night, 'sides which there's four men as said they'd come looking tonight – if'n their courage doant disappear into thin air when it comes to it! You'd best be staying in tonight, Master Barnaby, lest I 'ave to give one of them scoundrels the two *livres* and that there turnkey, Greuze, won't 'ave no reason tomorrow to leave 'is post.'

Barnaby nodded as he attempted to quash his impatience. It was several minutes before his expression became thoughtful, and he said, 'As you pointed out, Jacques, we cannot risk a mistake, for we might have no second chance. If the four men come up to the château tonight and see no ghost, there will be less credence for your sighting, so it might be well for you to return to the *auberge* and admit that you might – just might – have been mistaken! We do not want anyone abroad in the streets tomorrow night and the fewer who go ghost-hunting the better! Treat everyone to as much liquor as they want. Let it be known you are a spendthrift and might do the same tomorrow evening. That will keep them in the inn for certain! Now tell me about Master Titus? It is still proving devilish difficult for me to believe he is alive! Was he in good heart? Was his prison as odious as Monsieur Vermond described?'

'It were larmentable small!' Jacques said. 'But 'e were in axellent spirits. 'E'll be knowing well enough as I be aiming to get 'im out of there, Master Barnaby. I couldn't say naught about you for fear the turnkey might ask some awk'ard questions, though 'e were that dim-witted, I dursay 'e'd not know a jack from a jenny!'

'I am not so sure I would, either!' Barnaby said, laughing. He was so filled with excitement at the thought that his twin really was alive and not a league away, that he was unable to remain seated. He paced the small floor of the loft, wild with impatience for the next twenty-four hours to pass.

As Jacques departed once more for the village, Barnaby found himself thinking of Adela and the joy it would give her if he could take Titus safely home. He had every hope that he and Jacques would be successful in getting him out of the prison; but he knew that even then they had still to make the dangerous journey to the coast. He and Jacques had seen many more patrols on their journey through France, and with the whole nation seeming to have lost its reason, those without papers to identify themselves as worthy citizens of the Republic were being speedily eliminated by whatever means was to hand.

Barnaby tried now to keep such fears at bay, and his thoughts returned to Adela. He could picture the look on her face when she saw Titus again. It was a look of love he would well remember and one which he would give anything in the world to have been meant for him! He would never cease to love her; to wish that she had chosen to be his wife. Yet he knew now that she had made the right choice. Titus was strong . . . and he was weak. When he had come to be tested, he had failed to do the right thing and tell Adela immediately he regained consciousness that he was not his twin. It had been so easy to convince himself that he had allowed her mistake to go uncorrected for her sake; so much easier to say nothing than to face her distress. Somewhere deep within him, he had welcomed the chance Fate had given him to step into his brother's shoes; to hear Adela's voice whisper words of love in *his* ear; feel her gentle caresses as she tended *his* wounds.

If there were excuse for him of any kind, it was that he would never have countenanced such deception had he not believed Titus was dead.

For the hundredth time since he had left Dene Place, Barnaby asked himself how he was to explain this last year to Titus. Adela had made him promise to say nothing until their return home. He tried yet again to imagine how he, Barnaby, would feel were he in Titus' shoes and went home to find that the wife and brother he loved had been living as man and wife.

The happiness Barnaby had been feeling earlier gave way to a deep unease. Whether Titus forgave him or not, he must leave Dene Place as quickly as possible. He would return to his parents' home; or perhaps go to live by himself at the new house he and Titus had built but never inhabited. Perhaps Eugénie would come to keep house for him – she had proposed it when Titus and Adela were married. On hearing of this suggestion, Titus, half in earnest, had told him he should wed Eugénie and settle down to married life as he himself was doing. Eugénie, Titus had pointed out, was only two years older than they were and still a very beautiful young woman.

Poor Eugénie! Barnaby thought now. She had had such a sad life, losing both husband and child, as well as Adela's little half-sister whom she had mothered. As adolescents, he and Titus had argued over whom should be the one to marry her! Barnaby gave a wry smile, recalling their agreement that whoever lost Eugénie, would take Adela instead!

At least *she* had forgiven him, he thought wistfully. She had kissed his cheek and wished him Godspeed. She had promised, too, to look after poor old Gloucester. There had been barely time to give his dog a thought until now, yet the animal had come to mean a great deal to him. He knew it was unwise to give his heart to a dog which at best might live a dozen years; yet Gloucester had been his friend, his confidant, his companion for so many months; and with single-minded devotion, had laid claim to his master's heart. It would be a bitter blow if

Gloucester had died of the poisoning and was not at Dene Place to welcome him home.

With a sigh Barnaby withdrew his timepiece and saw that it was nearly midnight. Jacques should have been back long since, he thought anxiously. Where was he? Could he have been detained? Arrested on some trumped-up charge? Only yesterday Jacques had been relating how many of the villagers he knew had simply disappeared without known cause or reason.

Barnaby bit his lip and, closing his eyes, tried not to think that even at this eleventh hour, on the point of success, Titus might not after all be saved.

CHAPTER THIRTY-TWO

1793

Titus leaned his ear as close to his cell door as his foot chains permitted, the better to hear the voices outside. His face was tense with anticipation for, from the moment he read Jacques' note, he had known that an attempt would shortly be made to rescue him. Adding to his excitement was the suspicion that Barnaby might be Jacques' accomplice for who else but he would have devised such a plan as a haunting to divert his guards' attention? The prospect of being reunited with his twin was exhilarating and he was filled with impatience. Now, twenty-four hours later, he could distinguish the rough, coarse tones of his turnkey and the slightly higher voice of his valet.

Was he about to receive another visit? Titus wondered. It must be nearing nine o'clock for it had been dark for several hours. The farmers would long since have come in from the fields and having eaten what simple fare their families could provide, gone down to *Le Cheval Blanc* to hear the latest gossip. Thanks to the two turnkeys, who also frequented the *auberge*, Titus had kept abreast of the news. Distorted by rumour though it might be, he was nevertheless aware of the growing terror in the capital and of the people's wholesale destruction of their fellow countrymen.

According to his gaolers, the women in Paris now sat in chairs surrounding the guillotine, counting not stitches as they plied their knitting needles but heads as they fell into the waiting baskets! If the gossip were to be believed, sometimes as many as seventy executions took place in a single day. Tumbrels carried the victims from the Conciergerie – where condemned prisoners were held in vast numbers awaiting their fate alongside common criminals – past jeering crowds to their untimely deaths.

Even Greuze had looked awed when he related the rumour – that there were now as many as seven thousand prisoners awaiting death or trial by the Tribunal; and barracks, schools, libraries as well as palaces had to be used as prisons to accommodate so many, the existing gaols being hopelessly inadequate. It did not seem to have crossed the uneducated turnkey's mind that these so-called 'traitors' were innocents. In his opinion it was right that even the children of the guilty must lose their heads to Madame Guillotine.

It would not be long, Titus knew, before prisoners such as he were rounded up and escorted to Paris, no doubt to suffer the same unhappy fate as those Greuze had described. Jacques and perhaps Barnaby, too, had come to his rescue none too early.

His heart thudding, Titus strained to interpret the conversation taking place outside the door of his cell. It seemed as if Greuze was protesting that he could not leave his post; that he would be shot were he to do so. Jacques' voice was more clearly audible as he replied, 'I understand your situation, Citizen, but surely your prisoners are secured behind lock and key and there is little purpose to your remaining outside their door? That foreigner you took me to see yesterday, 'e were chained and could not possibly escape. I tell you, my good fellow, the ghost of the Chevalier is in the churchyard. I saw 'im with my own eyes but five minutes past, and I 'ave ridden apace to tell you afore I tells them as doant believe me in the *auberge*.'

The turnkey sounded doubtful as he muttered, 'You said the apparition was 'aunting the ruins of 'is château! What would 'e be doing now in the graveyard?'

'Looking for the resting place of his dead son, I dare say!' Jacques' voice was casual but became more urgent as he continued, ''Tis not to my liking to 'ave my word in doubt

– and there's those at the *auberge* as is making me a laughing-stock. I promised two *livres* to the first man as could prove I speak the truth, and now I am prepared to raise that sum to four – if only for the pleasure of seeing the look on the faces of those who doubt me.'

Outside Titus' door, the men were invisible to him, but Jacques' eyes were observing every expression on the turnkey's face and now he could see the avarice in Greuze's eyes as he scratched his head. His desire to do his duty was wavering.

'Those four men as went up to the château last night were in a right ugly mood when they returned,' Jacques continued. ''Tweren't my fault they'd seen nothing. 'Appen if I shows my face in *Le Cheval Blanc* this evening, there's one or two as might set upon me. See here, Citizen, 'tis but a short way from 'ere to the church, as you know. If you run fast, you'd be gone but five minutes. If it will ease your mind, I'll take charge of your keys for you and mind your prisoners.'

Jacques could see that the turnkey was tempted, but that his peasant caution prevailed.

'I might be seen! There are soldiers, officers still abroad in the streets. 'Tis too risky!'

Jacques made pretence of agreeing with him and then, rattling the coins in his pocket, he said, 'We could change clothes so's you'd look like me. We be the same 'eight. If'n you keep your 'ead down and doant speak to no one, you'd not be rekkernized, not nohow!'

There was a long pause whilst Jacques withdrew the coins from his pocket and pretended to count them. He was aware that Greuze was also counting them, and one by one, he put them back out of sight.

''Tis for you to decide, Citizen,' he said with a sigh, 'but if you be brave enough to go, you should make 'aste. I'd not want for you to reach the graveyard and find the apparition 'ad vanished. I 'id be'ind that there lych-gate and 'e didn't see me noways, so you'd not be in no danger.'

Jacques could see that Greuze was almost convinced; but

a shred of wariness prompted the fellow to ask shrewdly, 'What were *you* doing in the graveyard, Citizen?'

The question took Jacques by surprise. He covered his confusion with a laugh. It was but a second before the obvious answer occurred to him.

'Relieving myself, of course!' He removed his coat and *bonnet rouge* and offered them to the turnkey. It seemed to him that the fellow took an unconscionably long time to don them. It was only with an effort that he forbore the urge to hurry him for there was a danger lest the farmer, whose mule Jacques had stolen earlier, might discover his loss and raise a hue and cry. The animal was tethered in the orchard of the nearby *presbytère* and might at any time reveal its presence with its feeble hoarse cry.

With obvious reluctance, but governed by the belief that he would shortly be the richer by the princely sum of four *livres*, the gaoler put his bunch of keys into Jacques' outstretched hand. Jacques grinned.

'Good thing I know how to use that!' he said, pointing to the musket the turnkey had propped against the wall. 'Served in the Army some years ago. Won't no one get past me. Away with you now, my friend, and I wish you *bonne chance*!' As the turnkey still hesitated, his heart sank.

'We ain't taken no account of Citizen Bagout!' he muttered, nodding in the direction of the main door of the prison outside which he knew the second gaoler was standing guard.

Jacques breathed a sigh of relief and withdrew a handful of *sous* from his pocket.

''Ow d'you think I got in 'ere to see you?' he said grinning. 'If'n 'e asks any questions, give 'im a few more of these! These'll keep 'is mouth shut!' he added, rattling the coins. 'No need to tell 'im where you're off to – or why! But like as not, 'e'll think it's me and not ask no questions. You doant want 'im going off to see the Chevalier's ghost for 'isself and claiming the reward.'

Satisfied at last, the turnkey nodded. He was impatient now

to be gone, and as Jacques took his place on the stool in the guardroom, Greuze hurried out of the door.

Jacques waited only until he heard the second guard lock the main door of the prison behind the turnkey before hurrying across the passage to Titus' cell. His hands unsteady with excitement, he tried the keys one after another until the lock clicked and the door opened. Closing it quickly behind him, he turned to see his young master smiling at him.

'I overheard most of your conversation, my dear fellow!' Titus said warmly. 'But what of these?' He held out his chained wrists and shuffled the chains around his ankles securing him to a ring in the floor.

Jacques selected one of the smaller keys, his eyes twinkling.

'Watched 'im lock you into them cuffs yesterday, Master Titus, so I knowed the keys was on this 'ere bunch!' He set about unfastening the padlocks, and a minute later, the chains were lying in a pool on the stone floor. With obvious pleasure, Titus rubbed his ankles and wrists, and put his arm affectionately round his faithful valet's shoulders.

'What now?' he asked. 'What of the second guard outside? Do we use fisticuffs? I fear I may not have much strength in mine!'

Jacques gave him a reassuring smile.

'Best mek use of the musket. We dursn't risk a shot, but I rekkon a blow to the 'ead should do it! There's 'orses and a mule tethered close by the churchyard, so if'n we can reach Master Barnaby undetected, sir, we're good as home!'

Titus caught his breath.

'So Barny is the ghost of the Chevalier, eh?' he cried joyfully. 'I had the feeling it would be he. Is he well? In good heart?'

There was no time to answer such questions, Jacques said as he urged Titus to follow him out of the cell. They could come later once they were safely out of the prison.

'Sure you can walk, Master Titus? I've checked the back streets and we can reach the church wi'out going through the village. 'Tis bitter cold but Master Barnaby 'as a thick coat

and strong boots waiting for you.' He took up the musket and
pointed to Greuze's clothes he had donned in place of his own.
'I'll be the guard wot's escorting two English spies if'n we's
stopped on our way to Anse Goéland.'

Titus put his hand on Jacques' shoulder.

'It seems you have thought of everything,' he said. 'As for
warm clothing for me, if you had been shut away from fresh
air as long as I have, you would care as little as I if 'tis cold
enough to bring the knaves out!'

Grinning at the proverb and delighted to find his young
master in such good heart, Jacques eased open the main
door of the prison and raising the butt of the musket, brought
it down in a crashing blow on the unsuspecting gaoler's
head.

'We must not be impatient!' Adela said gently as her mother-
in-law rose to leave. ''Tis but three weeks since they left for
France, and at very best, they could not have reached Saint
Cyrille in less than a week.'

Frances Mallory sighed.

'You are quite right, my dear, and I do admire your compo-
sure! Of course, Barnaby cannot be quite as dear to you as
to us, and it is unreasonable of me to expect you to feel quite
the same degree of joy as we do.' She glanced briefly at her
husband who came to stand beside her. 'It is indeed a miracle,
is it not, for our beloved son to be returned to us when we
had believed—'

As she broke off, her eyes filling with tears, Adela turned
quickly away. She could not bear to think what this good,
kindly, God-fearing couple might think if she were to tell them
that they were wrong – it was Titus who was returning to
them, not Barnaby; and that she, therefore, had as much if
not more reason than they to be waiting impatiently for his
return.

Each day since Jacques and Barnaby had left, her in-laws
had either come to Dene Place or she had called at the

parsonage, for they were determined to be among the first to welcome their son. Each visit had been a torment for Adela as she listened to them speaking of *Barnaby*'s imprisonment; of *Titus*' courage in going to his rescue. Again and again they had perused Monsieur Vermond's letter which, to Adela's great relief, mentioned only his fellow prisoner's surname. He might so easily have written Mr *Titus* Mallory – and then she and Barnaby would have been unmasked.

As their carriage departed and the dark November night filled the house with shadows, Adela rang for the servants to light the fires in all the rooms and to bring more candles. It was bitterly cold and she was shivering, although she knew it was partially from fear. She wanted Titus back more than anything in the whole world – but not an unforgiving Titus who hated her. To see those laughing, loving eyes regarding her with scorn and derision was more than she would be able to bear. How would she ever find the courage, she asked herself for the hundredth time, to confess the lie she and Barnaby had perpetrated these past seven months?

Adela drew her shawl more closely about her shoulders as she paced uneasily in front of the drawing-room fire. It was ironic, she thought, that Lady Mallory had believed her to be 'composed', for in the twenty years of her lifetime, she could not recall when a greater conflict of emotions had raged inside her. Her longing to see Titus, to know he was safely home, to be able to touch him, hear his voice was overwhelming; yet combined with that impatience, was her fear of what the next few moments, hours, after his arrival might bring. Even were he willing by some further miracle to forgive her and Barnaby, would they really be able to hide the truth from the rest of the world? Suppose he had ceased to be his twin's double, and the deprivations of prison life had marked him? She had read that criminals who had been incarcerated for many years were shrunken, pale as death, easily identifiable as former prisoners. Although Barnaby had lost a great deal of weight and had new lines about his mouth and eyes, he had been healthy enough when he had left the house. And what of the tell-tale strands of grey in his hair?

As one of the housemaids came in to draw the curtains across the windows and make up the fire, Adela sat down and pretended to occupy herself with her tapestry work. It was so hard to keep up a pretence of normality in front of the servants and her in-laws, a necessary pretence, she believed, for it was unlikely she would be in so great a state of turmoil on account of her brother-in-law. Only in Dolly's presence could she allow her true feelings free rein, and Dolly was proving little comfort.

'Reckon as 'ow you be paying the price for wot you did, Miss Addy!' she had said. 'I know it were Mr Barnaby's fault too – you getting into this mess, but 'twere your idea, not 'is, to go on 'tending arter you knowed he weren't Mr Titus. 'Tweren't right for you, nor him neither and neither of the both of you 'ave been the 'appier for it. Now you be in a right pickle! One lie allus leads to another, Miss Addy, as we was taught in Sunday School at the orphanage – and it be true enough.'

Now she was about to tell another lie, Adela thought. She did not want to lie – least of all to Titus – but would he understand, forgive? Dolly thought it highly unlikely that any husband would believe his wife could share another man's bed and not be taken by him in adultery!

At least Barnaby had promised not to reveal anything to Titus until they reached home, she consoled herself. She could trust him to stay silent; and Jacques would not speak out. Meanwhile she could only wait, as she had these past twenty-one days, the joy that should have been unsurpassable marred by her indecision and her fears.

As she set aside her embroidery and stared into the glowing fire, Adela tried not to think beyond the moment when, God willing, Titus arrived and at least for the first few minutes of his homecoming, his eyes would be filled with love as he held her in his arms.

The clock on the tower of Dene church had struck the tenth hour and Adela was already in bed searching for the oblivion of sleep, when the sounds of Gloucester's barking and horses' hooves in the driveway reached her ears. She sat up quickly and lit the candle. A moment later Dolly appeared, her nightcap askew, her candle dripping wax on to the polished floorboards as she hurried towards the bed.

'I reckon 'tis my Jacques!' she said breathlessly. 'You awake, Miss Addy? I think 'tis *them* come 'ome!'

She hurried to the casement and threw open the windows. A rush of cold air blew out her candle and stirred the embers of the fire. Adela could now hear men's voices . . . a laugh . . . the snorting of one of the horses as it pawed the hard ground. Not waiting to put on her night-robe, she ran to Dolly's side, her excitement so overpowering that she was unable to speak. Her hands trembled as she gripped Dolly's shoulders for support.

The men below were but shadowy figures. She counted them . . . one, two, three. Was one of them Titus? The question burned in her mind as she strained the better to see. Then he spoke.

'Devil take it, Barny, will you help me down? I declare, I am as stiff as an icicle – and as cold!'

The sound of his soft laughter caused Adela's heart to miss a beat.

'Upon my life, I never thought this moment would come, though God knows I prayed for it often enough! I suppose Addy will be a-bed. Let us go and wake her, Barny, eh?'

Now Adela could make out Jacques' stocky figure as he took the horses' reins and led them away towards the stables. One of the twins mounted the steps and rapped on the door with his riding crop.

'I'll go down and let them in!' Dolly said excitedly. 'Oh, Miss Addy, they's back – Jacques and the both of 'em. Thanks be to God!'

Oblivious to the cold, Adela stood immobile by the casement.

She could not bring herself to drag her eyes away from the two figures below. One of them was Titus! In a moment, he would be here . . . here in the room with her!

Suddenly the bright transparent bubble of joy burst and fragmented into a void of fear. Titus was back and nothing, no one must mar this moment of his home-coming. She must go down quickly and make sure that nothing was said, no awkward questions asked that might arouse his suspicions. She must find out if he had changed in his appearance; if Jacques or Barnaby had, after all, spoken out.

Flinging her night-robe over her shoulders, Adela ran barefoot from the room and down the wide staircase, her face pale, her heart thudding in her breast. On the bottom step, she paused. The twins were surrounded by members of the household staff. All were beaming with delight as they welcomed them home. Above their heads, she could see the identical heads of the twins – which, she noted in the light of the candle flames, were *both* slightly tinged with grey. Then one of them turned in her direction and breaking through the cordon around him, came striding towards her.

As he took her in his arms, Adela had not the slightest doubt that it was Titus. Even had she not known it then, she would have been totally convinced as she felt his lips crushing hers.

'Titus, oh, Titus!' she breathed when he took his mouth away. 'I have missed you – so much!'

'And I, you, my sweeting!' Titus said happily. Drawing her close against his side, he called across to Barnaby. 'Did I not say this would be the happiest moment of my life?' he asked with a grin. 'We shall celebrate – all of us. Sutton, bring some brandy to the drawing-room; and the staff are to have as much of whatever you all fancy in the servants' hall. Come, Addy, my darling, and you, old fellow, for 'tis deuced cold standing here!'

As the servants departed, he drew Adela towards the drawing-room but paused when he saw that Barnaby was not following.

'What's amiss with you?' he asked. 'By the look on your face, anyone would think you were at a funeral!'

Barnaby threw an anxious glance at Adela.

'I think I should be going . . . home!' he said hesitantly. 'Father and Mother—'

'Demme if they cannot be left to sleep in peace!' Titus broke in. 'You can go and break the good news tomorrow. You and I are going to celebrate my home-coming with Addy. We will drink a toast to my beautiful wife; and to that fellow, Vermond, for had he not told you of my whereabouts, you would not have come to my rescue. Lud, man, but what is keeping you?'

Barnaby's steps were faltering as he followed Titus and Adela into the drawing-room. Avoiding his eyes, Adela clung tightly to Titus' arm.

Please, Barny, do not tell him! The words, unspoken, were a silent prayer. Tomorrow, perhaps, she would confess. Now, if only for a few hours, Titus must not know. His eyes as he regarded her were so full of love! *Must he ever be told?* God had been kind to her and as far as she could see, there was little outwardly to tell the twins apart.

As the thought crossed Adela's mind, she knew that even if she and Barnaby remained silent, it would be only a matter of time before Titus realized that those around him believed it was his twin who had come back from the dead and would be questioning Barnaby about his own imprisonment; who would be making reference to his, Titus', activities during the past seven months when supposedly he was living here as her husband.

No, she would have to confess just as she and Barnaby had known from the first. It was a moment of madness to think otherwise! But the presence of the living, breathing, laughing man she loved so dearly, had eroded her courage and more now than she had ever anticipated, she dreaded the prospect of destroying his happiness.

Titus drew her down on to the sofa beside him, and with his arm around her shoulders, he stared down into her face.

'So silent, my love?' he asked tenderly. 'You have not spoken one word. Are you not pleased to have me home?'

Tears sprang hot and stinging into Adela's eyes. She buried her face against his chest and heard the soft rumble of his laughter.

'Come now, my dearest, this is no time for tears! We are together again – for ever, God willing! If you knew how often I have dreamt of this moment. Have you missed me? Were you lonely without me? Barny has told me you all believed me dead!'

'Titus, do not talk of it, I beg you!' Adela whispered.

He wiped a tear from her cheek and lifted her face so that she must look at him.

'I will not have you weeping when we should all be rejoicing!' he chided her gently. 'By all means, let us not talk of my supposed "death", nor indeed of my near escapes from it! Let us talk instead of happier things.' He glanced across at Barnaby who had sunk into one of the armchairs opposite them. 'That vexatious brother of mine would tell me nothing of your doings this past year. He said I must wait and *you* would impart all the news to me! Demme if I could get a word out of him!'

Adela looked quickly at Barnaby and away again. At least for the moment, their secret was safe. She was saved an immediate reply by one of the servants arriving with a tray on which were glasses and a decanter.

'Pardon me, sir,' he said as he set it down on the sofa-table behind Titus and Adela, 'but I was asked to speak for us all, and we wish to say, Welcome home, and we think it were right brave of you, sir, to go back into Frenchie country and bring Mr Barnaby home!'

Having made his speech, the man bowed himself out of the room. Titus looked from Adela to Barnaby. Neither met his gaze.

'What the devil was the fellow talking about? He seemed to think it was I – not you, Barny – who deserved the praise!'

Adela gave a quick, nervous laugh.

'As, indeed you do, Titus, for it must have taken great courage to endure that terrible imprisonment. Monsieur Vermond told us – did he not, Barny – how each prisoner feared that another dawn might bring his death?'

Titus seemed to be successfully diverted for he began to speak of his French friend and how they had managed to keep one another's spirits up. Glancing at Barnaby, Adela noted that he looked as ill at ease as herself. She was aware that she was trembling. Titus regarded her with tenderness and self-reproach.

'Here I am talking about matters which you have told me distress you!' he said apologetically. 'Forgive me, dearest! Let me see you smile, for by my faith, it seems a century ago that I last saw those beautiful green eyes of yours aglow with merriment!'

Before she could speak, Barnaby stood up abruptly.

'Really, Titus, I think it is my duty to go home!' he said. 'You cannot realize how impatient Mother and Father have been to know we are both safe!'

'Confound it, Barny, of course I do! But you of all people must understand my need to have you here. You are my brother, the dearest of brothers, and I want to share my joy with you as well as with my darling Addy. 'Pon my life, I do not think there is a man alive who could be happier than I – and 'twas you as well as Jacques who made it possible!'

'Of course, of course, old fellow!' Barnaby said huskily; but he had time to say no more before the door opened and the same manservant came into the room. Straining on a leash by his side was the deer-hound, Gloucester.

'Pardon me, sir, madam, but 'e were going wild and we couldn't quiet 'im noways. Cook said 'as 'ow you'd be wanting to see 'im, sir.'

He got no further for the dog had torn himself loose from the restraining leash and came bounding towards the sofa. Spell-bound, Adela watched as the hound halted by Titus;

sniffed at his legs and turning quickly away, hurried across the room. Even before he had reached Barnaby's chair, he gave a great whine of joy and then sprang forward. Balancing his forelegs on his master's shoulders, rapturously he licked Barnaby's face.

In the doorway, the servant stood with a look of bewilderment on his face. The same bewilderment was on Titus' face as he turned from Adela's agonized eyes to stare at his brother. Tears were streaming down Barnaby's cheeks as he stroked the dog's head and murmured his name. When the animal ceased licking him, he turned to look at Adela.

'I am sorry!' he said brokenly. 'I could not . . . deny him a welcome . . . oh, God, Addy, I am so sorry!'

The dog's tail, waving furiously, now swept the decanter and brandy glasses off the table and on to the floor. In the confusion that followed as the three men moved simultaneously to prevent further damage, Adela sat frozen to her chair. In her long hours of scheming, she had forgotten the dog; forgotten the bond between Gloucester and Barnaby. She had trusted in words to smooth away any strange anomalies. Had she not succeeded already when the servant had praised the wrong twin for going to the succour of the other? *But animals were not deceived by words,* and the bond between Barnaby and his dog was far too great to be broken. There could be no doubt that Barnaby was his master, and if Barny left tonight for the parsonage, Gloucester would follow him there. Titus must soon realize – if he had not done so already – that his twin had been living here at Dene Place and not with his parents.

Dismissing the servant, and with Gloucester now lying relatively quietly with his great head on Barnaby's lap, his tail thumping the floor, Titus said quietly, 'I think the time has come for the two of you to do some explaining. Something has happened whilst I have been away, and whatever it is, neither of you wished to speak of it. Clearly that fellow thought the dog belonged to me; and equally clearly, the animal belongs to you, Barny. How comes it that Sutton was mistaken?'

Adela was now unable to control the trembling of her hands. She looked up at Titus in appeal.

'I will try to explain. I . . . beg you to try to understand. When Barny came back from France, he believed that you . . . we all thought . . . oh, Titus, we believed you were dead, and . . .'

At her halting words, Barnaby stood up. In a firm voice he broke in saying, 'Do you not think it would be better for me to make the explanation, Addy? After all it was I who was first responsible. Please trust me to know what is best – in this matter if in no other! I must be the one to confess. Titus, will you ask . . . ask your wife to leave us?'

Titus hesitated, looking from Adela's white face to the flushed cheeks of his twin. He turned back to Adela, but she was weeping softly and would not meet his eyes.

'Whatever this mystery, it is clear to me that it upsets you deeply,' he said uneasily. 'So please do as Barnaby suggests and leave us, Addy. We will sort matters out between us. Return to your bedchamber, my sweeting, and I will come to you presently.'

No man ever walked to the gallows with more reluctance than she now left the room and went upstairs, Adela thought, for however much Barny strived to vindicate her part in the deception, she knew herself as guilty as he. She had wanted to punish him for the pain he had inflicted on her; wanted revenge for allowing her to believe that it was Titus who had survived. When the truth was revealed, it had seemed at the time such a cruel trick for Barnaby to have played on her, and for a while she had hated him. In the end, she had suffered as greatly as he; and she had come to realize that it was love and pity which had prompted him, not selfishness or cruelty. She could and did forgive him his weakness; but Titus had always been the stronger of the two and she would be deluding herself by thinking that pity might prompt Titus to forgive her.

Looking deeply concerned, Dolly came into Adela's bedchamber to offer her mistress such comfort as she could;

but Adela dismissed her. There was no comfort to be had from crying on Dolly's shoulder. There were perhaps minutes left, she realized, before Titus would come striding through the door, a look of contempt on his face where only a short while ago, there had been such love! Would he rebuke her? Deride her? Worst of all, would he disavow her?

When thirty minutes had passed with still no sign of Titus, Adela could bear the suspense so longer. Taking up her candle, she crept downstairs and pressed her ear to the drawing-room door. The voices she could hear were muted, too quiet for her to distinguish one from the other. The dog whined, and afraid that she might be discovered, Adela hurried back upstairs. She returned to her lonely vigil by the fire, ashamed of herself, for only servants listened at keyholes! She could remember her father reprimanding her when she had been only a little girl for committing just such a crime. She had been no more than four years old when she had heard her parents speaking of the birthday gift with which they planned to surprise her on the day. 'We will discuss it further after Adela has gone to bed!' her father had said, and so after Nou-Nou had blown out her bedside candle, Adela had tip-toed downstairs to listen at the door. Her face softened at the memory, but only momentarily as her thoughts returned to Titus.

Would he wish her to leave this house – *her* home? she asked herself as a burning log broke in two and dropped in a shower of sparks on to the ash. It was Titus' home now, for since Kitty's death she had inherited Dene Place and her husband had become master of it. How brief their marriage had been! She had known the happiness of being a wife for so short a while! 'You are more than a wife to me!' he had said on their wedding night. 'You are my dearest friend and my lover. We are as one now!'

Oh, Titus, Titus, she wept. How shall I live without you? What will I do with my life if you disown me? It will have no meaning if you cease to love me!

The church clock sounded yet another hour. It was now two in the morning. Adela went to her door and opened it. From downstairs came the sound of footsteps – a servant moving from the pantry to the drawing-room. A door opened and now she could hear raised voices and . . . laughter? No, she must be mistaken.

Dolly appeared from the shadows of the landing.

'Shall I go down, Miss Addy?' she whispered, for she, too, had heard the noise from below. Adela nodded and stood waiting until Dolly reappeared by her door.

'Sutton says as 'ow 'e's just now tekken another bottle to the drawing-room. 'E said as 'ow the young masters is 'aving a right merry time in there. They bin laughing and drinkin' like there's no t'morrow! 'E reckoned the dog were the worse for wear, too! 'Appen you should go down, Miss Addy, and stop 'em afore they drinks theirselfs under the table!'

Too confused to move from the spot where her feet seemed to be rooted, Adela gripped her hands and pressed them beneath her chin as she stared down into the dark hallway. The opening of the drawing-room door broke the silence and made them both jump. They heard Gloucester's nails clicking against the hall flagstones and a moment later, they saw the dog's shadowy form as he lifted his leg against the newel-post of the stairs. Dolly grinned.

'Weren't no one thought to let 'im outside!' she whispered. 'Go on down, Miss Addy. Find out what they young masters is up to!'

One hand gripping the banister for support, the other holding her candle, Adela went slowly down the stairs. As she paused on the last step, Gloucester went past her and scratched at the drawing-room door. It opened almost at once, and as the dog pushed past him in his eagerness to get back to his master, Titus looked up and saw her.

'Devil take it, Addy, you startled me!' he said, moving towards her. 'Just as Barny and I were talking about his clever invention of the Chevalier's ghost, what do I espy but a white wraith on the stairs – albeit in a very fetching night-robe! Are you trying to scare the wits out of me?'

He took her hand and drew her towards him. His next words were so unexpected, she gaped at him in astonishment.

'Are you angry with me, Addy?'

'Angry!' she repeated stupidly as he put his arm round her shoulders and led her back into the drawing-room. 'I angry with *you?*'

Titus grinned.

'Every right to be angry!' he said cheerfully. 'I fear Barny and I have downed a few too many brandies . . . talking over old times . . . neglecting my beautiful wife! I love you very much, you know that? Always will!'

As he guided Adela into the room, Barnaby looked up with a sheepish grin on his face.

'I do apologize, Addy, for keeping Titus from you. There was so much to talk about, you see. My apologies!'

He had some trouble pronouncing the word and as he stood up, he appeared slightly unbalanced. At last Adela found her voice.

'You have told Titus . . . about us?'

Barnaby nodded. He did not look particularly unhappy, or even concerned.

'Silly of us both to have worried!' he said vaguely. 'Should've known Titus would understand. Should've known! He's my twin brother. Always understands!'

Titus grinned.

'Barny's right – we have always understood each other. 'Tis hard to explain but . . . well, we share feelings as well as opinions. 'Pon my soul, Addy, I would have acted no differently if I had been in his shoes. He is my twin and I trust him with my life.'

'*And* with your wife?' Despite herself, the question had burst from her.

'When I thought I was on the point of death I asked Barny to take care of you for me, Addy,' Titus said, adding with a half smile on his lips, 'Mind you, I am the happier for knowing that there was a limit to his solicitude. I would not have wanted him to usurp my husbandly duties! Come now, my sweeting, will you not take that glum look from your face? There is no harm done. Barny and I are agreed that he will play the part of the prisoner returned from the grave, and I, the devoted husband who left you only to search for him. Our parents need know nothing of this. As for that scoundrel, Gloucester, I shall say I have given him to Barny as a welcome-home gift.'

As wave after wave of relief flooded through her, Adela whispered, 'I was so afraid . . . that you would never forgive me . . . that you would never want to speak to me, see me, again!'

Titus put both his arms around her and laid his cheek against her hair.

'Nor shall I want to see you again – if you keep that worrisome look on your face. Demme if you do not remind me of that pesky old harridan who taught us our A B C! Do you not agree that Addy is looking much like her, Barny?'

'Indeed, I do not . . .' Adela began indignantly, but broke off as she looked up and saw the bright, golden flecks of laughter in Titus' eyes. She knew then with unquestionable certainty that all was well with them again.

'Don't do to tease Addy! Always was a little spitfire!' Barnaby muttered as his eyes closed and he fell back amongst the cushions fast asleep.

'I have better things to do than tease you, my dearest!' Titus murmured, and lifting her effortlessly into his arms, he carried her up to bed.

Love. Passion. War.
Family. Secrets. History.

Stunning timeless classics from the bestselling
novelist Claire Lorrimer.

Available in paperback and ebook.